I0665583

The Jazz Swinger

Lexi Haynes

The Jazz Swinger

Copyright © 2024 by Lexi Haynes.

All rights reserved. No part of this book may be reproduced in any form or by any electronic or mechanical means, including information storage and retrieval systems, without permission in writing from the publisher, except by reviewers, who may quote brief passages in a review.

This publication contains the opinions and ideas of its author. It is intended to provide helpful and informative material on the subjects addressed in the publication. The author and publisher specifically disclaim all responsibility for any liability, loss, or risk, personal or otherwise, which is incurred as a consequence, directly or indirectly, of the use and application of any of the contents of this book.

MILTON & HUGO L.L.C.
4407 Park Ave., Suite 5
Union City, NJ 07087, USA

Website: *www. miltonandhugo.com*
Hotline: *1- 888-778-0033*
Email: *info@miltonandhugo.com*

Ordering Information:
Quantity sales. Special discounts are available on quantity purchases by corporations, associations, and others. For details, contact the publisher at the address above.

Library of Congress Control Number:		2024910085
ISBN-13:	979-8-89285-130-5	[Paperback Edition]
	979-8-89285-129-9	[Hardback Edition]
	979-8-89285-128-2	[Digital Edition]

Rev. date: 04/19/2024

Contents

Dedication

I want to dedicate this book to two people
who I could not have done without them.

The first person is my husband. He gave me all the love
and support I could possibly ask for when doing this.

Second is my girlfriend, Nicole. She helped me
when producing ideas and editing. I could never
pay her enough for doing all that for me.

Italian Cheat Sheet

Mia Cara - My Darling
Stronzo - Asshole
Mio Figlio - My son
Mia Figilia - My Daughter
Mio Amore - My love (male)
Mia Amore - My love (female)
Per favore - Please
Mia Mamma - My mom
Bellissima - Beautiful
Fanculo - Fuck
Arrivederci - Goodbye
Ti amo - I love you.
Idiotis - idiots
Grazie - Thank you.
Sei mio per sempre, Mia Cara. Per favore, di che sei mio - You are mine
forever, My Dear. Please, say you're mine
Sono tuo per sempre - I'm yours forever
Ho bisogno di assaggiarti, Mia Amore - I need to taste you, my love
Voglio stare con te per sempre, Mia Amore - I want to be with you forever,
my love
Anch'io ti amo - I love you to
Io sono abbastanza - I am enough
Si, ti amo tesoro mio - Yes, I love you my darling

Meet the Teammates

Hockey
Dante De Luca - Goalie - #13
Stan Marshall - Right Wing - #26
Richard Quick - Second Goalie - #69
Steele Beauileu - Defensemen - #41
Jason Roberts - Center - #18

Football
Carter Quinn - Running Back - #11
Xavier Jackson - Middle Linebacker - #21
Jaden Andrews - Quarterback - #26

Baseball
Ivan Valdimir - Pitcher - #22
Cole Adams - Catcher - #42
Rick Roy - Shortstop - #7

Chapter 1

NIKKI

I am late. I am never late. I am meeting Ian for breakfast today to get the new dish on this guy I saw him with last night that he brought into my club. My club is the best jazz club, at least that is what my reviews say. I have worked so hard to have a place where I could perform whatever I want. I love to sing, even tried to get onto Broadway, but it just wasn't my thing. When trying to get into Broadway every director would bark orders and tear me down with every audition. So, what do I do, open a Jazz Bar where I can be whoever I want and not be criticized. I get the occasional heckler but being the owner, I can just kick them to the curb.

I pull out my mirror in my purse to check my makeup and hair. I have bright red curly hair and pale skin which can be a turn off for some but to others it can really get their motor running, not that I care. I am so busy with my club I am kind of going through a dry spell, a two-year dry spell. I decided to do a natural smokey eye and bright red lipstick. I check my lipstick and eyes to make sure none of it smudged and then put my mirror back in my purse. I get a text just as my cab is pulling up to the diner. Looks like Ian is getting impatient waiting because as soon as I look at one another comes in.

Ian: Hey girl! Can't wait to see you!

Ian: Bitch!!! Where are you?!?! I got all the dirty Deets!!

Instead of texting back, I pay my cab fare and run into the diner. No point in texting him when I am already here. I fixed my black sweater dress I threw on. The host greets me, "Hey Nikki, Ian is at table twelve practically jumping out of his seat."

"Thanks Tommy, I can find him. No need to show the way," I say with a smile.

I rush to the table and see Ian sitting there fidgeting with his silverware and bouncing his knee. Ian was always a pretty man and my gay best friend. His golden hair is always perfectly faded on the sides and styled up top. Gorgeous tan skin that looks like it was softly kissed by the sun and beautiful blue eyes. He is wearing his tailored three-piece suit in a dark navy and gray silk shirt. He is the top event planner in the city and lives the high life, but I am not jealous because he would give me the shirt off his back if it came down to it. He is from old money but when he came out to his parents at sixteen, they kicked him out. He worked hard getting his GED and starting his own event planning business. Now he is the life of the party and lives with no regrets being who he is.

"Well, hello handsome, is this seat taken?" I question with a snicker, which makes him jump in surprise.

"Bitch!! You are never late! You made me worried sick!!" He exclaimed as he hopped out of the booth to give me the biggest bear hug.

We have been coming to the Gold Eagle since we met five years ago. The diner is a mom-and-pop shop with the best breakfast in the city. They decked it out in retro eighties flair. The walls are painted a warm white. The booths and chairs have red leather upholstery and gold hardware. The tables and counters are deep oak. The floors were a fake white marble and were always sticky. The table we sat at every time was always wobbly, but we come here every Sunday for the great food. The food was the perfect remedy for a Saturday Night hangover. Not like we ever got to party on the weekend, with him having events all the time and with me running my own club. Our Saturday nights out are normally on Mondays but we always go to breakfast on Sunday mornings so we can touch base and make sure we are available for one another with our busy schedules.

"Sorry! My cab driver was an idiot. He took forty fourth street and traffic was a nightmare. I just got your texts when the cab pulled up and thought it would be dumb to text you back since I was here," I say as I sit down in our booth. He already ordered my cappuccino which I am so happy to see. I take a sip of my drink when we sit down. "Okay, give me the four one one."

"Soooo, I met this amazing guy last night at my event," he said inquisitively.

"Wait, pause, did you pick up a guy at an event you planned. Mr. I-don't-shit-where-I-eat," I said mockingly.

"I know, I know, but we just clicked. So, I planned this event for a famous hockey player, who is a sweetheart by the way, well his whole team was there to celebrate the start of a new season. Apparently, he is friends with a football star and baseball star, so their teams were there as well. I was running around trying to find the restroom when I ran into the sexiest man I have ever met. He was like a brick wall of muscle and then he was making jokes about how the place was too large and could not find anything in the house. We talked a good bit and then he said that he loved Jazz so I told him if he wanted to, when I was done with the event, that I knew the best jazz bar in the city we could go to," He then started blushing and rubbing the back of his head like he was hiding something.

"So does this brick wall of muscle have a name?" I asked, truly intrigued.

"He does but please do not freak out or tell anyone because he is a part of the hockey team and not fully out yet," he said reluctantly.

"When do I gossip?" I asked offendedly. I do not have time for that shit. Plus, I don't have many friends to gossip with. I really only have two, him and one of the bartenders at the club named Chloe.

"His name is Stan Marshall. He is the starting right wing to New York's NHL team," he almost whispered.

"Shut up!! You have to be kidding!! Stan Marshall?" I said a little too loud. He slaps his hand over my mouth. He knew I would freak out after I heard that. I love hockey! I never miss a game and if I do, I will record the game to watch it in my office while cashing out my bartenders and servers at the end of the night. He shushes me.

"Shut up, please. That is why once I saw you last night, I hid from you a little. I did not want to freak him out with your fangirling. I knew you would recognize him and then it would bring him unwanted attention and he really wanted to listen to jazz and have a few drinks. He is really sweet," he explained.

"So do you have a second date with him?" I asked. It is hard for Ian to date because of his parents. They made him feel like he was doing something wrong by being gay and I think that is why he always was reserved about dating.

"I do but I would not call last night a date," he said with a blush that was so bright you could see it from space.

"Call it whatever you want but you are seeing him again?" I asked, annoyed.

"Yes, he wants to go to dinner Friday and go back to your club for drinks after. He heard you sing, and he loved you. I told him you were a huge fan and my best friend. He wants to hear you sing again. I wanted to introduce him to you last night, but I needed to tell you to please play it cool before introducing you to him. I knew I could get around last night without introducing him but If I tried a second time, you would hunt me down like a lioness you are," he explained further but got quiet once the server walked up with our food. This is what is so great about this place. We never had to wait for our table, and we never had to order our food. They knew our order so when we walked in, they would start everything.

"Hey guys. I saw Ian walk in and thought I would get started on the usual. I got eggs benedict for Ian and for Nikki, I got you the biggest stack of chocolate chip pancakes with a side of bacon. Don't worry kid, I made sure no one over cooked your bacon," he said to reassure me.

"Hey Raymond, Thank you so much! You know me so well," I said appreciatively. He knew this was always a problem and the biggest debate ever with Ian. Crispy or chewy bacon. I like my bacon on the chewier side and Ian always says that is a sin. Raymond was the owner of the place but always brought food out to make sure customers were happy with the food and the place. Raymond left with a nod.

"I don't know how you can eat all that and not gain a pound," Ian says with a grimace as he stares at my bacon with disgust.

"Don't worry about my bacon. I need more information on your new boy toy. Do you want me to make sure I reserve the VIP booth that is close to the stage Friday? It is open so if you want it, then it is yours," I said, taking a big bite of my pancakes. I moan as the syrupy deliciousness touches my tongue.

"I would appreciate it! He might bring some friends and would like to make sure they are not bothered. I know you will be chill now that I have got to explain who he is," he said with excitement, taking a sip of his mimosa. I can't blame him. I am excited for him about this.

"I will be on my best behavior and will not be a fangirl. I won't even bother you unless you grab me," I promised him. "I will also take care of the tab for you and his boys," I go further into it.

"You do not have to do that," he exclaimed. He is always so proud about being able to take care of himself, but he knows better than anyone that I will get my way on this. When I do make someone my friend, I make sure to take care of them anyway I can.

"I will. If that is the only way to be your wing woman then that is what I will do. I do have one question. Do his friends know he is gay? I know you said he was not fully out so don't want to oust him to his friends by accident," I say reluctantly.

"His friends and family know but that is it. He just is not out to the press, and he wants to keep it that way until he has to. That is a big deal in sports as you know," he says, and I nod in agreement. It can be brutal coming out to family and friends, I could not even imagine how it would be having to explain it to a whole fan base that watches his every move. I mean the guy shares a locker room with other guys and that could make some of the other guys awkward knowing he is into men.

"Okay, sounds good! If you know any songs he likes, let me know so I can rehearse them this week to really seal the deal," I said with a wink.

"What I really want to do is set you up with one of his hot friends and get you out this damn dry spell," he says, not afraid to tell me how he sees it.

"Really, you do not have to do that. I mean I would love to meet his teammates, but I don't want to date or hook up with anyone. I have to focus on the club, you know that. It is hard to find good bartenders in New York, let alone jazz singers. I am having to do both while running the club," I said with a sigh. I have never met a guy who understands that I am a strong independent businesswoman. Running the club takes up most of my time, which is why Ian and I even started doing Sunday breakfast. We were both so busy with our businesses that we went months without checking in with each other so we made a vow that every Sunday we would come here so we could make time for one another. Plus, Ian knows my kink about wanting to be shared with several men. So, between working crazy hours and my weird fetish, no man ever stays long.

"Okay, but if you change your mind when you see them just let me know. You could use some good dick for a night," he said while downing his mimosa.

"I have a perfect dick and I call him Preston," I said referring to my vibrator in my nightstand.

"Your vibrator is not a real dick. Don't you miss a guy in your bed, throwing moves on you and trying the kinky shit?" He asked, knowing full well most men run when they hear I want more than one man in bed.

I don't know what it is, but my biggest fantasy is having more than one man in my bed. I don't want them to be into each other which I think is the misunderstanding when I tell a guy. I just want to be surrounded with all the men's focus on me. I used to have the occasional one-night stand with a guy just to kill the urge, but it is so underwhelming, and I just can't get there. So, I just fantasize about a harem of men at my disposal and do the work myself. Ian knows this though, but always tells me there is nothing wrong with a simple hook up to feel the warmth of a man in bed. I really think he just wants me to find love. One man just doesn't do it for me.

"You know why, no man ever wants to do that in bed. They think I want them to do stuff to each other and say it's gay. Then, they run for the hills. I would rather do it myself than get the weird looks and criticism I get when trying to explain what I want," I explain, starting to twirl a red curl with my finger.

"Okay girl, but please tell me if you change your mind. I am sure we can get you laid really quick. I mean you are a ten out of ten. If we did not play for the same team, I would be all over you," He practically yells the last part in frustration. He tells me all the time of how gorgeous I am, but it is hard to believe it with how much rejection I get.

"No, I am not! Otherwise, I would be so much better off bringing in a harem of men and living my dirtiest fantasies," I say with a scoff.

"You have a big butt and serious titties!! Then your belly is toned and flat. You are every straight guy's dream girl!" He yells for the whole diner to hear.

"Really! I am fine. Now can you please quiet down. I do not need the whole restaurant to know what I am into plus I need to focus on the club anyways so please let's just drop it. I got to get out of here shortly anyway. I have got to put in my orders for the club," I said, trying to drop the subject.

"Okay I will drop it, for now. I just want to see you happy and get all the love you deserve. You work so hard and have the voice of an angel. You are such an amazing woman and deserve the world," he says as we stand up to leave. We walk outside in silence, and I get lost in my thoughts.

I believe what Ian is saying, but when no man wants to give me what I need, it makes me think, maybe I don't deserve it. Maybe I am just asking for too much. I know I will probably never find what I am looking for, but I'm starting to feel that it's okay, because as long as I have Ian and my club what more could I ask for?

"Bye babe, I love you," he says as my cab pulls up. He pulls open the door for me to get in.

I give him a big hug, "I love you too babe. You are all I ever need in life. You are my soulmate."

I get into the cab and wave as I head to the club which is my other soulmate.

Chapter 2

IVAN

"Why do we have to go out?" I ask my friends, seriously rethinking my life choices right now, while we pregame in our penthouse. I take a sip of my vodka as we are sitting at the island discussing the plans for tonight.

I hate going into crowded places with a bunch of strangers. I blame it on my upbringing. I was in foster care in New York since I was four. Never knew who my parents were and had a tough time making friends since I was so reserved and shy as a kid. The Nuns at my foster home were always nice though. They were always so patient with me when I was socially awkward. Now, I donate fifty percent of my baseball contract to their foster home, God's Home for Children, to give back and thank them for raising me. I am a simple guy, it is not like I spend a lot of money on clothes or other expensive things. I watch my three friends and roommates as we spend time together in our penthouse discussing the bar they want to go to.

"You could use a night out. You never go out with us and have a good time, you are always staying behind. What? You don't want to be seen with us anymore," my friend Dante says, irritated with me.

I met Dante when I was ten. His family went to the same church the sisters took us to on Sundays. He was my first true friend and never judged me for being a socially awkward kid. He sat next to me in church one Sunday trying to talk to me, but I just stayed quiet. He did this for weeks till one day I finally opened up and told him my name and that I like baseball. You would have thought I gave him the best Christmas gift as his face lit up with the biggest smile I had ever seen. He continued to keep sitting next to me every Sunday and would ask one question about me and it would not even bother him if I did not answer every time, he did enough talking for the both of us. He started inviting me over for Sunday dinner with his family when he found out I stayed at the foster home. I never stayed for too long at the dinners though, I like my solitude with my books. Books cannot hurt you or abandon you like my family did. I never tried to look for them either. If they wanted to find me then they knew where I was. The sisters only told me that my parents could not take care of me, so they thought it best to leave me with them. They also found some information later on that they were Russian. Which could not have been that hard to find out. For fuck's sake my last name was Valdimir, it does not take a rocket scientist to figure out that is a Russian last name.

"Come on man, live it up for once! Also, last week's party did not count, you knew everyone that was there. Stan says the club we are going to is low key and we will not have to worry about being recognized. Since Stan is dating the owner's friend, we finally have a place we can chill," Carter says, trying to convince me this is a promising idea. He probably wants to hook up tonight like the man whore he is.

"I went because it was a private party with all our teammates. That was more like team bonding. This is a room full of strangers wanting to party," I say running my hand through my salt and pepper hair. I am not sure why my hair went gray, maybe it is genetic, but it is where I got my nickname for my team. I am known as the silver fox of baseball.

I met Carter through Dante. I was always jealous of how easily he could talk to women. I never know when a woman is trying to talk to me because I am a famous athlete or if they actually want to get to know me. Dante decided for us all to share a penthouse, so we are never alone. We only have one rule, we do not bring girls back to the house. It is an invasion of privacy that me and Dante like to have. Dante wants to find the kind of love his parents had so he does not want girls just coming in and out. Carter on the other hand has girls in and out of his life. He even has a list of the girls he has hooked up with while on the road so when he is in town, he knows who to message for a fun time. It also helps remind himself of what they look like. At least he is an organized man whore.

"I promise, it will be chill. We even got a VIP booth, so no one can bother us. Ian said the owner got our tab for some reason. We will go in and listen to some music, have a few drinks and then we can leave. Please Ivan, I really like this guy. I promise I will never interrupt your reading again," Stan begs me while sipping his grasshopper. I never understood this guy's drinking preference but hey, I don't have to drink it. We all had our drinking preferences. I blame mine for being Russian. Dante gets his taste for wine from his mom and Carter loves Guinness.

"Fine, I will go. But if I ever need a favor, you will help, no questions asked," I almost growled. I start walking away so I can get dressed to go out.

"I owe you so much for this!" Stan yells behind me.

I go to my room to get ready. I slip on a long sleeve dark green Henley shirt and a pair of jeans. I don't even want to go out, so I am not getting dressed up. I put on my black motorcycle boots and look at myself in the mirror. I run my fingers through my hair to comb it and give myself a glance over. I think I look decent, but when I walked out of my room and made my way to the kitchen to finish my drink, the boys apparently decided we were dressing up. Dante is in black trousers and a gray button up. He is sitting on the couch with his dog begging to jump on him. Instead, he tells the dog to sit on the floor in front of him, giving him head scratches. He owns a black and white husky with the most beautiful eyes I have ever seen. One is a muddy brown, but the other is a soft blue. Dante called him Tot, probably because that dog loves tater tots more than any human I know. Dante always brings him back some when we go out to eat. Carter is standing there drinking a beer in a three-piece blood red suit with a black button-up shirt. Stan is trying to play it cool for his date and is wearing ripped jeans and a white button up. I am going to stick out like a sore thumb, but I am not trying to impress anyone, and I am definitely not going to pick up chicks.

"You could have dressed up a little more. What if there is a dress code? What if you meet a girl you like?" Carter asked. I know I should put a little more effort in, but I just do not have anyone that I want to impress. Girls always get too clingy and talk all the time. I like my silence with an informative book in my library that is in the penthouse.

"Actually, you and Dante are over dressed for this place. It is a really laid back and chill Jazz Club. You folks look like you are going to a board meeting in your outfits," Stan says, coming to my defense, not like I asked him to, but it does make me feel better about what I decided to wear.

"I never know when I could meet someone special, so I like to be prepared and look good," Dante says, rubbing the back of his neck. He just wants to find the kind of love his parents had. That love that hits you so hard you are a lovesick fool. I do not know why, but it sounds like a pain in the ass to me.

"I am not trying to impress anyone. I am just grabbing a drink and listening to some music where it sounds like they are playing all the notes at once," I explain. I just don't get Jazz. I prefer to listen to classical music or opera, not that I will ever admit that to anyone. I normally listen with my headphones on, so the guys do not hear so they don't make jokes about my taste in music.

"I swear, this music is not like that. Plus, the headliner is a real cutie," Stan says while we walk out of the house.

We head to the garage where Dante parked. He is driving since his car will fit all of us. He has a black SUV with dark tinted windows. He hops into the driver seat as Stan gets in the passenger side and me and Carter get in the back. When hopping in the car, I realized tonight is really going to suck but I will try to make the most of it.

Chapter 3

DANTE

I pull into the side parking lot. There is a line all the way down the block. I am starting to get nervous about this. We don't tend to go out a lot because it can get annoying with fans, but I really want to be there for my teammate. Stan is not fully out yet but a secret like that could put a lot of stress on someone. I just want him out and happy, like this Ian guy he likes so much is.

"Ian said to go to the front of the line and tell the bouncer a password so we can bypass the line. It is how the owners' friends get in now that the club is super popular," Stan says as I look at the sign. In big bright purple neon, I see the name, Swingers. It doesn't look like a big club, but the line is all the way down the block of people trying to get in. I can even see a couple of girls trying to flirt with the bouncers to get in.

"So, what is the password?" I ask as we get out of the car.

"Don't laugh but it is Barn Burner," Stan says reluctantly. Carter throws his head back to laugh.

"Sorry man, I cannot help it. What does that even mean?" Carter asks when wiping his tears aways from laughing so hard.

"It is a term that a famous jazz singer used to use. When a woman was stylish and classy he would call them Barn Burners. This owner must really love music to know that term," I said, explaining further. The guys know I love music, but they don't understand that it is a full-blown kink. At first, I thought I just like to set the mood with music but later I found out I cannot even cum without music playing. I did my research, and it is called Melolagnia, it is a fetish for music. I never told the guys and don't feel like I need to. They just know I like music and have a bunch of random facts about music.

"Dude! Where do you store all those useless facts about this stuff?" Carter asked.

"Just like learning about what is behind the music," I say nervously.

We walk around to the side where two bouncers stand at the door with a purple velvet rope blocking the entrance. They are in black suits and purple button-ups. Jesus! These guys are huge! They were both well over six feet and definitely worked out. They look like fucking body builders. One is sporting dreads and the other has an afro. Stan walks up to one and says the password.

"You must be the guys' Ian is waiting on," The one the afro says with a smile. This guy can smile all he wants but he still looks intimidating as fuck. "Hey Donnie, watch the line will you. I am going to take these guys back to the VIP booth."

The other guy unhooks the purple velvet rope that is blocking the door. The guy leads us through the door and I am really liking the vibe of the place. There is purple velvet everywhere. There is a stage off to the right where there is a soft jazz band playing right now. There is a huge black bar with purple velvet bar stools with black legs to the left. The guy with the afro guides us through the middle where there is a dark wood dance floor. There are a few couples that are swaying to the music. We are led to a round booth that is blocked off with more velvet rope. It is off the left of the stage in a corner. There is a guy there with short blonde hair and a black three-piece suit and light blue silk shirt sitting in the booth already.

"Hey Jake! Thanks for showing them where to go!" The blonde yells to the afro guy, trying to talk over the crowd and music. He gets up to shake his hand in gratitude.

"No problem, Ian. Nik should be on soon," he says to the guy in the booth. He then let's go of Ian's hand and turns to us.

"You guys have a good night. You are in for a treat here shortly," He yells to us before he makes his way back to the door.

"Man, that guy was fucking huge!" I yell to the blonde and my friends.

"Oh Jake? He is like a bear," Ian says with a laugh.

"Big and scary?" Ivan asked with a scoff. Ivan is big himself for a baseball player, but he has got nothing on that Donnie guy.

"More like big and cuddly. He would not hurt a fly but if you start a bar fight, he has no problem kicking your ass. He also is the guy that will throw your ass to the curb if you say anything bad about the lead singer." Ian says with a chuckle. We take our seats in the booth. Stan sits next to Ian then I sit on the other side. Ivan and Carter sit in the chairs opposite of the booth.

"Is that the Nik he was referring to?" Ivan asks, with the permanent scowl that I do not see leaving his face anytime soon. He is always a grumpy guy when we are out. He hates meeting new people or going somewhere crowded. His perfect night is staying in and reading one of his books.

"Yeah, she is great! One of the best singers I know. Think of Dianna Ross singing Jazz," Ian says as our server walks up. She is cute with brunette hair and fake tan and tits but does not seem to recognize us. Thank God! When people know who you are because you are famous does not bring in great company.

I want to find what my parents had. My mamma and papa had that love that shakes the earth when you see each other. Then when mamma lost papa to a heart attack, I thought we were going to lose her just from grief. It was like her universe fell apart. It almost made me scared to fall in love at first because to have your entire world ripped away in the blink of an eye must be devastating. I was only sixteen at the time and I had to step up. I have two younger brothers, Bobbie, and Paulie, and they were just as devastated as mom was. I had to pick up the pieces that my papa left behind. I did not blame anyone though. In a big Italian family, when the head of the family dies, the next to step up is the oldest son. It is just how my family is.

Ivan really was there for me when I needed it though. He was basically our family too, since his family had bailed on him when he was young. Ivan would help my brothers with their homework, I was never good at school. He would watch my brothers when my mom was working, and I picked up the odd job here and there to help mamma with the bills.

Now that I make more than enough for my whole family, it was time for me to look for the love I always wanted. After everything, my mamma could see I was scared to fall in love and lose it like her. So, she sat me down and told me that she would not take her pain away even if she could. That it was rare for someone to find their soul mate and she was able to even if she only got to be with him for a short amount of time. This made me want to find my soulmate just like she did.

"Hey boys! What can I get you to drink?" The server asked with a flirty smile. Great. She does not seem to recognize us but that is not stopping her from flirting with us.

"I will take an old fashion," I said and then the guys ordered their usuals. Then she runs off to get our drinks.

"The food is great here too! It is not fancy but still it is greasy and delicious if you guys want some," Ian says offering the menu to us. I look over the menu and it is your typical greasy bar food that professional athletes should not eat. I will definitely have to get tater tots to go though.

Tot would look so sad if I did not bring anything home for him. Tot, I got once I moved into the penthouse with Carter and Ivan. They love him even if they don't say so. I even caught Carter snuggling on the couch with him one time. I made sure to get a picture of it in case he even gets annoyed with him so I can hold it over his head.

"I will have to get some for Tot," I say to the table with a smile.

"Who is Tot?" Ian asked with a confused face.

"It is his pup. The dog loves tater tots so much. He looks so sad when we walk in without them," Stan explained.

"That is so cute! I love dogs. I just can't get one with my crazy work schedule. I would feel bad about leaving them all the time." He says with a sad look.

"If you ever change your mind, I have a great dog sitter who will even come to your house to look after them. I always use her when I have to go out of town for games." I tell him while pulling out my phone to show him pictures.

"Oh my god, yes! I will have to get her information from you and once I have talked to her, I will definitely look for one!" He yells excitedly. The server comes back with our drinks. She sets them on the table and gives Carter a wink when handing him his beer. She walks away swaying her hips a little too hard so he will notice, and he does. He checks out her ass as she walks off to the bar.

"Hey, do not even think about it," I warn Carter. I am really liking this place so far and don't want him to screw it up but fucking some waitress here because he does not date. He only does casual hook ups and then she would get clingy anytime we came in the future. So, then we would have to veto this place all together.

"What?" He asks, like he has done nothing wrong. The nerve. My jaw clenches in frustration.

"Not here. The owner and Ian were nice enough to get us drinks and a VIP section. I also like that we are not bombarded with fans so I would like to come back here," I say sternly like I am his dad.

"Not getting what you are putting down," he states, like I did not know what he was thinking.

"Okay I will spell it out for you. Do not be a man whore with the staff," I say slowly so he can understand.

"Okay, Jesus Christ man," he says as he puts his hands up in defeat.

"Yeah, I would be scared of what Nik would do if you scared off a server," Ian says with a laugh.

"The headliner. Why would the singer care?" Carter asked, really confused.

That is when someone takes the mic on the stage. He is a small guy in a twenties inspired outfit in pinstripe suit with a fedora. "Alright. Alright. Alright. How is everyone doing?" He asked the crowd. The crowd cheers in response. "Great! You all are in for a real treat! So, our very own Nik is coming to the stage to sing for some incredibly special guest she has here tonight." he says excitedly. This makes us four sit up a little straighter. All I can think is please don't point us out, pretty please don't point us out. The crowd screams like it is a damn concert hall. Who is this chick that is about to sing? We keep hearing her name and that she is a great singer but that is really it. The crowd gathers on the dance floor ready to watch and listen to her.

"Now we are not going to point them out because they are here to hear her sing just the same as you. Now please welcome to the stage our very own Nikki," he says as he leaves the stage.

The stage goes dark for a second and the light in the bar dims a little. I see a shadow move across the stage in a floor length dress. We all wait in anticipation. Then the spotlight goes to the girl at the center of the stage.

Mine and Carter's jaws drop to the floor. There in the spotlight stood the most beautiful redhead I have ever seen. She has long curly natural red hair and pale skin. She is wearing a tight black dress that hits the floor with a slit that goes all the way up to her thigh. That dress is showing off some serious curves. Her tits are practically falling out the top and I can see enough of her ass to know it is perfect. Perfect little freckles dance across her face under the most beautiful bright green eyes. Her makeup is simple to not hide her natural beauty but has a bright red lipstick on. Is this what my papa felt when he saw my mamma? Is this love at first sight? I am not really sure, but I am quite sure the earth just shook. Even Ivan has a small smirk when she lights up the stage. Then she speaks.

"Hey everyone. I will be performing a special song tonight for my friend Ian and a special someone," she says and then the music starts softly. The music starts to play the intro to "Bound to You" from the musical Burlesque. It is one of my mamma's favorite songs. Then she starts to sing and now I know the earth shook. My dick is instantly hard. Her perfect red lips wrapped around each word. I could imagine how they would look around my cock with my hands clutching her bright red curls. Her emotion comes out in her movements on the stage. As she sings, I keep having to adjust myself. I am glad I am wearing dress pants instead of jeans. Jeans really would have been painful with how hard I am getting.

Then when she gets to the chorus to the end, I swear I almost cum in my pants like a teenage boy. I am half tempted to go fix this issue in the bathroom, so I am not walking around with a hard on all night. Then she finishes with the most beautiful smile, she is beaming. You can tell this is what she loves to do but why is she not singing somewhere bigger I wonder. With a voice like that she could even be on Broadway. Then she walks off stage with her bows while the crowd goes crazy. I turn to Ian immediately.

"Who is she?" I asked, I want to know everything about her, but I also notice Carter and Ivan looking his way too.

"Oh, you guys will meet her soon. She is my friend Nikki. She is just getting changed and joining us," Ian says with a smirk.

"She is only going to sing one song?" Ivan asked curiously.

"Oh, that's all she needs to do. Look at her audience, they all are enthralled with her. I mean look at your faces. Me and Stan were laughing at your faces the entire time," he laughs out.

I could care less if he was laughing at me. My angel will be here shortly, and I cannot wait to meet her.

Chapter 4

CARTER

I am gob smacked. The most beautiful woman I have ever seen is going to hang out with us. I cannot wait! Now, I am not a relationship man, the guys know this. I like to have my options and don't like it when a girl starts to get clingy, but I think I want to get clingy with this girl. She was drop dead gorgeous and has a set of pipes on her. She looked gorgeous in that dress. It showed off her curves and made her tits pop up. Then those beautiful green eyes. I feel like I could get lost in them if I get a closer look. The server came back with another round and some food the owner sent too.

"Here you go handsome," she says as she bends down to put my drink in front of me. Her boobs are practically in my face. She would be easy, but right now all I think about is a certain redhead. When I don't even look at her, she makes a scoff sounding annoyed. Dante's eyes widen when he notices my reaction. I just shrug my shoulders in response.

Any other day I would be on that server real quick, but I understand why Dante did not want me to. It is so hard to find a place where we can go and just chill. Screwing the waitress would make it complicated. Now if that girl Nikki comes onto me that is a whole other story. I will not be able to hold back with her. I got hard just imagining what I could do to that girl. I want to tie her to my bed and take dirty pictures of her to use them on the road when I need them.

"So, what sports do you guys play? I know Stan and Dante are in hockey but not sure about you all." Ian asked while sipping his martini.

"Well, I play football for New York and Ivan over here plays baseball," I tell him, still looking for this redhead that disappeared. I tried to be discreet while looking for her in the crowd, but I am sure the guys notice as I whip my head around. Ivan looks at me with an arched brow wondering who I am looking for. I could care less. I just want another look at her and maybe talk to her.

"That is really cool! I don't really watch sports, but I guess I will now that I know athletes are so cute," he says as he gives a sideways look to Stan. Stan blushes looking down at the table.

"Let us know if you ever want to come to a game. We can get you tickets," I say, trying to get into his good graces. If he is friends with this Nikki girl, then I need to be friends with him. I mean I still would have been nice to him for Stan, but I really want to get with Nikki, so I need to be extra nice.

"You do not need to do that. It is a sweet offer so thank you but actually Nikki is more of a sports fan than I am," he says, and this makes me sit up a little straighter.

"Really?" I ask, wanting to know if she would come to one of my games if I offered. I would love to invite her to a game. I could look up after every play and see her cheering for me in my jersey. My cock turns into steel as I imagine her that way. I have to adjust myself in my seat.

"She never misses a hockey game. Her dad is a pretty big sports guy, so she grew up around sports but fell in love with hockey," he says, keeping his focus on Stan. Fucking hell! That means she will probably be more into Dante than me. I have got to fix this if I want that girl in my bed. I need to find this girl and fast. Maybe I can talk to her first and invite her to a game to get her into my sport.

Then I spot her coming out of a door next to the stage. Even dressed down she still puts all these other girls to shame. She is in an ACDC vintage band crop top and high-rise black booty shorts. Then when I go down further, I notice fishnets and glossy tall black heels. I wonder what she would look like just in those shoes and nothing else. Good god, my dick is the hardest it has ever been, and I have not even seen this girl naked. I need to turn on the charm times ten because I need her to fix what she is doing to my dick. She walks to the bar and pours herself some Johnie Walker over ice. Ahhhh, she does have good taste. While she is pouring it, she talks to the good-looking bartender. He is about five nine and has long brown hair in a man bun. He is built but not crazy muscular. She laughs at something he says to her. Then, there is this feeling in my chest I have not felt before. I haven't even met the girl so it can't be jealous. Then she waves, telling him bye as she starts walking to our table. Her legs are walking to the beat that the band is playing.

"Hey everyone!" She says as she walks over to the table. She slips past me and sits next to Stan. She smells absolutely delicious, like strawberry shortcake. I wonder if she tastes as delectable as she smells.

"Hey babe!!" Ian yells at her. "Everyone, this is my friend Nikki. Nikki, this is Stan, his teammate Dante, and his friends Ivan and Carter." He says as he points to us as he introduces us.

"I hope you guys are enjoying my club," she says as she steals a fry from Ian's plate. A girl with an appetite, I love it. All the jersey chasers me and the guys put up with would not be caught dead eating anything fatty.

"Wait, your club?" Dante asked, with a look of shock on his face. Damn, this woman owns this cool club. She is way cooler than me and the guys. I am really going to have to work hard for this girl.

"Yeah, I am the owner. I wanted a place to sing so I opened this place," she says with a shrug of the shoulders.

"You are a great vocalist," Ivan says nonchalantly. Me and Dante just stare at him. We were expecting him to be silent all night, looking like he was going to murder someone. Then he smirked at her performance and now this. This is so out of character for him. I am not sure how to react to this, but Dante just keeps up the conversation.

"So, you own this place and you sing. That is amazing! That song is one of my mamma's favorites. You should be on Broadway with that voice," Dante says with such enthusiasm.

"I was, but I just didn't enjoy it. I was always told what to sing and how to sing it. I started to not like singing," she explains. What the hell? Anything she sang would be nothing less than perfect so I am having a tough time believing that anyone would criticize such a perfect woman.

"Why don't you try writing songs?" I asked, curiously. I would think with such an amazing voice she would not have a challenging time with that. Any record company would be lucky to have her as a singer.

"To do that you need to know how to play an instrument," she says with a laugh. Then sighs in defeat. "I really only know how to sing, never learned instruments."

"Well, you really are good," I said. Then under my breath I added, "and hot."

"Excuse me?" She says with a laugh.

Fuck! She heard me. Now I have to get out of this, so she does not think I am a tool. Dante gives me a look that says good luck. Ian and Stan are laughing in the center of the booth.

"You are gorgeous is all I am saying," I said with my flirty smile. I am gonna have to pull all the stops with this girl. I can tell she does not take shit from anyone. That's okay, it would have been boring if she just jumped in my lap.

"Nice save flirt," she said with a scoff and rolled her eyes.

"Not a flirt. Just stating the obvious," I tell her honestly. Am I trying to flirt with her? Yes, but it's god's honest truth that she is drop dead gorgeous, so I am just stating the obvious.

"Hey, you guys want to dance?" Ian asks. He gets up and offers his hand to Stan and he takes it to get up with him. This is my opportunity, and I am gonna take it.

"I would love to," I say as I get up from my seat and move towards Nikki. I put out my hand to the beautiful woman beside me.

"Want to dance?" I ask her, hoping she is not stubborn.

"Sure, why not," she says in a monotone and takes a hold of my hand as I pull her out the booth. Ian and Stan follow us to the dance floor while I lead her to the middle. The band on stage is playing a nice soft jazz song which is perfect for me. I stop us when we get to the middle and bow to her and that gets me a giggle. I love that sound. I cannot wait to hear other noises come out of her mouth. I grab her one hand and the other goes around her waist. We start to sway to the music. I can feel her warmth and my cock practically jump in my pants. I start to graze my hand closer to her ass and then she stiffens a little.

"Watch the hands flirt," she warns because she knew exactly what I was going for. I can't help but laugh at that.

"Sorry, must have slipped," I tell her innocently and give her a mischievous smirk. She is smart and can see right through my bullshit.

"I bet it did," she snaps back softly in a whisper.

We continue to sway to the music, and I ask her, "I got a nickname already I see. Do we all have nicknames yet?"

"Not yet. Need to talk to the others before I decide," She admits with a light laugh. "So, Ian told me you are an athlete but did not tell me your sport. What is your sport?"

"How about we make this a game?" I ask with my flirty smile. Seeing this as my chance to get her to one of my games.

"Oh, a game? What are the rules, Mr. Flirt?" She asked curiously.

"I will give you three guesses. If you guess correctly, I will give you season tickets to my games." I say with an evil grin.

"And what do you get if I don't get it in three guesses?" She asks, fighting back a knowing smirk. I lean down so my lips touch her ear.

"Oh, I think you know what I want," I whisper, ghosting my breath against her ear. Her body shivers from my breath. Still whispering in her ear, I tell her what I want, "A kiss from those beautiful red lips."

"You are playing high stakes," she says as I go to dip her. I dip her and then pull her back up close to me.

"It's no fun if you don't," I say, still grinning evilly. There is no way this girl can get it right. I have to win this game. I need to see if she tastes as good as she smells.

"Okay I'm down to play," she says with a laugh and continues, "Okay so I know you are not a hockey player so we can exclude that."

"Oh, how do you know that?" I ask her, trying to edge her on so she uses one of her guesses. I am not going to play fair if that gets me my kiss from this goddess.

"Well, are you?" She asked as we continued to sway.

"No and that counts as a guess," I say with a laugh.

"No, I already said you weren't," she says with her eyebrows furrowed.

"Too bad. I am not playing fair if it gets me a kiss from you. You will get wrinkles if you make faces like that," I move my hand, using my thumb to rub between her brows to get her to soften her face.

"Is this your idea of flirting? Telling a woman she is going to get wrinkles?" she asked with a scoff.

"Works with other women. Keep guessing sweetheart," I say in command. I cannot wait to boss her in the bedroom. I wonder if I can get her to switch my nickname to daddy.

"Okay. This is a shot in the dark but you're not a soccer player?" She asked second guessing herself.

"Nope and that was a waste of a guess. Does this body look like a foot fairy?" I say laughing hard.

"Ahhhh, I know now. You just gave yourself away," she says with a cocky smirk. My cock hardens even more. She gasps as I press myself against her so she can feel the effect she has on me.

"Oh, please tell me how I gave myself away," I say. There is no way she figured it out. I made sure not to accidentally give her any hints as to what sport I play.

"Well, I know you don't play hockey or soccer. Then your comment about your body actually made me think about how big it is," she says.

"That is not the only thing that is big," I whisper in her ear again. She starts to blush when she realizes what I mean.

"Then your cocky attitude just confirms it more," she says with another laugh.

"Okay so what sport do I play princess?" I ask. She moves so close I can almost taste her sweet scent. Fuck! She is rubbing her heat against my cock. I know she can feel it. I am going to be sporting a hard cock all night. Then she leans up, so her lips touch my ear.

"You're a football player," she says with a whisper in my ear. The music starts to fade out as she stops moving. I watch her as she walks back to the table. Well shit! So much for my kiss.

Chapter 5

Nikki

Oh, sweet baby Jesus!! I am so turned on by one dance. I need to fight this urge though. I am here to support my friend anyway I can, not screw his new friends. That would just make things complicated. Carter is such a flirt though and he is just looking for a night and not forever, I could already tell that about him. I slide into the booth with Ian and Stan and Carter tries to slip in beside me but is practically falling out of the booth. It makes me laugh. Carter leans down so his lips are right on my ear.

"What's so funny?" He asks in a whisper in my ear. I shiver as his lips graze my ear. I can feel his warm breath as he asks me.

"You know you can sit in the seat over there. There is no room in the booth," explaining further as I sigh in frustration.

"But it is so far away from where I want to be," he says with a devilish grin, he has been sporting all night. I can practically feel my pussy ache every time he gives me that smile and I feel like he knows that, but I am not going to give him the satisfaction. If he wants in my pants he is going to have to work for it.

"And where would that be, flirt?" I ask, even though I know where he means. He smells delectable. He smells the ocean, and I can almost envision the beach with the sand in my toes.

"Next to you," he whispers in my ear. I can feel the hair stand on my neck. He continues and this time it sends another shiver down my spine, "You smell like strawberry shortcake. Sweet and delicious."

"Okay Mr. Flirt but I need to go to the bathroom and get another drink," I state as I shove him out the booth. I can hear Ian and Stan snicker when Carter falls to the floor. I get up from the booth and extend my hand to him to help him up. I didn't mean to push him that hard, I was just trying to get him to move. He gets up and then sits in his chair that is across from the booth.

I rushed to the office, it is small, but I don't need a big fancy office. I painted it purple, my favorite color. I have a television hanging on the wall to watch hockey games for when I work late. Which is basically every night. I have some shelves here for storage in dark wood and a black desk with a back-office chair. I need a second to breathe and have a drink. I close my office door and take a deep breath. It was too much sitting in a booth with the most delectable men in my bar. I can literally feel my pussy pulsing at the opportunity to share those three men. Fuck no, you little traitor! I cannot go through that again. They would run if I even insinuated that with a joke. I can feel myself getting wetter at the images of the three of them surrounding me. I rush to my mini fridge and get a cold bottle of water. I really need to calm down and this is really my only option. I jump when I hear a knock on the door. I opened the door to see Ian.

"How's the libido now, love?" He asked with a laugh. He pushes in and sits in the chair that is in front of my desk. I have that so the servers can sit and talk to me while I cash them out for the night. It's more professional than sitting out front and doing it. The customers would see the money and might get the stupid idea to mug them as they walk out. I close the door with a sigh.

"What do you mean?" I ask in a squeaky voice. I could never lie. My voice always goes up an octave when I try. Ian laughs knowing me all too well.

"Oh please, as your best friend you cannot fool me. Which one is doing it for you?" He asked as he leaned back into the office chair full of himself. I go to the shelves where I have some scotch and pour us both a glass. Sadly, I don't have ice in my office, but it does not matter. I hand him his and slam back mine. I move to my office chair that is at my desk.

"Okay I will be honest. They all do beside your little guy," I told him truthfully.

"Wait, wait, wait. What do you mean by all of them?" He asked, so confused. Then we sit there in silence for a moment as I pour myself another glass of scotch and then I see the light bulb in his head go off when his face changes.

"Ohhhh!" He yells. I roll my eyes and then slam back my glass again. Then he asked, "So what are you going to do about it?"

"Nothing! For so many reasons!" I yell at him and then continue, "One, you want to get with Stan, and I am not trying to ruin it by hooking up with his friends."

"How would that ruin it? I think it would make it better to be honest. We would finally have a group of friends to hang out with," He says as he tilts his head to the side looking at me like I am not making any sense.

"And when it does not work out? If it doesn't then you will continue to see Stan and they guys are his friends so they will be around. It will make me feel awkward seeing them all the time." I ask. He stays silent as I continue, "Second, they are pro athletes. What would they want with a girl like me?"

"Bitch! Do we really need to have this conversation again? You are a knockout!" He yells frustrated. I know he is getting annoyed having to repeat himself about this, but I can't help it. I have insecurities and I blame it on the men that won't even think about what I want. I can just remember their judgmental stares when I ask them if they could even think about sharing me.

"Okay I will move onto number three. Third and most important one, if I tell them I want to sleep with all of them at once, they will run for the hills. I cannot deal with that reaction anymore! That is the whole reason I am insecure. I am not going to put myself through that. Again!" I yell the last word breathlessly. Ian gets up from the chair and pulls me out of my chair, so we are both standing. He gives me the biggest hug. He pulls back to look me in the eyes cradling my head between his hands, just to make sure I get the gravity of his next words.

"Listen love because I am only going to say this once more. You will find someone or multiple people that will make that fantasy of yours come true. I know this is hard for you and guys from your past made it seem like you are crazy for even asking but you are not. I love you so much and I want you to have the world. You have so much love in your heart and there is so much it would be too much for just one man. The right man will come along and give you that. You are absolutely beautiful and deserve nothing less. I hope one day you will think that too. Just know that, if you want to go after all of them you have my full support and if Stan is not okay with that, then he can kiss my ass. I would never put you before anyone else and you know that," he explained empathetically.

"I know but I am not going to do that. I will not be the reason to make you give up and lose this relationship. I see the way you look at Stan. I want to see that smile every day," I told him.

"I love you. Now let's go get me laid and possibly you!" He yells as he runs from my office. I laugh and follow him out. I run to the bar to get myself another drink that I desperately need, when I see the other hockey player come up to the bar. I pour myself another scotch on ice and pretend I do not see him coming.

"Hey Nikki, mind if I have one of what you are having?" He asked shyly with a hint of an Italian accent. He is blushing and it is so darn cute and innocent. This man is absolutely gorgeous too. He has dark medium length hair and a beard that I would love to feel between my thighs. My pussy is up and awake again. Down girl, I tell her in my head. He has beautiful tan skin and rippling muscles that bulge out of his dress shirt. It would be crazy not to get wet from looking at this man.

"Absolutely...." I say and shit! I am fangirling here and cannot get his name out. I am fucking this up and I promised Ian I would be cool. I go to pour him his drink as he tells me, "Dante De Luca." His accent is too much for my libido. He has a small Italian accent that makes me swoon.

"I am so sorry. You would think that owning a bar, I would be good with names. I do love yours though and with your accent, you must be a lady killer," I tell him truthfully, trying to play it cool. His blush goes even deeper.

"I would not call me that, Mia Cara." He says softly.

"Oh, and what should I call you?" I ask, wondering what he is going to say about my blatant question.

"Hmmmm... I would have to say I am a romantic," he says with a smile. This guy is just way too sweet. If he keeps it up it is going to be hard to stick to my promise with Ian that I would not touch Stan's friends.

"Then Carter is Mr. Flirt and I think I will call you Romeo," I tell him with a laugh.

"Anything but that, Mia Cara," he tells me with a serious tone.

"What does Mia Cara even mean?" I ask him with a snitty tone. I don't mean to come off as a bitch, but what if he is making fun of me. It does not matter how sexy his voice is when he says it. If he is insulting me, he should at least do it in English, so I know.

"I can see I won't be able to sneak anything by you. It is Italian for my darling," he says with a smirk.

"Oh, so you weren't insulting me then," I say looking down at my drink, blushing. He reaches over the bar to grab my hand and waits till I look at him.

"There is nothing about you to insult, Mia Cara. You are absolutely perfect, and I think I want the next dance," he says and pulls me around the bar. I followed him to the dance floor forgetting our drinks. The band is playing a more upbeat jazz song now. I am kind of stunned at what he just said. He barely knows me and is already calling me perfect. He will learn how imperfect I am soon enough though. They always do. He grabs my hips, and we start to sway to the beat of the song.

"Once you get to know me you will find out how wrong that statement is," I say as I look at our feet avoiding his eyes. One of his hands leaves my hip and moves under my chin. He forces me to look at him. His eyes go black with lust, but I can still see the beautiful warm brown in them.

"No, Mia Cara, that is where you are wrong. I think once I learn more about you it will just prove how perfect you are," he says deeply and then moves his hand back around my waist. I am so glad it did, because to be honest, I almost swoon when he said that. I lost my footing a little, but his strong hands hold me in place and then we went back to swaying.

"With lines like that I am not sure how you are single then," I say, and I just gave myself away. I can feel my face warm as I blush. God fucking damn it!

"And how do you know this?" He says with a smirk.

"I love hockey so to be honest I already knew who you were before meeting you. I swear I am not a stalker," I say defensively looking down at our feet again. I don't need him thinking I stalk him. It would just make seeing me in the future more awkward.

"I thought you forgot my name," he says with a laugh like I said the funniest joke. This makes me whip my head up to look him in the eyes. My face softens as I see his beautiful smile.

"If I am being fully honest here, I could never forget the best goalie in the league. I just couldn't get it out because I was nervous meeting you," I say with a nervous chuckle turning my head not wanting to see his reaction.

"See, I am learning more about you and you are the perfect girl. There are not many beautiful women who can talk hockey with me. Also please look at me. I do not want to miss a second of those beautiful green eyes looking at me," he says and that makes me turn to look him in his eyes. I get lost in his warm brown gaze and can tell from his gaze that he means what he says.

"You really know how to test a woman then," I say, still gazing into his eyes.

"How am I testing you, Mia Cara?" He asks almost with concern shining in his eyes.

"Well, I already told Ian I did not want to go past friends with you all because tonight is about supporting him and Stan. You guys are making it exceedingly difficult to stand by that," I say with a giggle. He leans down to my ear.

"Well, I am going to make it my mission that you don't keep to that Mia Cara," He whispers so close to my ear I can feel his breath. I am sure he can feel my whole-body shiver. Then I feel his hand move up my back and rest on my bare skin that is showing from my crop top. We start swaying again and he leans back to look at me.

"So, since you are a hockey fan would you be interested in some tickets? I have my own private box that my family uses sometimes but other times they cannot make it. I would love to have you at one of my games wearing my jersey," He offers, looking so excited it is almost so hard to say no.

"No, you don't need to do that really. I have a television in my office, so I never miss a game. Plus, I would not want to kick your family out," I said reluctantly. I would love some hockey tickets, but I don't need to be in a private box with his family. That seems a little too intimate.

"Well, if you don't want box seats, I do have tickets for behind the bench. That would be even better because then I can see you the whole game and have Mia Cara so close," he says with a wink. Fuck! I won't be able to keep it together if he keeps coming at me with that Mia Cara crap. I am barely keeping up with his accent let alone with how sweet he is. "Please Mia Cara, just one game?" He asked so sadly. Yep, I am done for.

"Fine, one game and not the box seats. Also, it has to be a weekday game because of the club," I say, and you would have thought he was a kid in a candy store with the smile he is sporting. I am going to have to ask my main bartender to close up the bar for me, but Chloe never minds helping me out. Plus, she is always telling me I need to take a day off for myself.

"Yes! Perfect! We have a home game on Monday. I will have my driver pick you up at five. He will have the tickets and your jersey," he said excitedly. Then the last part hit me.

"I have a jersey. You don't have to get me one," I say nervously. I don't want him to think he needs to buy me things to get my attention.

"Oh, and whose name is on the jersey?" He says as he arches one eyebrow.

"It's Quick, the other goalie," I say, and I can feel my blush creep up on me again.

"No, Mia Cara, I will not let another man's name be on your skin. The only jersey I want to see you in is mine from now on," he says with a scowl. It is actually kind of scary, but it looks like Mr. Romance has a dark side and it is doing wonders to me. I can feel my pussy almost dripping at his possessiveness so I will play along for now.

"So, it is true what they say about hockey players?" I ask with a smirk.

"What is that?" He asked, confused.

"That hockey players are very possessive and that you hate to see your woman in any other jersey but your own," I say and instantly regret it.

"So, you are my woman?" He asked, sporting that dazzling smile. The music starts to fade. I get on my tip toes so I can lean up to his ear so no one can hear me.

"That is still to be determined, because I don't know yet if you can handle me as your woman," I whisper. I get off my toes and he is standing there stunned. I rush back to the table with him following close behind. I make sure to sway my hips a little hard as I walk just for him.

I slip into the other side of the booth, so I am next to Ian and across from Ivan. This man is bigger than the other men at the table. He has beautiful salt and pepper hair and green eyes I could get lost in. He is not like his other friends, they have no problem flirting and striking up a conversation. Also, his friends are decked out in designer clothes, and he is in just a green long sleeve and a pair of jeans. Even dressed down he is handsome. I wonder what he would like in gray sweatpants and nothing else. Wait no! Bad pussy, I scorn my pussy in my head. I do not need those images right now. I am curious because all night he has been looking like he could kill someone if they talk to him. Well, let's poke the bear. I turn to him and look him straight in the eyes not backing down.

"Hey Mr. Grumpy, you are the only one I have not danced with. Want to come dance with me?" I ask with my best smile. Something I said must have been right because I can tell he is fighting back a smirk.

"I don't dance," he says seriously.

"Do you not know how?" I ask, trying to tease him. One side of his lips twitch up. Got him!

"No, I know how but I choose not to," he says still smirking. All his friends are all wide eyed and their jaws dropped. Interesting, I wonder why. I get up and grab his hand to pull him up. Like I said, this guy is big, and it takes a lot of effort on my part to yank him out of his seat.

"Well, I want to dance with you, so come on big guy, live a little," I say and pull him towards the dance floor. He hesitantly follows me. The band is playing a soft jazz song. I have his hand and then with my other hand I hold onto his shoulder and his hand goes to my waist.

"So, Mr. Grump, why no dancing?" I ask when we start to sway.

"This is just not my type of music," he says with a scowl.

"Oh, and why is that? Do you not like my club?" I ask with a raised eyebrow. I have never really seen a negative review about my club, so his statement is kind of shocking.

"No that is not it. I just really don't like Jazz, is all. Some of the songs sound like they are trying to play all the notes at the same time. I don't hear the rhythm," he says trying to fight off a smile. We start to turn and when I see his friends, it is like they are frozen as they were, wide eyed and jaws to the floor. This is going to be interesting.

"Okay so what kind of music do you like?" I ask curiously. I want to figure out this bear of a man and what makes him tick.

"I don't really tell people. I will tell you, but you must promise not to tell anyone else," he says nervously. I am not sure why, but this man's reactions are fascinating to me.

"Of course, but why would you want to keep it a secret?" I ask. It can't be that bad, unless it is something embarrassing like screamo.

"You will know once I tell you," he says looking nervous. After a moment of him watching me, I hear him say lightly, "I like opera." It was so low, I almost missed it.

"Why is that a secret? That is cool!" I tell him. It looks like a weight was just lifted off his shoulders as he relaxes.

"Oh really? Not a lot of people like opera and classical music so I don't tend to tell anyone. When I was in high school a kid found out and made fun of me for it," he says admittedly. This has my jaw dropping. Why would someone make fun of a kid for their type of music? Oh, right kids can be little shits.

"That is awful! You should not listen to them. That is the music that made all other music what it is today. Who is your favorite opera singer?" I asked, super excited. I have never met another opera fan. Now it is not my favorite music, but I do enjoy it.

"Maria Callos," he says, and his grin gets wider. I have cracked Mr. Grump's walls a little and I am enjoying every second of it.

"Oh, I love her, but I am a huge fan of Luca Pavarotti. I know a drag queen who performs his songs, and it is amazing," I tell him.

"That's cool I guess," he says as he starts to build those walls again. Nope, not gonna let it happen. I just started to see behind the grump facade, and I am not going to let him build these walls back up.

"So, what sport do you play?" I ask, wanting to know everything about this man.

"You don't know?" He asked, looking amused.

"I hate to tell you big guy, but if you do not play hockey, I don't know your name," I tell him honestly. I looked up and he has the biggest smile I have ever seen. It is almost shocking since he looked so grumpy all night.

"You don't know how happy that makes me," he tells me with excitement. It is probably so refreshing to meet someone who is not falling to his feet because of the fame of his sport.

"Oh. Do you not like being a pro athlete?" I asked him looking into his eyes. I want to understand this man, he is so different from his friends. He is also not the normal cocky athlete. I can almost see the trauma in his gaze when he looks all grumpy.

"I think I like that you don't know. I think I will keep it to myself," he says with a cocky smirk. My mouth is gaping as he lets go of me and walks back to the table. This is not at all what I was expecting. The other two are so far up my ass I literally had to push one out the booth, but this guy is so different. Now I want Ian to make it work with Stan so I can see these guys more. I will make sure to always have a VIP booth anytime these guys come in. I want to see how this plays out.

I follow him back to the booth and I would like to stay for the night, but I have so much to do for the club. The list is never ending. I sit for about another hour and make sure my focus is on Ian and Stan and not on the three men that are staring at me. I need to focus! I cannot deal with this kind of complication. I can see it now, they are not going to want to share me, they are going to want to own me for themselves. Well, I can tell them right now it is not in the cards, but I don't want to ruin Ian's night. Tonight is all about him and I need to make sure I keep it that way. So, the best thing I could do is just excuse myself and go to my upstairs apartment and work on stuff for the club up there.

"Ian, babe, I think I am gonna call it a night," I tell him as I get up from the booth. The three guys get up with me and I look at them confused.

"This early?" Ian asked disappointed. Stan on the other hand looks just as disappointed, probably because now his friend won't have a toy to keep them distracted.

"I have a ton of orders to write up for Sunday and have to start getting everyone's pay together. I am going to do it upstairs so I can focus on it. Enjoy the rest of your night guys, we are not closed till two so you still have two hours to party," I tell them and hope they would just let me go.

"Okay love. I will see you on Sunday, right?" Ian asked, like I would not show up on our one definite plan.

"Of course! I wouldn't miss it even if the world was ending," I tell him with a big smile. He rolls his eyes at my exaggeration.

"I think it is time for us to go anyway. I have to meet with the trainer tomorrow," Carter says while he rubs the back of his neck like he is nervous. It's kind of cute compared to the cocky football player I met. I giggle which makes him look at me in surprise. We all get out of the booth, and I give Ian and Stan a group hug. They are so cute, and I cannot wait to hear how the rest of the night went on Sunday.

"It was really nice to meet you all! I hope I get to see you a lot more and never be afraid to come to the club. Here, I will give you my number so you can text me when you do," I hand Stan my phone and he gives me his so we can swap numbers. Ian looks so happy that me and Stan are getting along. I hope he wears that smile more now that he met a nice guy that likes him for him. I turn to the other guys to say bye but then Dante pulls me into a hug and slips something in my pocket. I am a little shocked that he did that, but I embrace it, enjoying his delicious smell. He smells like forest, I get hints of fresh pine. I let go so I can say goodbye to the other two. I go to give Carter a quick hug, but he pulls me in close to whisper in my ear.

"Goodnight, beautiful. I cannot wait to see you again," he whispers in my ear, which sends goosebumps down my neck. He must feel my reaction because he quietly laughs in my ear then lets me go so, I can turn to Ivan. Ivan surprises me the most with what he does. He grabs my hand and plants a wet kiss on my knuckles. I look at him surprised.

"Good night, Nikki," he says softly, dropping the whole grump act.

"Goodnight!" I squeak out. I practically run up to my apartment. I slammed the door behind me and slid down so I am sitting on the floor. I am so fucked!

Chapter 6

Ivan

I am sitting in the back of the SUV while Dante drives home. Carter is in the passenger seat, but I am too deep in thought about what happened back at the club to worry about them. Stan went home and took Ian with him, so I have an idea what they are doing. I didn't mean to eavesdrop. I was just looking for the bathroom when I heard voices. My legs lead me to the beautiful voice I wanted. She said she wanted all of us. The thought actually was intoxicating. I could imagine taking her deep from behind while she is on her hands and knees. Then having Dante there in front of her claiming her mouth. I am so hard behind my jeans that it is uncomfortable. I try to adjust myself to take some pressure off, but it is no use. It is obvious that they were into her, but I am not sure they will be into what she is into. I need to talk to them beforehand.

Rage surges through me at the thought of all these men before me that made her feel like she was undeserving of her fantasy, which caused her to have self-doubt. She deserves everything we have to offer, and I plan to give it to her. I have never felt so pulled to a woman before. Do not get me wrong I have urges just as much as the next guy. When I hooked up with a girl and I lay it out that there will not be another night. No one can abandon you if you leave first. We pulled up in the garage and we get out of the car. I finally say, "We need to talk when we get upstairs."

"That we do because we need to talk about Nikki," says Dante. I figured they noticed too. We all went after her tonight fighting over her like a couple of horny teenage boys that saw a girl for the first time. We make our way to the penthouse in silence. Once the door is closed Dante speaks first. Tot is so excited to see us, he jumps on Carter when he sees he has a takeout box. Carter goes and opens the box to give him a tater tot. Carter puts the box in the kitchen, and we all make our way to the living room and sit down.

"Okay so what do you have to say since you brought it up first," Dante says while looking at me with furrowed brows.

"First, I need you guys to keep an open mind when I tell you about what I am about to say because it is a bizarre idea," I say, rubbing the back of my neck with one hand and the other with a fist at my side.

"If it is about Nikki I can," Dante chimes in. We both look at Carter who looks at me with his head tilted.

"Sure, I think I can do that," he says as he sits down on the couch and still has a couple tots to give to Tot that he must have pulled out of the box before sitting down. Tot waits patiently in front of him wagging his tail as Carter gives them to him one at a time.

"Okay first thing is first, I need to know if you guys like Nikki and if you want to pursue her," I ask them, and they look at me like I have ten heads, but I do not care. I need to know this first.

"I think that would be obvious," Dante says with a laugh. He goes to sit on the couch with Carter.

"I need to make sure before I continue," I say in seriousness.

"Yes," they both say excitedly. Then they look at each other with a scowl. This is what I was afraid of. Dante always had a possessive side and Carter is so blind when it came to girls he actually liked, which was few. Nikki doesn't want three men fighting over her, she wants them to show her how much she means to them by not letting jealousy get in the way and share her.

"Okay so, when I got up to go to the bathroom, I heard a conversation Ian and Nikki were having in her office," I say, and both sit up straight. I continued, "She is into all of us but that is not the only thing she said."

"Okay what else did she say," Carter says interested now.

"So, this is where I need you to keep an open mind. She wants all of us, but she wants all of us together. She has a fantasy about having multiple men at the same time. She is not going to ask us though. Apparently anytime she offers it the guy runs with his tail between his legs. This has caused some insecurities for her, which I hate. That girl is so amazing, and I have never felt like this before. Like, I want to give her the world," I tell them honestly. They look at me like I am crazy, but I could care less. I expected this reaction, but we needed to have this conversation because I don't want them to make her feel like she was not worthy of this. She is a goddess and deserved the entire world on their knees offering this to her.

"That... is different," Carter says, shocked.

"I just needed to talk to you guys because what if we offer this?" I ask them and I cannot get a read on Dante, but Carter looks so surprised by this.

"I would offer it to her if I knew that is what she wanted," Dante says admittingly. I know that was hard for him to admit with his possessive side. He must really like her like I do.

"Okay so how would this work," Carter finally chimes in and then continues with his concerns, "Would we have specific days with her? Like I get her on Monday and Dante Tuesday? I don't think she would like to get passed around."

"No, we would all share her together, that is what she wants. I know that is weird, but it is what she wants and if you care about her, you will let this happen and not sleep around. If you have any doubt at this moment, me and Dante will pursue her and you back off," I tell him in warning. I am already pissed about how men make her feel and I will not let Carter make her feel that way.

"What is that supposed to mean?" He asked in shock that I would say that. I roll my eyes at him because he is so open about being a manwhore it is laughable that he is asking surprised.

"You know what I mean. Look I am not going to sugar coat this. You are kind of a man whore, and you know that. If we do this, we need to focus on her like she is the sun and we revolve around her," I told him. Dante nodded his head in agreement.

"Okay, I know that is what I am like but with her I don't want that. She needs a better guy and I think I would like to try to be that guy," he says nervously. Wow, I did not see that one coming. I thought he would bow out. He must really like this girl.

"That is what I wanted to hear so the next step is how do we do this?" I ask them. I had planned to bring this up but did not want to get ahead of myself and start planning what to do to make this happen.

"Well, I am not gonna lie, but I did invite her to Monday's home game. We need to ease her into this. Like each one has a one on one with her and then all of us come together after," Dante suggests. It's not a bad idea. With how judged she has been for this it is an innovative idea to take it slow. If we rush it, she might think it is us messing with her.

"That sounds great! We can feel her out individually and then once she is comfortable, we can bring her back here and talk to her about it. I don't want her to have insecurities with us. I really hate all the men that came before us made her feel that way," Carter says and tenses up.

"I agree because if we just ambush her, she might take it as us messing with her for wanting this. So, Dante has Monday with her. Carter, you don't have a game tomorrow?" I ask him and his face lights up.

"Nope, what are you thinking?" He asks as his anger melts away at the thought of seeing her. He is practically wiggling on the sofa with excitement. I can't help but let out a chuckle because he kind of looks like Tot waiting for a treat.

"Can you go to the club tomorrow and kind of ease her into it? I am going to invite her to an opera on Sunday night for our one on one," I tell him the plan and then both their eyes widen. I should not have told them my plan.

"Wait what? Do you listen to opera? That is so cool!" Dante explains.

"I did not tell you guys because kids used to make fun of me for listening to it in high school. So, I learned to keep that to myself, but I think I am done hiding. I mean if I have the guts to tell you guys, I want to share a girl then I should have the guts to tell you this," I explain. We have always been close, but I have a hard time letting people in, scared they would leave just like my parents, but I need to get over this bullshit fear.

"Man, you never have to keep anything from us! We all get judged in our own way, but you should know that me and Dante will never judge you for what you like," Carter says with pity written all over his face.

"I know man but back to what we were talking about. You meet up with her on Saturday, I invite her Sunday night and Dante has his game with her," I tell him, so we all understand our plan.

"Agreed," They both say at the same time.

"Now I have to figure out how to invite her Sunday," I say defeated. I never got her number and neither did either of the guys.

"I slipped my number to her because of Monday but she has not texted me yet and I don't think she will until last minute Monday," Dante tells us, also defeated.

"Wait! We know one person who has her number!" Carter practically screams, causing Tot to run to Dante scared. We patiently wait and he looks at us like idiots. "Stan!"

I already have my phone out calling Stan the second Carter said his name. He did not answer the first time, so I redial and put on speaker. Then he picks up and I can hear his moan and his annoyance. It makes me laugh.

"What do you want? I am kind of busy here!" He snaps and I hear Ian laugh in the background.

"You know that favor you owe me? I want to cash in," I tell him with a snicker.

"Right now?" He says still annoyed. I know I am an ass for interrupting him and Ian, but we have to get the ball rolling with Nikki.

"Yep, and you're on speaker so try to keep this call PG please," Carter says, throwing his head back with a laugh. As much as he is a dick for pointing that out, I can wholeheartedly agree. I exactly don't want to hear Stan and Ian fuck.

"Fine, what do you want?" He asked defeated because he knows I will just keep calling him till he gives me what I want.

"You got her number right?" I asked.

"Whose number?" He asked curiously, which earned an eye roll from Dante.

"Don't play dumb! You are the only one that got Nikki's number and we want it," Dante says annoyed.

"Hold on! Give me that phone!" We hear Ian yell in the background. I hear some rustling as Stan gives Ian the phone and he asks, "What do you guys want with my Nikki?"

He comes off more possessive. Ah, he must be Nikki's gate keeper. I can respect it because he is just trying to protect her. He did seem to like us when we were there, but I am not sure what he will do now. He probably has seen her get her heartbroken with these fucking idiots that she has dated so he might not trust us, so I am just going to tell him the truth.

"Okay I am not going to fuck around with you on this. I was looking for the bathroom and her office is right by it, and I heard the whole conversation in the office. Now that we are being honest, we want to give her what you guys talked about," I tell him, and he goes silent for a moment. I had to check my phone to make sure we did not get disconnected.

"You guys are seriously going to offer her that?" He asked skeptically. He wants to protect her and us three can respect that. We try to do the same in our little circle we created.

"Yes," all three of us say in unison.

Then Dante continues, "We have all talked about it and we want to offer it because that woman is so amazing she deserves the world. We want to be the ones to offer what she wants and see where it goes. We have never done this before, but we want to try, with her." Ian stays silent like he is contemplating letting Stan give us her number. I am biting on my bottom lip nervously. I am praying to God that we convince him we are serious about this.

"Fine, but if any of you hurt her you will answer to me, you understand? That poor girl has been through enough with men promising her the world and coming up short. It has caused that girl to have so many insecurities that just do not make sense because I mean you have seen her," He adds that last comment with a laugh. Then he yells out to Stan, "Hey babe! Can you send Nikki's and my number to the guys?" I can hear Stan in the background groan and say fine. We hear Ian hand back the phone to Stan and then we hear all our phones go off with her contact information.

"Okay happy? Can I go back to fucking Ian?" He says, annoyed. We all laugh.

"Yeah, sorry to interrupt you guys," I tell him with a laugh.

"Also please do not screw this up. It will make it awkward for me since things are going well with Ian and I like Nikki," He warns us.

"We won't," Dante yells. With that Stan laughs and hangs up.

"Well that went well," Carter says with a chuckle.

"Well at least we can get started on this plan. Carter, you text her first and then we will go from there," I tell him, but he looks skeptical. I glare at him while we wait for him to get moving. He better not be backing out after promising Ian we would not hurt her.

"I will wait till tomorrow. She is probably overwhelmed with all three of us coming onto her. Let's let her breathe," Carter says with a sigh and heads to his room.

"He's not wrong. I am sure it was too much for her and that is why she ran off towards the end of the night. It just confirms we have to do this the way you said and take this slow," Dante says and puts a hand on my shoulder for reassurance. I am frustrated. I just want to start with our plan, but I sigh because he's right. Her head must be reeling with all three of us coming on to her at once.

"Okay he's right. I am going to call it a night," I tell him, and we head to our rooms. Once I am in, I can still feel my rock hard erection that I have been sporting all night. It was a semi when I first saw her and then it went to steel when I was dancing with her. I was trying to keep my distance when we were dancing because I did not want her to feel the effect she had on me. Now that I think about it, I should have pulled her closer so I could show her what she was doing to me. I grew even harder thinking about dancing with her and grinding myself against her. I don't think a cold show is going to help.

I still need to shower so I headed into my bathroom and stripped all my clothes off. My bathroom is simple. It is painted black with a white sink and white marble floors. I always liked the monochromatic look of our penthouse. I am a simple man, so I like simple decorating.

I head to the walk in shower and turn it on. I don't wait for the water to get warm. I hop in and the water is freezing. The icy water hits my skin while my cock aches. I can just imagine her next to me. I start to stroke the base of my cock, imagining it was her touching me. The water finally started to warm up as I continued to stroke my cock and imagine her getting on her knees begging for a taste. I pick up my movement and start rubbing the full length of it as I envision her mouth on my cock while she touches herself. I can almost see her dripping as she takes my cock deeper into her mouth. I feel my balls tighten because I am so close. Then I can hear her moan my name, "Ivan" she moans out and that does me in. I am cumming so hard I see stars. It shoots out so hard it hits the walls of the shower. I watch as it goes down the wall and into the drain. I cannot wait to make this fantasy into a reality.

I dried off in the bathroom and headed to bed. I am a hot sleeper, so I like to sleep naked. I lay in bed unable to sleep because of the excitement I felt about our plan. I toss and turn for a little bit while. I think about what it would be like to have her sleeping in my bed. I bet if she was here, I would have no problem falling asleep. I cannot wait to snuggle the shit out of her in my bed as we fall asleep together.

Chapter 7

CARTER

I woke up after a long night of thinking. I did not sleep too well with the anticipation of today. I kept trying to figure out how I was going to convince this goddess to give me a chance. I had a reputation of a dog with me sleeping around with women. I have never regretted my reputation till this moment. I have never met a woman that makes me want to give it all up but here I am contemplating all my life choices. I sigh in frustration.

This morning wood is not going away anytime soon but I might need to take care of it. I don't want a hard on when I go see my trainer. Rachel might get the wrong idea. She has been trying to convince me for months to give her a go and I might be a man whore, but I don't fuck my coworkers. That can get messy. I lay on my back and lower my black boxer briefs. My cock bounces on my stomach when I free it from my briefs. I grip my cock at the base. This is the only way, I don't want to screw this up by trying to find release in another girl. To be honest I don't want another girl to begin with because I really think this girl is the one. God what I would not give to have Nikki on top of me, using me till she found her own sweet release first and then mine. I start to stroke up and down just imagining her riding me. I start to go fast as my imagination runs wild. Her on top with that sassy mouth moaning my name. Her perfect tits bouncing as she rides me faster. My balls tightened as I found a sweet release with her. I am so close,

I grab a towel I found on the floor from my shower last night. I bring the towel to my cock as I start to spurt out so much cum, it is ridiculous. I sigh in relief, if jerking off to her feels this good I cannot wait to have her. I get up and put the towel in my hamper. I get dressed in heather gray sweatpants and a white t-shirt that is tight on my arm muscles. I sit on the bed and slide on my white air force ones.

I get up from my bed when I am fully dressed and grab my phone that was on the end table. I decide to wait to text Nikki so I can talk to the guys first, so I make my way down the hall to the kitchen. Dante is in the kitchen making us protein shakes for breakfast while Ivan is sitting on the couch with Tot reading one of his books. Dante is wearing jeans, and a dark navy t-shirt and Ivan is in black sweats and a light blue t-shirt.

"Look who finally decided to wake the fuck up and grace us with his presence. Did you text her?" Dante asks, impatient as ever. I can't really blame him. I am sure I am not the only one tossing and turning all night thinking about our plan.

"Well good morning to you," I tell him with an eye roll. I go to pick up my protein shake when Dante grabs it just before me.

"You can have this when you answer my question," he tells me with a stern look as he holds my protein shake hostage. This is not fair. I need the caffeine that is in that bloody thing. We always add ice coffee to our morning protein shakes to get us going.

"Fine! I have not texted her yet. I wanted to talk to you guys first. Plus, she owns a club. I don't think she would be up this early anyway," I tell them with my hands waving in the air frustrated. He must be content with my answer because he hands me my protein shake and I down it.

"What are you going to text her?" Ivan asked while one of his eyebrows arched. I take my hand and wipe my upper lip to get any protein shake off before I speak.

"I am not sure. I thought about texting her about coming to the club again tonight to see her sing. I want to keep it casual and not come on too strong," I tell them, hoping my idea is okay. I have never been so nervous to text a girl. I am a ladies' man and liking her so much is throwing me off my game.

"Okay that is perfect. You can see her sing and hopefully the club won't be too busy where she can sit and talk to you. Don't talk to her about us. We want to ease her into this," Ivan says excitedly. I am a little taken back by his reaction. I have never seen Ivan so excited let alone so excited by a girl. I go to sit on the couch and I pull out my phone so I can text her.

Carter: Hey Beautiful!! It is Carter! I got your number from Ian because I would love to come to the club tonight to hear you sing again. I don't need the VIP booth since it is just me. I hope you don't mind that Ian gave me your number. If it helps, he was very protective. LOL

I wait patiently as I see the three dots form on the screen and disappear several times. I can just see her writing a text and then deleting it with self-doubt. Biting her plush bottom lip with nervousness trying to think of what to say back. I don't want her to feel that way with us but then the message finally comes through.

Beautiful: Hey Mr. Flirt! It's okay and I have a booth available so if you would like you can come in and tell the guys your name and they will take you to the booth. I am not singing tonight, just to warn you. I normally have the guys on because I am too busy on Saturdays. I hope it is not a disappointment.

No! I have to convince her to give me one on one time even if it is a few minutes. I contemplate on how I am going to convince her to give me the time of day. I need to turn up the flirt.

Carter: Really you do not need to do that but I would like to talk to you for a bit. What would be a good time to come in so I get a moment with that beautiful face?

Beautiful: Smooth LOL! I will save the VIP for you and I will serve you because it is probably the only way for me to talk to you. Saturdays are the busiest night of the week for us. If you can, come in early before the crazy crowd comes in.

Well at least she is not telling me to go fuck myself. I figured she would with the reputation I had but then I think she must be interested because she has even offered to be my server so she can talk to me. I will take anything she will give me.

Carter: See I knew you liked me beautiful! I will come in after training. I should be there around 5 if that is okay.

Beautiful: That should work! I will let the guys know up front. Just give them your nickname and they will take you to the table. See you tonight!

Wait, did she just say my nickname! I have to tell the two biggest guys ever that my name is Mr. Flirt! I text back as fast as I can before I lose her.

Carter: Wait! I have to tell those 2 big guys my name is Mr. Flirt! Please don't do this to me!

Beautiful: Don't worry. I could give you a different name if you want but I don't think you would like it Think of it as my way to make sure you are serious about me. If you don't come in because of that it will say you are not that into me.

Fine! She wants me to prove myself then that is what she will get. I can understand why she would need me to. I am pictured with many girls I go home with all the time, so we need to work on the trust. I can play this game.

Carter: Game on princess! I can take anything you throw at me.

Beautiful: We will see! See you tonight!

I finally look up from my phone and see Dante and Ivan crouching over to look at my phone. I pull it to my chest like I have something to hide.

"Can I help you?" I ask as I tuck my phone away.

"This is funny as shit! You are trying to text a girl you like and you say game on. I am dying here!" Dante says as he throws his head back in a laugh. I look at Ivan who looks just amused.

"Just don't fuck this up. You are our starting player in this so you will be setting the mood for all three of us," Ivan says smiling.

"I won't! Worry about your own dates and I will worry about mine. I have to go see my trainer," I say with a sigh and get up to leave. Then both their smiles fall into a frowns.

"Don't let her rile you up," Ivan warns. He knows I have a short fuse with this bullshit. I may have vented to them once or twice about Rachel.

"I won't," I say with a sigh and continue, "I will make sure my focus is on Nikki. I want her to know I am serious and don't want to fuck this up for any of us. I know I have a reputation for being a dog but I can't change my past. I can only work towards my future and I want her in it."

"We know man, this is new to all of us, but we will work on this together," Dante says in order to comfort me. I let out a grunt of frustration because this is not going to be fun.

"Okay I am going to head out!" I yell behind me as I head for the door and make my way to the garage. I have a purple Lambo. I love my toy.

I get into the Lambo and start the car hearing the sweet purring sound of the engine. I rush through the city, and I start thinking about Nikki and trying not to get hard. Let's just say I am not winning. I pull into the arena and park in the private parking garage for players. I'm still hard from thinking about Nikki so I start to think of football plays to calm down. I do not want Racheal to think she did this to me and give her the wrong idea. It finally goes down so I start to make my way to Racheal's office. When I walk in she turns my way and gives me a flirty smile. I let out a small groan of frustration. When is this girl going to get that I will not be with her. She has long tan legs and blonde hair. She looks like one of those blonde bimbos I used to sleep with but not anymore. I will not fuck up any chance I have with Nikki for this bitch.

"Hey handsome! I have been waiting for you," she says as she crosses the room to stand right in front of me. She places a hand on my chest and I am quick to bat it away.

"I'm here. The coach wanted me to come in since my back has been sore. Let's just get this over with," I say with no interest.

"Okay go lay down on my table and make sure you take your shirt off," she says and licks her lips with that last part. This is going to be a nightmare. I head to her table and leave my shirt on because I don't really want her ogling me.

"Forgot the shirt, handsome," she reminds me with a wink.

"Can you please be professional? I have a girl I like and don't want to deal with you on top of it. If you cannot keep it professional then I will go report you," I say sternly.

"I have no idea what you mean. I am nothing but professional," she says as she bats her eyelashes and puts her hand on my chest again. I grab her hand before she can run it down my torso and push it away harder this time so she can get it through her thick head. She looks annoyed with me and I am okay with this.

"Okay this is what is going to happen. You are going to keep it professional and not flirt because I have a lady now. You will do the exam and be respectful. Before I let you flirt because it was harmless but now, I have a woman to be faithful for and you are not going to fuck that up. It is disrespectful to flirt and touch another woman's man inappropriately,"

I say with a growl because she needs to realize that it does not only affect me when she does this now but Nikki as well.

"Fine," she says in defeat. I lay on the table and lift the back of my shirt so she can have a look without me showing her too much. She starts to massage, and I hold back my moans. The only person who gets to hear my moans is Nikki.

"So, who is this girl? She must be pretty amazing for the great Carter to change his ways," she says with a laugh.

"She is the best," I say with the biggest smile.

"You know you are just going to get bored with her right? That's fine though because when it happens, I will be here waiting," she says as her hands go lower and start to massage my ass. Okay that's it. I get up from the table and get in her face.

"Okay you are going to listen and pay attention this time. I am not going to get bored with my beautiful princess and even if I did, I will never sleep with you and you want to know why? I don't want you. I never have and never will. You could be the last girl on earth, and I still would not be with you," I tell her and push past her with rage. I stop at the door and glare back at her while I continue with, "Also, I would start looking for a new job because I will be reporting you to the coach and until you are gone, I will go to someone else for my back."

"You can't do that! I would lose my job and have nowhere to go if I get fired," she yells after me.

"You should have thought of that before you sexually harassed a taken man," I add, and I practically run to my car. Once I am settled in my car, I pull out my phone to text my coach about what just happened.

Carter: Racheal has been sexually harassing me and I am done. She just inappropriately touched me as well so get a new trainer or I breach my contract.

Coach: Consider it done. I will have her gone in the next 24 hours. Texting owner now.

I sigh in relief and start the engine. This nightmare is over. I then smile because I need to get ready for my date.

I pull up to the club nervous. I am never nervous about girls but it shows how much I like my princess. I decided on black slacks and a white button up and I made sure not to button it up too high so you can see the top of my chest a little. I think I showed the guys a hundred outfits when I was trying to get ready. They kept telling me I looked fine, but I don't want to just look fine when I see her. I finally just gave up and settled with the last thing I had on. It is not too busy yet, there is still a line to get into the club though. I see the guys from the other night watching the door. I walk up to them and tell them my name.

"Carter," I tell them.

"Sorry my man. You know what you have to say to get in," Donnie says with a laugh. Damn it! She really wasn't fucking kidding about that.

"Fuck it, Mr. Flirt," I whisper to one of the guys. They both laugh.

"I don't think I hear you man you might want to speak up," Donnie says with a snicker.

"Mr. Flirt!" I yell with frustration because they are fucking messing with me.

"Fuck! I had a hundred bucks with Nik that you would not say it. You must be a desperate man," Jake says as he pulls down the purple velvet rope.

"Have you seen Nikki? I am a very desperate man." I say with a laugh as I follow Donnie back to the same booth we were sitting in last night. As soon as I sit I look for my beautiful princess. Then I spotted her behind the bar and with that one look, she took my breath away. Her red curly hair is crazy and she is in a short black sweater dress. She has black thigh thigh-high boots that are so damn sexy. I work quickly to take a picture with my phone. I take it out fast and snap quickly, so she does not think I am a creep taking her picture. I check to make sure it is not blurry and send it to the guys. I save it for myself, but they should see how hot she is. I have an instant hard on, looking at the picture. Down boy, I curse at my dick. We are supposed to be going slow for multiple reasons. One, we have to ease her into the plan we have and second, I am sure she doesn't trust me if she has heard anything about me. She spots me staring at her, so I give her a small wave. She smiles and heads my way with her hips swaying to the music the band is playing. Once she gets to the booth, she slides right in next to me. I give her a hug and when I pull away, I keep one arm wrapped around her back with my hand on her hip.

"Hey princess," I whisper in her ear. I can feel her shiver with delight.

"Well hello to you too. I am not gonna lie, I thought I was gonna lose my bet," she says with a cute soft laugh.

"You have made me a very desperate man princess. You underestimate how much I want you," I tell her honestly. She has no clue how wrapped around her finger I am. I really would do anything this woman asked. If she asked me to get on my knees and worship her I would.

"I can see that so what can I bring you to drink? Guinness, right?" She asked and that made me lift one brow in amusement.

"You remember what I drink?" I ask her, surprised.

"Of course! Do you want any food tonight?" She asked with a laugh.

"Yes please! If you ask the guys I am a bottomless pit. Just bring me what you think is good and add it to my bill. I trust you," I tell her. Which is the truth, I do trust her. That is hard for me. Someone is always trying to use us for money, connections or our fame. It is hard for us to find someone who wants nothing to do with that and Nikki is one of them. She slides out of my hold and out the booth.

I watch her as she walks away to pour my beer and I miss her already. I don't like this feeling in my chest as a man at the bar is trying to flirt with her as she pours my beer. I want to get up and knock the shit out of him, but I know that will cause issues. She shrugs him off and comes my way. She sets my beer down in front of me and looks like she is going to leave, so I grab her wrist before she can go.

"Leaving me already princess," I tell her with a smirk trying to hide my anger. I don't want her to go back to the bar with that guy still there. He just seemed like a creep and I was not even close to him.

"I just need to grab Donnie to kick out this guy who is being a creep at the bar. I promise I will be back. I need to check on your food I put in once I am done with that," she tells me with a smile like she can read my mind about that guy. I let go of her wrist and nod thankful that she is kicking that guy out.

I watch as she goes to the door to grab Donnie and he follows her in with a frown. This Donnie guy is scary even with a smile on his face. He looks extra terrifying now that he means business. She taps the creep's shoulder to get his attention and then sneaks off to go to the kitchen to grab my food. Donnie wasted no time. He picks up the guy and throws him over his shoulder and walks him outside. It is funny to watch as the little guy smacks Donnie's butt to get loose. Then my princess comes back with three plates full of food. I lick my lips hungry. It looks amazing as she sets down the plates and then slides in next to me.

"So, I got you a bit of everything. There is a German pretzel with beer cheese, then deep fried mac and cheese bites and just in case you have to watch what you eat I brought our Tai crunch salad," she explains as she sets down her own drink.

"Please tell me you will help me," I say with a laugh. I know I am a big boy and I can kill a lot of food, but Nik brought so much even I am doubtful I can finish it all. She slides into the booth close to me. I can smell her delectable scent of strawberry short cake. Slow! I have to go slow! I keep reminding myself and I am sure I am going to have to do it all night.

"Yeah, I made sure an extra bartender came in so we could talk since you were coming in just for me," she says, bouncing her knee nervously and biting her bottom lip. I want to suck on that bottom lip. No, fuck! I should not be thinking like that. Slow!

"Princess, are you nervous?" I ask her as I glide my thumb across her bottom lip so she will release it from her teeth.

"Can I be honest with you?" She asked as she released her bottom lip from her teeth.

"Absolutely!" I yell a little too loud.

"Your reputation scares me a little," she says, not wanting to look at me. I wrap one arm around her shoulders and the other goes to her chin so I can look her in the eyes when I tell her this.

"I understand princess. If I could take it all back, I would. I don't want to live like that anymore," I tell her and she looks concerned.

"What made you change your mind?" She asks with confusion in her eyes.

"You did," I tell her in all seriousness.

"Me?" She says and her eyes widen.

"Yes, you. I know it sounds crazy since we just met yesterday and I know I have a rep but when I saw you and got to know you it made me want to be a better person. I know I am going to have to earn your trust by showing you. So, from now on you are my priority unless you tell me to fuck off, I hope you are okay with that," I admitted to her hoping she does not say that right now. I wouldn't blame her if she did, but it would crush me.

"Okay," she says in a whisper. My heart skips a beat at that one single word.

"Okay? Okay to what princess?" I ask with excitement. I feel like I just won the super bowl.

"Okay we can be friends and then when I know I can trust you we can see where this goes but you should know I do have plans with Dante and I don't want you guys to think I am a whore jumping between you guys," she explains further and I am so excited I couldn't help it. I peck her quickly on her lips. My heart is beating out of my chest at the fact she is giving me even a small chance.

"I know he already told me and I would never think that way about you," I tell her with a big goofy grin on my face. She smiles at my response. I let go of her so we can start digging in. I start with the pretzel while she starts the salad. This food is so good! I know I should not be eating badly during the season but it is so worth it.

"So why did you open this place?" I ask her in between bites, wanting to know everything about her.

"Well, I tried the whole Broadway thing and I hated it. I hated how it made me feel. The directors were always degrading and then the critics were awful. I use singing to make myself feel good about myself. I see it as an outlet to my emotions but with Broadway you can't do that. You are told what to sing and how to sing it. I started to hate singing so I quit and opened this place so I could have a safe place to sing. I let all of my singers do the same. I only have one rule, they just need to run what they are going to sing for the night by me first but for the most part I let them sing whatever they want," she says with such passion in her eyes. Her eyes are dilated with the excitement, and she has a small smirk because she is trying to hold back a big grin. I can tell this is what she was meant to do.

"That is amazing! I can tell how passionate you are about this. To give a safe place for singers to perform what they want," I tell her. I love that she is letting me in and trusting me with this information. She is showing me her insecurities which cannot be easy for her to do.

"Yeah, I never want someone to feel like I did when working on Broadway," she says and focuses on her glass like she is hurt.

"How did they make you feel?" I say with concern. I think I know where this is going but I don't want to assume anything with this girl. Plus, if she admits it, it means she is letting her walls down so I can get to know her.

"Like I was never enough, but that is in the past," she says with a small smile. I can relate with that statement. She is trying to put the past behind her like I am doing with my reputation.

"Okay what musicals were you in?" I ask her wanting to know. Dante's mom is obsessed with musicals so I have seen a few when she comes to the penthouse to visit.

"I was in two different productions. I was in Burlesque and then I was in Phantom of the Opera. My favorite was Burlesque. The song I performed last night is from that show," She says and her eyes go dreamy.

"I know," I tell her, which makes her jaw drop. She looks so cute.

"Wait, does Mr. Flirt watch musicals?" she asked amused and snuggled closer to my side. I am so thankful for Dante's mom right now. I will never complain again when she puts one on.

"Yes. Dante's mom loves musicals and when she comes to visit, she will put on the occasional musical and make me, Dante and Ivan watch. She says it makes us more cultured," I tell her, and her jaw is still gaping open and eyebrows raised. It makes me laugh. I put down my pretzel so I can put my hand on her chin so I can close her mouth. I lean down so I can whisper the next part.

"You are so cute when you make that face. I bet you will make that face when I have my face between your thighs," I say low and raspy. I can hear her breath hitch as I turn her on with my words. I want to slide my hand up her thigh and see if she is wet, but I know that would ruin everything we are working towards. I kiss her cheek and go back to my food.

"Are you messing with me?" She says a little breathless. She is practically squirming in her seat and I want to fix her urges but that will have to wait. I need her to want me entirely and not just for sex.

"No," I say with a laugh. "I for once in my life, I am trying to use restraint with you. You do not trust me enough yet to let me touch you and I do not want to mess this up by rushing things. I want to take things slow and once you tell me you trust me completely then it is game on princess," I tell her and look into her eyes so she can see I am being honest.

"Why do you call me princess?" She asks, I have been waiting for this question. I plaster on a big goofy grin again.

"Because I wanted to be your Prince Charming the moment I saw you," I tell her and that makes her make that cute face again. I cannot help it, I kiss her cheek again.

"Okay Mr. Flirt, I need to get a head start on my orders for tomorrow and I know being a football player you have a game tomorrow," she says as she gets up from the booth.

"Are you going to your apartment for it?" I ask her as I get up as well and run my fingers through my hair.

"Yes?" She says like a question, wondering what I was thinking.

"Can I at least walk you to your door?" I asked her hopefully. I just want to make sure she makes it home okay even if it is just upstairs.

"You don't have to do that. I just have to walk around the building and up some stairs and I am there," she says with a giggle. The fact that she has to go around outside with all those people and creeps only makes me want to do it more.

"That makes me want to even more knowing you have to walk outside. Please?" I whisper in her ear.

"Okay," she says in defeat and starts to turn away. I pump my fist in the air in triumph. Then I rush after her and grab her hand. We walk in silence as we make our way outside. We round the building to some stairs that are on the side of the building. I follow behind her and I try to not stare at her ass. Fuck! It is an amazing ass. Her small black dress clings to every curve, it is so inviting. I am so tempted to grab it and make it mine. We make it to the top step and she turns to me. I grab both her hands not wanting her to go.

"Thanks for tonight. I had a lot of fun and I normally don't have time for fun," she says like she is contemplating staying with me.

"No, princess, thank you for letting me take my shot. You will not regret letting me in," I tell her in truth.

"It's easy to talk to you, especially when you dial back the flirting," she says with a laugh which causes me to laugh. She is so sweet and no one would ever know unless they got to know her.

"I will always want to flirt with you," I say, which makes her giggle. Then she does the one thing that I least expect. She leans in and kisses me. She tastes like she smells, like strawberry shortcake. The kiss is soft and sweet. It is over too soon and she pulls away. I give her a hug and whisper in her ear, "Goodnight princess, remember to leave your window cracked in case I have to save you from your tower."

"Goodnight my prince charming," she says and turns to get into her apartment.

I feel like I'm on top of the world. She let me in and the realization kicked in. I cannot fuck this up. I head to my car and speed through the city with the biggest grin on my face. My face hurts because of how much smiling I did tonight. I better get used to it because I think I am going to do a lot of smiling with my princess.

Chapter 8

IVAN

God! How long are me and Dante going to have to wait to know what happened? I texted him a hundred times wanting to know how it is going. I pull out my phone to check it for the millionth time and still no word from Carter. All he has done is send a picture of Nikki looking hot as fuck behind the bar.

Ivan: Hey! How is it going?

Ivan: Wanting to know how it is going.

Ivan: Hey asshole answer!

Ivan: Dante is pacing back and forth. I want to give him something so he can stop foaming at the mouth.

He never responded, which I am taking as a good sign. It means he is taking this seriously and focusing on our girl. Dante, however, is a nervous wreck. He has been pacing in the kitchen since Carter left. I sit on the couch with Tot lying next to me. I am trying to focus on my book, but he is making it impossible.

"Can you please just sit down and chill the fuck out?" I ask him, putting my book down annoyed.

"I can't help it! What if he comes on too strong? What if she doesn't like him? This could ruin everything!" He says running his hands through his hair. Then we hear the ding for the door security. Carter strides into the kitchen with the goofiest grin I have ever seen on him. Me and Dante sit there in shock as he ignores us while pouring himself a glass of water.

"Good night?" I ask him with a smirk.

"The best! She opened up to me and she even gave me a goodnight kiss," he says as his smile grows bigger behind his glass.

"She kissed you?" Dante asked not believing him. I am having a tough time believing him too. I mean he is a man whore so I thought she would make him grovel a little.

"Don't be an ass. She already told me she has trust issues because of my past but she agreed we could start as friends and then when I show her, she can trust me, she will give me a shot. It was an innocent kiss so chill dude," he says with an attitude.

"This is good Dante. Relax because this is our plan. Do not let your possessiveness lose sight of that. This is what she wants and so we will give it to her," I reminded him.

"Okay you are right, Mia Cara deserves it," he says, relaxing his shoulders.

"So, it is your turn Ivan but be careful, because she told me she felt bad for seeing me and then seeing Dante on Monday. I just want to make sure she is happy. She thought I was going to judge her once she told me. So, we need to be supportive in that, show her it is okay that we are all pursuing her and that we all want her," Carter explains and this makes my heart drop. This amazing woman is always judged for doing what she wants and that is not okay. This goddess deserves everything we have to offer.

"Okay I am going to text her next and will make sure she is okay," I tell them and get up to head to my room.

"Where are you going?" Dante and Carter ask at the same time. I ignore them and make it to my bedroom. I lay on my bed and reach for my phone.

Ivan: Hey Nikki! It's Ivan. I have an extra ticket to an opera tomorrow and need someone to go with me. Would you mind coming with me?

I am so nervous. It takes several minutes before I see the three dots. I wait patiently but I am rethinking how I asked. Maybe I was too forward or maybe she doesn't like me. Then my phone pings and I cannot help the grin that takes over my face.

Little One: Let me guess, you got my number from Ian?

Ivan: I can't give out my resources lol So you in little one?

Little One: I would love to, but I have a confession to make…

Oh god! She doesn't like me. This is going to hurt but I wouldn't like me if I was her. I mean all I did was scowl last night so I wasn't really welcoming. She probably likes the other guys more and she deserves them. They are nice and family oriented. I am just a broken lost boy. When she does not continue, I ask her.

Ivan: What is that little one?

Little One: I was with Carter tonight at the bar and I am seeing Dante Monday. I just want to make sure that is okay before I agree.

Thank fuck! I finally let go of that breath that I did not realize I was holding. She is just worried that I didn't know. This makes me want to kill any man that came before us and did not worship the goddess she is. I have to think about what I should text back with. I want to ease her insecurities about multiple men pursuing her, but I don't want to come on as strong as Carter. It is not my style.

Ivan: I know, little one. We tell each other everything and it's okay. You don't have to worry about that. So, will you go with me?

Little One: Wait, you're okay with that?!?!

Okay I might need to pull a Carter for this one. Fuck! I am bad at flirting, but I need to charm the pants off her.

Ivan: I don't mind sharing. They know I am asking you out and I know they asked you as well. Now what do you think about going to the opera?

The three dots appear and disappear so many times. Oh god! I came on too strong. I am such an ass. I kept asking if she wanted to go like a jackass. I probably sound like a broken record. I should have let the guys help me with the text. I throw my phone and then I hear the ding. I rush off the bed to pick up my phone, praying that she will come.

Little One: What time daddy?

I practically jump up and down on my bed in excitement but wait. I have to read the text ten times just to be sure I read that right. She just called me daddy and that is everything. She doesn't know but I love being a Daddy Dom in bed. Must come from getting gray hair. I am rock hard just reading the word, imagining her there in my bed begging for her daddy to touch her. I shake my head to come to my senses and text her back.

Ivan: I will pick you up at 6 PM. Also, Daddy?

Little One: I'm sorry! I hope you don't mind my flirty ass.

Ivan: Little one, YOU can call me that anytime. Preferably in bed.

Little One: Well now I have to take a cold shower. See you tomorrow!

Ivan: Goodnight little one.

This is Fantastic! She is starting to get eased into our idea and I have time with her tomorrow. I am smiling so big as I get up to go to the kitchen to let the guys know and when I go to open my door, they are standing there with worried looks. What idiots. I push past them and make my way to the kitchen to get something to snack on. They follow me like sad lost puppies.

"Well!?" Carter asks with his hands in the air.

"She agreed to come tomorrow and I started to ease her into the idea of all of us," I tell them with a shrug. I grab my water that is on the counter and chug it. I am so turned on by our flirty texts I need something to cool off.

"Wait, she knows we all want to be with her?" Dante asked with concern in his eyes. I can understand the concern especially after what Carter said. I pull out my phone and give it to Dante so he can see our text. As he reads, I can see his worry just melt away as a smile starts to grow on his face. Carter reads over his shoulder and throws his head back with a laugh.

"What's so funny?" I ask Carter with a scowl.

"Little one and Daddy?" He asked while wiping the tears away from his eyes.

"Oh, don't start. At least it is better than princess and Mr. Flirt," I tell him, punching him in the shoulder and he starts to blush.

"Hey! I got upgraded to Prince Charming," he says defensively.

"Anyway, I have more to plan for the opera so if you don't mind I am going back to my room to plan," I tell them as I make it back to my room. Once I am in, I lay on my bed and start to think how I can make this a memorable date. I want us to look back on this date when we are old and gray and remember our perfect first date.

I have to plan this accordingly. I want to impress her but don't want to scare her. I make sure to order a car and driver for tomorrow because I don't think it would be appropriate to show up in my beat-up jeep. This will also give us time to talk in the car. They serve dinner at the opera because it is a dinner theater so I email them beforehand, so everything is taken care of. Then I think, what if she does not have a dress for the opera? I got an amazing idea to seal the deal. I rush out of bed and go to Carter's room. I slam the door open and immediately have to put my hand over my eyes because he is jerking off in his bed.

"Fuck! Man, seriously?" I yell at him in frustration with my hand still over my eyes. Yep, I am now scarred for life.

"Hey! At least it is my hand! I don't want to screw up with Nikki so if this is what I have to do then I am doing it! You didn't see her tonight. That tight black dress. Knock next time!" He yells and throws a pillow at me.

"Okay, is it safe to look?" I say with a laugh.

"Yes asshole! The second you walked in I put my dick away. Now what do you want?" He asked with a groan. I take my hand off my eyes. He is standing in front of me with no shirt and basketball shorts he must have thrown on when my eyes were closed. He looks at me curiously waiting for me to tell him why I barged in.

"Do you still have that personal shopper?" I asked him, rubbing the back of my neck. I hate asking for help, but with us working together on this, I am going to have to get used to it.

"Yes, why?" He asked, looking at me up and down. I can understand why he is confused by my question. I have never cared about my clothes or appearances before. I only have one suit for game days for Christ sake. All the rest of my clothes are pretty plain.

"I want to get a dress sent to Nikki for tomorrow as a surprise," I admit to him. I want her to feel special to us and this is the cherry on top.

"Wow. You are really pulling all the stops out for the princess," he says as he pulls out his phone and sends me the information. Then he continues, "Okay so if you can find a picture of her my shopper should be able to help but I would just text Ian to make it easier. He said he wanted this for her so I am sure he will have no issue with telling you her sizes, so it is perfect for her."

"Thanks! I will!" I yell as I make my way back to my room and pull out my phone.

Ivan: Hey Ian! It is Ivan. I am getting Nikki a present for our date tomorrow, but I do not know her size. I am needing a gown that she could wear to the opera.

I waited a few minutes, nervous that he won't think it is a good idea and then I see the three dots appear.

Ian: Haha! This is too funny! You boys have it bad for my girl. She is a medium in her outfit, but I am not sure about gowns.

Ivan: So, I am using Carter's personal shopper so if you can send a full body picture and with the size you gave me she should be able to determine the size.

Then the most beautiful picture of my little one comes in. She is in a strapless silver sundress and purple heels. She is on the beach and the dress is sparking in the sunset that she is looking at. Well, I am keeping this picture for later. Might even send it to Carter as a thank you for letting me use his shopper.

Ian: Here you go! Hope the date goes well! I am rooting for you all! This is the first time she is going to get what she wants and I will help you guys anyway I can! I will be with her tomorrow and she will shit a brick when it comes but I will be there to talk her off the ledge and make sure she understands that it is okay to get gifts.

Ivan: Thank you! We are going to give that gorgeous woman whatever she wants! Have a good night!

I plug in my phone in my nightstand after I text the personal shopper everything for Nikki. I told her to send pictures of the options. The personal shopper was quick. I can already hear my phone go off multiple times with images of clothes, shoes, and jewelry. I decided to get her a little of everything to be safe. She won't even have to think of what to wear tomorrow with the whole ensemble I have for her. While lying in bed I think about Ian's text. She doesn't like presents. Maybe I shouldn't have done this, but I just want to give this woman everything I have to offer. Well, she better get used to receiving presents because between three men trying to get her attention, she is going to get a lot of them in the future. Now I just need to not screw up tomorrow.

Chapter 9

NIKKI

To say I have had a weird weekend is the understatement of the century. I am in a cab on my way to Gold Eagle. I put on a bright purple sweater dress and my combat boots. On the way to the diner all I could think about were the three guys that seemed to not care that they were all coming onto me. I don't want to get my hopes up because the second I tell them I want them to share me I know I am going to get that judgmental look. It is just so odd because they share everything it sounds like, and it is making me think they wouldn't mind sharing me. I am not going to tell them that though. I promised myself I would not put myself through that again. The cab pulls up and I run inside to tell Ian all the juicy tidbits of the weekend. I walk in and go straight to our booth and Ian is already there looking like he has some hot gossip. He turns to see me and looks relieved.

"Finally! Thank God! I know you are not late, but I know you have some tea for me and I am dying to hear," he says as he gets up and hugs me.

"This wouldn't happen to be about the three guys you gave my number to?" I ask with a smirk. He lets me go with a smile, so we slide into the booth and our drinks are already there. He must have gotten here early with everything going on.

"Okay so you already know and since you did not text me, I am going to assume you are not going to kill me," He says with a laugh as I sip my latte.

"No, but why did you give them my number?" I ask him with one eyebrow arched. I know he does not give out my number to just anyone. He is way too protective for that.

"Okay look if I tell you something you have to promise not to say anything to them and let everything happen naturally," he says with defeat. This is bizarre but I just nod my head and let him continue.

"So, after I went to Stan's place he got a call from the guys asking for your number. I jumped in on that call real quick because I am always going to protect my girl. I asked them what they want with my beautiful Nikki? Then Ivan explained that he was looking for the bathroom and heard us talking in your office," he says and I can feel my face go white. I want to throw up. I can feel the tears in my eyes because I know they are done now. They already know that I am a freak and have weird taste. Ian jumps up and slides into my side of the booth to hug me.

"Babe! Don't look like that till I get to the end," he says as he leans back to finish. Our food comes out and Raymond looks pissed when he sees my face.

"What are you doing to my girl?" He asked as he set our food down. Raymond keeps to himself for the most part but he kind of adopted me as his surrogate daughter so when he sees me like this, he can get a little protective. It takes a lot for me to get upset and he knows that.

"Hey, she was my girl first and I am telling her something and haven't gotten to the good part yet so don't worry. She will be leaving with the biggest smile once I am done," he says with an attitude and Raymond looks between us and then turns to me.

"Yell if you need anything, love," he says with a nod and leaves. Ian slides out and goes to his side of the booth again.

"So, like I was saying, Ivan heard our conversation and they want to share you. I was skeptical at first but then they reassured me they want to give you your fantasy," he says with the biggest smile I have ever seen.

"They want to share me? Like on opposite days where they can pass me around like a personal whore?" I ask furious now. How dare they suggest that? I have half a mind to text them all right now to go fuck themselves.

"No no no no no," he repeats like a child and then continues, "They want to share you in the sense you want. One bed for all four of you." He wiggles his eyebrows. Then it hit me, I said what I wanted in the office, and they still pursued me. I am in shock as I think about this. I did not scare them off.

"Ohhh and they were okay with that?" I ask, biting my bottom lip. No one has ever wanted to do that for me and now here they come offering what I want like it is no big deal. It sounds too good to be true.

"They are more than okay with it. They want to give you what your heart desires most," he tells me with a puppy dog look in his eyes.

"Oh Fuck! I don't know what to do now! I hung out with Carter last night and now I'll be with Ivan tonight!" I yell in shock.

"Now we are getting to the good part! How was hanging out with Carter?" He asks as he dives into his eggs benedict. How can he eat at a time like this?!

"It went well. We flirted and I told him his reputation bothers me. He told me he wanted a chance to prove that he has put that behind him. Even if we are just friends at first and we work towards something more. I may have kissed him when he walked me to my apartment," I tell him, and his mouth opens in shock and eyebrows raised.

"Wait back up! You kissed him? Kiss him how?" He asked, dropping his fork. I blush at his questions. I should not have told him that.

"Calm down! It was just a peck on the lips," I explain with my hands up in defense.

"Okay but have the others texted you?" He asked, fully enthralled by my dating life.

"Yes, Carter first before we hung out and Ivan invited me to an opera tonight. He had an extra ticket so he asked me if I could come," I told him and he hopped out of the booth and grabs his jacket. I am starting to think he lied about the extra ticket thing. He probably only said that, so I agreed to go but I won't hold that against him. I know I can be stubborn.

"Girl, we are leaving right now and finding you something to wear!" He says as he pulls me out of the booth and leads me outside.

"Tommy, charge my card on file! We got to go!" He yells as he rushes me outside. He calls us a cab and tells the cab driver my address and slips him a fifty-dollar bill to make it fast. Then the cab takes off to my place and I stay quite lost in my own thoughts. This is really happening? I have three beautiful men that want to give this a serious try. Would we just be fuck buddies or do they want more? If we go into a relationship what will their families think? We pull up to the club and make our way to the apartment. Ian rushes out the cab, makes it to the door, and unlocks it with his key. I gave him one for emergencies and to Ian this is an emergency. When inside we kick our shoes off and Ian runs to my closet in my bedroom and starts pulling out dresses.

"I r-really don't have anything for an-n opera. We should h-have gone shopping," I say with a stutter.

"No, you have plenty and we are going to look through everything," He says bound and determined. Then my doorbell rings. I look at Ian confused and he just pops his shoulders with a shrug. We make our way to the door and I open it to a tiny girl with a huge black box and purple ribbon just sitting there.

"Are you Nikki?" She asked with a smile.

"Yes, can I help you?" I ask with an eyebrow arched.

"This is a present for you. There is a note from the sender as well," she tells me as she hands Ian the big box and me the note.

"It was nice to meet you and I am sure I will see you again soon," she says and before I can ask her what she meant, she makes her way down the stairs. Ian puts the box on my glass coffee table and smiles so big.

"Well read the card," he says with a knowing smug smirk. I narrow my eyes at him and he gives me a mischievous smirk.

"You knew, didn't you?" I ask. I know he knew. He played it off so cool at first.

"Just open the note bitch," he says with a roll of his eyes. I open the envelope and read the note in shock when I get to who it is from.

My little one,

I wanted to make sure you did not have to worry about a single thing. I made sure to check with Ian on this to make sure it fit perfectly.

Love, Daddy

I am in shock and then Ian gets up and reads the note over my shoulder. He starts to laugh and almost falls over.

"Daddy?" He asked.

"It's an inside joke and I am mad at you. You acted like I needed to find something to wear and you knew he was doing this," I tell him sternly and with a glare.

"Okay be mad at me. Just go open your present! I have not seen it yet," He yells, pushing me to the couch so I can open the giant box on my coffee table. I gape at the box and am nervous. He did not have to do this. I am awful at accepting gifts. I have a fight with Ian every Christmas on gift giving. I like giving gifts, not receiving them.

Ian knows this, so he moves behind me and helps me take the ribbon off the box. We lift the lid together and see a mix of black and purple tissue paper. We start to move it out of the way and the most gorgeous purple gown sits before me. I gently pull it out of the box with my mouth gaping in shock. It is a silk purple full length gown with a deep v down the front of it. It has long sleeves, and the sleeves flare out towards the wrist. There is also a slit that would go to the middle of my thigh. As I picked up the dress to show Ian, I notice two other small boxes. I open the bigger one first, the small box scares me because it looks like a jewelry box. I hand Ian the dress and pick up the other box. It is purple too. I am noticing a theme here. I open the box and find name label, black velvet pumps. Okay so if this was in the big box I am even more scared of what is in the jewelry box. Ian gives me an eye roll as I stare at it with wide eyes.

"It is jewelry woman, not a wild animal," he says with a bit of a sarcastic tone. He grabs the box and opens it and his jaw drops. He turns it to me and in it lays the most beautiful black velvet choker with a glorious silver pendant with amethyst jewels and matching earrings. It is all stunning and too much. I am on the verge of having a panic attack. Ian can see me start to panic and my wet eyes.

"It is just an outfit love, it will be okay," he whispers to calm me down.

"I cannot accept this, Ian. It is too much. I am going to text him right now so I can give it back," I tell him frantically. I search for my phone in all the tissue paper, but Ian grabs it first.

"Hey that's mine!" I yell at him trying to get it out of his hands. He lifts it up in the air. He is six feet and I am five six so he is going to win this one, but it does not stop me from trying.

"No, you don't! I want you to keep it. Do you know what Ivan told me about this date? It is all about you and he wants everything to be perfect for you. They want to give you the world love and I am not going to let you sabotage it because you are scared of a few gifts. Just please keep them and wear them tonight," he says with the biggest puppy dog eyes he has ever given me, still holding my phone in the air because he doesn't trust me with it yet. Little Shit! He knows when he makes that face, I can't argue.

"Fine but I need you to do my hair and make-up, so I don't look crazy," I tell him with a sigh. I am not good at accepting gifts, but these guys make more money in a year than I would in a lifetime plus I do not have anything fancy enough for an opera.

"Bitch! Like I would have it any other way. Okay so go get in the shower and then I will do your hair first and cute purple make-up to go with the dress. It is go time people!" He yells, pushing me into the bathroom. I get a shower and start to think. Is this really happening? They all want to share me in one bed. I make sure to shave because with that beautiful daddy, I don't know what the night might bring. I get out and go to my bedroom in just a white towel where Ian has laid out my dress, jewelry, and shoes. I sat at my black vanity table reaching for my phone because I was so shocked I forgot to text him thank you.

Nikki: Thank you, Daddy. You did not have to do that but I appreciate it. No one has ever done something so extravagant for me before and I was shocked to be honest.

I stare at my phone nervously waiting for a response. I hope he is okay with the daddy comment. He just gives off daddy dom vibes with his dominant personality and silver hair to match. Then his nickname for me just seals the deal for his name to be daddy. I start to chew on my bottom lip as I see the three dots appear.

Daddy: You deserve the world little one. I am glad you liked it. I am glad I held back then. You were almost dripping with jewels tonight, but you did not seem like the type who would like that. I just wanted tonight to be perfect.

Dripping in jewels? Me? I would never. Just a dress had me freaking the fuck out, let alone the other two gifts. I go to type a reply and I decide to play with him a little. He deserves to squirm a little with this gift.

Nikki: I will be dripping daddy but it will not be in jewels.

Daddy: Behave little one or I will take you over my knee. I am not trying to rush. I want to take my time with you.

My mouth goes dry. I have to lick my lips, but it does not help. I can feel myself getting wet at the thought of being over his knees while he spanks me till I am red. This man is daddy dom, and I cannot wait for another date. I know that they want to go slow, but I don't think I can go slow with this man.

Nikki: Is that a promise daddy or a warning?

Daddy: A promise. Now get ready little one while I go take care of what you started. I cannot wait to see you in that dress. See you tonight at 6.

For the first time in a long time, I am excited for a date. I yell out to Ian, "Bitch get in here! I need all the help I can get!"

Chapter 10

IVAN

The driver pulls up to her place and lets me out. The nerves are starting to kick into overdrive. I make it up her steps with a bouquet of purple roses in hand. I had to search all over the city for purple, but I can tell that is her favorite color. I made fun of Carter for taking so long to get ready last night to meet her, but I did the exact same thing. I decided on a black suit with a purple button-up that matches her dress perfectly. I freeze as I am about to knock. What if I did too much? What if the outfit was going overboard? Then the door is wide open, and I am frozen in place. She is an angel. The satin purple dress hugs her curves in just the right way. Her hair is not wild and crazy, she has her hair pinned up. I want to pull out each pin, so her beautiful fire red curls are free. She did her eye makeup to match the dress with the brightest purple lipstick she could find. I wonder if it would stain my cock purple. No stop. We are supposed to be going slow, but how can I when this vision is standing in front of me? I must be staring too long because she pulls me out of my trance with her buttery voice.

"Are those for me, daddy?" She asks with a smirk that could bring the strongest man to his knees. I am really reconsidering skipping the opera and just spending the night on my knees worshiping this goddess, but I have to work on the plan, not just for me, but my friends as well.

"Who else would they be for, little one?" I ask her, trying to channel my inner Carter. I am not good at flirting or at least I don't think so. She grabs the flowers and hugs them while taking a big whiff of the floral aroma.

"Thank you, they are beautiful. You want to come in so I can put these in water?" She says and I just nod as I walk into her space. It matches her perfectly. It is a small two bedroom from the look of it. The walls are a bright purple but everything else is black. I walk into the living room where a black velvet couch sits with a small glass coffee table beside it. She has a small TV in the corner, but what has me impressed is the big wall with shelves and on it a library of books. I pick one up and read the back. It is about mafia brothers who share a girl. Oh, my little one likes dirty girl books. I can just imagine her sitting on the couch with one of these books touching herself. She walks in before I can put the book down and smiles at me.

"Oh, I see you found my smut books. That is actually a good one," She comes over and grabs the book out of my hand. When our hands touch, I can feel a shock of electricity and she pulls back like I burned her. So, she felt that too. I grab the book and put it back on the shelf. I lean down and wrap my arms around her while putting my mouth to her ear.

"Do these books make my little one wet?" I ask her in a low gravelly voice. I will have no restraint if she tells me yes.

"Yes daddy, I get all hot and bothered from my books," she says breathlessly. Her breath gets shallow, and I can almost hear her moan at the end. I cannot hold back. I kiss her ear and then down her neck as I make my way up her jaw line. When I finally hit her lips it was like something in us explodes. She wraps her arms around my neck to deepen the kiss. I lick her bottom lip and she opens so willingly. I explore her mouth for the first time and it is magical. It is wet and so warm. I thought with her sass I would have to fight for dominance but my angel melts into me. I pull away because if we continue, there will be no date. I rest my forehead on hers as we remember how to breathe.

Lexi Haynes

"We need to go, little one. If we continue, I will say fuck the opera and ravish you," I whisper.

"I don't see a problem with that," she says and then I growl.

"No. I told you little one, I want to take my time with you and show you how special you are," I tell her as I lead her to the door. She grabs her little black purse and locks up. We go down the steps where the driver is waiting.

"Wow you have your own driver," she says inquisitively.

"Not every day. I just wanted to impress my angel," I tell her honestly as I open the door for her. She slides into the black SUV and then I get in behind her. The driver already knows where we are going so no need to speak to him. I want to get to know my little one better.

"So have you figured out what sport I play yet?" I asked her, wanting to know if she was thinking about me as much as I do her. It feels like she is consuming every thought I have. Like I had a brand meeting today and kept thinking what she would like when planning than what I like.

"Well, I have been thinking about that all day. I didn't want to google you because that would be cheating but I think I figured it out," she says with a smirk. I grab her hand smiling.

"Oh, and do tell little one," I say, coaxing her to continue.

"Well, I figured out you don't play hockey or football. I was never giving the inkling that you play with the other guys because they would have told me already. It is also November, and you haven't talked about a game or practice coming up, so it sounds like you are in your off season. So, then I started to think about your personality, and I think you play baseball," she says and this lets me know my little one is a smart one.

"Well done and did you deduce what position I play?" I ask her knowing she probably won't get it right.

"I take you for a pitcher. You are profoundly serious all the time and always in charge so that fits you best," she says, and it makes me frown because what if she thinks I don't know how to have a good time or have fun. She pushes her finger to my forehead to lessen the scowl that is forming.

"Relax, Ivan, I can hear you thinking," she says and that makes me smile again. This woman can make my emotions do a three sixty with just a simple touch.

"Sorry little one, I tend to overthink things especially when interacting with people. I have lived a very solitary lifestyle and so I have a tough time reading people," I tell her honestly. I don't want to get into this now. It is too soon to show her that all I am is a lost soul. Once she figures that out, she will think I am broken and leave. She just reassures me with a nod.

"We don't have to get into your back story now but just know when you are ready to tell me I will be here for you," she says softly. That makes me want to tell her more. I gulp down a hard swallow and continue, "I was an orphan. My parents abandoned me at a church orphanage. The nuns that took care of me told me that they just did not have the means to keep me. I don't know much about them. All I know is that they left me and that they were Russian. I have not looked for them because if they wanted to know about me, they would have looked for me."

She squeezes my hand and says, "That is their loss. They missed out on what a great guy you are."

This amazing goddess always surprises me. I thought she would have retreated when she heard this, but she moved closer. She leans up and kisses my cheek.

"That is actually how I met Dante. He would sit with me at church and talk to me even though I was socially awkward. I was able to find my surrogate family," I tell her honestly.

"Sounds like a win there. I have my dad but that is really it. My mom took off when I was younger, she and my father had a one-night stand and had me by accident, but it made me want to surround myself with people that choose to be in my life," she says with a frown and then it registers. She is a little lost soul just like me. The driver pulls up to the opera. This is an amazing theater. The driver comes and opens the door for us. I get out first and then give her my hand. She grabs it and when she steps out her jaw is slacked as she takes in the theater.

"I have always wanted to come to this theater but never made the time," she says in awe.

"Only the best for my little one," I tell her as we make our way up the steps. When we walk in, I am even shocked with how amazing it looks. This theater was modeled after the theater in the Phantom of the Opera. There is white and tan marble everywhere. In the entry ways there are red velvet curtains pulled to the side. The lights are statues of women holding the illuminating lights. There is a huge double staircase that meets in the middle up top, lined with red carpet. I lead her up the stairs because it looks like she is overwhelmed with everything.

I let out a small chuckle as I led her to the best box, I could get my hands on. It is decked out in red velvet carpet and there is a table in the center with our food ready. The table and chairs are gold and have a Victorian flare. I go in and pull out her chair as she sits, still holding her breath. I push her in and lean down to her ear.

"Breath, little one," I tell her with a chuckle. I go to my seat and grab her hand across the table as she takes a deep breath.

"This is amazing! So, what are we seeing tonight?" She asks, as the server came up behind us and lifted the lid to our plates, then walked out giving us privacy.

"Well, I may have asked Carter what you might like and this opera house performs Phantom of the opera," I tell her as I rub the back of my neck nervously. She is jumping in her seat.

"Really? I was in the Broadway version of Phantom of the Opera!" She squeals, excitedly. I stop rubbing my neck and smile at her.

"He said you did, and I thought you would enjoy watching it instead of performing it. I even got you opera glasses," I tell her as I hand her a small box that was on the table.

"Oh my god! I love them," she says when opening the box. She looks so happy, and I want to keep it this way. My angel should always feel this way when she is with one of us. The theater goes dark as the lights come on at the stage. She holds the glasses to her eyes as she starts to watch the opening number, but I am not watching the show. My eyes have been on her all night. We don't even touch our food as the performance goes on. Then the lead female comes out in a big pink Victorian dress to perform the song, think of me, and I swear I see Nikki's eyes water as the music moves her. I would love to see her perform it. I bet she would do ten times better than the woman performing it now. We continue to watch as the opera goes on. Then it is over, and the performers come out for the final bow. Nikki stands up to clap and I join her. We make our way down the steps and while waiting for the car she turns to me.

"Thank you for tonight. I had a lot of fun," she says in a low tone.

"Anytime little one, now time to get you home," I tell her as the car comes around. I lead her in and slide in next to her and then we are off to her apartment.

As we pull up to her apartment I lean down and whisper into her ear, "I don't want this to be over."

"It doesn't have to be," she tells me and pulls me out of the car and leads me to her door. She unlocks it and ushers me in. I can already tell where this is going. I told myself we would not do this tonight. I planned just to walk her to her door, give her a peck on the lips and go rub out my hard on that I have had all night.

"Little one, I said we will go slow," I tell her in a low, raspy voice.

"What if I don't want to go slow," she says and leans in to kiss me. I know I should stop her and just kiss her goodnight and leave but I can't after this. She gets on her tiptoes and then our lips connect. Her lips are so soft and inviting. I pick her up, so her legs wrap around my waist and then she licks my bottom lip asking for entrance. I open my mouth willingly and our tongues clash with passion. My hands go to her ass to anchor her against my hardening cock. She pulls away a little, sucking on my bottom lip causing me to groan.

"You should text your driver that you don't need a ride home. I was promised a spanking, daddy," she teases as I put her down and text the driver, we are good for the night. She saunters into the bedroom, and I follow like a lost puppy. She stands there waiting for me to lead. I walk to her and grab her hips and kiss her neck.

"Are you wet for your daddy?" I ask, whispering in her skin. She whimpers and I cannot wait to see what other noises she makes.

"Yes, I have been since we texted earlier," she tells me which makes me moan in her neck. I let her go and sit on her bed. I pat my lap for her to sit on it. My little vixen stands for a moment contemplating something in her head. I hope she doesn't want to stop. My cock has been aching all night, but if she says stop, then we will. Then she has me shocked as she slips off her dress and saunters over. She has stunning black lace lingerie with a pair of black stockings clipped to it. She keeps her heels on that I bought her, which is doing things for me. This is exactly how I envisioned her when I bought them. She sits on my knee, and I can feel her hot wet heat through my pants. I groan as I wrap one arm around her waist and the other goes to her chin holding her there as I look into her beautiful green eyes.

"We can't have you not taken care of but if this is too soon, I understand," I tell her. God it would fucking suck to stop now. Talk about some serious blue balls but I would never pressure my little one into anything she didn't want.

"I want this. Please daddy make your little one feel good," she says breathless already.

"Okay little one, but if at any time you want to stop, you tell me and we will stop," I tell her sternly and she nods with excitement in her eyes.

"Okay, I won't, but I will tell you if we need to stop. Now I was promised a spanking, daddy," she says with mischief glinting in her eye. This makes me growl in the back of my throat.

"Well, I need to give my little one what she wants. Bend across my knee angel," I tell her in a low and deep tone. She gets up for a second and then lays across my knees with her ass in the air, eager. I can't help myself. I lean down and bite her ass. She yelps at the touch of my teeth. I laugh sitting straight up. I press my hand to her perfect back side and start massaging it.

"Are you ready?" I ask her and she nods.

"Use your words, little one," I tell her growling.

"Yes daddy," she says while shaking her ass in the air. She is really trying to tempt me, and you know what, if she wants a punishment then that is what she will get.

"I think ten spanks will be enough of a punishment," I tell her, spanking her once hard and then rubbing the pain away.

"Punishment?" She asked with a moan.

"Yes, punishment, little one. It is for looking so damn tempting and getting me so fucking hard before we left," I tell her with another swat and rubbed her pain away.

"That's not my fault daddy. You bought me the dress and if I am not mistaken you started that earlier," she says with a sass. I swat her harder but don't rub it out this time. Fuck that, she is going to learn not to talk back to her daddy.

"Are you talking back to your daddy?" I ask as I swat her again twice without rubbing the pain away. She moans from the pleasure and pain.

"I would never," She gasps out as I deliver the fifth blow to her bottom. Her ass is starting to get pink, so I rub this one.

"I was going to do ten, but I think I want to play now," I growl out, guiding her up so she is sitting up right. My beautiful little one is flushed in the face and eyes dark with lust. I don't have the patience to fully punish her right now. I am ready to play.

"That wasn't too bad daddy. I thought this was a punishment," she taunts with her tongue out to lick her lips. Oh, so my little one can play?

"Are you testing your daddy?" I ask as I pick her up and stand her on her feet. I take off my jacket finally. I go to start unbuttoning my shirt and she stops my hands.

"Let me," she says as she starts to take over unbuttoning. As she gets the last button, she rubs her hands up my chest. I groan trying to let her take the reins but as she rubs down, she starts to play with my belt.

"Those don't come off until you at least have one orgasm," I tell her with a growl. She looks shocked as I throw her to the bed on her back and I climb on top of her. I go to unclasp her bra so I can worship those amazing breasts. Once I get it off of her, I just stare at her in awe. I thought this woman was gorgeous with clothes on, she is unbelievable with no clothes. She catches me gawking and giggles.

"See something you like?" She asks with a knowing grin.

"Oh, you have no idea. I have imagined you like this since we met," I tell her. I start kissing her neck and working my way down to those glorious tits. Her nipples are already stiff peaks of pink. I cup one with my hand as I suck on the other nipple. That gets me a moan from that beautiful mouth. I switch hands so I can worship her tits. Then I pull up just a little so I can feel the weight of both breasts in my hands. I kiss her hard as I grope her then I go and twist both nipples. She gasps into my mouth. I start to kiss down her neck, then when I get to her shoulder, I suck hard leaving a mark. I want every man at the club to know she is mine. Once

I am satisfied with the mark I left, I work my way down her chest to her stomach, biting and kissing till I am right above her panties.

"Please Ivan," she begs with a whimper.

"That is not my name, little one. Beg your daddy properly," I tell her, kissing her through her panties.

"God! Please daddy take them off. I need you," she begs. I take off each heel, kissing her arch on her foot. Then I slowly slide her panties down, taking her stockings with them. Grabbing her ankles, I slide her to the edge of the bed, and throw her legs over my shoulders as I get on my knees. I kiss up her thighs and just stare at her cunt. It is dripping already with her arousal. I am captivated by this beautiful pink pussy I am about to ravish. I kiss her and she gasps, shivering at my first touch. I can't take it anymore, I need a real taste. I dive in like a starving man. Sticking my tongue in her tight wet pussy. Her sweet juices dripped down face. God, I need some relief. I pause for a moment to kick off my shoes then go back to eating my angel. As I eat her, I undo my belt and my zipper releasing my painfully hard erection. Once I get my pants down, sliding my boxers with them, I see my little one's eyes go wide. I lift my head a little so I can slide two fingers in and curl. Her head leans back as she moans yelling daddy.

"Don't worry about me, little one. You don't get this till I get at least one orgasm," I tell her, moving my fingers in and out. I suck on her swollen clit. I can feel her pussy clench on my fingers, so I know she is close. I slide a third finger in to stretch her out for me. Then she screams as I feel her let go. As she is shaking from her orgasm, I pull out my fingers and slide them up to her lips brushing them along her bottom lip.

"Suck, little one. Taste how sweet you are," I tell her. My little one is such a good girl, without hesitation she takes my fingers into her mouth and sucks and licks all her cum off my fingers. I go back to licking her as she comes down, breathing hard, trying to remember how to breathe.

"You cum so beautifully, little one," I tell her as I kiss up her body. I kiss her hard again making her taste herself on my lips. I can feel my precum leaking out from watching her. She pushes me up, so I am on my knees and butt on my heels. She looks in my eyes and I see the need to touch me.

"You got to taste me and now it is my turn," she says, kissing my chest and making her way down my stomach. I moan as she licks the precum from the tip. God this woman is going to be the death of me. Her beautiful bright green eyes peered up at me full of lust as she sucked the tip in licking and sucking. I groan as she grips the base of my cock as her head starts to bob up and down. My hands go to her hair holding her head. I start to push her head down to the base. She doesn't even gag, she just moans around my cock. The vibration of the moan has me almost cumming. I grasp her hair and tug her up.

"Baby, if you keep going, I am going to cum in your pretty little mouth," I tell her out of breath. At this rate I am going to embarrass myself.

"I don't see a problem," she says, cocking her head in confusion. She continues while stroking my cock, "Well I don't have a condom and with how you keep saying we are taking it slow I don't think you have one either so let me finish my meal daddy."

She moves her head back to my cock going full force. She is deep throating me and I can feel the back of her throat on the tip of my cock. She does not gag once. This girl is a beautiful wet dream, sexy as hell and no gag reflex. I start to feel my balls tightening as I start to pull her hair. I am so close and she sucks even harder knowing I am on the edge. Then I feel it, I shoot in her mouth and my gorgeous goddess just takes me deep sucking every drop of cum. When I am finally done, my little vixen licks my cock from base to tip, kissing the tip before sitting up and wrapping her arms around my neck. We both fall to the bed and I wrap my arms around her waist while she keeps her arms around my neck.

"I didn't take you for a cuddler daddy," she says with a giggle. I flip her so we are spooning.

"Only with you little one," I whisper in her ear. I never was a cuddler but with her I would take any chance I got to hold her. She nestles her ass on my cock which is already getting semi hard. That is the fastest refractory time I have ever had, but I ignore it because this was not supposed to happen anyway. I wanted to take it slow and show her that this is not just about sex. She wiggles more back putting pressure on my hard cock.

"Ignore it baby. Let's cuddle each other to sleep and then I will make breakfast in the morning," I tell her, kissing her ear.

"Well, aren't you just the full package," she says with a yawn. Then she cuddles close, and I swear I hear her purr like a little kitten. She is so goddamn cute. She starts to drift off to sleep and I am not too far behind her.

I am woken up by ringing. My phone keeps ringing and I know exactly who it is. They probably did not sleep all night waiting for me to come home. My phone goes quiet and then starts ringing again. Nikki pulls the blanket up over her face.

"Make it stop," she grumbles, which makes me laugh. I slide from the bed and search for my phone. I pull it out from my jacket pocket and I'm not surprised by the face I see. I get dressed and walk out to her living room to sit on the couch. I sigh and accept the call. When I put it up to my ear the yell that comes through is so loud.

"Where the fuck are you?" Carter yells in frustration. These idiots know where I am, so I have no fucking idea why they are asking.

"Did the asshole finally answer?" Dante yells in the background. I have to hold the phone away from my ear. I place it back on my ear when they are done yelling.

"Well good morning to you too," I say with a laugh.

"And you did not answer my question fucker. Where the fuck are you?" Carter yells again.

"You know where I am," I tell him annoyed. I hear shuffling in the background. I can only assume the idiots are fighting over the phone to hear how the night went.

"Soo what happened?" Dante asked as calmly as he could, but I know he is foaming out the mouth because I did not come home last night. Nikki saunters in and goes to her kitchen, I assume to make coffee. I desperately hope so because I am going to need caffeine to deal with these fucktards.

"It went well and I will talk to you guys when I get home," I say and then hang up. Nikki walks into the living room in a black silk robe and two cups of coffee in her hands. She hands me one and then sits on my lap. I catch her by the waist with the hand that does not have coffee. She leans her head onto my shoulder.

"Are they mad that I slept with you?" She asks with a sigh.

"I did not tell them, little one. It is none of their business what we did last night and if it makes you uncomfortable, I will not tell them," I tell her while taking a sip of my coffee. She sets her coffee down on her glass coffee table and wraps her arms around my neck. I put mine down so I can wrap both arms around her waist. Her gorgeous green eyes are peering into my soul.

"You can tell them as long as you are serious about sharing. Sorry, Ian might have told me your guy's plan," she says and I see a small glimmer of fear in her eyes. She glances down at the floor not wanting to see my reaction. She is nervous to bring this up and anger surges through me at every guy before me. I put my hand on her chin to make her look me in the eyes again.

"I would not joke about that babe. We don't mind that you like all of us and we don't mind sharing you. Even at the same time if you want. We just don't want to rush this because we want to share you in every sense. Meaning this is more than just sex and I think you know that. We want to take you on dates and get to know you as a person," I tell her.

"But you are all in the public eye. What will your fans say, what will your families say?" She rambles on about being seen with all of us. This selfless woman is not scared to do it, she is scared we will get backlash from the press. I put my hand to her mouth to quiet her.

"We will deal with it one problem at a time. I don't have a family to worry about, so you are good on that front. Carter's family I am not sure, but I have never seen him like this. So dedicated to one woman. Dante's mom will just be so happy that he found the kind woman to share a life with. The press we will figure out as we go but we have to be honest with each other and talk everything through. No secrets or second guessing. All we have here is honesty," I tell her and plant a kiss to her forehead. I move my hands so she can speak now.

"Okay, as long as you all are okay with it and we figure this out as we go, I think we can do this. Also, I wanted to tell you thank you," she says.

"For what little one?" I ask, raising one eyebrow with curiosity. If anything, I should be the one that should say thank you to her.

"I may have found out that you heard me and Ian in the office and that you took the lead on trying to give me what I have been looking for. It takes an utterly amazing man to even consider it let alone have three that agree to it. You are all so wonderful and kind. I cannot wait to hang out with all three of you together," she tells me with such happiness in her eyes and the biggest smile I have ever seen on her. My chest swells with pride knowing I could put that look on her face.

"So, what can I make you for breakfast?" I ask her with a laugh.

"Yeah, we may need to take a rain check on breakfast. I don't have much and today is grocery shopping day," she says, all shy and cute. I can't help but kiss the tip of her nose because of her cute reaction.

"Okay little one. Make sure to get a ton of breakfast food for our next sleepover," I tell her with a wink. I continue, "I should probably get going anyway. I am sure Carter and Dante are climbing the walls wanting to know what happened."

I pick up my coffee and slam it back and then place my empty cup on the coffee table. I pick her up, so she is standing beside me. Then, I lift her up and she wraps her legs around my torso. I kiss her so deeply till we have to pull away for air. I rest my forehead to hers.

"I will miss you little one," I tell her, sighing.

"I will miss you too, but you have my number and we can video chat whenever you want," she says, kissing my cheek. I set her down, so we are standing there just holding each other. Seeing who is going to pull away first.

"Fine, little one. Don't think I won't call you every night while we are apart," I tell her with a wicked smile. I give her a quick wink.

"Oh, I am counting on it, big guy," she says with a snicker. She walks me to the door and gives me a quick kiss and hug bye.

"Have a wonderful day baby. I'll call you later," I tell her as I make way down the steps, I pull out my phone and dial. I hear her pick up, but she does not say anything confused why I am calling.

"It's later, love," I say.

"You are impossible," she laughs and I hang up. I get on the street and hail a cab. The cab driver probably thinks I am crazy with my smile. I cannot help it, I got my angel.

Chapter 11

Dante

That stronzo! We agreed to go slow and he got to stay the night at Mia Cara's house! I am a possessive asshole and I know we agreed to share her, but this is the hard part. They both got their time with her and here I am twiddling my thumbs waiting my turn. I am literally sitting on the couch twiddling my thumbs waiting for him to come home. Carter is just as bad, pacing in the kitchen as we wait for Ivan to get home. Tot hops on the couch looking for pets. I start to pet him and I hear the beep from our security system that someone was coming in the door. Me and Carter bum rush the door before Ivan can even close it.

"Well?" Carter asks him. Instead of answering, Ivan pushes past him to the living room to see Tot, with the same smile Carter had last night.

"You gonna answer him?" I ask him. I mean out of all of us I don't think that Ivan would be the one to scare her away but with our scared little Nik I am just not sure. She is just so scared we would judge her that anything could set her off.

"It was fantastic! I told her this morning and she agreed to see where this goes," he says and my anxiety melted away.

"You mean sharing her?" I ask with enthusiasm.

"Yeah, and before you ask we did not fully sleep together. We did not expect to fool around and did not have a condom. No condom, no ride. I am getting some today that is for damn sure," he says annoyed. I could understand the frustration. I would be pissed too if I didn't have a condom and Nikki was in my bed. I made a mental note to pick some up today too.

"My turn!" I say and run to my room for my phone. I know we made plans, but I want the reassurance that she is coming.

Dante: Hello Mi Cara! It is Dante! I just wanted to check you were still coming tonight.

Mi Cara: Hey!! I was about to text you. BTW it was pretty smooth to slip your number in my pocket LOL

Dante: My driver will pick you up at 6 and will have my jersey for you. I am going to make it a shut out for you! Also do you have plans after the game?

I am full of adrenaline. I know she agreed to the game but now it feels like I am asking her on a real date. I really want some one-on-one time before we get into sharing. I want her to see me and get to know me as a person before we come together as a group, but I know it is just going to get even better when we do. I had to jerk off last night and started to imagine what it would be like to share her, and it was so fucking hot.

Mi Cara: I don't. I am gonna be honest I thought we would hang out after but if you don't want to that is okay. I am sure you will want to party with your team when you guys win.

Dante: We are absolutely hanging out after the game. My driver will have a pass for you to come to the player waiting area. Also I heard Ian is coming as well for Stan. Your seats are right next to each other. I cannot wait to see you.

I had already made reservations at my favorite Italian restaurant. I want to have something set up so that way we can have our privacy, so I rented one of their rooms in the back. Then once we have dinner we can meet my team to party later. I really hate going partying with the team anyway. Any time we go out, the puck bunnies swarm us, and I want nothing to do with them. I am looking for love and all I will find with them is gold digging cunts.

Mi Cara: I can't wait either! Yeah, Ian is excited to see Stan almost as much as I am to see you.

My heart is beating out of my chest. She can't wait to see me and I can't wait to see her. I didn't believe it at first. I have to read the text three times just to be sure I was reading it right. This woman owns me and she does not understand that, but she will tonight.

Dante: I will make sure I come out early to see you walk in. I bet you are going to look hot with my name on your back.

Mi Cara: I don't know I think I might want to wear my jersey.

I feel a growl in the back of my throat as I read her text. This woman.

Dante: You are trying to kill me, Mi Cara. I will kill whose ever jersey you are wearing so I would think before you do that

Mi Cara: Well, I don't want you to kill someone and miss our date. I guess I will have to appease you Romeo. Go get ready for your game! I will see you when I get there.

I toss my phone on my bed to start to get dressed. We are required to wear suits on game day. I normally keep it simple with a black suit and white shirt but today is different. I have a special suit that I don't wear often but it is perfect for this. It is a plum suit and then put on a white silk shirt. Then I go to my jewelry drawer in my dresser. I don't wear it too often, but I am pulling out all the stops for Mi Cara. I put on my gold Rolex and matching gold chain. My grandfather would call me a real Italian chooch. I grab my backpack and make my way out to the kitchen for breakfast. The guys are already there making protein shakes and they just stare at me.

"Wow," Carter says.

"What?" I ask, snapping at him even though I know why.

"We have never seen you so suited up for a game. You normally like to keep it basic," Ivan explains.

"Is it too much?" I ask them. Did I go too far? I want to impress her but don't want her to think I am a materialistic man.

"No, man, you look great. So, what is the plan?" Ivan asked, concerned. I can understand his concern because this is finally my one on one and this can set the tone for how this little plan is going to go.

"My driver is picking her up after he drops me off. Then we are going to go to dinner and then might go out with the team. I rented a private room at Lucciola, so we won't get interrupted by fans," I tell them.

"You are going out with the team?" Carter asked with his brows furrowed.

"We might, why?" I ask.

"Just be careful. We have not discussed going public with this and it might put us in a position Nikki might not be comfortable with," Ivan explains. I can feel the color in my face drain and I am sure I look pale from Ivan's statement. Shit! I did not even think about it. There are sure to pops there and if they get a picture of me and Nikki, she will be plastered all over magazines. They have never caught me with anyone so it will surely be front page news.

"Okay I won't go out with the team but what are your suggestions because I don't think just dinner is going to do it for me," I tell them. Ivan thinks for a moment, rubbing his chin. Then his eyes light up.

"I got it! Invite her back here!" Ivan exclaims.

"Wouldn't that overwhelm her," Carter says with wide eyes. We have never had a girl in our space that was not family but I will break that rule in a heartbeat if it means getting Mi Cara in my bed.

"We won't bother them. Dante sends us a text when he is on the way, and we'll hide out in our bedrooms so you can have your time with her. Then if she stays over then we can have a serious talk about being with her over breakfast. It is perfect!" He says with excitement.

"What if she is reserved about coming over?" I ask.

"You got this man. Just tell her why because she was concerned about the press too so if you explain why she will understand," Ivan tells me putting a hand on my shoulder.

"Okay sounds like a plan!" Carter says with enthusiasm. He is just excited that he will see her at some point. We down our protein shakes that Carter made.

"Okay I am going to head out and get ready for the game," I tell them, picking up my backpack and heading for the door. I call my driver to pick me up and when I get in the car I get a video call from my mother. She always calls before a game.

"Hello Mamma," I say with a smile on her face.

"Hello Mio Figlio! We are so excited for the game!" She says jumping up and down. Great, I was hoping they would miss this game since I have Nikki there, but it is okay. She continues with, "We are all coming! Will we see you after the game?"

"Mamma, I have to tell you something and you cannot freak out, okay?" I tell her with a stern look, so she knows I am serious.

"What is it, Mio Figlio?" She asked with a curious glint in her eye. My mother looks like your typical Italian mother. Long, dark, flowing hair, tan skin, and dark eyes. My father used to say I was the spitting image of her.

"I won't be able to see you tonight because I have a date after the game. She will be there and it is our first official date, so I don't want to overwhelm her with meeting you guys just yet," I tell her, keeping a stern look.

"Oh my! My son has a girl at a game and a date! When can I meet her? Will she be sitting in your box with us? What does she look like? What does she do for work?" She kept firing off question after question with no room for me to actually answer them. I pinch my nose in frustration. I knew she was going to be like this. This is why when I go on a date, I don't tell her. She just gets so excited for me to find what she and my father had.

"Mamma! Breathe!" I yell into the phone. She takes a deep breath and waits for me to answer all her unanswered questions. "Mamma, it is our first date so please do not go looking for her. She is not sitting in the box because it is still new and we need to get to know each other before I introduce her. Once the game is over, I am taking her for dinner so please once the game is over you can go and we can hang out after another game."

"Okay but I want to meet this girl!" She says with mischief in her eyes, so I know she is up to something. I rolled my eyes because she did not listen to a word I said. I love this woman, but man can she be frustrating.

"I know, but when it is time, I will introduce you to her. Please mamma," I beg not wanting Mia Cara to deal with my overbearing family.

"You know I cannot promise you anything. I got to go pick up your brothers! Have a wonderful game, Mio Figlio!" She exclaims and hangs up immediately. I know she is going to find some way to get to Nikki, but I have a plan for that. I video call my brother Bobbie and lucky me, Paulie is there too.

"Well Hell! What do we owe for this pleasure, brother?" Bobbie asked.

"I need a favor from you guys tonight at the game," I tell them.

"Oh, and what is the favor before we agree?" Paulie says with skepticism. I can understand why he is like this. I have never asked anything from them. I am the big brother, so I have always supported them. They watched me in high school working odd jobs to help mom put food on the table when papa passed. I have paid for both of them to go to college when I finally got drafted for the NHL. Now they run their own construction company in Philadelphia and just opened another branch here in New York.

"I have a girl coming to the game tonight and I need you to keep mom in check. I told her I did not want to introduce them to each other yet because it is our first official date, but you know how mom gets," I tell them with a desperate look. They both crack up laughing on the phone.

"This is too funny!" Paulie says while throwing his head back to laugh.

"Why did you invite the broad if you knew we might be there?" Bobbie asked, slapping Paulie on the back.

"Hey, watch your fucking mouth brother! You will not call Mi Cara a broad! Do you understand me?" I yell, shaking with anger. Then both their mouths gape.

"Did you just call her what I think you just did?" Paulie chimes in. Shit! They understand that for me to call a woman by that name is serious. It is the name my father used to call my mother to show his love to her.

"Yeah, I did," I say, running my hand through my hair, stressed.

"Shit! You love this girl, don't you?" Paulie asked because Bobbie still looks in shock.

"I don't know, but I have never felt this way about a girl and I just want everything to be perfect for her. Which means I don't want her to deal with an overbearing mother and you two dick heads," I tell them and it is true. I want to say I love her but I have never been in love before, so I don't know. Also, if I do, I will not admit it to these two stronzos before her.

"Fine we will try to keep mom at bay, but you know how she gets. I don't know if we can actually stop her if she is determined to meet this girl," Bobbie says with a laugh. I know he is right but at least we can try now that they know.

"I know, but you guys can at least try to distract her, so she doesn't try anything with Nikki. Thank you, brothers, I owe you one," I tell them and then both of them look sad all of a sudden.

"You don't owe us anything and you know it. Consider this repayment for helping raise us," Paulie says with a soft smile. They always feel like they owe me because of everything I did for them when I was a teen, but they don't. I was just doing my job as the head of the family.

"You know you guys don't have to repay me. We are blood and you look after your flesh and blood. Now I have to go. We just pulled up to the stadium and have to get ready for this game," I tell them and give them a waive.

"Don't worry brother, we got your back!" They yell and hang up the phone.

I laugh and head into the stadium.

It is game time in a few minutes. I need to focus, we are playing our rivals tonight, Philly. They just redrafted almost an entire team so it should be an easy win, but they love to fight. I don't need them trying to knock out one of my teammates. I am sitting next to Stan as we suit up for the game and he is bouncing his knee nervously.

"What's up man?" I ask him. Steele and Jason come to us because they are just as curious about what is going on with him.

"I need to tell you all something because I really need advice on what to do. It also kind of will fall back on you guys too," he says, still bouncing away but looking down. It's like he can't look us in the eyes admitting this. This just makes me even more curious.

"You can tell me anything, you know I don't judge," I tell him trying to get it out of him. He looks up at me finally.

"I am thinking about coming out to the press," he says, running his hands through his hair.

"Dude! That is awesome! I am sure it will feel great being out in the open with nothing to hide!" Steele yells. We just want what is best for our teammates. I couldn't imagine trying to hide a big part of who you are to the world.

"Yeah, whatever you want to do we will support you a hundred and ten percent," Jason tells him.

"Thank you, guys! My publicist already has it ready for when I give the go ahead but did not want to do it before the game," he explains.

"But isn't Ian coming with Nikki?" I ask him and instantly regret it because Steele and Jason's mouths drop in shock.

"Wait back up! Who is Ian and who is Nikki?" Steele asked, still in shock.

"Ian is a guy I met, and Nikki is with Dante," he says with a shrug.

"Hold on! You two never bring people besides family to games!" Jason yells. Then Quick comes around the corner.

"Who has who at this game?" Quick chimes in which makes me roll my eyes. I love all my teammates, but Mi Cara said something about wearing his jersey instead of mine which really irks me.

"These two punks brought people they are seeing and acting like it is no big deal," Jason says pointing at me and Stan.

"Oh, you finally found someone you want to bring to games. Is she hot?" Quick asked and it just strikes the fire of my rage too far. I grab his shirt and pin him up to the lockers.

"Watch your mouth!" I yell at him and he smirks, but I can see the shock in his eyes. It's not his fault that Nikki taunted me.

"What the fuck did I do?" He asks and I let him go taking a deep breath. I have to count to five in my head to calm myself down.

"Sorry man. She made a comment about wearing your jersey tonight and it pissed me off," I explained brushing his shirt out.

"Shit! You're jealous because your girl has my jersey and not yours!" He says with a laugh.

"Fuck off! I fixed it though! I got her a jersey and not just any jersey. I gave her my actual away jersey," I tell him with pride swelling in my chest. I stand ready to start warmups.

"Let's go kick some asses!" I yell at them and make my way out of the locker room with the team behind me. We start to make our way to the tunnel. We wait for the announcer to call each of our names. When he calls my name, I skate out and my eyes go straight to the crowd looking for her. The announcer finally calls all of our names, so I skate to the bench since she is sitting right behind it. She is gorgeous. She is in black combat boots and tight ass jeans. I bet her ass is phenomenal but what gets me is her in a black and white jersey. I skate up to the glass and twirl my finger at her. She blushes and stands. As I see her back and get instantly hard from seeing the name De Luca. She has a shy smile as she sits down. I need to make this the best game for her! I skate to my goal for warmups when Stan skates up to me.

"This is weird having people here for us, that is not family," Stan says looking at Ian with a grin.

"Well, my family is here. I told mom to stay away from Nikki because this is our first date and don't want to scare her away," I tell him and he almost falls on the ice laughing like I told a good joke. I look at him confused and ask, "What is so funny?"

"You! You told your mom!" He exclaims while falling to the ice laughing.

"Yeah, your point?" I ask, still confused. He finally gets up and gains his composure. He pats me on my shoulder.

"Okay, I see I am going to have to explain slowly. You told your mom that you are bringing a girl to a game. One that she will be at as well?" He says almost as a question.

"Yeah?" I ask.

"Okay and when has your mom ever once been known to refrain herself with something like this?" He asked and concern hit me.

"I asked my brothers for help to keep her in the box and then leave after the game," I tell him to try to convince myself I got this.

"Your mom might be little, but she is a bulldozer. When have you or your brothers been able to stop that woman when she has her mind set on something?" He asks and skates away with a smirk. Shit! I look up at my box and don't see my brothers or my mamma. He is right I am fucked!

Chapter 12

Nikki

This is crazy! We are right at the players bench like Dante said. Not that I did not believe him, it's just that I normally sit in nosebleed seats when coming to games, so to be this close to the ice is crazy! Me and Ian grab a couple of beers and snacks. We have the works, we got popcorn and candy galore. They start to announce the players and when Dante comes out, I just stare with my mouth wide open. He looks so hot in all his goalie equipment. I just want to take him home and tear each piece off to get to that amazing body. He skates up to the glass looking pleased with himself. He waves and then gives me a finger twirl. Fuck! He is really doing this. He wants to make sure I wore his jersey and not Quick's. I blush and I hear Ian snicker. I stand and twirl slowly and make sure to pause when my back is to him. I look over my shoulder and he has a smile so big and full of pride. I am sure my panties are drenched from his gaze. I sit back down as he skates to his goal so he can do his warmups.

"I love this for you!" Ian yells laughing.

"Shut the fuck up! The whole arena can hear you with how loud you are!" I yell back at him. I turn my attention to Dante. He and Stan are talking and then I see concern flash across Dante's face as Stan falls over laughing. Oh god! I hope it is not about me being here. Stan skates away still laughing and Dante shakes it off and then does his warmups and good lord. I never thought watching someone do groin stretches could be so hot. As he gets up from his stretches, he looks at me and smiles. I have to clench my thighs together. I am so hot and bothered.

"I have something to tell you and it is very important," Ian says which snaps me out of my gawking. I look at him and he looks so concerned about what he is going to tell me.

"What is it, babe? You can tell me anything," I tell him and that is the honest truth. He could tell me he killed someone, and I would be there to help him hide the body. It is just how our relationship works.

"So, Stan is coming out tomorrow morning," he says and looks over to Stan and Stan gives him a huge smile.

"Wow, that is big. How are you feeling about it?" I ask him, trying to give him all the support he needs.

"I feel okay, but I am concerned for him. I agreed to come out as his boyfriend. The article is getting published first thing in the morning," he says looking down at his feet blushing.

"That is amazing! He is willing to come out because he cares for you so much and wants the world to know," I tell him bouncing in my seat. I am just so happy for him! He finally found someone that cares for him like I do.

"I know but he is going to get ridiculed by fans. What if he resents me for it? What if they don't accept him? What if we break up because of it? What if his family doesn't like me?" His questions keep going, not breathing between them. I grab his hand and squeeze it, so he stops.

"That is a lot of what ifs babe. Just take a deep breath," I tell him and I can see his chest rise and fall as he takes a deep breath. I continue, "That is better. Now I am going to tell you this and this will be hard to hear. This is going to be hard on you both. Just try to focus on the now and then battle the what ifs when and if they come up. I can see how much he cares for you. He is willing to battle this with you by his side. I have never seen someone willing to do this for you and I want you to stick with it. Just know whatever happens, I will be here for you to love you."

"I love you, Bitch!" He yells and tackles me for a hug. When he pulls away, I can see the tears forming in his eyes.

"I love you too! Now let's watch our men win!" I tell him, taking his hand.

"Our men? Huh?" He says with a smirk.

"What?" I asked confused and then it hits me. I just said our men. I just staked my claim to Dante, and I immediately blush again. I told him what happened with Ivan and how it was the best orgasm I have ever had.

"So now you have a harem?" He asked with a laugh.

"I guess I do. Ivan told me they don't mind sharing and that we can all be together like a family, and I really like that but we all need to come together and have a conversation. We need to make ground rules and discuss how we are going to go about it," I tell him, twirling a loose strand of hair.

"This is perfect! We are getting what we want for the first time. You with your harem and me with a boyfriend that doesn't want to hide me," he says, and he is right, we both found great men. The game starts and we watch holding each other's hands. The puck drops and Stan takes off. He is fast! It is amazing, he gets a goal in the first thirty seconds of the game. Then something happens that not only surprises me but Ian as well. The camera pans to Ian, and he is on the jumbotron and Stan points to him dedicating the goal to him. It makes me laugh as Ian blushes, but I don't let go of his hand. This is so wonderful for him, but I know he is going to need a lot of support from me as they come out.

"That boy is so in love with you! I guess he is done with hiding who he is," I tell Ian with excitement. Ian blushes so red you can see it in outer space. We continue to watch. Stan does a hat trick, dedicating every goal he makes to Ian. It is so cute but then I realize that Dante is trying to impress me too. Every saved goal he looks and winks at me. Then in between the second and third period he skates up to the glass. He points to me and yells, "I am going to make it a shut out for you Mia Cara!"

I slump back in my seat and blush. He just laughs and goes into the player's tunnel. When we get to the end of the third he keeps his promise. It is a shutout and Stan wins with a hat trick. That was a crazy game. Ian and I make our way to the waiting area for family and friends, finding a high top to sit at. While I'm sitting there, I am not sure why, but I get this weird sense like someone is watching me. I look around and I see a beautiful older woman staring at me. She has long dark hair and gorgeous tan skin that would make anyone jealous. There are two men with her that are the spitting image of her. She starts to make her way towards me with the men trying to stop her. I am so confused. When she finally can shake the men off of her, she tails it to me.

"Hello! My name is Maria!" She says excitedly when she finally makes it to our table.

"Ummm, hello, I am Nikki. I don't mean to be rude, but do I know you," I ask her confusedly. She just looks so familiar.

"Oh, good lord! You must think I am a crazy lady! Completely understandable!" She yells and then the two men that are with her stand right behind her.

"Mamma please don't scare her," He tells her and then leans in and whispers, "She is a crazy lady, but she is harmless."

The other guy chimes in, "Dante is going to kill you mamma. You promised him you would not bother them."

"Dante?" I ask them.

"I apologize, we are being rude. I am Dante's mamma, and these two idiots are his younger brothers, Paulie and Bobbie," she explains, almost jumping for joy at the chance to meet me. It's actually really sweet and makes me giggle.

"It is really nice to meet you Mrs. De Luca!" I tell her and hop off my stool to hug her.

"Oh, please call me Mamma!" She says hugging me back with a laugh.

"Okay mamma you met her. Can we go now so Dante does not kill us?" One of the guys asks. She swats him on his chest.

"You are being rude Bobbie!" she yells at him and then turns to me.

"So how long have you known Dante?" She asks as she sits down with me and Ian. Ian has just been giggling under his breath this entire time. I shoot him a glare to back off. Then turn my attention back to Mrs. De Luca.

"Not long. We really only met a few days ago," I tell her.

"Oh, so love at first sight! Where did you meet?" She asks and her first statement shocks me. My mouth goes dry. We just met so it is way too soon to be saying the "L" word. Can Dante really love me already?

I lick my lips and tell her, "He came to the club I own. It is a Jazz club I opened for me to sing at." Her eyes widened. I am just praying she does not judge me. I mean it is not a big career, but I am proud to be a small business owner. Then the smile that grows on her face says she is not.

"That is wonderful!! What do you like to sing?" She asks, still wiggling in her seat. Her sons are still glaring at her in between looking for Dante, wanting to leave.

"I used to sing on Broadway, so my favorite is any number from Burlesque," I tell her and her eyes are practically bugging out of her head.

"That is my favorite musical! I take the boys all the time!" She yells then I see her frown, along with her sons. I look where they are frowning and there is an incredibly angry Dante headed our way. Oh no! Is he going to be mad at me? Does he think I planned this to get closer? I am sure he has had crazy puck bunnies try this before. He makes it to our table and does not even acknowledge his family. He puts his arm around me and pecks my cheek.

"Has my family been bothering you, Mia Cara?" He asks with concern.

"Not at all," I tell him with a smile. It was the truth. I was nervous at first, but I was enjoying talking to his mother. She is a kind and caring woman. His attention turned to his brothers.

"I thought I told you guys to leave after the game," he says with a growl.

"Hey! We tried but you know mamma. When she sets her mind to it nothing is stopping her," he says and winks at me. It causes me to giggle. Dante looks at me and his expression softens. I think I am understanding now. He did not want his mother to scare me off. Little does he know, it will take a lot more than his nosy mother to scare me off. I grabbed his other hand that is not around my shoulder and gave it a squeeze, trying to reassure him this is okay.

"I was just telling your mother about my singing, and she was telling me that her favorite musical is Burlesque," I said to him with a soft smile.

"Oh, did you tell her the song you sang when we met?" He says with a mischievous smile. I turn to his mother and she looks so intrigued.

"What was it?" She asks, bouncing in her seat again.

"I sang Bound to you from Burlesque," I tell her and her eyes widen with joy.

"That is my favorite song! It was me and my husband's favorite song to dance to. The boys probably know it by heart," she says with a small frown though. I am not sure why and it makes me want to ask but then Dante cuts in before I could.

"Okay mother, Nikki and I have dinner reservations and I do not want to be late," Dante says as he pulls me out of my seat. Shit! I forgot about Ian too! I was so distracted by meeting Dante's family. I notice he is not in the seat across from me anymore. I look around to find him and Stan standing in the corner holding hands. My heart swells at the image. Stan was not kidding, he is not hiding anymore.

"Ready to go, Mia Cara?" Dante asks, whispering in my ear. I turn to him and give him a nod. I turn to his family before he tries to usher me away.

"It was very nice to meet you Mrs. De Luca, you as well Paulie and Bobbie," I tell them and then Dante's mother glares at me. She is just as scary as Dante when she looks like that.

"I told you, please call me mamma. Mrs. De Luca sounds so formal," she tells me when her expression softens.

"Okay, Mamma," I mimic her and her face lights up.

"Nice meeting you too, Mia Figlia," she says with the warmest smile. I am not sure what she just called me, but I can tell it is endearing. The sons usher her out of the stadium. Then I turn to Dante with a confused look.

"What did she just call me?" I ask him and he barks a laugh.

"I am kind of embarrassed to tell you," he says while pulling me to the exit.

"Why? It didn't sound bad. It wasn't right?" I ask him. The car pulls up and we both slide in. He grabs my hand once we are buckled in.

"Not bad, Mia Cara. Quite the opposite. She called you, Mia Figlia. It means my daughter," he tells me blushing now. It is so cute to see the red flush on his beautiful tan skin. The car starts to move toward the city.

"You played great, Romeo," I tell him, and he groans.

"Mia Cara, you know how I feel about that nickname," he says and glares at me. I giggle even though he looks pretty mad because he is always so composed. It is nice to see this side of him.

"Well, if not Romeo, then what?" I ask him, still giggling like a little school girl.

"I prefer to be your, Mio Amore," he says with a mischievous grin. I don't by any means know Italian but have heard enough Italian opera to know what that means. Now it is my turn to blush. I turn my head to the side so he wouldn't see it but then his other hand goes to my chin to stop me. He looks into my eyes with such passion it could make any woman melt for him.

"Say it, Mia Cara," he says and dips his head so his lips ghost over mine. I hesitate for a moment but then I realize that he is Mio Amore.

"Mio Amore," I whisper against his lips. Next thing I know his lips crash to mine. He licks at the seam of my lips, begging for entrance. I part my lips and he devours me. I start to wiggle in my seat and then he groans into my mouth. I can feel the passion behind this kiss. His claim. He pulls away, only slightly. I can still feel the warmth of his lips. I lick my lips and his gaze drops to them.

"We need to stop, or we won't make it to dinner," he whispers.

"I am not hungry anymore," I whisper but then my stomach betrays me. It makes a low growl. He just smiles and continues with, "I need to feed you, Mia Cara."

He slides away but grabs my hand. The drive is killing me. I want this man and I want him alone. He glances at me while I wiggle in my seat looking for some kind of friction that I desperately need. He dips his head to my ear and whispers, "There will be time for that later." Then nibbles my ear and pulls away with a huge grin. The car comes to a stop and when I look out, I see a little Italian restaurant. There are beautiful stained-glass windows with warm wood around the paneling. In bright, red, neon lights above I see the name Lucciola. Dante gets out first and then grabs my hand to help me out. We walk in and I blush realizing I am not dressed for a fancy dinner. I am just in jeans and his hockey jersey. While he is in a gorgeous plum three-piece suit.

As we wait for the host, Dante leans down and whispers in my ear, "You look beautiful, Mia Cara."

My blush deepens. It is like the man can read my mind. I start to look around at the decor. The walls are lined with beautiful warm bricks. There are tables of every size lined with white tablecloth. There is a small bar to the left with red leather stools. The host finally walks up with a big grin.

"Good evening, Mr. De Luca. We have your room ready for you," He says and leads us through the establishment.

"Dante, what does he mean by room?" I asked him confused. He just ignores me and grabs my hand as the host walks us to a back room. He moves the red velvet curtains that are in the archway of the room, and I gasp. There is a table set up for two but what gets me is there are candles everywhere and beautiful red rose petals on the floor. There is a small table in the corner with the biggest bouquet of red roses and sunflowers. Dante leads me to the table that is in the middle of the room and pulls out my chair for me. I sit and then he rounds the table to sit in his chair that the host holds out to him.

The host stands at the edge of the table and asks, "What can I get you to drink, Mr. De Luca?"

Dante looks at me and asks, "Do you like wine, Mia Cara?" I just nod speechless.

"Per favore, get us a bottle of your Poli Cleopatra Moscato Grappe," He tells the host in his delicious Italian accent. The host hands us menus and then goes to get the wine. He turns to me and grabs my hand across the table and holds it.

"Would you like me to order for you Mia Cara or would you rather look at the menu and pick something out?" He asks with a sweet grin. It is obvious he has been here before.

"I am not picky and it looks like you know what is good. You can order. I bet it will be delicious," I tell him and our server comes in with a bottle of wine. I just watch as the server pops the wine and pours us both a glass.

"My name is Isabella, and I will be taking care of madam and sir," she says with an Italian accent. She continues, "Are you ready to order or will you need a minute?"

"We will have the Burrata Salad and Melon Prosciutto skewers to start. Then for the main course let's do the Penne al Voda and the Chicken Conchiglie. For dessert let's do the Tiramisu with two espressos per favore," he tells our server, and I am enticed with his voice. His accent comes out when he orders each Italian dish. I would swoon if I were not already sitting. The waiter takes our menus and scurries off. Dante turns to me, and his warm brown eyes go dark passion. They almost look black in this lighting.

"Mia Cara don't look at me like that," he says with a grin.

"Like what?" I ask but it comes out as a squeak. His voice alone can have me wiggling in my seat.

"Like I am the meal. If you don't stop, I won't be able to hold back," he says with a warning. I laugh now.

"Well, you did look so delicious on the ice tonight which I did not get to congratulate you yet. Congratulations on your win, Mio Amor," I tell him and add his new nickname to tease. That earns me a dazzling smile but then frowns.

"I am sorry about my family," he apologizes, which I don't understand. It is not his fault that his mom showed up curious about me.

"Don't apologize, silly. They were lovely," I tell him and the frown melts off his face and then smirks.

"I feel like I do. Mia mamma can come across as overbearing and I love her, but it can be too much for some people," he says with an apologetic smile.

"She just wants to protect her son and I can understand why. You wear your heart on your sleeve with me and she does not want some puck bunny to come in and hurt you or use you," I tell him with an honest smile.

"I don't think of you as a puck bunny or would use me," he says with a frown looking at our intertwined hands. I pull his hand to my face and kiss the back of his.

"I know but your mother is sweet and kind. She did not scare me off, quite the opposite actually," I tell him to ease his nervousness. Our waiter comes back in with our appetizers, and they look phenomenal. There is a plate with vibrant tomatoes, cheese, and basil and then the other plate had these skewers with melon, mozzarella cheese balls and what looks like ham. Both plates are drizzled with balsamic glaze. My mouth is watering just looking at them. The waiter sets down the plates in the middle and refills our wine.

"Will you need anything else, Mr. De Luca?" She asks. Without tearing his gaze from me he gives her a quick headshake and she runs off. He lets go of my hand to serve up both appetizers on the little white porcelain plates the waiter left.

"This all looks amazing. You really did not have to do all of this, Dante," I tell him blushing.

"You deserve the world, Mia Cara so yes I did have to do all this," he tells me like I am crazy for thinking otherwise. He hands me my plate and I lick my lips starving.

"This all looks delicious, Mio Amor. I cannot wait to taste the rest of it," I tell him and take a bite of the skewer. It was amazing! My eyes are practically rolling back in my head. It is so good. I really need to think about serving better food at my club. Maybe I will talk to my cook about adding some more fancy food.

"What do you think?" He asks with a smirk and then takes a bite out of the tomato salad.

"It is amazing! It is making me think to revamp my menu at the club," I tell him while taking another bite.

"Just don't take tater tots off," he says with a faint laugh. I look at him like he is crazy.

"Why?" I ask cocking my head to the side.

"My dog loves tots, which is actually why I called him tot," he explains.

"I love dogs! What kind of breed is he?" I ask loudly with excitement. Dante pulls out his phone and hands it to me.

"He is a husky," he tells me while I look at the photo on his phone. It is a beautiful black and white husky. One eye brown and one blue. He is laying on the couch cuddling a passed-out Carter. It is so adorable. Dante lets out a small laugh and says, "Don't tell Carter I showed you that. He doesn't even know I have it. I am saving it in case Tot ever annoys him and he wants to get rid of him. I can show him that to shut him up."

"He is so cute! What a little puff ball. I can't wait to meet him," I tell him and Dante's eyes light up with excitement.

"You will love him. He loves to snuggle, and we go for walks in Central Park. You can come with us and throw the ball for him," he says practically jumping in his seat. His reaction is so cute and you can tell how much he loves his fur baby.

"I would love that," I tell him as our waitress appears with the main courses. She takes the plates we are done with and places the new plates in the middle again. We make it through eating the main courses and to be honest I am watching Dante eat. The man is even seductive even while eating. I have to squeeze my thighs tight together from the aching that my vagina is doing. He catches me gawking and smiles.

"What did I say about looking at me like that, Mia Cara," he says with a mischievous grin, and he takes another bite of his food.

"I can't help it," I say with a gasp because now I feel his hand on my thigh. It is slowly making its way up. He leans down to my ear and whispers, "If you don't stop, I will have to bend you over this table and show everyone who you belong to."

He lets go of my thigh and adjusts himself. Then he goes right back to eating like he did not whisper those dirty promises in my ear. Two can play that game. I lean up and whisper in his ear, "I think we should skip dessert because I am not hungry for food anymore." He groans as I sit back in my seat. The waitress comes back in to check on us and Dante tells her to make dessert to go. I can feel my pussy pulsing with want. I need this man in bed right now. Then a big guy with a chef's coat comes in. He has long dark hair that is pulled into a man bun and I can see his muscles practically ripping through his coat.

"Cousin, how was everything?" He asked Dante. Wait! Time out! Did he just say cousin?

"Everything was delicious as always, Antonio," he tells him with a glare. The big guy turned to me with a wink.

"And who is this Bellissima?" He asks me but I really feel like the question is pointed at Dante.

"My name is Nikki," I reply. Antonio grabs my hand and places a kiss on my knuckles. Dante grabs my hand from him and intertwines our fingers again.

"That is enough cousin. Nikki, this is my second cousin, Antonio. Antonio, this is Nikki. I am sure mamma gave you the full report already," he says with an eye roll. Wait! What does he mean by full report?

"Your mamma may have called right before you got here. I just wanted to meet the girl that has my cousin all up in knots," he says with a soft laugh. Dante rolls his eyes again.

"Okay you met her now, so we will be on our way," Dante tells him and then grabs the box out of his hands and then with the other helps me from my seat. He leads me out of the restaurant as we are walking out the car is pulling up.

"We did not have to rush out, Dante. That was rude," I tell him, annoyed.

"Trust me, Mia Cara. He was annoying me touching you and right now I want you all to myself. No sharing tonight. Just me and you," he says and my annoyance melts away. I shiver with excitement. Not at his possessiveness but at his promise of sharing. These men know just what to say to get me wet. Dante helps me into the car and he tells the driver to take us to his house and to make it fast. Then he looks at me with concern, "Is that okay, Mia Cara?"

"It's fine but won't Ivan and Carter be there? Won't they hear us?" I ask, concerned that they might think it is wrong that I am there with him. I don't want them to think I am a hoe.

"Don't worry, Mia Cara. They promised to stay away tonight so it is just me and you. I wanted to take you out with the team but did not want you to have to deal with the pops that would show up. Besides I am sure they will be happy to hear you there," he says and then nibbles my ear. I blush and go silent. Trying to wrap my head around what he just said. I think he is telling me his friends want to hear us fuck. God I am so wet at the thought. This will be the closest I have ever come to my fantasy. I could practically envision me and Dante in his room being as loud as we could and then Ivan and Carter in another room stroking themselves at the noises we made. I am getting so wet I have to wiggle in my seat to feel some release. Dante notices and lets out a soft laugh under his breath. I glare at him because here I am all hot and bothered and he is not helping a girl out on the way. The driver finally pulls into a parking garage which I am assuming is their building.

The driver pulls into a parking space and Dante helps me out. I look around the garage and there are so many beautiful cars lined up. There is a black SUV with tinted windows, a brand-new Ford Bronco, and shit! There is even a Lamborghini! I look up to Dante and say, "Wow a lot of people must live in your building."

"There is but this is our private garage, so these are all ours," he says with a soft laugh. I drop my jaw in shock which makes him laugh harder. He leads me to what looks like a private elevator because there are only two buttons. One for the garage and one that says PH. Oh shit doesn't PH stand for Penthouse! We ride up the elevator just holding hands but just that alone is making my heart flutter. The door opens to a beautiful penthouse. It is very monochromatic with white walls and black big sofa in the middle. It is a two-story penthouse with floor to ceiling windows. To the left is a big kitchen with white marble countertops. The floor is a warm wood floor. No really when I take off my shoes my feet feel warm. They must have heated floors. Dante grabs my shoes and leads me up the stairs and down the hall. There are four doors. He stops at what I assume is his bedroom.

"I will give you a full tour tomorrow, Mia Cara. Right now, all I want to see is you in my bed," he whispers and then opens his door to his room. I walk in and the decor goes with the rest of the house. The walls are white and there is a huge, big black bed in the middle with black sheets and comforter. I do see a small dresser to the side that has a retro record player and next to that a big black bookcase that is full of records. There are still big glass windows everywhere that give you the perfect view of Central Park. The view alone takes my breath away. I get lost in the view but then I feel Dante standing behind me and wraps his arms around my waist and rests his chin on my shoulder. I can feel his hard cock push against my ass. He bends down so I can feel his breath on my ear.

"I am going to play some music, why don't you get comfortable on my bed Mia Cara," he whispers in my ear so softly I can't help but feel the shiver run down my spine and the hair on the back of my neck stand up. He lets me go and goes to the record player and starts to play soft jazz. Well, he did say get comfortable. I slowly take off my jeans and be sure to bend down really slowly to take them off, giving him the perfect view of my ass in my white lace panties. I look back and the feral look in his eyes has me licking my lips. He is leaning back on the dresser with his arms crossed. I giggle as I get back up from taking off my jeans and hop on the bed in just his jersey. I go to take it off but then he rushes towards me and is there to stop my hands grabbing my wrists.

"No, Mia Cara. I want you in this and nothing else when I finally fuck you," he tells me. His voice is low and raspy. I do as he says and stop. He gets up a little to take off his vest and shirt. He slides them off slowly as I am kneeling in his bed with my ass on the heels of my feet. Then he goes to undo his buttons on his shirt and I hop up.

"Let me," I say softly. His hands drop to his side in fist. He is trying to hold back. I graze my hands up his shirt and start to undo the buttons. I go slow one at a time, when I am finally done, I rub my hands up his torso feeling every muscle. I go up to his shoulders and slide off his shirt. His tan skin with all his muscles is making me wiggle on the bed. I rest my hands on his pectorals but then I notice a tattoo on his chest. There is a beautiful black cross with beautiful lines and details. Then I look at the center of it and there is a year going through it. I can see the pain in his eyes when I trace over it following the decorative line work. I stop because I can see in his eyes that he got this out of pain for a lost loved one.

"Who did you get this for?" I ask, wanting to know everything about this man. His happy moments but also his sadness.

"I got it after my pappa died," he whispers.

"We don't have to get into this now but later I would love to hear about him. It is obvious that he meant a great deal to you, and I want to know all about him and how he influenced the man you became today," I tell him, grabbing both his hands. He relaxes in relief.

"Thank you, Mia Cara," he whispers. He guides me down, so I am laying on the bed kissing my neck. I am sure he can still see the marks that Ivan left on me. I hear him growl into my neck at the sight of them. He carefully brushes his lips across my neck and to the other side. He sucks and it's hard. I gasp with how hard he is marking me. He leans back to look at his work and groans.

"Now you have my mark," he says and then adds, "The only one to mark you is us, Mia Cara. No one else."

He drops his head to kiss me. He devours my mouth as our tongues clash. I whimper in his mouth and he swallows my whimpers as he continues to explore my mouth. I moan in protest wanting more as his lips leave mine. His one hand starts to stroke down my torso then slides into my panties. I feel his rough hand start to dance around my entrance. Then, when his thumb is rubbing against my sensitive nub, he slides one finger inside. I am already so close with our banter from earlier. It was like our whole dinner was our foreplay.

"You are so tight Mia Amor, so wet for me," he whispers into my neck. God his words alone have me unraveling. My walls tighten around his finger as he pumps them in and out of my core. I come so hard I see stars.

I am breathless when he pulls his hand from my panties and then sucks them. Making sure not one drop of my juices is wasted. He groans as he pops his fingers from his mouth.

"You taste so sweet and tart. Like a strawberry," he moans out. I am breathing heavily like I just ran a marathon. He gets up from the bed and goes to his black end table to pull out a condom. He tosses it to me to open as he undoes his belt and pants. He drops his pants to the floor with his black boxers and I just stare in awe. He is bigger than Ivan which I was not expecting. He grabs the base to relieve some ache. I go to stroke it with him but he takes a step back, so I am just out of reach of him.

"Sorry Mia Cara but if you touch me, I might explode before we even get to fuck," he growls out. That only makes me want to touch him even more.

"Really?" I ask out of curiosity.

"Really. Now come to the edge of the bed on your hands and knees. I want to watch you take my cock with my name on your back," he says, grabbing the condom out of my hands. I do quick work and get on my hands and knees wanting to feel him inside me. He lifts up the jersey, so it is up my mid back. He slowly slides my panties off and we just sit there for a few breaths.

"Everything okay, Mio Amor?" I ask him. I look back and he is on his knees staring in awe at my dripping wet core. He then lifts his head, and his gaze is so intense I had to look away.

"I am just admiring you, Mia Cara," he says, and I can feel his breath on my pussy. I shiver at his words. He then stands and I feel him lineup his cock so he can plunge into me. Then I feel the tip of his cock rub against my slick folds. I moan as he slides the tip in.

"Fanculo, Mia Cara. I am not going to last long," he tells me, and his words are making me gush around him. The power I have over this man. I love the fact that this will be fast because it shows how much I affect him.

Most girls would hate that it would be over so soon, but it is giving me the extra confidence I need. I look back at him and his eyes are closed and jaw clenched. He is trying to hold back so he will last.

"That only makes it hotter that you can't hold back," I tell him honestly. His eyes shoot open and the feral look he gives me says it all. I turn right around and he starts to pound into me, hard and fast. I can feel his hands grip my ass as he goes even harder. Then one of his hands lets go and then I feel the sting of his hand as he spanks one cheek. I moan at the pain and pleasure. My head drops to the bed when I feel my second orgasm coming. I arch my back, so he is hitting just the right spot. My whole body starts to shake as I start to cum. I clench his cock with my pussy as it pulsates from the build.

"That's it, Mia Cara. Cum around my cock," he growls and his words send me over the edge. I am cuming hard as he finds his release himself. We sit there for a moment trying to catch our breath. He slowly starts to slide out of me and walks to what I assume is his private bathroom to clean up. I crawl up the bed till my head finds the pillows and I crash into them. He comes back nude in all his glory. He has a damp washcloth that is warm. He guides it up my pussy to clean me. So, this is after care? I have never had a man that would do this for me. I moan as he wipes me down.

"Keep making those noises, Mia Cara and we will have to do that again," he warns.

"I can't help it. No one has ever done this for me before and I think I love it," I tell him honestly. This aftercare is making me all hot and bothered again in ways that I can't describe. He gets up after wiping me down with a big smile on his face and throws the cloth in a hamper that is in a corner of the room. He then tucks me in under the comforter and then slides in next to me. We face each other as his hands go around my waist.

"Well, you better get used to it now that you have us," He says as he places a sweet kiss on my forehead. I rest my head on his chest and fall asleep to the sound of his heartbeat.

Chapter 13

NIKKI

I am woken up by the boys yelling. From what I can hear they are yelling about what is for breakfast. I shot up when I realized where I was. I am still in Dante's bed, but he was missing. Shit! Now I have to do the walk of shame in front of Ivan and Carter. I need to make a quick getaway for sure. I look around for my pants and panties and they are nowhere in sight. Where the hell did I put them? I guess I will have to ask Dante. At least the jersey is big enough to cover everything. I get out of bed and take a deep breath as I open the door. I will not be ashamed of what I did. That is my past talking and these men have already told me they are okay with this, but talking about it is different from seeing it. I make my way down the stairs to see the boys in the kitchen. Ivan is making pancakes and Dante and Carter are sitting at the breakfast bar drinking protein shakes.

"I told you I would order her breakfast when she is up. We don't even know if she likes pancakes," Dante yells at Ivan. It is so sweet that they are fighting about what I like. I can't hold back my giggle because that is what I eat most days.

"I love pancakes," I added and all the guys looked my way. All tension leaves their faces and smiles replace them. They all look delectable. Ivan's hair is messy like he just woke up. He is in black sweats and a tight black t-shirt that shows off all his delicious muscles. I can practically feel myself drool. I turn to the other two and they are in gray sweatpants. Carter is in a white shirt and good lord Dante is not in any shirt. I just gawk as I look over his ripped torso. Dante springs to life and walks up to me to wrap his arms around my waist.

"Good morning, Mia Cara," he says with his voice sultry. He gives me a quick peck on my lips. I look at the other guys and they don't look mad or sad. Carter and Ivan just grin.

"Where is my good morning kiss, Princess?" Carter chimes in as Dante leads me to the counter where Carter is sitting. I look to Dante because I am not sure how to react to Carter's request. Dante does not look mad, he just points to Carter.

"He asked for a kiss, Mia Cara," he says and I turn to Carter. He smirks and pulls me to him and kisses me. It is not a peck like Dante, he deepens it. I wrap my arms around his neck and get lost in the kiss, forgetting the other men that are watching us. He pulls away and then lifts me up on his lap, so I am sitting on it. I look at other guys and there is no anger in their eyes. All I can see is hunger, like they liked watching us kiss.

"That's better," Carter whispers in my ear as Dante slides into the seat next to him. Ivan puts a plate stacked high with chocolate chip pancakes in front of me. My mouth waters at the sight of the pancakes.

"Ian said this is your favorite, little one," Ivan adds when he hands me the syrup. I douse my pancakes and then take a big bite.

"So, we wanted to talk to this morning, Princess," Carter says in my ear. Oh god! They are going to stop this. I feel like I am finally getting a taste of what every other man refused and then they are ripping it away. I would have rather them just not pursue me at all if that is the case. The dread in my face must have given me away. While sitting on Carter's lap Dante grabs one hand and Ivan the other.

"Relax, Mia Cara," Dante says, kissing the back of my hand.

"Okay what do we need to talk about?" I try to keep a calm voice when I ask but it comes out squeaky.

"We just want to talk about some ground rules, little one. We have never done this before and want to make sure we talk about what you want. We want this and want to make sure we don't scare you off," Ivan says, trying to reassure me.

"Okay what kind of ground rules do you want?" I ask them.

"We don't want to hide this but understand the press can be crazy. We understand if you want to keep quiet about this. If that is what you want, Mia Cara," Dante says shyly. Are they worried that I don't want this but then his words hit me. They don't care if people know about me.

"What about your families? I don't want them to judge you for wanting this," I tell them worried their families might want to cut ties when they find out what kind of relationship we have. I mean when Ian came out to his family, they completely cut him off and even kicked him out as a teen.

"They won't care, Princess. From what I hear Dante's mom is already in love with you," Carter says and I turn to see his face. His smile is so big and dazzling.

"What about your family?" I ask him nervously.

"My parents will be so happy I want to settle down. Also, they will be happy as long as I am happy. I'm sure my sister will have her jokes, but it will be out of love," Carter says trying to reassure me.

"I don't want to keep it a secret, but I want to ease into this. This is a first for me as well and I want to take it slow so we can take the punches as they come," I tell them and they all nod.

"So, we won't show too much PDA till you want to. We can hold hands in public and small, sweet kisses, stuff we can deflect until you are ready, little one," Ivan says sweetly and lowly and the other two nod. I look around and my smile grew. This is happening. I found my guys that care about me so much and would not give me up for something as silly as jealousy. Then the happy moment is broken when I hear my phone ring on the counter where it is charging. One of the guys must have plugged it in to make sure it was charged for me this morning. Ivan goes around the counter and hands it to me. Shit! It is my dad calling. I have to answer it because he will just keep calling till I answer. I hit the accept button.

"Hey daddy!" I say and the guys stiffen at the words. I put it on speaker to reassure them but put my finger to my lips to tell them to keep quiet.

"Hello, my little lion," he says happily. He continues, "I am in town for a fight this week and wanted to see if you wanted to go to dinner later."

"I would love to see you! Who are you fighting this week?" I ask him. My dad was a professional boxer. He lives in New Orleans now but whenever he was in town he would call to see me.

"It's the fucker Rodrigez. He has been talking shit saying I am too old to fight so I had to come to New York to retain my title," he says and the guys look at me in shock. Their reaction is so cute I can't help but let out a soft laugh.

"Okay daddy, when did you want to meet?" I ask him. Carter goes to my neck and starts to pepper it in kisses. I giggle again and he smiles into my neck.

"You okay little lion? You seem distracted. We can spend time together another time if you are busy," he says through the phone.

"No! I don't get to see you that much. If you want we can go to dinner and then you can come check the club out. I have your favorite singer performing tonight," I tell him the plan.

"Oh, my little Chloe is singing? That sounds perfect! I will pick you up at six. Love you my little lion," he tells me.

"Love you too, Daddy," I tell him and hang up the phone. The guys just stare at me and I shrug my shoulders.

"I am going to need to talk to your father because I need to tell him I am your daddy, little one," Ivan says and kisses me on the cheek. I giggle at his words. I know he is joking but part of me thinks he is serious.

"Wait so your dad is a fighter?" Carter asked.

"You could say that. He currently holds the belt for heavyweight champion for boxing," I tell them and all their jaws drop in shock.

"Wait so your dad is Andrea Bell?" Dante asks with a stunned look and I look at him still laughing. I normally keep my dad's profession a secret because as soon as a guy I am dating finds out they want to meet him and could care less about me. I know I don't have to worry about them because they are already famous athletes in their own rights so I am sure they would not care about who he is.

"Yeah, that's daddy," I tell them with a shrug.

"You call the heavyweight champion daddy? I am dead!" Carter says with a laugh.

"He is really a big teddy bear once you meet him," I say laughing because I can understand why it is so funny. I call a big crazy looking guy daddy, but I have always called him that since I was little.

"Wait, we get to meet him, Mia Cara?" Dante asked with an arched brow.

"I was going to invite you guys to the club to meet him if you like. There just won't be that many chances for you to meet him since he lives in New Orleans," It comes out more of a question. I get nervous and start playing with my hair. Maybe that is too soon for them. Ivan reaches for my hand to stop my nervous tick.

"We would love to, little one. We just don't want to rush you, but we are all in," Ivan says with such sincerity. They just want me to be happy and that makes my heart flutter for these three men. This is more than just sex to them, and they are proving that this morning. The guys down their protein shakes and I eat half my breakfast. Ivan made too much for me. Once I am done, I hop off of Carter's lap.

"Hey Mio Amor, I could not find my jeans this morning. Do you remember where I threw them last night? I have to get going soon because I have interviews for new bartenders," I ask him and he walks off. He comes back a few moments later with my pants and panties neatly folded. This aftercare thing is really doing wonders for my pussy. I walked up to him and pecked him on the lips but before I could pull away he deepened the kiss wanting to explore my mouth. When he finally pulls aways he hands me my jeans and underwear. I rushed to his room to get dressed. When I come back out Carter is dressed in jeans and a t-shirt.

"I am going to drive you home, Princess," he tells me as he walks up and winds his hands around my waist. He pecks me on the cheek.

"Ready to go?" He asks. I look over to the other guys in the kitchen. I am feeling bold this morning with how they are treating me.

"One second," I tell him, walking out of his grip. I rush over to Dante and give him a peck on his cheek and then go to the kitchen and do the same with Ivan. Ivan grabs me by the waist to stop me though.

"See you later, little one?" Ivan says as a question. It makes me giggle like I would go back inviting them.

"Yeah, big guy. I will text with the details," I tell him to reassure him. He smiles and lets out a soft laugh. Then kisses me hard on the lips. I pull away from Ivan with Dante groaning in protest.

"That's not fair, Mia Cara. I didn't know my kiss was coming," Dante complains pouting his bottom lip. He is so stinking cute.

"You will be okay, Mio Amor. You act like that is the last kiss you will ever get from me," I say with a smirk. His annoyance melts from his face and is replaced with a smirk at my promise of more kisses. I rush over to Carter, who is still waiting for me with a smile. I give him a quick kiss on the lips.

"Now I am ready," I tell him. As we walk out the door I yell to the other guys, "Bye big guy, bye Mio Amor!"

Carter leads me to the garage where he walks up to a stunning purple Lambo and opens the passenger door. I stand there for a second in shock. He laughs and then grabs my chin to close my mouth.

"This sex on wheels is yours?" I ask him.

"Yes, Princess. I did not take you for a car girl," he says in a whisper.

"It comes with being raised only by my father. He was always into taking me to car shows when I was younger so learned all about them," I tell him as I slide in and buckle my seatbelt. Carter rounds the hood and then slides into his side. He starts up the engine and pulls out of the garage.

"So, was it just you and him?" He asks softly.

"Yeah, it was just me and him against the world. He taught me all the important things like cars, hunting, fighting all the boy stuff and then I taught myself all the girl stuff," I tell him nervously. Great Nikki! He is now going to think I am a tomboy. When I was growing up, I was but then when moving to New York I finally had the freedom to learn all the girl shit I wanted. Ian helped along the way teaching me about clothing, dating and just being more feminine.

"You're kidding! Your daddy taught you how to fight?" He asked with amusement.

"Yeah, why? Is that a terrible thing?" I ask him, twirling my hair nervously. He grabs my hand that I was twirling my hair with and interlocks our fingers in his lap.

"It's sexy as hell, Princess! I mean at least me, and the guys will never have to worry about some punks messing with you at the bar now, but knowing us we will still worry," he says with playfulness in his eyes.

"Thanks! Most guys hate that I can kick ass," I tell him with a smirk.

"Not us! Hey, if I get you a Black Widow costume will you kick the other guy's asses in it and then play with me?" He asks and his pupils get big and dark with hunger. Fuck! I am wiggling in my seat because I could just imagine that role play. He could be a sexy KGB agent and I can be black widow. I move his hands to my lips to kiss the back and nibble on one of his fingers.

"I will take that as a hell yes, Princess," He says with a laugh. I giggle as I suck one of his fingers into my mouth. He is staring at me while sucking on his finger and swerves almost crashing the car.

"Fuck, Princess you need to stop before I crash in the middle of Downtown," he says low and raspy. He turns his head so he can focus on the road.

"Okay since we are on the subject, and I am kind of curious. What is your kink?" I ask him with the most flirty smile I could manage.

"My kink?" He asks with a soft laugh.

"Yeah, Charming. Everyone has one. What turns you on the most?" I ask him, trying to egg him on to answer.

"Well, I don't really tell many people because most girls are not into it," he says nervously. I could care less what it is. I just want to return the favor because they want to give me my wildest fantasies and I intend to return the favor.

"Please, Charming! I promise I won't judge. Shit! You all are not judging me on my kink," I tell him honestly.

"Okay, well shit. It's pictures. I love taking pictures with someone if they let me, but they never do so never got to try it," he says gripping the wheel so tight that his knuckles go white.

"I love that!" I tell him with excitement.

"Really?" He says in shock.

"Yeah! I mean it makes sense that would be something you are into. You have to travel all the time so you would need something for the road to save for later and I would rather you get off to a picture to me then some random naked chick on the web," I tell him to reassure him and it is the god honest truth. I know it is hypocritical but I get jealous so easily so I would be down to do this.

"Fuck, Princess! You cannot say things like that when I am about to travel this weekend. Here I am trying to be your respectful Prince Charming," he says with a groan.

"You are still my Prince Charming but not in the bedroom. I will be sure to send you sexy pictures when you are away," I tell him with a wink. He pulls up to my apartment. I go to open my door but then he locks the doors and hops out. He rounds the hood and unlocks the doors with his key and opens my door. He holds out his hand to help me out. I get out and we hold hands walking to my door.

"Thank you for bringing me home, Charming," I tell him to go unlock my door. He then grabs my waist and pulls me into a hug.

"I will miss my Princess," he whispers in my ear. My hands go to wrap around his neck. He continues, "Do I get a kiss goodbye too?"

"Of course!" I squeak out. I go to kiss his lips, but he does not give me the chance to give him a quick peck. He deepens the kiss, licking my lips asking for entrance. I part my lips and he is eager to devour my mouth. His tongue is so inviting, wet and warm. When he goes to pull away, he bites my bottom lip tugging lightly. I moan into his mouth. I am so wet and bothered from one kiss. It is unreal. I don't mean to but my body grinds against his in need. He groans when I rub against his hard length.

"Fuck me, Princess. Your body is so responsive. I cannot wait to have you in my bed and take all the naughty pictures of you," he growls out and then sighs. He loosens his grip around my waist.

"Sounds like a plan to me," I tell him softly, trying to pull him closer.

"I need to let you go to get ready for your dad, but it is so hard to let go of my Princess," he says softly and I can understand his words. It was actually really hard to leave them now that I have them. It's like I am scared that if I leave them for a moment they will disappear.

"I understand but you are coming tonight, right?" I ask uncertainty.

"Of course, Princess but that is hours away!" He says with annoyance. It makes me giggle because he does not want to be apart for a single moment.

"You're a big boy. I think you can manage a few hours apart," I tell him and lean out of his grip to open my door. Once my door is open, I turn to give him a quick peck on the cheek.

"Have a good day, Charming," I tell him.

"Bye, Princess. Have fun with your interviews," he says and then turns to leave. I walk into my apartment, and I miss them already.

Lexi Haynes

I dress casually for the interview. I dress in one of my vintage band tees and some high waisted dark denim shorts. When you're the owner you really don't have to give a fuck when it comes to stuff like this. I am not a huge fan of meeting new people anyway with my trust issues so I would rather be comfortable. I am sitting in the VIP booth waiting for my first interview to arrive. They are already ten minutes late. Yeah, that is not a good sign. I need someone reliable to work for me, but I will still give them a few minutes because traffic in New York can be unpredictable. Chloe walks in early for her shift. Why can't I find another Chloe to work here? She is the most amazing employee that anyone can ask for. She walks up with a shy smile.

"Hey, are you still waiting on your interview?" She asked worriedly.

"Yeah, with how late they are there is no point in doing the interview. Being late is not something I can excuse, especially since it is the first time meeting them," I tell her frustratedly. "It is so hard to find good help. Can I just clone you? You're the perfect employee!"

"Oh, you don't want a second Chloe running around trust me," she says with a chuckle. "So, the girl outside is not here for an interview?"

I looked at my paper and the person I had lined up was a guy. I look at her curiously and ask. "What girl?"

"There is a girl outside who said she was looking for a job and asked Donnie if she could talk to the owner about applying and doing an interview, if possible," she says with a shrug. Well, that's convenient. I am not going to pass up this opportunity.

"Do you mind grabbing her for me then? Since my other interview is a no show might as well give her a chance," I tell her. She smiles and nods. She makes her way to the front door and tells Donnie to let the girl in. When the girl walks in, I can't help but think she is pretty. She is tall and lengthy like a model. She has blonde hair and blue eyes. She looks like one of those snobby models. I roll my eyes. She is pretty so she could sell drinks, but I am just praying she is not a bimbo. She walks up to me and waves off Chloe. Chloe looks shocked but just lets out a scoff of breath and goes to put her purse up in the office. Yeah, that is strike one. If she does not get along with Chloe that is a problem because Chloe is here to stay no matter what. Then she does not say hello or even introduces herself, she just sits down in front of me like she owns the god damn club. Yeah no, confidence is required for a job like this because drunks can be a little mean, but I don't tolerate arrogance. Strike two. She crosses her arms and waits for me to speak. I am a little taken back but shake my head and recompose myself.

"Hello, my name is Nikki, and I am the owner of the club," I tell her and wait for her to introduce herself but she just sits there. She looks at me up and down checking me out. In her intense gaze it almost looks like she is sizing me up. Yeah, I am getting a weird feeling about this. "So, I hear you would like to apply? What kind of position are you looking for?"

She softens her face and gives me a small smile. "I heard remarkable things about this club. I would love to work here."

Yeah, she still didn't answer my question. "Okay...... So, what is your background? What are you good at?"

"Oh, I am good at anything you can give me and I have a medical background but they had to let me go for budget cuts," she says with some sass. Yeah, strike three. Me and Chloe have enough sass, we don't need anymore. I get up from the booth and put my hand out to shake her hand and politely decline her for a position. She stares at my hand and keeps her arms crossed with a glare. Okay so no handshake. I pull my hand back and ball it into a fist at my side. I swear this girl wants to get punched with the disrespect she is showing me.

"Okay so I don't think you would be a good fit. I am sorry but thank you for coming in. You can see yourself out," I tell her and walk back to my office. I need a drink after that weird interaction. I go to my office to find Chloe already with two drinks poured. She poured two scotches for us. Thank fuck this woman can read my mind. She hands me my glass with a smile.

"Did I tell you how much I love you," I tell her with a chuckle. I move to my office chair and slam back my drink.

"Yeah, with my interaction with her I thought you might need that," she says with an apologetic smile. "So, what was her name?"

"Oh, I never got that far to be honest," I tell her, straightening in my chair. I am not sure why, but she never gave me her name.

"Well then I guess she is not hired," she says, and we both throw our heads back in laughter.

"No, she most certainly is not," I tell her, still laughing. There is a knock on my office door which makes our laughter die. "Come in."

Thank god Donnie walks in.

"Hey, your interview is here," he tells me. Yeah, that is not happening. One he is thirty minutes late and second I don't have the energy dealing with that one girl.

"Yeah, tell him the position is not available anymore because he was late," I tell him and he gives me a nod and leaves closing the door. Chloe dies in laughter, almost falling to the floor. I sigh. "Hey, my dad is in town. Do you mind running the club and closing it?"

She stops laughing and gives me a flirty smile. "Absolutely but promise you will bring your sex on stick daddy for me. Tell him I will be singing tonight."

"Okay I will bring him but please don't flirt with my dad," I say with a grimace. She gets up to get her shift started.

"No promises!" She yells behind her as she leaves my office. I sigh in frustration. God tonight is going to be a long night.

I got ready pretty fast, so I was on my couch finishing up orders for the club when there was a knock on my door. I decided to wear my black knee-high velvet boots and a tan sweater dress. I rush to the door and there is my father. He is in jeans and a black t-shirt with his tattoo sleeves showing. He has light tan skin and dark hair that is in a high and tight military style cut. I jump into his arms and give him the biggest hug.

"Hey, little lion," he says in my ear. I pull away from the hug and lead him into my apartment. He laughed as he saw my purple walls.

"I don't why you are obsessed with the color purple, but I like the new paint," he says still laughing.

"It is my favorite color!" I yell at him.

"Ready to go, little lion?" He asked.

"Yes, Daddy," I tell him and blush. Calling him daddy now just feels awkward because of what Ivan said. I am also filled with nervousness because I have to explain that I am seeing three guys. He hated it when I would bring one guy home and now I have to introduce him to three. We make our way out of my apartment and go to the street to hail a cab. I tell the cab driver to go to the Gold Eagle. My father scoffs at my request.

"What?" I ask him with a glare.

"You know I can take you somewhere better than the diner, little lion," he tells me with an eye roll.

"I know but I like the food and the service there. Plus dinner is on me," I tell him and he arched one eyebrow curiously.

"Oh and why is that?" He asked.

"I have some news and giving free food to a boxer normally softens the blow," I tell him with a giggle.

"What news?" He says and his face goes serious.

"Just wait till we get to the diner," I tell him. The cab makes its way through the city and we stay silent the whole ride. I don't think my father wants to talk till I tell him what I have to tell him. We finally get to the diner. We slide out of the cab and enter the diner. The host sees me and laughs.

"Cheating on Ian" Tommy says as he comes up to greet us.

"No more like I am cheating on my dad with Ian," I tell him with a scoff. Tommy guides us to my normal table. We sit down and Tommy takes our order. He dashes to the kitchen to tell Raymond. I look to my dad who has not dropped his serious expression.

"Okay we are at the diner so talk," he says not wanting to make small talk. I sigh.

"Okay I need you to keep an open mind for what I am about to tell you," I tell him in all seriousness. Tommy comes and drops off our drinks and then leaves. He probably can feel the tension between us and wants to give us space.

"You are scaring me, little lion," he tells me with a worried look.

"I am seeing someone," I tell him and he instantly relaxes.

"Oh is that all?" He says but he can tell I am not done.

"Well more like three someone's," I say, closing my eyes not wanting to see his reaction. I wait for a moment and when he stays silent I open one eye. His face is in complete shock. I continue, "It just kind of happened and I like them."

"So you have more than one relationship? How does that work?" He asked and his expression went back to serious.

"I guess the proper term is I have a polyamory relationship with them. They all date me and don't see anyone else but I date all three of them," I say. My mouth goes dry. I hope he is okay with this and supports me.

"Well, do they treat you well, baby?" He asked.

"They treat me with so much respect and love it is crazy. It can actually be overwhelming sometimes. I thought it was just going to be a physical relationship but they want more and so do I so we are taking it slow and making sure there are ground rules," I tell him and he grimaces when I say physical.

"Okay, first TMI on the physical part and second are you happy?" He asks and his expression softens.

"Yes, Daddy, I am," I tell him and grab his hand across the table in reassurance.

"That's all that matters, little lion. It is unconventional but all I ever want is for you to be happy and I am so delighted that you trust me to know this," he says with a smile and squeezes my hand giving all the love and support I need. Raymond comes over with our food. I get my normal and dad gets steak and eggs. Raymond arches a brow looking at my dad.

"Ray this is my dad Andrea. Daddy this is Raymond he is the owner of the diner," I tell him as he puts our plates down. His face softens and just gives my dad a nod and then leaves.

"Man of few words. I like him," he says as he dives into his eggs. I start to eat my bacon.

"So, what do these men of yours do?" He asked and paused eating.

"Well let's see, Ivan is a baseball player, Dante is a hockey player and Carter is a football player," I tell him with a shrug but then his eyes light up.

"Wait a second! They are all athletes?" he asked with shock.

"Yes, they are all in the pros too," I added with a soft laugh.

"Fuck! How am I supposed to be the intimidating father figure when they are all probably as big as me and outnumber me!" He exclaims and that has me rolling over laughing.

"Well, I know you will love Carter because you already do," I tell him. He was a crazy football fan and crazy enough Carter was one of his favorite players. His eyes go wide in the realization of who he is.

"Now wait a fucking second! One of the men in the Harem is Carter Quinn?" He yells and I shoosh him.

"Will you calm down! Yes it is him but we are keeping quiet while we figure things out," I quietly yell so no one would hear us.

"Okay when do I get to meet them?" He asks softer.

"Actually, I invited them to the club tonight so you can meet them before you leave," I tell him. Then he rushes to eat, I can only assume to get to the club faster.

After he takes the last bite, he says, "Okay done, can we go to the club now?"

It makes me laugh. He is acting like a little kid who is going to meet his hero. I nod as we go to pay. When we are on our way to the club in a cab I create a group chat with the guys and text them.

Nikki: Me and my dad are on our way to the club. You guys are more than welcome to come now. Daddy is excited to meet you guys

They all type at once and I am nervous because meeting my dad is not really taking it slow like we said. Then all three messages come in at the same time even though I know they are together.

Dante: Can't wait to meet him, Mia Cara

Ivan: On the way, little one. Also what did I say about calling him that?

Carter: Wait! Is he okay with us Princess? I was expecting for him to be pissed and be overprotective.

I laugh at all their reactions. My dad looks at me with an arched brow but I just shrug him off and text them back.

Nikki: Well, it might help that he is a football fan and his favorite player is Carter

Carter replies almost instantly and I can feel his shock in his text.

Carter: Wait, maybe I read that text wrong! Did you mean to say he was a fan of mine, Princess?

I roll my eyes as Dante and Ivan text come in. I mean it is not that hard to believe. Maybe he is worried about his reputation for sleeping around.

Dante: That's not fair! He already likes Carter and not me!

Ivan: I can see Carter's head swelling as we speak little one LOL

Nikki: Yes, Charming! He is a huge fan of yours which I think softened the blow of the news. I will see you guys soon

I put my phone away as we pulled up to the club. The line is not too bad tonight. It is only Tuesday but the weekend the line would be around the block. My dad helps me out of the cab.

"Looks like the club is doing good, little lion," he tells me as Donnie unhooks the velvet rope to let us in the club. There is soft Jazz in the air as we make our way through the dance floor to the VIP booth. We sit down and my dad coughs which get my attention.

"So, is there anything else I should know about these men I am about to meet?" He asks as my favorite bartender/singer comes over to take our drink order. She is a triple threat. She is gorgeous, can sing, and can make a killer cocktail. She has a killer body and light pink hair.

"Hey Nikki! Oh my god is that my big daddy Andrea?" Chloe asks with a shriek. She practically jumps in my dad's lap. He laughs and hugs her in a big bear hug.

"Chloe I know you love him but maybe not sit on my dad's lap? Kinda creepy," I tell her with a look of disgust. She lets go of him and gifts me with the biggest eye roll.

"You know I would make the best stepmom. Now what can I get you to drink?" She asks with a laugh. I grimace at the word stepmom but dad looks amused at the word. Lucky me dad never brought women home. He always told me I was his main woman and no one else would ever compare to his little lion. I will be forever thankful I did not have to deal with that.

"Can you just bring a bottle of Johny Walker with two glasses of ice," I tell her and she scurries off to get our drinks while laughing. I turned back to my dad to continue our conversation before Chloe had to scare me for life.

"Nothing too crazy but you can ask them anything when they are here," I tell him. Then before I even see them I feel their presence. It is like the air shifts then I see them walk in. Well here goes nothing!

Chapter 14

CARTER

I am so excited! We all got dressed up, even Ivan put a little more effort to impress her dad. We all decided on buttoned up and slacks. I decided on a white shirt and tan slacks. Ivan did a basic white shirt with black pants and Dante of course had to be different and put on a lavender button up and dark purple pants. It's okay though because I am so confident with my Princess' text. Her dad is a fan and I would take any advantage given to me. I was full of nerves until her text. We pull up to the club and all get out of the car. We walk up and Donnie is there.

"Hey Donnie! We are here to see Princess," I tell him and he arches his brow.

"You know what you got to say man to let you in," he says with a smirk.

"Come on man! You know us, do I really have to say it?" I ask him with a groan and sigh when he stays silent.

"Mr. Flirt," I say with a sigh.

"See, was that so hard? Until Nikki tells me otherwise you gotta use your nickname. Also, Nikki is in the back with her dad, normal booth," he says as he unhooks the velvet rope. We walk in and the club is busy on a Tuesday night but my Princess has the best club, so I am not surprised. We make our way through the dancers and there is soft jazz playing then I see her. I swear every time I see her, she just gets more gorgeous. She is in another sweater dress and thigh-high boots. Shit! I wonder if she will let me fuck her in only those boots. No! I cannot get hard in front of her dad. The guy is a crazy boxer and can kick my ass. We walked up to the booth and Nikki and her dad looked up. She has the biggest smile and then when I turn to her dad, he does not look happy. Fuck me! Even though he is a fan I can tell this is not going to be fun. He is a big guy with tan skin and dark hair. He keeps his hair in a military high and tight but has a little on the top to style. The man is covered in tattoos on his arms. He has torn jeans and a white button up. We may have overdressed.

"So, this is your harem, little lion?" He asked her and she looked down and blushed. She is so cute like this. She is normally so strong and stubborn so seeing her nervousness and blushing, it does something to me.

Dante chimes in with a smile, "That would be us."

Nikki slides closer to her dad, and I rush so I can sit next to her. Ivan and Dante give me a glare and sit in the chairs across from me. Once I sat down, a bartender came up to us with a bottle of my girl's favorite liquor and two glasses of ice. She smiles at us and for once in my life I pray she doesn't flirt with me. Just to make sure I grab Nikki's hand and intertwine our fingers and just for reassurance I put our hands on the table. I want to make sure she knows I am with Nikki. She sets the bottle down between Nikki and her dad and gives them their glasses. Nikki looks up at her with a smile.

"Thanks, Chloe! Do you mind grabbing these guys their drinks and then I will leave you alone so you can get to the stage," Nikki says with a soft laugh. The server turns to us still smiling.

"What can I get you guys?" She asks.

"Tell you what you can just bring us what they are having. Is that okay with you all?" Ivan asks us and we both nod our heads.

Then Nikki chimes in with, "You can just bring them glasses as well and we will just share this bottle."

Chloe nods and rushes off to get our glasses. The table falls silent and awkward. I shift in my seat uncomfortable. I always hated awkward silence. I have to break this awkward silence.

"So, Mr. Bell, I heard you are a football fan," I tell her father. I hope he takes the bait because I really want Nikki at one of my games soon. My plan is to hook her father up with tickets and then she can come with him. I can see he is torn with emotion with my statement. It's like he wants to be a fan and ask all the questions but at the same time he wants to be that rough and tough daddy figure. He finally gives in and smiles.

"Yeah, I never miss a New York game. I am not going to lie, I am kind of fangirling right now but at the same time I need to be a protective daddy for my girl," he tells me and it has me rolling over laughing. Hook, line, and sinker.

"Well, if it helps I was going to invite you to a game. I have a private box that you and Nikki can use for a home game or if it is an away game I can get you guys a box in that city too. I know Nikki is more of a hockey princess, but I figured if you come she would want to come too," I tell him and his eyes go wide.

"You're serious?" he asks in complete shock.

"I mean if you don't want the box…" I trail my words off hoping he takes the bait. Do I want Nikki at my game? Yes, but inviting him will get me in his good graces. I am all for it. I can tell it is working when his expression changes to a worried look.

"No wait, I want to come!" He yells like a kid taking it back. I even hear Nikki giggle next to me. I turn to her and look at her like she is the only one in the room. Her sweet giggle is becoming my favorite sound in the world. I turned back to her dad with a smile.

"Well, it just so happens that I have a game in New Orleans this Sunday. I can get a box for you guys and then I can have Princess fly down Sunday so you both can come," I tell them and both their eyes go wide in shock.

"I can't just leave! I have a club to run!" Nikki yells at me and I knew she was going to do this so I already have a plan in place. I turn to her and put on my best sad puppy dog look.

"Well, I already have you covered. So, you will fly in that morning and then a flight back first thing Monday morning so you will only be gone for twenty-four hours. The club is not open Sunday or Monday and I know you like to do your orders on Saturday night, so you won't miss a thing," I tell her, still trying to look sad to convince her. I even stick my bottom lip out to pout to seal the deal. Her anger melts away and a smile grows and that is when I know I have her.

"Okay, Charming," she says with a sigh.

"Okay?" I ask her, wanting to confirm this is not just a dream.

"Okay, I will come to your game in New Orleans," she says with annoyance, knowing I won this battle. I throw my fist in the air to celebrate this win. I am so excited! She is going to be at my game, and I have to get her a jersey. I think I will give her my alternate jersey that I have. It will drown her, but it is going to be sexy as hell to see my name on her back. I wonder if she would do a sexy photo shoot for me in nothing but my jersey. Shit! I am getting hard again. I close my eyes and run through plays in my head trying to get myself down. Once my dick finally calms down, I open my eyes to find Nikki looking at me confused but then I glance at her father who is glaring at me. Fuck! He knows exactly what I was doing. Chloe comes with our glasses which distracts her dad for a second but just to be sure I try to steer the conversation to him.

"So, I hear you have a fight this week?" I say and luckily, he takes my change of subject. He smiles and nods.

"I do! It is on Thursday night. The fucker who I am fighting keeps calling me out that I am too old to fight saying my movements are to slow and that I should retire once he beats me. No way in hell am I gonna let some fucker look down on me," He says with anger in his eyes. Fuck, we really don't want to be on this guy's bad side with his daughter. He continues but his expression goes serious, "Now I don't just fight in the ring either. If any of you assholes decide to mistreat or hurt my daughter I will personally bring the ring to you guys and fuck you up."

"Daddy!" Nikki yells at him with her eyes wide. She looks like a deer in headlights.

"It's okay Mia Cara. We can understand where your father is coming from," Dante says and turns to her father. "We would not dream of hurting your daughter, sir. We genuinely care for her and want her to be happy. Also, if I or my guys do hurt your daughter, I will personally take the beating because anyone that could hurt this beautiful daughter of yours deserves any punishment you dole out."

Me and Ivan nod in agreement. Her father's expression softens and laughs.

"Shit! I like this kid! You have some serious balls telling me that. You are welcome to my ring anytime! You must be the hockey player if you don't mind a beating," He says, and I got instantly jealous. Damn, why does Dante have to be the smooth talker? I desperately needed her dad's approval and I thought I had it inviting him to my game. I try to think of a way to get on his good side. But then he turns to Ivan. "So, I know this guy is the football player and that guy is the hockey player. That must make you the baseball player?" He asks Ivan. Ivan smiles at the chance to bond with her father.

"Yes, sir," Ivan says. He is a man of very few words. He has always been like this since Dante introduced us.

"I did get a chance to google all you and you are the most impressive. I saw you donate half of your makings to charity. I did not get a chance to find which one," he says. Shit! He googled us and that means he saw all the news about me being a player before Nikki. Now it makes sense why he wants to be the big strong dad.

"I donate all of it to God's Home for Children. I grew up there when my parents took off when I was younger. I owe the Nun's everything for raising me so it is the least I can do," Ivan tells him, and Nikki looks at him like he is the only man in the room. I mean it is impressive and makes the man look so selfless so I will give him this one.

"That is remarkable since I know you are the highest paid player in the NBL. The Nuns must be awfully grateful for any donation you give them," Her dad says.

"They actually tried to rip up the first check to be honest saying they were just doing God's work by taking care of me but then I made sure I went to the pastor and told him to make sure the Nuns use it for the foster home they run. He now takes the money and does not tell them where it comes from but they figured it out. You should have heard them yell at me when they figured out it was me," He tells her dad with a soft laugh. Then her dad turns to me with a frown. Fuck me! Here it comes.

"I was less impressed with you. Don't get me wrong, I was a fan of yours before my little lion told me you were the one she was dating but I am not a fan of your reputation. You are kind of a man whore to be honest," he says with no amusement in his eyes.

"Daddy! Please stop!" She begs her dad. He just gives her a shrug because he is not wrong for calling me out on my bullshit and I know that. I take a deep breath and grab Nikki's hand.

"I completely understand. Before your daughter, I was. There is no point denying it when the proof is there in black and white, but you also need to understand that is the old me. I would never do something to hurt your daughter. I know the reputation I made for myself, and I am working with your daughter to prove I am done with that. I told her we can go slow so that way we can build trust in our relationship. I never plan or intend to hurt her, I can promise you that," I tell him putting everything I have into it. It's the truth I never intend to hurt her but there will be disagreements. No one is perfect but as long as we are open and work through it, I know everything will be fine. I look over to Nikki and she looks absolutely enthralled with me. Her eyes are glossed over and her face shows me the most beautiful smile. I am head over heels in love with this woman. There is no denying it anymore, but I hold that feeling in because I do not want to blurt that out to her in front of her dad. Chloe takes the stage and starts to sing her Rendition of New York by a famous jazz singer. This is the moment I have been waiting for. I get up from the booth and hold out my hand to Nikki.

"Want to dance, Princess?" I ask her with the biggest smile. She nods with a smirk. I look to her dad for approval as well. He looks at me with a knowing smirk and just gives me a slight nod. Nikki takes my hand and I guide her out the booth to the dance floor. I wrap one hand around her waist and the other is intertwined in her hand. Her other hand goes to my chest and we start to sway to the music. Nikki bites her lip nervously and she is silent, lost in her own thoughts. Well, that won't do.

"What's on your mind?" I ask her.

"I'm sorry about my dad giving you a hard time," she says, still nibbling on her bottom lip.

"It's okay, Princess. I expected nothing less than a protective daddy," I say with a soft laugh and that gets her to laugh too, letting go of her bottom lip.

"I know he is crazy protective, but he should not have called you a man whore. That is none of his business because we have already had talks about it and you have proved there is no one else besides me," she explains, and it warms an ache in my chest. My Princess is always going to be in my corner no matter what. I wrap both arms around her waist to make our dancing just a small sway. Both her hands go to my chest.

"I know but your dad just wants to protect you and I completely understand that. All I want to do is protect you as well, but I made some mistakes in my past and I have to deal with the consequences. If that means having to take some shit from your father, I will do that because you are worth it Princess," I tell her and I lean down to kiss her. It is a sweet kiss, but she tries to deepen it. I pull away slightly. I want to reciprocate but I don't want her father to kick my ass for making out with his daughter in the middle of the club. I look into her eyes, and she has a mischievous glint in her eyes that has me groaning.

"Why did you stop?" She asks me with a giggle.

"Because I don't want to get my ass kicked by your dad for making out with his daughter in front of him," I tell her with a serious look. I love her but I am not trying to die from her father today.

She leans up to my ear to whisper, "Well then I think it is your turn for a sleepover."

This has my heart racing. Good god this woman is trying to kill me! I lean back to look at her. I can't fight the hard on that I have now while I can feel her breath on my ear as she whispers dirty promises.

"Are you sure, Princess? I do not want to rush you and don't want you to think this is just sex for me. You are so much more," I tell her.

"Oh, don't you worry about that. That little speech you gave at the table took care of any fears I had about you. It might have been for my daddy but it sure as hell did things for me," she tells me almost purring the end. Good god! Yep, I am dead. Her hands slowly go up to my chest and wrap around my neck. Her hands go to my hair scratching my scalp which feels so fucking good. I cannot hold back the moan that forms in my throat.

"I only have one question, Charming," she says softly.

"What is that, Princess?" I ask her with curiosity.

"Do we invite the other guys, or do you want me to yourself?" She asks with a mischievous smirk. This makes me laugh because as much as I want her to myself, I don't want to be selfish. I got her all to myself this weekend and now that I know she is coming I am going to make it so special so I want to give her fantasy while I am still in town. I give her a quick peck on the lips.

"We should all stay over. I don't want to be selfish. I hope your bed is big enough, Princess," I tell her with a soft laugh. The music starts to slow but neither of us move, like we are caught in a trance.

"Well, you should know I have a very big bed that can fit all four of us, Charming," she says with a wink and then walks back to the table, swaying her hips as she goes. Jesus Fucking Christ! This is really happening. We are finally going to be all together tonight. I am scared but also excited. Once I gather my thoughts I make my way back to the table. Her dad is gone and Ivan took his seat next to Nikki. I go to slide back in next to her, but she hops up saying she needs to go to the bathroom. This gives me the perfect chance to talk to the guys about staying over. She rushes off and I sit while we wait for her.

"Where did her dad go?" I ask them both.

"He left so he can go train for his fight," Dante says.

"Okay good because I need to talk to you guys about Nikki," I tell them, running my hands through my hair nervously. They both straighten and their faces go serious.

"What about Nikki?" Ivan asks with an arched brow.

"It's nothing bad guys so chill the fuck out," I tell them. It's not but I know they will be as nervous as I am once I tell them. They both relax briefly but stare at me waiting for what I am going to tell them. I take a deep breath and say, "Nikki asked if we want to stay over."

They both looked excited and shocked all at the same time. It makes me laugh but I stop and explain further, "She asked me if I want to stay or all of us. I think she was trying to make sure I get my alone time with her but how I see it I will be getting her in New Orleans this weekend. I did not want to be selfish so I said we can all stay over if she wants, and it made her so happy. Hope you all did not have plans in the morning."

They both looked shocked with mouths gaping and I can understand why. I can be a selfish person when it comes to girls but with Nikki and them, I do not feel that way. She makes me want to be a better person for her. That means not being a shit head and taking her for myself. They finally both have shit eating grins.

"That's incredible man! Thank you!" Dante says excitedly. He is practically jumping in his seat.

"Carter, this is great! We can finally ease her into this, and we can figure out our dynamic but you made a hard choice and for that I am grateful," Ivan says more relaxed but I have never seen the man so happy.

"It's okay guys. It was hard but I am really trying. She makes me feel things I have never felt before and I want to make sure she is happy and that does not include me being a selfish prick," I tell them with a shrug. Then I continued, "But the real reason I wanted to bring this up is because we have never done this before and I have heard it can be awkward if we don't have a game plan going in. We need to work as a team, so the movement is fluid and not a mess."

"Have you been doing research on this?" Dante asks with a laugh. I just shrug because I have. I want everything to be perfect for Nikki and since we have never done this before I had to look it up, so it is for her.

Ivan nods and says, "I agree. This is going to be all about her so I think we take your team analogy and run with it. I think every time we pick a captain so they can be in charge of the room. I mean we know about each other enough to make that work. We know Dante is all about setting the mood with music, you like pictures and I have my Daddy Dom thing with her. So, who is going to be captain tonight?"

We all sit there and think and then it comes to me.

"Ivan, I think you should be the one who is Captain most of the time," I tell them and Dante looks at me stunned.

"Why not me?" Dante says offended.

"Listen man it is not that you would not make a good captain for this, but I think because of Daddy Dom here would be better at taking charge of the room. Think about it. We can stand back a little while he gets her started so I can get the pictures I want, and you can figure out how to do the music in her place. Then when we are done with our stuff Ivan can back up and then take control of our movements from the sidelines so someone can make sure the movements flow better. It's just a better play if you think about it."

He takes a moment to think and I can see when it hits him that it is the best plan we have got. He smiles and nods. Then I turn to Ivan, and he looks just as happy.

"So, Ivan is Captain for tonight and then in the future we can decide who is Captain when we are with her. Shit, once we get more of a flow, we can even make Nikki Captain too!" I tell them and we all nod in agreement. Nikki finally comes back at the perfect time, so I scoot out of the booth for her to sit but she just smirks at me and shakes her head.

"Nope I think I am ready to be alone with my Harem," she says with a purr. She grabs my hand and Dante's and leads us outside to her apartment. Ivan is not far behind. Our little Princess is so excited. I can see her pulse beating at the base of her neck. She leads us up the stairs and unlocks the door. Dante lets go of her hand and holds the door. Nikki grabs Ivan's hand and pulls both of us in, then Dante follows and locks up for her. Ivan grabs her and puts her over his shoulder. She laughs so hard smacking his ass.

"Put me down, big guy!" She yells as he leads us to her bedroom. He throws her to the bed and climbs on top of her. Jesus! I have had a semi all night but now I am hard as a rock. I have to palm my cock through my pants just to relieve some of the throbbing ache I am feeling. I look over to Dante who is having to do the same thing. He moves to her stereo and plugs up his phone. The dip shit put on Pony by Ginwine. A little on the nose for me but we put him in charge of tunes. I roll my eyes at him and he just shrugs.

"That is not my name and you know that. What is my name, little one?" He asks her in a low, raspy tone. Holy shit! This guy is daddy dom. She blushes and hesitates for one second to look at me and Dante nervously.

"Don't worry about them at the moment. Now, what is my name when you are with me?" He asks again sternly. He takes his role as daddy very seriously. She turns his attention to him and whispers, "Daddy."

Ivan groans and kisses her senseless. Ivan slowly takes off her sweater dress and reveals the most stunning body I have ever seen. Her skin glows under the soft yellow light from her lamp on her bedside table and hot damn she was not wearing panties. Ivan growls at the sight.

"Little one, were you not wearing panties all night?" He asks her with an arched brow.

"Well, I wanted to surprise my guys. Did I do good, Daddy?" She asks Ivan with a smirk and gives him a quick wink.

"You did extraordinarily good, little one. Be glad that none of us knew you did that though because we would have been fingering you under the table with your father present," He says with a smirk and that has her blushing. He starts to explore her body, his mouth goes to her neck and sucks so hard I can hear it.

"Where are the condoms, Mia Cara?" Dante asks her. Dante wants to make sure she got some.

"They are in my nightstand, top draw, Mio Amor," she tells him. Dante goes to the nightstand and pulls out three. He hands one to Ivan and then goes to toss one to me. I highly doubt we are all going to need them but he just wanted to be sure, so we are ready for whatever comes up. Ivan goes to undo it but then thinks for a moment. Then he looks at our girl and tilts her chin up.

"I think we need to try something new just for our little one," Ivan says and her eyes go wide.

"What is that, Daddy?" She asks him not knowing what is in store. God, I hope it is fucking good because I need relief ASAP. He looks at her with such hunger and I am sure I am looking at her the same way.

"Well, I know how your sweet hot mouth feels like and Dante knows how your tight wet pussy feels like. I think we should put you on your hands and knees and he can see what he is missing, and I can feel you tight wet pussy. How does that sound, little one?" He explains and good god it really does sound amazing even if I just watch and wait my turn. She looks to me anxious.

"What will you do?" She asks me and I know exactly what I am going to do. It's still sweet that she is worried about me because I am the only one that has not been with her sexually, but I need to show her I am okay with anything that we do right now.

I tell her without hesitation, "I am going to take some hot photos of you, Princess. Is that okay?"

She looks at me and she does not have to think because she is nodding the second I am done talking. That makes me have a shit eating grin I am sure, but I cannot help it. No one has ever trusted me enough to take pictures of them. This just confirms that she trusts and cares for me. Me and Dante start stripping while Ivan warms her up by fingering her deep. I know he is hitting just the right spot for her by the way she is moaning and yelling his name.

"God you are so wet for us," Ivan growls out and picks up the pace of his fingers. Then she hits her first climax and I make sure I pull out my phone so I can take a picture of her cuming. She looks so beautiful as she moans loud, and her mouth goes to make the perfect O shape. Ivan is a gentleman and waits till she comes down from her orgasm before pulling out his fingers. He goes and sucks all her sweet juices from his fingers. She licks her lips and when he is done, he kisses her hard. It is the hottest thing I think I have ever seen. She kisses him back chasing a taste of herself. Then he pulls away but drags her with him. Ivan flips her so she is on her hands and knees. I go to her side and unclasp her bra and shimmy it down her shoulders. She lifts her hands slightly so I can get rid of it. Once I throw it across the room Dante moves to in front of her and Ivan gets the condom around his dick.

I lean down to whisper in her ear, "Don't worry about me, Princess. I am going to take pictures and rub my cock so I can cum all over you."

She shivers with the dirty things I whisper. It makes me let out a soft chuckle. I start to rub my cock as the boys get ready. Ivan has gotten undressed and slips on the condom. When he is ready, he lines up at her entrance.

"Ready for me, little one?" Ivan asks her and she just nods.

"Use your words, Mia Cara," Dante warns her in a deep tone. This is fucking hot. I never thought it would be so hot to watch but it's like I am getting my own little porno.

"Yes, I want you so bad, Daddy," she moans out. Ivan goes and lines up at her entrance. He sticks his tip in and groans.

"Fuck me, little one. "You are so warm and tight for me," he groans out and then thrust into her completely and she lets out a gasp as he fills her. He waits while she adjusts to him being in there completely. I take a few photos for myself and keep rubbing my aching cock. I make sure to keep my pace slow, so I don't blow too early. Once she stops moaning, he starts to thrust into her full force.

"God! She is so fucking tight," Ivan moans out. Then Dante kneels in front of her gripping his cock at his base. He lifts her chin up, so she is looking at him in the eyes.

"If it is too much, Mia Amore, you tell us and we stop," he says but her reply was not in words. She launches forward and licks his tip.

"Fanculo!" He yells and tilts his head back with pleasure. She starts to suck and get in a rhythm with Ivan and Dante, and it is the hottest thing I have ever seen. As Ivan thrust, she takes Dante deeper. Then when he pulls out, she lifts her head to Dante's dick. It's like Ivan said, we need to work as a team. I recorded a little video because how can I not. Once I am done recording, I start working on my cock. I don't think I will last much longer. I throw my phone to the side completely forgotten. Then she comes undone again moaning around Dante's dick.

"Mia Amore, you are going to make me cum moaning around my cock," Dante says in warning, and she just takes him deeper. I watch as he cums in her mouth and she sucks every last drop of him. When he finally relaxes then it is Ivans turn to let loose. His thrust becomes fast and shallow.

"Fuck, scream for your daddy," Ivan tells her with a growl.

"Cum for me, Daddy," she screams and then Ivans cums hard. I can practically see the stars in his eyes. I start to feel my balls tighten and I know I am close.

"Flip her over on her back, Ivan," I tell him because I got an idea for my princess, I know she will like. Ivan quickly pulls out of her and flips her. She has barely any time to register when I move next to her and cum all over her tits. I feel like I am claiming her, cuming on her. All I thought while my cum came out is, *mine*. I almost fell over from my legs giving out, I cum so hard. Then she does the kinkiest thing and starts to rub it all over her skin moaning. Once I have feeling in my legs, I grab my phone really fast to take a picture of my dirty little angel. She smirks in the picture, and it is absolutely perfect. I lean down and give her a soft kiss.

"That was perfect, Princess. You did so good," I whisper on her lips. Her smile is beaming but I can tell she is drowsy as she closes her eyes, almost falling asleep already. I give her a soft laugh as I pick her up. I look at the guys as she snuggles into my chest.

"I will do after care," I tell them and leave and realize I don't know where her bathroom is. I look down at her and she hums happily.

"Princess," I say when I shake her softly. She looks up at me through her long lashes and tilts her head inquisitively. She is so precious looking like this.

"Which room is your bathroom?" I ask her with a laugh.

"Down the hall at the very end," she says, going back to snuggling my chest. I go to where she says and open the door. My princess must love relaxing in her bathroom because when I open the door it is like a spa. Her whole apartment is purple and black, but this is completely different. It is all white and lavender. The walls are white and then she has a stand-alone tub which looks like it has jets. The bathroom sink has white and purple marble. It is covered in bath bombs, shower fizzes, and tons of skin care. There are shelves with white and purple candles. She has a white stone shower that is so big that it could fit all four of us in there. It even has a rain shower head.

I set her on the edge of the tub so I can turn on the shower. I let it warm up for a bit and I go to her collection of shower fizzes and grab a eucalyptus and mint one. I toss it in the shower and let the scent fill the air. She perks up now that the scent hit her. I pick her up and bring her into the shower. I grab her loofa that is hanging in the shower and squirt some shower gel she has that smells just like her. It smells exactly like a strawberry shortcake with a mixture of vanilla, sugar, and strawberries. I started to lather her up and clean my cum off her tits. She lets out a soft moan and I am already getting a semi with her sounds.

"I am going to need you to not make those noises. I am trying to take care of my princess and get you clean," I tell her with a growl. She giggled softly.

"I can't help it. It feels so good to have someone take care of me," she tells me and it infuriates me because it sounds like no one has done aftercare with her.

"Princess, has a guy never done this for you before?" I ask her with a glare. She just shrugs. I bring her close to me, wrapping my arms around her. Her arms go around my neck.

"Well Princess, get used to it. If you don't think we won't do this all the time you have another thing coming," I warn her and she just gives me the biggest smile with a nod. I finished washing her and myself and yes, I used her body wash. I could give a rat's ass that I smell like a girl. I get to smell like my Princess all day tomorrow and I was not missing that opportunity to smell like her all day. I dry her and myself off. I wrap the towel around her and slip my briefs back on. I picked her up, bridal style again and carried her to her bedroom. Dante and Ivan already put their briefs back on and slide in under her bedding.

"Don't you two look comfy," I tell them with a scoff. I place her in between them and slip the towel off her. I keep having to tell myself not to be selfish. I got to have my time looking after her so they can cuddle her to sleep. Ivan is on her right and cuddles into her back with his face in her damp hair and Dante her front with his face in her chest. I go next to Dante, and she sits up.

"Where do you think you are going?" she asks with an arched brow.

"Well, you only have two sides to cuddle, Princess. Don't worry I will spoon Dante for you," I say with a laugh. Dante looks at me in shock.

"You will do no such thing!" He yells at me, and Nikki has a giggle fit. She then twists her waist a little and spreads her legs. She pats between her legs.

"You can sleep right here and use my tummy as your pillow," she says and hot damn I don't have to be told twice. I dive right in, and she lets out a breath like I knocked the wind out of her.

"Jesus, asshole. Don't hurt her," Ivan tells me in his dad voice.

"Sorry, Princess," I tell her laying on my stomach and snuggling into her tummy.

"It's okay, Charming. I know you were just excited, like a puppy," she says with a soft laugh. She continues, "But if you don't think I won't make that your new nickname when you act like this you are crazy."

"What? No way that is such a downgrade from Charming," I say with a groan. She pats my head.

"Night, puppy," she tells me with a yawn. I groan but she could call me whatever she wants as long as she stays this happy with us. I fell asleep perfectly happy between my woman's legs.

Chapter 15

NIKKI

Fuck me! Why am I so hot this morning? Oh right, I have three grown men cuddling me. I will have to remind myself to turn off the heat the next time we have a sleepover. Ivan is behind me with one arm draped over my hip with his face buried in my hair. Then Dante is in front of me with his face buried in my chest and his arm is just above Ivan's on my waist. Then I have my sweet little puppy. He is laying on his stomach, face on my stomach, between my legs with both his arms wrapped around my thighs. I know it does not sound comfortable, but I could not resist letting one of them be by themselves. I wanted all my guys with me and to be honest, it was the best night of sleep I have gotten in a while. I don't want to wake them, but I really have to pee. I peek one eye open and realize I must have shifted when waking because Dante lifts his head from my chest and stares at me with contentment in his eyes.

"Good morning, Mia Cara. How did you sleep?" He asks with worry.

"Actually, it was the best sleep I have gotten in a while," I tell him with a smile. He beams at my answer with a dazzling smile that could make a girl swoon. I start to twist my legs a little to get in a more comfortable position but then I hear Carter groan.

"Princess, five more minutes," he groans out and cuddles into my stomach. He has a death grip on my legs to make sure I don't go anywhere. Then Ivan starts to move and places a kiss on my neck.

"Good morning, little one. As you can see Carter is not a morning person," he says laughing into my neck.

"Shhh, people are sleeping," Carter tells him in a sleepy voice. I just giggle because normally I am like Carter in the morning. Groggy and too tired to do a thing, but I feel like I have had ten cups of coffee waking up to them so sweetly.

"Actually, puppy, I need to get up and pee," I tell him and that just has him looking up at me through his lashes.

"You can do it right here. I don't mind," he says with a soft laugh. I know he is joking but gross. I look at him with disgust which only has him laughing harder into my stomach. Ivan gets up, picks up Carter, and throws him over his shoulder like he weighs nothing.

"There we go, little one. Me and Carter will go make breakfast. You went shopping right?" He asks and I get up to go to the bathroom and throw on a lavender silk robe I have. I watch as Ivan throws Carter onto the couch and he just pouts at me.

"I did. I also got some of you guys' protein powder delivered yesterday when I saw what kind you all had yesterday morning. I did not know if you and Dante were on a strict diet since you are in season so wanted to make sure you all had some here if you needed it," Ivan and Carter look at me in shock. Like it was crazy for me to do that. I am not sure why. They have done so much for me, something as small as buying protein powder should not be that big of a deal. Then I feel Dantes arms go around my waist behind me and he rests his chin on my shoulder.

"Mia Amor, you did not have to do that," Dante says in my ear. I lift my hand to cup the side of his face.

"Well, you guys have done so much for me. I don't want you to think this is one-sided. I know it is not much, but I want you guys to feel welcome and cared for while you are here," I tell them with a shrug. Dante grabs my waist with his hands and spins me around and looks so happy. Like he won the damn lottery.

"No, Mia Amor. It does not matter what the size of the gift. It is how much thought you put into it. You saw what we use for our shakes and made sure you remembered the brand that we use. You came home and made sure you got it delivered that day, so it was here for the next time we are here. It might not be that much, but to us that is so thoughtful and meaningful. This is why you are Mia Amor," Dante says with such sincerity. He wraps his arms around my waist and then I feel the other two on the other sides. Dante leans in and gives me a soft kiss while the other kisses either side of my neck. My body shivers with all their mouths on me. I have to clench my thighs together to relieve my throbbing cunt. Dante pulls away slightly with a mischievous glint to his eyes.

"Later Mia Cara. We need to feed you and you need rest after last night," Dante says. Ivan slips away to the kitchen and Carter pulls me to the couch and sits me on his lap. Ivan saunters in with my coffee which smells amazing. He hands it to me, and Carter wraps his arms around my waist. Before I could even take a sip, Carter puts his lips on it and takes a sip.

"Hey, that's my coffee! Get your own!" I yell at him, almost spilling it. He just smiles at me with a devilish grin.

"Well, someone woke me up early so I need at least a sip," he explains but then Ivan comes in with another cup for him.

"Here and don't get used to me bringing you coffee. I only did it so little one would not have to share," he tells Carter and then kisses the top of my head.

"What would you like for breakfast little one? I saw you got a lot of breakfast stuff like I told you," Ivan says which makes me blush. I would do anything he told me to do but him praising me for it, is making me feel embarrassed. I looked at him and then I remembered he had asked a question, and he was waiting for me to answer.

"Just make whatever you all want to eat is fine. There is bacon, eggs, and pancake mix. So just make whatever," I tell him with a shrug.

"How about I make eggs and bacon?" He asks.

"Sounds delicious, daddy, but don't overcook my bacon!" I tell him with a big smile. They all look at me like I have ten heads.

"What? I like chewy bacon," I tell them and they all laugh. Now it is my turn to look at them like they are crazy.

"It's like you were made for us, Princess. It is how we eat it too," Carter whispers in my ear and nibbles on it once he is done. I shudder but smile at the thought that they like bacon the same way I do. I can't help but think we were made for each other. Ivan goes back into the kitchen to start breakfast. I stay on Carter's lap but then Dante comes over and sits next to him. He pulls my feet into my lap and then something dawns on me.

"Oh no! Who is watching Tot?" I ask Dante with a worried look. I would hate to be the reason that precious creature was alone all night without his daddy. He just gives me a warm smile.

"Are you worried about my fur baby?" He asks, still smiling.

"Of course! I did not even think about you staying and leaving that poor baby alone!" I yell at him, but he does not look worried.

"Don't worry, Mia Cara. I have a dog sitter who I pay a lot of money for that watches him when we are not there. I texted him last night and he stayed with Tot. He fed him breakfast and took him to the park for the day so I can stay with you," he says to reassure me.

"You know anytime you have an away game he is more than welcome to stay with me," I tell him and his smile grows even bigger. His smile is making me wet in all the right places. I wiggle in Carter's lap and that makes him groan as he takes a sip of his coffee. I can feel him growing hard underneath me, but I try to ignore it and focus on my conversation with Dante.

"Are you sure, Mia Cara? Tot can be a lot. He is a very naughty dog, and I don't want you to have to deal with that," he says looking sad. Well, this won't do.

"No, I want to! Sounds like a match made in heaven to me," I tell him with a shy smile. His sadness melts away as he thinks. He rubs his chin with his hand thinking about a way to make this work. Then I see the light bulb in his head go off.

"I got it! If you are really determined to watch Tot when I am at away games, you can stay at our place to watch him. It would make me feel better knowing he will not destroy your apartment but ours," he says with a laugh.

"Is that okay? I don't like being there when you guys are not there. I don't mind him tearing up my place. He is so cute, I don't think I could ever get mad at him," I tell him blushing. It makes me nervous being there when they are not. It feels like it is an invasion of their privacy. Ivan walks in with a plate of scrambled eggs and bacon that smells absolutely scrumptious. He hands me the plate and places a soft kiss on my head.

"It is absolutely okay, little one. In fact, here," He goes into my bedroom and comes back a second later with a key in hand. He holds out his hand handing me the key. I look at him in shock. My mouth is hanging wide open, and my eyes are bugging out of my head. I look at him while he is still waiting for me to take it. I just shake my head and then he frowns with his eyebrows furrowed in confusion.

"I can't take that. Isn't it too soon for me to have a key to your place?" I ask them and they all shake their heads.

"Mia Cara, we agreed to go at your pace since you don't want to go public with this yet, but it will make us feel better if you have that. You can come over whenever you want and then we won't have to worry about you not being able to get in. We will tell security to add you to the list of approved guests and then you can have the key to use our private elevator. Please, Mia Amore," Dante begs. I sigh and finally grab the key out of Ivan's hand. I hop up from Carter's lap and stroll to my door where I keep my keys. I pull my keychain from the hook on my wall and then add the key to my ring and put it back on the hook but then stop. You know what if they trust me enough to have a key, I could at least return the favor. I pluck my spare key off the hook and saunter over to them. I hand the key to Ivan.

"I sadly don't have three spare keys, but I have one. You all can just make copies for each other," Ivan takes the key but looks confused.

"You don't have to do this, little one. I didn't give you a key so you would feel obligated to do the same," he says with a concerned look on his face.

"No, I am not doing this out of obligation. It just feels right. I am working all the time so if you guys ever want to come over while I am working up here you can or if you come home late from an away game decide you missed me. You are welcome here anytime," I tell them with a smirk. They all look at me like kids on Christmas. I still cannot believe how happy I make them doing these little things. Carter stands and grabs the key from Ivan.

"I want the key. I am off today so I will make copies, but I want the first key," Carter says and Ivan glares at him. I roll my eyes and laugh.

"Fine but I want my copy tonight. You better not forget to do it," Ivan warns, and it makes me laugh. Carter pulls me back to his lap and puts my plate back on mine.

"Eat, Princess. You need the calories after last night," he says with his devilish smirk. I laugh and dig into my food again. Dante stays next to us, and Ivan sits in my armchair next to the couch. We eat our breakfast and then Dante turns to me.

"I have another game tonight. Will you come again?" He looks so cute and hopeful I can't deny him anything. He could have asked for anything looking at me like that and I would do it.

"Sure! I would love to!" I exclaim because there is nothing else, I would rather do.

"Perfect! Do you want to be in the box seats or near the ice again?" He asks sweetly. I got nervous because it might cause me to see his family again but then I decided I don't care. His family was sweet and he promised his family would be okay with this.

"Whichever you want, Mio Amore. I already met your mama, and she was so sweet but if you want me closer to the ice so I am closer to you that works too," I tell him and he was beaming at the fact that I did not mind his mother I am sure.

"Please use the box. As much as I love it when you are close, I would feel better with you in the box so some drunk guy doesn't mess with you. Plus, they feed you and have free booze," he says and it almost sounds like begging.

"You do know I own a club, right? I deal with drunk men all the time," I say to reassure him but then he stiffens at my last comment. I look at them and Ivan and Dante look pissed, so I look away and turn to Carter who has a smile plastered on his face. I look at him with an arched brow confused. He laughs softly.

"I think our girl can handle herself," he says to the other men in the room. I giggle because I know what he is referencing. I told him Daddy taught me how to fight so putting up with drunks is nothing compared to training with boxing champions. The other guys look at him confused.

"What do you mean?" Ivan asked with his brows furrowed. It only made me laugh harder.

"Our little Princess here learned how to fight from her daddy, so we don't need to worry about her getting taken advantage of by some drunk," he explains to them. They looked shocked but also relieved at the same time.

"Is that why your father calls you little lion?" Ivan asks with a small smirk.

"Yeah, he says I fight like a lioness that protects her cubs and will protect them by any means necessary," I tell him with a shrug.

"As hot as that sounds, Mia Cara, I still would feel better with you in the box," he tells me, and I nod but then want to get to know him better.

"You know what. Let's make a deal. I will use the box tonight as long as you invite your team to the club," I tell him and his jaw slacks and just stares at me. I continue, "And don't think it's me wanting your team to come in as publicity. I just know you guys like the club because I don't allow puck bunnies in and I think the guys would like a break from women throwing themselves at you. They can just relax after the game and I get to know you better and meet them." His face softens and gives me what I call a panty wetting smile. I have to wiggle in Carter's lap again and he groans.

"Mia Cara, you got yourself a deal!" He says excitedly.

"They won't mind coming to the club?" I asked him nervously. They might not want to come to my small humble club. They probably want to go to some crazy Manhattan bar downtown. I start to twirl my hair as my nervous tick. The guys see right through it though. Dante reaches for my hand that is twirling a red curl. He pulled my hand from my hair and intertwined our fingers.

"What is wrong, Mia Cara?" He asked worriedly.

"Nothing is wrong," I tell him and he shakes his head.

"You always twirl your pretty red curls when you are worried about something. Tell us what is wrong, little one," Ivan chimes in.

"Oh, if your team does not want to, that is fine. I know my club is not a crazy party club, but I thought it would be nice to meet your team to get to know you better," I tell him blushing. I hate showing my self-doubt, but I worry about their feelings for me sometimes. I blame it on the years of men that made me think I was crazy for even proposing what I want. They made me feel like I was never enough. Dante stops my train of thought by kissing me hard. He does not give me a chance to deepen it because he pulls away too quickly. I moan in protest which makes him smile big.

"I am only going to say this once so listen and listen well. The team will love your club. They will love that they won't have to look over their shoulder for pops or puck bunnies. We can just spend time together and be ourselves which we never can do when going out. Plus, your club is amazing. It is not some crazy club where we cannot even hear each other talk. We can just chill and have a drink after the game. I will even text them right now so you know how many will be coming," he says to give me reassurance.

"You don't have to do all that. I'm sorry, I am just so used to this self-conscious issue I have. I always have self-doubt in everything I do. Shit! When I quit Broadway, I sat in my apartment at the time crying for a week eating my weight in ice cream and Ian had to drag me out kicking and screaming but it was great. He talked me into opening the club and helped me with the business side of things so I had a free space to sing. Now I make it my mission to do that with all my singers and bands I have at my club. Like Chloe, she actually collaborated with me on the musical I quit from. She quit right after me saying the director was an asshole who did not know a good singer if it kicked him in the ass," I tell them with the god honest truth. I loved Chloe as much as I loved Ian when she did that. When I opened the club, she was my first hire. I pay her way more than most small-time singers or bartenders but she deserved it after what she did for me. She also brings in a pretty big crowd when people know she is singing. I had to start using her as a surprise singer and I think that is why my club is busy every night. People come to make sure she is or is not singing.

"No more self-doubt, Princess. You are amazing at everything you do. You run a successful business, you are an amazing singer and to be honest hot as hell. The full triple threat," Carter says as he kisses my neck. I shiver with his touch.

"I don't think it will ever go away, but you guys are definitely helping with it," I tell them. Ivan gets up and pushes Dante out of the way and places a kiss on my forehead.

"I know, little one but we will be here every day to remind you of how beautiful and worthy you are of our love," Ivan says, the last word makes me freeze. We have danced around the word, but it feels so soon. I gape at the other two guys, and they just nod in agreement.

"Yes, we love you, Mia Cara. I think we fell in love with you the first night we met you," Dante says softly. It just makes me smile. Who cares if it's too soon? If you feel it, you feel it.

"I love you guys too," I whisper to them. I continue speaking with a little more confidence, "And I am not saying it because you all said it. I really do love you guys and I know this is unconventional and it puts more pressure on you guys, but I think that's why I love you. You don't care that I love all of you and don't think that I love you any less that there are three of you. I have enough love to share with all of you. You make sure that I feel like I am the most important thing to you and that there is no one else."

They all look so happy it makes me happy. They give me a group hug, but I still am worried. As they pull away, I caress Dante's face with both hands and he freezes but does not pull away from my touch. After a second he finally leans into my hand.

"Are you sure your family is okay with this? I mean with me being with all three of you?" I ask him. I worry that his family might judge me for this. It is so hard to read his face but then he looks pissed. I regret asking now. I feel the heat from my blush. I am sure I am red in the face and chest.

"How many times are you going to make me repeat myself? You know what we are ending this issue right now," he trails off and grabs his phone from the coffee table and facetimes someone. Then I hear her voice.

"Mio figlio! What a pleasant surprise! How is mia figlia?" His mother said with such excitement. I love how she does not even ask how he is doing and goes straight to me. I am starting to think I am her favorite. He takes a deep breath and then starts.

"Hello, mamma. Mia Cara is actually why I am calling," He says nervously and that made my nerves shake. He is going to tell her now.

"Please tell me you did not mess up, mio figilo! I like her! You better do whatever it takes to make her happy!" She yells at him and I bite my lip to hold back my laugh. I cannot see her, but I can just imagine her waving her hands around frustrated at him.

"Jesus, mamma! I have not messed up and me calling you is me trying to make her happy!" He yells at her, annoyed.

"Okay, what about mia figlia?" She asked more relaxed.

"Well, she likes having unconventional relationships. She is technically with me, Carter, and Ivan," he tells her with worry all across his face as he looks at the phone. I then peak over his shoulder and see her stunned. Fuck, this is what I was worried about. Then she smiles.

"Are you happy?" She asks and his worry melts away and a big smile plastered his face.

"Yes, mamma. I am so happy, and I officially asked her to go out," he tells her softly, like he is dreamily thinking of me, even though I am there with him.

"Well, I am happy for you then and I like Carter and Ivan. If anyone can make mia faglia happy it is the three of you. Yes, it is unconventional but if you are happy then I am happy! You are finally experiencing something you have always looked for, true love. Will she be at the game tonight?" She asks with excitement. I can see her jumping in her seat in her car with anticipation. I giggle when Dante points the camera at me.

"I don't know. What do you think, Mia Cara?" He asks with a smirk. I grab the nearest throw pillow and hit him in the face. He tries to duck but is too slow.

"Hey! That is not nice!" He yells with a pout but is laughing so I know he is not hurt. Well maybe I hurt his ego. I grab his phone and angle it to my face and Carter is showing in the background.

"Hey, mia faglia! Please tell me you will be at the game! It will be so much more fun if you are there!" She yells into the phone.

"Yes, I am coming, mamma. Dante invited me and told me to use the box. I hope you don't mind my company," I tell her and started to twirl my hair again. Carter smacks my hand down, so I stop playing with my curls. I really need to start remembering to stop doing my nervous tick around the guys.

"Carter Quinn! You did not just smack that young lady's hand!" Dante's mom yells and she looks pissed. I look at Carter and his face pales a little.

"No ma'am," he says like a little kid that got caught doing something naughty. I giggle and come to his rescue.

"It's okay, mamma. It is an awful habit, and the boys are trying to help stop," I tell her and she nods but still looks torn to yell at him.

"Fine, but to answer your question I would love for you to be in the box with us. I was going to tell you I would not have it any other way. You had your fun last game being close to the ice but now you need to be in the family box since you are family," she tells me. Man, this woman is pulling all the mom tricks. She is looking at me sternly like I do not have a choice in the matter. The words are stuck in my throat so I just nod. She then smiles so big like I made her the happiest woman on the earth just by nodding.

"Wonderful! Also don't worry about Dante's brothers. They will be on their best behavior this time," she tells me.

"Oh, don't worry about it! They were great last time," I tell her and before I could go on the phone was plucked out of my hand by Dante.

"Okay, mamma. Stop tormenting the girl. You will have plenty of time at the game. Love ya," he tells her and hangs up. I go to grab another pillow to chuck at him, but he catches it this time. He grabs my plate and puts it on the coffee table. He yanks me out of Carter's lap and into his. He buries his head in my neck and bites down.

"I said that was not nice, Mia Cara," he whispered into my neck. It has me squirming again. He groans as I feel him getting hard again. I go to give him a kiss and he stops me by caressing my head between his hands.

"I'm sorry, Mia Cara but I have a morning skate here shortly. I am running late already but wanted to make sure I spent some time with you before I went," he tells me.

"No..." I tell him with a whimper. I know I sound like a whiney teen complaining her boyfriend is going away, sue me.

"Yes, Mia Cara. I know it is not ideal. If I could, I would shrink you and keep you in my pocket always," he tells me sweetly. Sad thing is, I believe it.

"What? We're not enough for you, little one?" Ivan asks and plucks me from Dante's lap. He lifts me and my legs automatically wrap around his waist and my arms loop around his neck.

"No, big guy that is why I have three of you," I giggle out when he tickles me. Dante goes to get dressed and when he comes back and god, he looks like a Greek god. His shirt almost looks too small for his muscles as he goes to button his cuffs. Then he looks at me and smiles because he knows that he caught me gawking.

"You guys want to come to the game with Nikki? I know you're not busy Ivan but was not sure about you Carter," Dante says to the guys. Ivan pins me to the wall, and I am gasping to feel his hard thick length pressed against me.

"I will be there," Ivan says and starts to devour my breast with his mouth. Like he could not be bothered by Dante's question.

"I have practice, but I should be able to make it," Carter chimes in from the couch but then gets up to get dressed.

"Perfect! I will stay here and ravish, little one while you guys are busy," Ivan says into my neck, but I have to make sure the club will be okay for one night.

"Put me down for a second, big guy. I need to say bye to them and call Chloe to cover at the club while I am at the game," He sighs and puts me down but does not let me go.

"Fine but once that is all done you are all mine," he says with a growl. I walk over to Dante and Carter to say goodbye. I hug Carter first and give him a quick kiss.

"Bye, Princess. I love you. I will be back right before you leave so I can ride over with you guys," he tells me and gives me a quick kiss on the forehead. I saunter over to Dante and he gathers me in his arms.

"Wish me luck?" He asks but it is sounding more like a demand coming from him.

"Do you need me too?" I ask him with an arched brow. He is one of the best goalies in the league. He does not need his girlfriend to wish him luck.

"I don't need it, Mia Amore but it does not make me want to hear you say it any less," he tells me. I put my hands on his chest so I can push him slightly back so I can look him in the eyes.

"Good luck, Mio Amore and I love you," I tell him and place a soft kiss on his lips.

He lets me go and says, "Just for that I will have a surprise for you at the game." I look at him with wide eyes.

"No! You guys have gotten me enough already just by being with me and loving me. I don't need any more presents," I tell him and try to keep my voice calm, so he knows I am serious. I don't need anything from them, just their love.

"Nope this will be a good surprise I swear and if I want to give you a gift, I will give you a fucking gift," he says and his voice is so deep and stern. Fuck me, he is turning me on. This is not fair I swear!

"Fine but it better not be expensive. Now go before you are so late, they won't let you play," I tell him and his face lights up.

"Arrivederci, Mia Cara. Ti amo," He says, giving me one last hard kiss. This man is going to be the death of my pussy if he keeps talking in Italian. They go and I wave goodbye at my door as they drive away. I walk back inside to find Ivan sprawled out on my couch in his skivvies but that isn't what has me frozen. He picked up the latest book I am reading and it looks like he is reading the scene I was on. It was a crazy sex scene where the girl is getting eaten out by a famous baseball player in the locker room. I may have picked it up after me and Ivan's date.

"Well, little one now I see why you read these," he tells me with a devilish smirk. His eyes are big and go dark with lust. I laugh and walk right over to him. I grab the book right out of his hands and throw it on the coffee table. I go to straddle his lap and can feel him grow hard under me. I lean down and place kisses on his chest and he moans.

"Oh, really and why is that Daddy?" I whisper into his chest. Before he answers me, he picks me up with him as he gets up and I wrap my legs around him again.

"It is giving me all sorts of ideas of what to do with my little one," he says as he starts to walk to my room. Yep, these men will be the death of my poor pussy.

Chapter 16

IVAN

Fuck me! I never thought a book could make me so horny, but it did. I was so close to grabbing my dick and jerking off on Nikki's couch. The scene was unbelievably detailed. It was a love story between a baseball player and his nanny. The scene I just read, he got his nanny into the locker room after his win and ate her out. Sounds like he got two wins. Then my beautiful woman comes in and straddles me and rubs her hot core against my dick. It was too much, I needed her. I whisk her away to her bedroom. I throw her to the bed, and I hop on top of her, covering her little body fully.

"You have been a very bad girl, little one," I whisper in her ear and nibble on her earlobe.

"Oh, and what bad thing did I do, Daddy?" She asks as a taunt. It makes me growl in lust that she thinks she can defy and play with her daddy like that.

"You did not tell me you were reading about another baseball player. Should I be jealous?" I said with a soft laugh. I slowly peel off her silk robe that had been gorgeous on her but not as gorgeous as seeing her naked.

"You never have to be jealous. You just cannot be here all the time Daddy so my books will have to do," she giggled out.

"Oh, I don't know. I think I need to remind you who your daddy is, little one," I tell her. I pop up and start looking around the room. She looks at me with an arched brow.

"And what are you looking for, Daddy?" She asks, but then I look under her bed and find what I was looking for. Women always hide their dirty secrets under the bed.

"Nope, found what I was looking for," I tell her as I slide the box out from her bed. It is a vintage black wooden box with silver latches holding it closed. As it hit the bed her eyes went wide, which gave me confirmation that this box is exactly what I was looking for.

"Well, well, well. Look what I found," I tell her while I open it. Oh, now this is a good box. I slowly started to pull out each thing. A couple of vibrators, a couple bottles of lube, a flogger, a black silk blindfold, but then I find exactly the thing I was looking for. She has purple fuzzy handcuffs. I will get back to the flogger I think laughing in my head. I grab them, throw them on the bed, and put the box down on the floor but leave it open just in case. You never know with my beautiful little vixen. I climb back on top of her straddling her like she did in the living room. I run both hands up her soft arms and pin them to the bed together with one of my large hands. She moans at my touch. The other hand grabs the cuffs that were off to the side. I latch them on her wrist but then I see a hook on her black wooden bed frame. Oh, I knew my little vixen was kinky but now I am excited. I hook the chain of the cuff on the hook. She looks at me surprised, but I can see her pupils dilate with lust as they get bigger.

"Now my baby girl can't go anywhere," I tell her as I get up to go to her box. She looks at me and I decide to make her give into trust. I pluck the blindfold out of the box and find a soft black feather. Oh, this could be fun. I grab the feather as well and go back. I put the blindfold on her.

"Please, Daddy. You are killing me with how much I want you," she begs but I cannot give in. My sweet vixen is a glutton for punishment. I don't go back to touching her. I take the feather and start gliding it across her chest. She arches her body up as much as she can while being restrained. She moans and whimpers as I swirl it around her nipple.

"Please, Ivan. I am dying here. I need to feel you," she gasps as I take the feather to her stomach.

"Not yet, little one. This is your punishment for not telling me what you are reading," I took the feather lower, so it was touching her clit. She gasps at the sensation of it touching her swollen wet clit. The feather is soaked with her wetness. God, I know this sounds bad, but I take the feather to my face and sniff in her delectable scent. My other hand goes to my cock to stroke it. I grip the base and slowly move my hand up and down.

"Daddy?" She asks. Shit I must have been too lost in the scent of the feather and touching myself that I forgot about the goddess before me, needing me. I kneel between her spreading her legs.

"Are you ready for your daddy?" I ask her as I position myself between her slick folds.

"Fuck yes!" She yells so loud I am sure her neighbors would hear. I go to reach for a condom on her end table but then she stops me by clenching me with her thighs. This is keeping me in place. I am kind of shocked, so I pull the blindfold off to look into her beautiful green eyes. Then she shocks the hell out of me by saying, "I don't want to use one with you. I want to feel all of you. I am on the pill. I am clean and I know you probably get screened a lot being a pro athlete but if you really feel uncomfortable about it you can use them."

I am shocked but don't say anything. I show her how okay I am with this by thrusting into her completely to the base. God, I almost nut right then and there. She moans as I start to find a pace that feels amazing. My sweet little one feels so good I have to stop for a second and focus on not cumming too soon. I am so glad I put those cuffs on her now because if she was able to touch me, I am sure I would lose it. Once I gain control over my body again, I start to move again. She is so warm and wet.

"Daddy," she moans out.

"What do you need, baby?" I ask her, wanting to give her what she needs. I could not deny this woman anything. She could ask me to kill someone, and I would ask her to point where.

"Harder, faster," she moaned out. She can't say those things. I am already on the edge. It is taking everything to hold back as is.

"If I do that love I am not going to last," I tell her, kissing her neck and sucking. I have this primal need to mark her whenever I can. She moans as I suck hard.

"I don't care, Daddy. It just shows me how much you can lose control with me. I want you unraveled by me," she whispers. I can't take it anymore with her filthy sweet nothings. I pull out of her and I can feel her pussy clenching wanting me to stay in her. I unhook the cuffs and kiss each wrist as I undo the cuffs. Making sure they did not hurt her. Then I flip her, so she is on her hands and knees in front of me. I put my hand between her shoulder blades and pushed her down softly, so her head hit the mattress. Her hands grasp the sheets as I slide back into her. Once I was fully in her, I pick up my pace and slam in and out of her. She wanted hard and fast and that is what she is going to get. As I slam into her, I can start to feel her pussy spasming and that is my queue. I know she is cumming. Her hand slides down to her clit and messages it as her muscles tenses.

"Daddy!" She screams as she cums. That does me in. Having my little one scream my name as she comes undone. My balls tighten as I cum inside her perfect cunt. We sit there trying to catch our breath. We are trying to remember how to breathe but it wasn't hard as we breathe together. I slowly slide out of her and watch as my cum starts to seep out of her. I growl, wanting it to stay inside of her. Like the sick fucker I am,

I gather my cum with my fingers and push it back into her. She moans as my fingers slip back into her.

"I love the way you look, little one. You on your hands and knees, filled with my cum but I need to clean you up," I tell her picking her up and she giggles as I pick her up like a new husband would carry their bride through the threshold.

"Nope, Daddy. You distracted me and I still need to call Chloe to cover at the club and reserve the VIP section," she tells me, and I set her down with a groan. She giggles and gives me a quick kiss on the lips.

"Don't be like that, Daddy. If you are good and let me, make my quick phone call we can play in the shower as we clean up," she whispers against my lips.

"Fine," I snap like a little kid. I let go of her and smack her ass as she leaves the room. I grab my phone so I can text Carter to bring me a change of clothes when he comes over.

Ivan: Hey, can you do me a favor and bring a change of clothes so I can hang out with Nikki for the day?

Carter: Go get your own damn clothes! It's not fair you are not in season so you get to spend the day with her.

I scoff at his message because there are five emojis at the end of his message. If this man could just speak emojis he would. I know him well enough how to get to him though. I laugh as I type out the message and send it.

Ivan: Fine! You call your princess and explain why I had to leave her to pick up clothes when we both know you are running home to change. Poor princess having to be home without one of us. You know what I will tell her, so she knows what an ass you are.

Then his messages come in instantly in rapid recession.

Carter: Don't you DARE!!

Carter: FINE!!!

Carter: What do you want me to bring you asshat?!?!

This guy is too easy to mess with.

Ivan: A white button up, black pants, socks, and a pair of boxers please!

Carter: AND just so you know I am not doing it for you. I am doing it for Princess! Tell her how nice of a boyfriend I am!

Ivan: Don't worry, I won't! I will tell her how much of an ass you are.

Carter: DON'T YOU FUCKING DARE!!

I laugh as I toss my phone to my bed and make my way out to my little one who is finishing up her phone call. I can hear the constant pinging of my phone, probably Carter blowing it up, but I could care less. Little one wants to play in the shower, and I cannot deny her that.

Carter finally brings my clothes and I go to change. Not only that, but he also brought spares to keep at little one's place so we can have something here. He walks in with a duffle and hands it to me. I walk out from changing as Carter is explaining it.

"Princess, I hope you don't mind that I brought us all spare clothes to keep here. I just want to make sure we have some if we ever spend the night," he says nervously with his hand rubbing the back of his neck. She walks over to him on the couch and sits in his lap and gives him a peck on the lips.

"I would not have it any other way. You folks are more than welcome to bring more over so you guys have options. I just need to make space in my already packed closet," she says with a laugh. I chime in then.

"We don't want you to go out of your way to make us comfortable," I tell her, placing a kiss on her forehead.

"No, I want to! I was going to today actually but then the big guy kept distracting me," she says with her cute giggle.

"I did not hear you complaining, little one," I told her, shooting a glare her way as I sit down in her armchair next to the couch. I pick up her book so I can read it as we wait to go to the game. I can see her eyes go wide out of the corner of my eye.

"You don't have to read that!" She squeaks out and then Carter looks in between us confused.

"Am I missing something?" Carter asks us and Nikki blushes a bright red in embarrassment that is so cute.

"Our girl likes dirty girl books. The scenes are quite descriptive," I tell him as I try to continue to read but he breaks my concentration.

"What? Really?" He asked Nikki, stunned.

"Yep, that is what distracted us earlier. I got so turned on by the scene she was on, that I could not help myself but get my hands all over our girl," I tell him with a shrug as Nikki gives me a death glare.

"That is so hot, Princess," He tells her with a smile but then she points her glare at him before returning the glare at me.

"Why are you still reading it?" She asked me dropping her glare and replacing it with a curious look. It has me laughing.

"Because, little one, I want to know how it ends! You got me hooked plus then I can get more ideas. The locker room scene has me wanting to pull you into my locker room next season to try it out," I tell her honestly. I would love to have our girl come to my game and pull her into my locker room to recreate the scene. Carter gets up and sits her on the couch to go to her bookcase to investigate further. He plucks the one that she had told me about the night I took her to the opera. He goes back to the couch and opens it to start to read. She just sits there stunned as she watches both of us reading her book. Carter must have gotten to a good scene because his eyes go wide and mouth slack, gaping at the book.

"Fuck me, Princess! This is hot as shit!" He exclaims to her. She gets up from the couch with attitude and grabs her purse. Shit! I embarrassed her. I didn't mean to do that, but I will be spanking her later because of her sass so it is a win win really.

"You guys are ridiculous! Let's go before we are late," she says, making her way to her door but she does not get far as Carter grabs her by the waist.

"Princess don't be mad. We are not making fun of you. On the contrary, will you read one to me one day while we play?" He asks with such sincerity that she has to take him seriously.

"Really? You would want to try that?" She asks with the anger fading away.

"Of course! That book was better than porn! You can read one on the phone when I have to go to away games!" He says with excitement, and I am kind of jealous I did not think of that. I chime in just to reassure her.

"Me too!" I tell her, dropping the book on the coffee table and make my way to her and Carter by the door. We both wrap our arms around her, him in front of her and me behind her.

"Okay, I think I want to try that too," she sighs out and Carter opens the door, but I keep her in my arms.

"And if you don't think I am spanking you later for giving us attitude you have another thing coming," I warn her, making her shiver with lust but she surprises me with a dazzling smile.

"As long as you use my flogger," she suggested. Damn, I am going to be hard the whole game waiting to get my hands on her. We all walked out following her to the SUV.

"This is going to be the longest hockey game ever," I tell Carter.

"No kidding!" He says to me and it has our girl giggling at us. We both groan because we sure as hell want to skip the game and share her at home.

Chapter 17

NIKKI

We pull into a private garage at the arena. It is a prime parking spot. The last game I was so happy that Dante had me take his driver. If me and Ian drove, we would have to park all the way in the back lot. I wore his jersey because I am sure if I wore anything else he would have killed me... or punish me. I would prefer the latter. Ivan drove and held my hand the entire way. It was nice and sweet which I did not expect from him. Each guy gives me something I need. Dante is my sweet romantic, Carter is my funny, frustrating man and Ivan is my calm serious one. I went to grab the handle as Ivan put the car in park, but Ivan quickly locked the doors. I looked at him and he shook his head. These men really don't think a woman can get their own door.

"Carter," he growled and quickly unlocked the doors. Carter just nods and gets out of the back seat to open my door. I laugh.

"You know I can get my own door," I tell them, and they both just shake their heads no. Carter grabs my hand and helps me out of the SUV. Then when I am fully out of the car Carter cradles my head between his hands.

"Princess, just because you can doesn't mean you should," Carter says, placing a sweet kiss on my lips but he does not linger, probably to respect the ground rules we set. I don't care at this moment, I deepen the kiss to show him how much I appreciate what they do for me. He lets me deepen it for a second then he pulls away biting my lip.

"Later, love. I am really trying to respect your boundaries, and this is making it really hard and me hard for that matter," he says with a laugh at the last part which has me giggling. Ivan comes around to join us.

"What if I tell you I don't care anymore? That I want the world to know I am yours, both of yours," I tell them and they both nod with excitement. I thought about this all yesterday after we agreed over breakfast. What we were doing was not wrong. Will the press suck? Yes, but I am not going to let the press scare me. These men should be able to scream it on mountain tops if they want. Actually, as I admit this, I am sure they will.

"Okay, little one. We just need to include Dante in this conversation. We will talk about it later when we are at the club. I just don't want him to feel left out about us having this conversation without him," Ivan says and that makes me hop out of Carter's arms and hug Ivan. He wraps his strong arms around me returning the hug.

"Of course! I wouldn't have it any other way. I love you both," I tell them and they return it with I love you too, at the same time. It was so cute. How can I not love them? They have always made sure I came first and always made sure I could have anything I could ever want in the short time we have been together. We make our way to the elevator where I run into a familiar face. The door opens and then I see Ian. I squeal and hug him.

"What are you doing here?" I asked him, still squealing. This is amazing he is here!

"Well, you should thank your boy toy that's not present. He asked if I would come since you were nervous about hanging out with his family, so he wanted to make sure you had a friend here. I know you have your harem but sometimes you just need your gay best friend," he says with a laugh pulling away. He continues as we ride up the elevator, "These guys are keepers. I am just saying."

"Oh, I know! I am keeping them forever," I tell Ian as I grab both my guy's hands for reassurance. They just flash dazzling smiles telling me they like what they hear. Carter turns to me.

"Trust me, Princess. If you ever broke it off with me, I would chase you to the ends of the earth as your white knight," Carter tells me with a big grin.

"How very stalker of you. Oh, new nickname! You are stalker boy!," I joke with a laugh. Even Ivan throws his head back in laughter. Carter doesn't take offense to the new nickname.

"Well, I would stalk you so be careful, love. Also at least it is better than Mr. Flirt," he says with a growl at the first comment. As the doors open to the elevator I am bum rushed into a hug by Dante's mom. I just laugh as I let go of the guy's hands and hug her back.

"Mia figlia! I am so happy you are here!" She is practically squealing. She is the sweetest woman I have ever met.

"I am happy to be here, mamma," I tell her, reluctantly calling her mamma. I know she told me to call her that, but it feels so informal. She pulls away and hugs both of the guys.

"Nice to see you boys too," she says softly and then turns to Ian.

"You must be Nikki's friend I heard so much about from Dante," she says and goes to hug him too. I am a little shocked. Dante talked to his mom about Ian? I guess it was to tell her that he was coming but then she says, "I heard you helped these idiotis out getting sweet Nikki."

"Oh, if it was not for me, they would not even have a chance," he says with a snicker as the boys give him a death glare.

"Well come on the box is ready," mamma says, grabbing my hand and pulling me all the way there but something she said is playing in my head. The box is ready. Ready for what? We get to the box and mamma opens the doors. I am overwhelmed by the scene I see. The whole box is decorated in purple streamers and balloons. His mother walks into the room with arms wide to me almost displaying the room like Vanna White. Then I realize that his mother is in a purple turtleneck sweater dress with black flats and his brothers are in lavender button ups and black slacks. His brothers don't look upset about having to wear the outfits though. They almost look as excited as Dante's mother. Dante must have coordinated with them. I am stunned silent while looking at Ivan and Carter and they have smug looks on their faces. I come out of my shock and glare at them.

"You knew all this was happening didn't you," I tell them, keeping my glare at them. They just laugh and nod. Ivan grabs me by the waist.

"It wasn't too hard to distract you while Carter and Dante took care of everything," Ivan says. Damn him! All the amazing sex was a distraction so I would not be texting or calling anyone and ruining this.

"Asshole," I whispered to him, giving him a hug. Carter must have heard me because he laughs. I turned to him.

"You are not off the hook either, Mr. Flirt," I tell him using the nickname he hates to punish him. He groans at the nickname but then mamma pulls me to a small table in the corner of the box. It is decorated with a black tablecloth and a magnificent bouquet of purple roses. I am starting to realize these are my favorite flowers. Then I look over the table and there is a gift bag on it. I look at mamma confused.

"It is something the boys got for you, and I am so excited to see you open it," she says jumping up and down, unable to contain her excitement. I start to pull out the tissue paper from the bag slowly because I am still in shock with everything, but mamma must have been feeling impatient because she starts helping with rapid speed, pulling out a jersey. I am stunned as she holds it up so I can get a better look at it. It is a jersey that has Dante's name and number on it, but the colors are wrong. It is a black jersey with purple detailing. He got me a custom jersey in my favorite colors. I can feel the tears in my eyes forming. This is just so astonishing. Dante knew I would feel a little uncomfortable about his family but agreed to make him happy so he made sure to do everything he could to do in his power to make me feel relaxed. Mamma hands me the jersey and points at a door in the box.

"There is a bathroom through there so you can change," she tells me, practically pushing me into it. I start to change and when I am done look in the mirror. I pull out my phone and take a picture of me in my new jersey. I sent it to Dante with a message.

Nikki: I know you probably won't see this till after the game, but I wanted to say thank you for everything. I love you and cannot wait to see you after you win! Good luck Mio Amore

I waited for a moment, but I highly doubt he has his phone right now. To my surprise the three dots show up and then a message.

Dante: Mia Cara, I love you too! We all do and we wanted to show you how much we care for you and love you. BTW you look hot as hell in your new jersey I cannot wait to get you in bed in nothing but that jersey. How do you like my new gear?

I read his message and then a picture came through. It is his goalie helmet and it is repainted. It is beautiful. It is a black base with purple roses with green stems and thorns weaving throughout the helmet. Then he sends a second picture of the back and on one of the stems in black calligraphy is the words Mia Cara on it. I cannot hold back the tears that have been building through this whole experience. I know I shouldn't do this, but it is still a little early. I Facetime him on my phone. He picks up after the first ring and he is beaming with the most beautiful smile but then turns to worry as he sees me.

"Mia Cara, what is wrong? Why are you crying? Do you not like your surprises?" He asks with concern seeping through his voice. I just shake my head and let the tears go.

"I know I shouldn't be calling you before a game and I don't want to get you in trouble, but I needed to call you to tell you something," I tell him with my voice cracking. His expression softens.

"Mia Amore, you can call anytime. My coach is not here yet but even if he was, I would answer. You do not come second to anything. The only time I do not have my phone is when I am on the ice and don't make me tempted to break that rule just to prove a point," he says sternly to make sure I understand what he says. I slowly nod and he smiles.

"So, you said you called to tell me something, Mia Cara?" He asks with a smirk because he knows exactly why I am calling.

"I wanted to say thank you for all the wonderful things you did. Also wanted to see your face when I say good luck and that I love you," I tell him honestly, twirling a red curl that is loose from my ponytail that I pulled up before we left. I can feel the heat of my blush on my cheeks. He glares at me which is not the reaction I was expecting.

"Hey, you know you are not to twirl your hair around us, Mia Cara. I am sure I can convince Ivan to spank you every time you do it," he says with sternness in his voice. I immediately stop and drop my hand. He goes back to smiling when my face goes red at the comment about Ivan spanking me.

"I am sure you could," I say shyly.

"That's my girl. You're welcome and there is still one more surprise that has not shown up yet but should be there any minute," he tells me and I drop my jaw in shock.

"No, you have done enough! You don't need to do anything else!" I yell into the phone. He just laughs.

"Well, I just got a text that it is there so I can't take it back. Go Mia Amore and enjoy your last surprise. I love you and will miss you," he says, and I just roll my eyes.

"You just saw me a few hours ago," I tell him, but I have to admit I miss him too.

"So, I don't like being separated for a second. The second I left this morning I started to miss you," he tells me with such honesty in his eyes. Then all of a sudden the phone is taken from him and I see a new face. It is Richard Quick! He has short dark curly hair and some scruff on his face but not a full beard. His hair is messy and has pale skin. I laugh as I see his smug face and hear Dante yelling to give his phone back.

"Marshall, hold him while I talk to my fan," he says smugly.

"On it," He yells back but can still hear Dante yelling for his phone.

"Well, hello. I heard you threaten to wear my jersey on your boyfriend," he says with a laugh. I blush because I did buy his jersey and wore it every game but never thought of him as cute. I just like his stats.

"Well, you do have ninety five percent in goal saves," I tell him and his jaw drops, stunned that I know his stats.

"Holy shit! Your girlfriend knows my stats! No wonder you hated me when she said she would wear my jersey!" He says laughing so hard he drops the phone, but it is picked up quickly and a new face is on the screen.

"Hello, I am Jason Robertson! I heard we are coming to your club after the game! I am so excited, I have never been to a jazz club!" He says excitedly, like he cannot wait to see the club. He has short black hair and looks Asian descent. I love that he introduces himself even though I know all the players on the team.

"It's no problem! I am happy that you all want to come and don't worry I have really good security so you guys can actually relax and chill after the game," I tell him and can still hear Dante struggling trying to get his phone.

"You don't know how much we appreciate that! I promise to tell you an embarrassing locker room story about Dante," he says with a soft laugh.

"You will not!" Dante yells from behind the phone.

"Oh, I will hold you to that later," I tell him, giggling.

"Hey Quick you come hold Dante! I want to say hi to my best friend!" Marshall yells in the background. Then Marshall is on the screen. His brown hair is slicked back, probably to keep it out of his face when he plays.

"Best friend?" I ask him with a laugh. He blushes a little about calling him out.

"Hey Nikki and yes you are my new best friend. Hope you and Ian have fun tonight!" He says making sure to include Ian.

"Of course, we are already having so much fun!" I tell him with a laugh. He looks nervous though. "Is everything okay?"

"Well, I have my jersey coming to the box for Ian and I was hoping he would wear it," he tells me looking down at his feet. He is so cute!

"I will make sure Ian wears it! It might not go with his three-piece suit but I am sure he will wear it no matter what," I tell him with a smile and that has him smiling with excitement.

"He does not have to if he does not want to…" he says but I cut him off.

"No, he does and he will want to support his man! He just did not want to wear it because he thinks it will embarrass you, so he waited until you offered it," I tell him. Me and Ian have had this conversation over text, and he explained he wanted to wait till Stan was ready.

"Oh, he was waiting on me?" Stan says with surprise in his voice.

"Yes, this is new for you. Coming out and all so he wanted to make sure you were comfortable and ready before wearing it. Trust me, I offered to buy him one for the games he comes to, but he turned me down saying this needs to be on your time," I tell him and I can practically see hearts in his eyes. He sighs with a breath of relief.

"Okay, thank you! It is my alternate jersey, so it is the real deal. I do not want my boyfriend wearing some store-bought jersey," he tells me. Then the phone is plucked from his hand and Dante comes back in view.

"Okay that is enough. Stop messing with my girl," he warns them.

"Oh, we have all night to do that later," Quick chimes in the background. Dante looks at him with anger.

"You most certainly will not!" He yells at them. He looks at the phone now and is pouting and says, "Tell them to be nice, Mia Cara."

"If you all could stop messing with him, at least till after the game," I added and is still pouting. "Don't give me that look. I love you and you need to go to get ready."

"Fine, I love you too, Mia Amore," he says with a small smirk.

"Bye!" I tell him and hang up. I walk out and see Ian first. I just snicker because he is already in the jersey. It must have been delivered when I was talking to Dante. Then I can see my last surprise. There is Raymond in the box giving chocolate chip pancakes to my dad while he is talking to Dante's mom. What the hell? Is this a two for one deal! I run over to my dad and give him the biggest hug.

"Well hello to you too little lion," he whispered in my ear with a soft laugh.

"What are you doing here? I thought you had to get ready for your fight tomorrow?" I ask pulling away to look at him.

"I trained today and the boys invited me so we can hang out before the fight," he told me with a smile and then I turned to the second part of the surprise and hugged Raymond.

"And you? I am assuming Dante asked you to come," I ask Raymond. Raymond never smiles but I see him fighting back a smirk.

"He asked if I would come so you would have food that he knows you would like. I like this kid," Raymond tells me, handing me my favorite. A big stack of chocolate chip pancakes and chewy bacon. I am not going to cry, I am not going to cry. I tell myself but I can't hold back the stinging in my eyes. Ivan and Carter run up to me like something is wrong.

"What's wrong, Princess?" Carter asks as Ivan wipes the tears off my face. They both looked so concerned. They both wrap their arms around my waist, Ivan in the front and Carter behind me. I am just so overwhelmed by them sometimes. We show our love by doing simple things. I got them protein shakes and gave them my key. Them being extreme they do all of this.

"I'm sorry these are happy tears. I just never had one man show me how much they love me besides my dad and now here the three of you come in and show me so much love, that it is overwhelming," I tell them. I cuddle into Ivan's chest trying to hide my face and tears. I look like a mess now that I have been crying. Ivan grabs my face and lifts it so I can look into his eyes. He smiles at me, but I get lost in his beautiful green eyes. I don't think I have ever seen such bright green eyes.

"No hiding, love. You look beautiful and we are keeping our promise," he says with such a declaration in his voice.

"What promise is that?" I ask them, my voice shaky from my emotions.

"We promised to give you the world and that is exactly what we intend to do, Princess," Carter says nuzzling into my neck. I lift both my hands, one cupping Ivan's face, which he then pushes into my touch. Then the other goes behind me to cup Carter's face.

"I don't need the world. The only thing I need is the three of you. I love you all," I tell them, and the tears start to subside as I declare my love for them. They both unwind their arms, and each grab a hand to grip my hands tight.

"We love you too," Ivan says.

"And not going anywhere," Carter says right after Ivan. I smile at them and then everyone in the room. Everyone is watching us with so much love and understanding, even Dante's brothers. I always felt so disappointed in the men I chose and now I understand why. I was waiting for these three guys to show me what true love really is. Then I hear my dad slap his hands together.

"Now that we got all the mushy stuff out the way, let's watch some hockey, little lion!" He yells with excitement. We go to our seats with our food and when I go to sit in my seat Carter grabs me and sits me in his lap. I squeal at the sudden movement. Then Ivan sits in the seat next to us that I was about to sit in and grabs my hand.

"You know I can sit in my own seat," I tell them and they both shake their heads.

"I would rather be your seat, it makes it easier to feed you," Carter says with a smirk. He grabs my syrup coated pancakes and cuts a piece off. He all but makes the airplane noises while giving me a bite. I eat it up though with a smile. Ivan holds my hands in his lap because he knows I would try to eat myself if they let me. I don't want to say I am a control freak, but I have always had control when it comes to my life. I was always the one making decisions for me and my dad. Believe it or not until he moved to New Orleans, he would always check with me about a fight before accepting. I don't think the boys are trying to control everything but I think they are trying to make decisions, so I don't have to, so I don't have to stress on what is the right move or wrong move. When I quit Broadway, I nearly had a panic attack everyday till I figured out what I wanted to do with my life. Carter goes and feeds me a piece of bacon and I moan at the delicious piece of meat in my mouth. It is fatty, salty goodness. Carter and Ivan scowl at me when I moan which has me cocking my head in confusion. Ivan leans down so his mouth is by my ear. I shiver when I feel his warm breath on my ear.

"Keep making those sounds and see what happens," Ivan whispers in my ear. I snap my head up to make sure my dad is not looking. He looks like he is in deep conversation with Dante's brothers. I turn to Ivan with a smirk.

"Oh, and what are you going to do about it, Daddy?" I whisper, calling his bluff. I am starting to realize I made a mistake when a mischievous grin grows on his face, but I don't falter.

"Do you need a reminder of who is in charge, little one?" He asks softly so no one but Carter and I hear it. Carter groans though.

"Can you two not talk dirty while, princess is on my lap? I am seriously getting hard and won't be able to get up with her dad and Dante's mom here," Carter says, sounding almost out of breath. I wiggle in his lap and feel him growing harder underneath me.

"Princess," Carter says growling as a warning. It just makes me giggle. I throw up my hands.

"Hey, that's not my fault. He started it," I tell Carter pointing at Ivan. He just lets out a sigh.

"And I am ending it. There will be plenty of time to play later princess," Carter whispers in my ear.

Carter continues to feed me and I hold back my moans because I am sure Ivan is not making idle threats about my sounds. He is a guy who will follow through. Ivan grabbed my hand while I was eating and was playing with our combined fingers. The announcer comes on and starts to announce the team. Ian practically screams when Stan skates out when he is announced out. Then they call Dante's name and I do the same. I hop off Carter's lap and run to the edge of the box screaming his name and waving like he can see me, but he shocks me. He waves towards the box and blows me a kiss. He really is the sweetest man I have ever met. I go back and sit in Carter's lap. We watch the game just like this. The boys talk to my dad and Ian and make small talk, but I cannot focus on that. I am zoned in on the game.

Dante is great at what he does. He blocks everything that is coming at him, and Stan has scored two times already. They go into the third period and Stan does the unthinkable. He scores a Hat Trick! Stan better get a raise in his contract with these past two games. I would like to think it is because he is more relaxed being out in the open. That could put a lot of stress on a person. Ian has the biggest grin and almost looks proud as the fans throw hats onto the ice to celebration at this trick. I am so happy that he has finally found someone. It almost has me crying again when he cheers his man's name as loud as he can.

It is down to the wire. The other team doesn't stand a chance. The other team decides it is time to try to get the man advantage. They pull their goalie, so it is a six on five on Dante's side. There is only one minute left in the game. The puck drops and New York wins the face off. Stan makes it to center ice but is checked. The other team's member who checked him grabs the puck and rushes at Dante. I know they won already but nerves set in as this huge guy charges down the ice with no one on him. It is just him and Dante. The crowd goes quiet as Dante skates up to him and jabs the puck with his goalie stick. The puck is flying down the ice and through the players on the ice and into the other goal. Dante scored a goal! When the puck is in the net the buzzer goes off. That is a game! Dante, a goalie, did the hardest thing possible. He shot a goal! I keep saying it in my head because it is so hard to believe. Then on the Jumbo Tron in big lettering is the goal dedication. Mia Cara. This has me crying again and rushing to the edge of the box cheering for Dante. He skates to center ice and points his goalie stick at our box dedicating the goal to me. He then is thrown down to the ground by his teammates into a big hot doggy pile.

Dante's mom is freaking out and his brothers are trying to calm her down. She bum rushes for me and hugs me.

"Thank you," she whispers in my ear which confuses me.

"For what mamma?" I ask her. She just looks at me with tears in her eyes. I hope it is tears of happiness and not sadness.

"He has always played great but with you he plays even better," she tells me with a nod and lets me go. That can't be right. I haven't done anything. I have only been to two games. His brothers came up to me to confirm.

"She is right, you know," Bobbie says with a smirk.

"Yeah! I mean so far since he has been seeing you, he has had two shutout games and now he has even scored. The little shit is going to be bragging about it for years!" Paulie complains and his mom elbows him in his gut. He hunches over like she knocked the wind right out of him. Okay do not get on this woman's bad side.

"Don't call your brother little shit!" She yells and smacks the back of his head as he is hunching over from the elbow. He finally is able to come up for air.

"But he is!" Paulie yells and it has me laughing. This is nice. They really make me feel like I am a part of their family and don't judge the relationship we have. This is what I have always dreamed of having and now these three men are making that dream come true.

Chapter 18

DANTE

I can't believe that happened! I, the goalie of the New York Knights, scored my first ever goal. The only thing better than that is that Mia Cara was there. It was hard to see her since the box was center ice, but I could see when she would rush to the edge of the box in her beautiful new jersey and scream my name. Surprisingly, the jersey was the hardest part of my surprise. I made my first call to my assistant and told her what I was looking for and that I needed it today. She was a little apprehensive at first saying it would be impossible to get it done today. I told her I don't care how much it cost and to get it done. With that she made the impossible possible. She cleared it with me, and I was so pleased. I had to match so I cleared it with the coach and PR people about changing my helmet. It got painted first thing in the morning so it would dry for the game. Now everything else my mother insisted on helping me with. So, I told her the necessities and that she can do whatever the hell she wants with the rest. I make my way to the locker room, but the coach stops me before I go in.

"Coach?" I ask him. He is older but used to be one of the best goalies in the NHL before he had a groin injury that made him retire early. He is one of the few coaches that does not wear a suit. He wears black dress pants, black button up and a New York Knights sweater. He says he wants to be comfortable while he is running around coaching and he can't do that in a suit. He has short salt and pepper hair like Ivan's and wears small, framed glasses. He looks at me with seriousness.

"I know I don't say this often, but you did a great job these past couple of games and wanted to say how proud I am to have you be a part of my team," he says which is kind of shocking. Coach can be a hard ass, so he rarely praises anyone.

"Grazie," I say while gaping at him.

"Whatever you have done recently, keep it up. I can tell there is a difference about you. I can only assume it is a woman by what you got painted on your helmet," he says fighting back a smirk. This makes me grin.

"Yeah, she is amazing," I tell him with a sigh.

"Well for the sake of this team try not to screw it up and lose her. Your contract renewal is next year and with how you are playing I am sure you will see some added zeros to the amount," he tells me and pats my back as he walks past me.

"I will never lose her," I whispered to myself. I go into the locker room needing a hot shower, so I don't stink for Mia Cara.

I took the fastest shower trying to hurry to see Nikki and my mom sent me photos of everything. I am kind of jealous I missed out. There are photos of the box fully decorated in purple and black with Mia Cara watching the game with an intense gaze. She also sent pictures of her dad, Ian, and Raymond. Looks like everything went perfectly! I go to grab my suit since I am only in a towel from the shower so I can meet everyone at Nikki's club but then I hear my phone ping.

Mia Cara: What are you up to?

That is an odd text from her. She should know what I am doing.

Dante: In the locker room getting dressed...... Why?

Mia Cara: Anyone in there with you?

I look around and it looks like I am the last one.

Dante: No I think all the guys rush to get to the club to check it out.... Again, why?

Then the door to the locker room opens and Mia Cara is standing there looking like a goddamn snack in my jersey. I instantly go rock hard under my towel. She closes the door and locks it so no one else can come in. I turn my gaze to her face, and it is full of mischief. She slowly walks up towards me one step at a time.

"Hi," is all she says when she finally makes it to me. I am having a hard time finding my words as she brings her hands to my chest and slowly wraps her arms around my neck, but I muster up a few words.

"How did you get in here?" I ask her as I wrap my hands around her waist. She lets out her adorable giggle.

"Ivan and Carter knew the way and I may have asked Stan to take the team to the club to distract them so I could sneak in," she tells me her grin getting bigger. This little minx. "I wanted to come say thank you for all my wonderful gifts and surprises you gave me today."

"Mia Amore, I would do anything for you," I promise her, leaning down to kiss her neck. I kiss her right on her pounding pulse which has her moaning.

"Oh, I know, it doesn't mean I don't want to sneak in here and show you how much I appreciate it, Mio Amore," she says, yanking the towel off my waist. I look at her gaping. My girl always knows how to keep me on my toes. I go to kiss her but she just steps back and shakes her head a little with a grin. I tilt my head confused. Maybe I misread what she meant but then her grin grew as she knelt in front of me and kissed the tip of my cock. Ohhh. That is what she meant. I rake my hands through her hair and groan as she licks me from base to tip.

"Don't tease, Mia Cara," I warn her with a growl, and she tilts back on her heels. This woman is beautiful on her knees.

"Who's teasing?" She says and then leans forward to swallow me whole. Good god! Sometimes I forget that this woman has no gag reflex. She takes me all the way to my base. I have to start thinking about anything other than what she is doing so I don't embarrass myself. She moves her head up and down in rapid motion. I start running plays in my head. Going through drills but my mind stops as she slows and takes me as deep as she can. I almost lose it when I feel my tip hitting the back of her throat. This woman is like a wet dream sitting here sucking my cock.

"Slow down, Mia Cara. I want this to last longer and you are going to embarrass me with how close I am," I tell her. She pops me out of her mouth but is still close to my throbbing cock.

"Sounds good to me, Mio Amore. Better not get caught," she whispers and I can feel her hot breath on my cock and has it twitching with need. She goes and gobbles me whole again which has me swearing. Her mouth is heaven. It is hot and wet.

"Fanculo!" I yell. I always switch to Italian when I get angry, but I guess it happens when I am too turned on too apparently. I am feeling all the feelings, and I cannot hold back the sweet nothings as she bobs up and down peering up at me through her thick dark lashes.

"Sei mio per sempre, Mia Cara. Per favore, di che sei mio," I ask her softly, but she takes me out of her mouth and looks up at me with such endearment like she knows what I am saying.

"Say it with me, Mia Cara. Sono tuo per sempre," I tell her, and she does not miss a beat.

"Sono tuo per sempre," she whispers and that does me. Before I cum all over her face she wraps her mouth around the tip of my cock sucking every last drop from me. I start to soften but it never goes fully soft. I don't think I will ever be fully soft again having my Mia Cara with me. When she finally pops me from her mouth again, I grab her under her arms and lift her up so she is on her feet. I wind my arms around her waist and give her a hot and hard kiss. I can taste myself on her lips. I know that sounds gross, but I could care less. I need to show her how much she is mine. She moans into my mouth which has me going hard again. She pulls away though.

"We better get going otherwise someone is going to catch us," she whispers against my lips and it has me growling in protest.

"But I was going to show you how much I missed you," I tell her and pout with my lower lip sticking out. That gets me a giggle and a soft kiss.

"You can show me later, love. We need to go and meet up with the other guys. I cannot wait to hear all the embarrassing stories your teammates have for me," she tells me with a soft laugh.

"Fine but later you're mine just like you said earlier," I tell her and her eyebrows fly up in shock.

"Is that what I said? You little sneak," she says with a smirk. I pick up the towel and toss it in the bin. Nikki sits on the bench waiting for me. I can't help myself. I slowly start to get dressed at a leisurely pace. I grab my boxers and slowly bring them up then followed by my pants. I look at my angel and she is licking her lips. It makes me laugh.

"See something you like, Mia Cara?" I ask her with an arched brow. She has the biggest grin on her face and tells me, "More like something I love."

That has me hauling ass to get dressed so I can get Mia Amore home and alone. Once I am dressed, I grab my bag out of my locker and close it. I pull her up to give her a quick peck on the lips and then pull her out of the locker room. I lead her to the car waiting in the back of the stadium and luckily since we stayed a little longer there were no pops outside. I hold the car door for her as I wave the driver off. He normally opens the door for me whenever he drives me, but no one is going to open her door but me and my friends. I am a possessive asshole like that. She slides in and I slide in right beside her. I put my arm around her shoulder, and she snuggles into my chest like a purring cat.

"I wish I could freeze time in these moments with you," she says softly into my chest.

"Me too, Mia Amore, me too," I tell her as the driver takes off into the city.

The driver pulls up to the club and I look at Nikki confused as we see the team is still waiting outside. We get out of the car and walk up to them.

"What are you all still doing out here? It is freezing," Nikki asks the guys. I grab her to keep her warm. I don't see Ivan or Carter anywhere.

"Well Ivan and Carter beat us here and they did not give us the password to get in so your security would not let us in," Quick says which has Nikki pissed.

"I will manage this," is all she says and makes her way to the guy Bobbie that watches the door. She puts her hands on her hips with all the sass in the world. I am getting hard just watching her.

"Bobbie, What in the actual fuck?" She yells at him and he looks at her in shock.

"What is wrong?" He asked, confused. She just scoffs.

"I made sure to let you guys know that the hockey team was coming so why are they sitting out here in the cold saying they are not able to get in asshole?" she asks him and damn. This big guy looks like he is about to wet himself. Now I understand why her dad calls her little lion. She is a vision of a strong lioness protecting her cubs. It makes me so happy because her cubs are my team. This is hot but I don't want to cause issues with her security if I ever want to get in. I sneak up behind her and wrap my arms around her waist and I feel her relax into me.

"It's okay, Mia Amore. They are hockey players, they can withstand a little cold," I tell her. She relaxes a little, but I can still feel a little tension in her body.

"No, it is not okay. It is disrespectful and appalling that your teammates were made to wait,' she says glaring at Bobbie. She is still trembling with anger. I need to calm her down somehow.

"It is but please, Mia Cara. I don't want this to ruin such a perfect night," I tell her, placing a soft kiss on her neck. I finally feel her completely softening as her anger melts away.

"Fine," she mutters. She turns to the big guy and glares. "You gonna let them in now or do I have to do it myself."

He moves fast, unhooking the purple velvet rope in the entrance.

"I-I am so sorry, it will never happen again," he says, almost stuttering and fumbling over the words. Nikki just sweeps past him grabbing my hand.

"See that you do," she quips as we make our way into the club with my teammates following. We make our way through the club to the VIP section where Carter and Ivan are sitting.

"Hey what took you guys so long?" Carter asks my teammates as we all sit down.

"Bobbie apparently did not get the memo about the team coming and had these poor guys waiting out in the cold," she snaps but Carter knows she is not mad at him, so he just grabs her and places her on his lap in the booth. I'm sorry, am I missing something? I thought we were being more discreet. I look at them in surprise, but Ivan and Carter just smile with goofy looking grins.

"Do you want to tell him, little one?" Ivan chimes in, smiling at me.

"Tell me what?" I ask Nikki with a raised brow. She just smiles.

"Well, I didn't want to talk about this in front of your team but since Carter is not playing nice I guess I will tell you now," she says and starts twirling her hair. I know it is bad if she is twirling her hair.

"Hey! I am being nice, Princess!" Carter yells. She just rolls her eyes at him and then turns to me with a smile. I scoot next to them in the booth with a nervous look.

"Well, I decided that I don't want this to be a secret. I want the world to know I have all three of you and all three of you have me," she says with a nervous smile. Holy shit! I grab her out of Carter's hold and pull her into my lap and kiss her hard. I pull back and look at her with a shit eating smile.

"Are you sure, Mia Cara?" I ask her to make sure. I don't want her to regret this once the press gets a hold of this. They can be brutal. She just pears up at me through those beautiful lashes.

"Yes, I don't want to hide away from something so perfect. Sono tuo per sempre, Mio Amore," she tells me, and my chest becomes tight. These are the moments I live for. I kiss her again and Carter comes in and kisses the side of her neck and Ivan grabs her hand and brings her knuckle to his lips. She pulls back and has a beaming smile that can melt any heart. Then I turn to my teammates, and they look shocked to say the least.

"Can we help you?" I ask them with a laugh, but I look at Nikki and she is embarrassed. She put her hands on her face to cover her blush. I grab both her hands and place them on her lap when she tries to pull them to move them back to her face. I hold them tighter and shake my head at her. The guys sit down and Quick is the first one to speak.

"Soooo... I am going to be that asshole. What is going on here?" Quick asks. This jackass! He can see that Mia Cara is nervous and embarrassed but still asking. Well here goes nothing.

"All three of us are dating Nikki. Not much more I can explain. That a problem?" I ask them almost growling. I love my team, but they are pissing me off with how they are upsetting my Nikki. We all love her, and she loves us. We should not have to explain anything more than that. All the guys throw up their hands in surrender.

"No man! We are not judging but you know it is a different situation," Jason says hands still in the air.

"Well, we love her and she loves us so get over it," Ivan says with a sternness.

"Okay man we get it no more questions," Jason says. Then Chloe comes over and that relaxes Nikki.

"Hey Chloe! Everyone this is Chloe and Chloe this is the hockey team," Nikki says, and Chloe looks around the table and gaze stops at John Quick. They stare at each other for a moment. Hmmm that's interesting. Chloe shakes her head and resets herself with a big smile.

"Hey everyone! Can I get you guys something to drink?" She asks and Nikki just orders a couple bottles of different liquors. She scurries off to grab our drinks and John is quick to follow her like a lost puppy to help her. Nikki softly laughs to herself.

"What is it, Princess?" Carter asks with an arched brow.

"Chloe is going to chew him up and spit him out," she says, still laughing.

"Maybe that is what he wants. I don't think he will mind being in her mouth," Ivan says and Nikki just elbows him but misses and hits me. She is strong because that almost knocked the wind out of me. I cough and Nikki freaks out.

"Sorry! Are you okay?" She asks, looking me over on my lap.

"I'm okay. It takes more than that to hurt me, Mia Cara," I say with a snicker. Chloe and Quick come back with our drinks. They are laughing and flirting away. I will have to ask him about that. I grab Nikki and slide her into Ivan's lap, and she looks at me confused.

"I have to run to the restroom. I will be quick," I tell her, getting up and placing a quick kiss on her lips and running to the restroom. I make quick work trying to pee with a hard on. Ever try it? It is uncomfortable. After I wash my hands, I bump into a girl outside in the hall.

"Oh, I am sorry ma'am," I say and then look at her. Wow this girl looks exactly like Mia Cara but I can tell that she put effort into her looks as Mia Cara is a natural beauty.

"Oh, I'm not you can run into me anytime handsome," she says trying to cling to me. I push past her though. That was really weird. I make my way to the VIP table. Mia Cara is still in Ivans lap on the chair and Carter gets up so I can slide into the booth. As I slide in my face must say it all when Carter asks, "You good man? You look weird."

"I am not sure. I ran into a girl on my way out of the bathroom and it was weird," I tell him and Nikki's head pops up with a smirk.

"Oh, should I be jealous?" She asks with a quirked eyebrow. I just laugh softly.

"Never, Mia Amore," I tell her honestly. I would never leave her and let her think otherwise. Then I see the girl make her way towards us. I point her out to them, "That's her."

I look at Carter and his face drains of all colors and goes pale. What the hell? Does he know her? She finally makes it to our table and before any of us can ask her what the hell she is doing she plops right into Carter's lap. What in the actual fuck? But before I can say anything Nikki comes to protect her cub.

"Who the fuck are you?" She snaps at the girl in question. The girl in Carter's lap just snickers and wraps her arms around his neck. She looks like she is trying to latch onto him when Nikki is obviously staking claim.

"I am a friend of Carter's," she says and that finally snaps Carter out of his stunned look and vibrates with anger. He is quick to push her off his lap and she falls to the floor.

"We are not friends, Rachel," he says standing up to tower over her. Then it clicks for me and Ivan. This is the trainer that would try to flirt with him. She must be one crazy bitch to follow him here and confront him after he got her fired. I mean he literally spelled it out for her, and she still did not get the hint.

"What would you call us then? I miss rubbing you down on my table," she says with a smirk. This fucking bitch! I thought Carter finally got rid of her when he reported her. I move to stand with Carter but then Nikki stops me by putting a hand on my chest to keep me seated. She moves and helps Rachel up.

"I don't know who you are and how you got past my security, but you need to fucking leave and leave my men alone," Nikki tells her with a growl. Damn now is not the time to get hard but angry Nikki is doing things to me. Plus, it's hot how she staked her claim on not just Carter but us as well. Carter moves next to Nikki and wraps his arms around her waist.

"It was really easy to be honest. I just said I was with the team and your security let me right in. Carter, tell this bitch to back off. We are perfect for each other. I even changed my look for you," Rachel says which has me and Ivan join them. Who does this bitch think she is?

"You really think changing your hair and putting contacts in to look like Nikki would make me want you? Let me cut this short," Carter says and gets in her face. "We were never a thing. I never liked you and I thought you would get the hint when I got you fired so let me spell it out again for the millionth time. You will never be like Nikki. I love her. You will leave and never come here ever again."

She starts to actually cry. I don't think she will ever get the message. This chick is seriously fucked up in the head.

"Don't say stuff like that. You love me. You were always so kind to me during our sessions. That bitch is messing with your mind," she is sobbing out.

"Call her a bitch one more time and see what happens!" Carter yells, shaking with anger. Shit! I go and grab him to hold him back before he does something stupid but if I am being honest, I want to lay this cunt out myself.

"Let me go man! You heard what she said," he says to me.

"You need to calm down before you do something stupid like hitting a chick," I tell him and look at Rachel who has an evil smirk with tears streaming down her face.

"She is a bitch and you're an asshole for ever making me think I had a shot," Rachel says and apparently, I am holding the wrong person because Nikki lungs for her. She tackles her down and does a quick and hard punch to her nose. You can hear the crack of her nose breaking.

"What the fuck did you call him?" she yells, laying a punch on her eye now. I see blood running from her nose, and I am sure Rachel will also have a black eye tomorrow. "You can call me whatever you like but you will not insult any of my men! Bobbie!!"

She yells for her security and Bobbie shows up fast. Probably trying to make up for the mess up earlier. Nikki grabs Rachel by the hair and pulls her up and tosses her towards Bobbie. She falls and Bobbie grabs her arm to stop the fall.

"Get this cunt out of my club and don't worry about being gentle with her. Also, we are going to have a serious talk about who we let into my club. First you don't let the guys in and then you let this psycho bitch into my club just because she says she is with the team," Nikki warns him with a glare. Damn poor guy cannot catch a break to save his life. Bobbie leaves quickly with Rachel and I cannot help myself. I let go of Carter and rushed to Nikki to give her a hot kiss. Our tongues clashing. I am so lost in the kiss I forget we are in public till my teammates start to whistle at us. We pull apart gasping for air.

"That was hot," I told her with a groan. She giggles but I can still feel her shaking. Carter and Ivan join us, surrounding her. Carter grabs and cradles her face.

"Are you okay, Princess?" He asks her with such endearment.

"Yeah, I am. She did not even lay a scratch on me," she says with confidence leaning into his touch.

"I don't mean physically, Princess. You kicked her ass, but I am worried she caused doubt. I know I had a rep, but I never touched her," Carter tells her and Nikki just nods understandingly.

"Okay I trust you. I told you I love you and will not listen to her, but it does sound like there is a story there. If you could explain, it will calm my nerves," she says. Carter nods voraciously.

"Of course, Princess. You want to come to the penthouse tonight so we can talk more privately?" He asks, concerned.

"Yeah, Chloe is covering tonight so she can close up. Can we go now? I don't feel like celebrating anymore because I soured the mood," she asked and that could be further from the truth.

"We can go now but you did not sour the mood, Mia Cara. Rachel did that," I reassure her and grab her to lead her out of the club. Well, there goes my victory sex. Fucking thanks Carter!

Chapter 19

CARTER

Well, this night went to shit fast. I just wanted Dante to have a good night because he had such an amazing game. I feel like utter shit taking that away from him. He hasn't said he was angry, but I can tell by looking at him that he is mad. The drive to the penthouse was filled with tension. Dante's driver is zooming through the city. I opted to sit in front while Ivan, Dante and Nikki are in the back. I wanted to sit in the back, but I figured she would need space till I explained myself. I look in the rearview mirror and see Ivan holding her hand and Dante's arm wrapped around her shoulders. A pang of jealousy hits my chest. All I want to do is comfort her, hold her, and ease all the uncertainty that Rachel might have caused. The driver pulls into our private garage, and we get out. I go to Nikki and grab her hand. I am starting to think I need reassurance more than her. We make our way to our elevator and the ride up feels like the longest one ever. Nikki surprises me and cuddles into a hug with me. It takes a second for me to process what is happening but once I snap out of it, I wrap my arms around her. She pops her head up from my chest with a big smile.

"You looked like you needed that, Charming," she says softly into my chest as she buries herself further into it. The ache in my chest melts away and all I feel is the warmth of her hug. God, I love this woman so much.

"I love you so much, Princess," I tell her and mean it. I never thought I would meet someone that would make me want to settle down, but this girl flipped my world upside down. She looks up at me through her long lashes.

"I love you too, Charming. Just don't worry about what you're about to tell me. I want honesty no matter how bad it is. It won't change how much I love you," she says with all the love in the world. The doors finally open and I hook one arm around her knees to carry her to the couch. Tot bum rushes to her and hops on the couch with her when I put her down. Ivan and Dante are not far behind us.

"I am going to make tea. Would you like some, love?" Ivan asks her. I am not a tea person but if it helps calm my nerves I am down.

"I would love some! Do you have Chia? That is my favorite," She asks him and I can see that it relaxes her a little.

"I don't have chia. I'm sorry love. I will run out tomorrow and get some but for now I have English Breakfast and Lavender," he tells her apologetically. I get it, if we did not have to talk about this situation, I would run to the store right now to get it for her or at least get it delivered.

"Lavender will be lovely. Thank you!" She calls out to him from the couch as he makes his way to the kitchen. I guess let's get this over with.

"So where do you want to start?" I ask Nikki, nervously rubbing my hands up and down my knees. She is quick to notice and she moves closer and grabs both my hands. She moves them to her lap.

"Let's start with who is she?" She asks, biting her lower lip. I let out a deep sigh.

"She used to be a physical therapist slash trainer for the team," I tell her.

"Used to?" She asks, curiously.

"Yeah. She was the trainer for years and she always flirted with me. I just ignored it because she never crossed a line but that changed," I tell her with another deep sigh.

"What do you mean changed? She touched you?" She asks in shock. She starts shaking with anger. To be honest if she wasn't trying to comfort me, she would probably run out and hunt down Rachel for doing this.

"Nothing crazy. My back was sore, and the coach wanted me to get it checked out, so I went to see her. She asked me to take my shirt off so she could massage me which is normal but then her hands started to wonder. That is not what did me in though," I tell her and she starts to play with my hands because she can tell this is hard for me.

"What made you finally snap?" She asks softly.

"It was what she said. The day after we met you is when I finally reported her. I told her to act professional because I have a girl that I don't want to screw up with," I say to her, placing a kiss on her forehead. "But that is not what hurt me. She said I would get bored with you and come back to her. That will never happen, and I need you to believe that."

"Of course I believe you!" She yells almost offended.

"You do?" I asked with an arched brow. I don't mean that she shouldn't but if I was her, I would not trust me. I built up this reputation that is not pretty. She stands up and kneels in front of me and I just look down at my lap. She grabs my legs and squeezes, but I cannot look up. How can I? Here is this beautiful angel that loves me with her whole heart and she has to be dealing with all the baggage that comes with me.

"Baby, please look at me," she whispers but I can hear her elongate out the please like she is begging. I look up and I get lost in her beautiful green eyes. I lift my hand to cup her cheek and she leans into it which makes me relax a little. She is not turning away from my touch. "I believe you. I know we have not known each other for long but in that brief time you have shown me how much you have changed. We all have a past and I will not fault yours. It is about the man that you are now with me. Since our first date, you have been nothing but devoted to me. Some bitch coming in and spouting nonsense is not going to change that. I love you baby and thank you for telling me all this must have been hard."

I tackle her to the ground in a big hug. She just laughs even though I am sure that it probably hurt her. I pull back and place a hard kiss on her luscious lips. Then I pull back so I can sit us both up on the floor and cup her face.

"I love you so much! Thank you for listening to me and believing in me. I could not ask for a better partner," I tell her without hesitation. Ivan sets her tea on the coffee table, and I look up and Dante is waiting patiently so we can have our moment. Ivan finally chimes in.

"Not to ruin this moment but I have a question," Ivan asks with a seriousness about him. I sit up with Nikki on the floor and we both lean on the couch. Tot is happy because now Nikki's face is right next to him. He licks the side of her face. She could care less. She smiles at him and pets his head.

"What's up man?" I ask him.

"If I remember correctly, you told me she was blonde when you were complaining about her one time but she looks a lot like our Nikki," Ivan says still not asking a question. I roll my eyes.

"I thought you had a question," I said, annoyed.

"So, she changed her look based off of Nikki so you would fall for her but how did she know about little one?" Ivan asks and we are all stunned silent. You could hear a pin drop if Tot wasn't breathing so heavily.

"You think she is following me?" I asked out of fear. It is stupid for me to ask because I know the answer.

"Kind of redundant question but yeah," Dante says with a scoff. Nikki then head snaps up in recognition.

"Wait, did you say she was blonde? Did she happen to have blue eyes?" Nikki asks me and this makes me scared.

"Yes," I say slowly, nervous about what she is going to tell me next.

"Remember when I said I had interviews the other day?" She asks and we all nod but our faces go white. I feel like I am about to throw up. "Well one was late but a girl who looked similar to her but had blonde hair and blue eyes showed up asking for a job. She had a big ass attitude and she seemed off. She never gave me her name and if it was her, she looks so different now that I did not recognize her. I am not sure how she knew to come there but this is more serious if that is the case."

"So, what should I do?" I ask them because I really don't know what to do but if she already found Nikki something needs to be done for her safety. I have had some crazy fans, but I never had a stalker. This is new ground for me, but I need to do something because it is obvious that she is going to start coming after Nikki. I feel my whole body go cold and clammy. I look at the guys and they just nod like they know what I am thinking. She is going after Nikki. The woman made herself look exactly like her just to try to get my attention. I turn to Nikki again with a heavy sigh.

"Princess, I need to ask you to do something. It might be soon, but I need this," I tell her and she looks at me with curiosity. It is a need for this situation but I am not going to lie, I do want this too. She nods waiting for my request.

"Will you move in?" I ask her and her brows shoot up in surprise.

"WHAT?!?" She yells and hops up, so she is standing in front of us now. I get up and wrap my arm around her waist.

"Move in with us," Ivan adds with a shrug.

"But it's a little soon and why all of a sudden?" She asks and turns to me. It makes me swallow hard.

"I am not going to lie to you, Princess but I need you to not freak out when I explain," I tell her, grab her hands, and put them on my lap. She takes a deep breath to prepare for what I am about to tell her.

"Well, it looks like that bitch has been following me because she changed her whole look to look like you to get my attention. I am not saying it is coming to this, but she might be placing her anger towards you since you got me to finally settle down and not her. Her changing her look and showing up at the club is not a coincidence," I tell her and her face pales with dread. Fuck me! I hate myself for putting that look on her face. This is all my fault, but I need to protect her. Then I start to ramble on. "You can keep your apartment, but I want you to move in even if you are only comfortable as just thinking it is temporary. I don't want it to be temporary and I think the guys agree that you could move in permanently, but I don't want you to feel trapped either. I just want to feel safe. We don't know what Rachel is capable of. I also want to hire more security for your club for when you are working. I can cover that since this is all my fault, but I would feel better if you did."

"Carter!" She yells which stops my rambling. All three of us look at her in shock but then she continues, "Breath, baby."

I listen to her and take a deep breath. She wraps her arms around my neck and gives me a sweet peck on the lips. When she pulls away, she has a big smile which calms my nerves.

"I will do anything to make you all feel better about this situation. If that means I move in with you and beef up my security then let's get to it," she says, and it makes my heart flutter. "But what are we going to do about her? We can't just wait for her to show up again."

They all turn to me, but I am not sure where to start.

"I am going to be honest I never had a stalker, so I don't know where to start, Princess," I tell her rubbing my chin to think.

"Well first you need to go to the police station and report her," Ivan says and that makes me freeze. God the press is going to have a field day with this!

"I can go with you so you feel more comfortable plus in the report I will have to explain why I hit her," Nikki tells me with a devilish smirk. We all laugh.

"You did more than hit her, love," Ivan says with a smirk.

"Hell, yeah you did! You kicked her ass!" I yell with a laugh. I was right before, we will never really have to worry about her, but we still will.

"Remind me never to make you mad, Mia Amore," Dante says with a devilish smile.

"After talking with the police, do you want help with getting your stuff?" I ask, turning to Nikki.

"If you guys don't mind, or I can ask Ian for help," she says, twirling her hair again. I can't help but grab her hand to stop her. She should never be nervous to ask us for help and I will make sure she knows.

"Well since I am in my off season I can help. I have nothing going on, but I do need to make a stop somewhere on the way," Ivan says.

"Where are we stopping?" She asks with an arched brow. I have to admit even I am curious.

"That is for Daddy to know and for you to find out," Ivan says with a wink. Kinky Bastard.

"Fine," she says with a harrumph and turns back to me.

"I will grab the necessities tomorrow and slowly bring stuff with me when I work," she says but pauses. "If you change your mind, or I become too much, please tell me. I will respect your space and stay the night at my apartment."

We all looked at her in shock. She could never be too much. I mean shit, I missed her every time she would leave for work. I know that sounds crazy, but I do. Dante finally breaks the silence, "We won't but if it makes you feel better, we will agree."

Ivan and I nod in agreement.

"Okay so we are really doing this, this is crazy, but I am excited," she says honestly with a beaming smile. "Now the only thing to figure out is which one of your beds I want to sleep in."

She gets up with Tot and walks towards the kitchen leaving us stunned and looking at each other. Dante gets up in one swift move. He darts to the kitchen and picks her up over his shoulder, so her face is eye level with his ass.

"I call the first night! I won and scored a goal!" He calls back to us. Nikki starts swatting at his ass.

"Put me down big buffoon or at least carry me in a way so your ass is not in my face!" Nikki yells, still swatting.

"Ah, ah, ah, Mia Cara. I am the winner so what I do and say goes," he tells her with a loud laugh.

"I swear to god if you fucking fart in my face I will make my other two men kill you!" She yells but laughs. This has me and Ivan rolling on the ground in laughter. Ivan has never been really happy but seeing him like this makes me glad. We were friends but he was always isolated to protect himself. I could understand that. His parents upped and left him as a kid and never really had a family till Dante forced his family on him. We really found our missing piece with Nikki.

"I am a gentleman! I would never fart in your face but now that you were mean I am going to put something else in your face," Dante tells her with a growl. We watch as they make their way to Dante's room. Me and Ivan stay put though. Dante was right, he earned some one on one for the game he had tonight.

Dante

Fucking finally!! Enough with the heavy shit! I have been half hard all night in anticipation of being alone with Mia Cara. I was still on the adrenaline rush from winning and scoring a goal. Then watching Mia Amore fight was such a big turn on and now she was going to live with us. I would think I was high with the excitement from the night's events. I carry her to my bedroom and make sure the guys are not following before I kick the door shut. I finally flop Nikki to the bed. Fuck... she looks like a wet dream in her new jersey, but I need to feel her skin. I kneel in front of her while she sits on the edge of the bed. I slide both of her boots off and toss them to the side. Then I make quick work of her tight ass jeans. The jersey is a little long and covers what I am dying to see and taste. She bends down and kisses me frantically, our tongues clashing. I move my hands to her hips to find what I need to tear off. Lace? Silk? Nothing. I don't feel any panties on her hips. I pull back a little letting out a deep low growl.

"Congratulations on winning, Mio Amore," she whispers with a quiet giggle. She moves her hands, so they are wrapped around my neck.

"Is this my present for winning?" I ask her, my voice raspy with lust. Best fucking present ever!

"It was one of them," she says and I arch a brow at her. She lets out a heavy sigh. "I was going to also sneak you to my office as the other but then that bitch had to ruin it," she says with a little rage in her voice.

"It's okay, Mia Cara. I would much rather fuck you in my bed but first," I tell her and move so that I was laying on the bed with my head on my pillow. "I need you to sit on my face to make up for the lack of office sex. Ho bisogno di assaggiarti, Mia Amore."

She blushes and shakes her head while inching up, so she is straddling my waist.

"And why the hell not?" I asked pissed because I have been wanting this all fucking day. I swear to god if this more insecurities I am going to kill someone.

"I am too heavy for you. I am sure I would suffocate you," she says and is bashful by turning her head slightly. These fucking men she dated have been twats, I swear. Who wouldn't want to die that way? Death by pussy sounds like a dream to me.

"You not fucking to heavy, and I fucking swear if some man told you that I need a name," I tell her which has her turning around to look at me shocked.

"No one has told me that but why would you need a name?" She asks, still in shock.

"So, I can kill the man that ever made you feel less of yourself. You are the most gorgeous woman I have ever met, and you need to understand that," I tell her more like a warning. Before she could argue, I slide both arms under her thighs and in one swift move slide her up my body, so her pussy is right in my face. I could smell her arousal and it was intoxicating. I brush my nose on her clit taking in her delectable scent of sweet and tart strawberries. I don't know how she smells so good, but I could fucking care less. She moves up so she is hovering over me. I let out a sigh. I move my hands to her thighs and press down so she is forced to sit. I feel her full weight on my mouth and then get to work. I start eating her like I am a starved man, licking long strokes and sucking. I move to her clit and suck hard. She screams out in pleasure.

"Mio Amore!" She yells. I can feel her dripping on my face. It makes me groan. The vibration from my groan makes her even wetter. I let go over her thighs slightly.

"Will you cum for me like this? Be my good girl and cum," I tell her with a growl. She looks down at me in surprise and is blushing. Oh, she liked it. "Do you like being called a good girl?"

She is still in shock but nods. I can work with this. I press on her thighs again, so her full weight is on me again. I move so I can start thrusting my tongue into her. I thrust in and savor her taste. She is so close already. She slings the jersey off before I could protest. She also makes quick work taking her bra off. Her boobs bounce out once she wiggles out of it. I move my hands quickly up her body needing to feel the full weight of her breast in both my hands. I keep eating her as I massage her breast. Then I pluck on one nipple and that sends her over the edge. She screams out again as she hits her climax. I lick her through it trying to get every last drop of her. She finally sighs coming down off her high. She swings her thigh, so she is not straddling my face and flops on the bed next to me. She is trying to catch her breath.

"Oh my god! I think you broke me," she says and points to her legs that are still shaking from her massive orgasm. I laugh because I think she broke me too. I almost came in my pants from eating and touching her. "We need to do this every day!"

"Of course, Mia Cara. Whenever you like," I say with a soft laugh. I also feel a warmth of pride in my chest from her losing one of her insecurities. If this helps with them, I will demand to do this every day. She sighs and relaxes into my side. I nudged her a little, "We are not done yet, don't fall asleep on me just yet."

I get up from the bed and strip as fast as I can. She just sits there with a smile and enjoys the show. Her eyes go wide when I take off my boxers and suit pants in one foul swoop. I don't blame her, my dick is red from being so hard. She licks her lips wanting a taste, but I want to be inside her so bad. I go to my end table to grab a condom, but Nikki stops me by grabbing my arm and pulling me to the bed. I land on top of her and she spreads her legs, so I am nestled in between her. I can feel her heat radiating on my dick.

"I want to feel you, Mio Amore," she whispers, placing a kiss on my chest where my tattoo is. She wraps her legs around me and digs her heels into my lower back so I can't pull away from her. "I am on birth control, and I am clean."

Her words make me freeze. I have never gone bare, not once. Even if a girl asked me too I never did it because people always want to use us for being famous. I have even heard of puck bunnies trying to do this so that the guy has to stay with them because they get pregnant. Mia Cara would never do this though, but it is still a big step.

"Are you sure?" I ask her to make sure I understand.

"Yes! I want to feel you bare. If you are unsure, I understand," she says with a little disappointment. Well, that won't do. I slide right into her and she screams again. I bury myself deep but stop because I feel like I am about to cum right there. I pause and run through plays again, so I don't embarrass myself yet again.

"Running through plays again?" She asks with a knowing smirk.

"Maybe, I have never been bare and it feels so good to be connected to you in this way," I tell her with a groan as I finally grab control. I start to move in and out of her slowly gritting my teeth.

"More, Mio Amore," she moans out.

"More what, Mia Cara? Faster or harder?" I ask her, quickening my pace.

"Just more," she yelled out. Well, I have to give her what she wants even if it means it will be short. I dig my nails into her hips, and she moans from the prickle of pain. I start to go faster and harder. God I just want to live like this every day. Buried deep in Mia Cara sweet tight pussy.

"Ti amo," I tell her, driving into her. I am so close, and I feel that she is too. "Say it back, Mia Amore."

"Ti amo," she yells out and we both lose control. I feel her pussy clench down on my cock and that has me skyrocketing into her. I slow my movement as I fill her. Her whole body is shaking from her intense orgasm. Once I came down from this fantastic high of my girl I put a sweet kiss on her forehead.

"Voglio stare con te per sempre, Mia Amore," I whisper with my lips to her forehead still.

"Forever sounds good," she whispers back and that has me taken back. I lean back and look at her in shock. She just giggles. "I may have been taking Italian lessons on an app on my phone since I have met you and your mom was able to get my number somehow, so I call her when I am not sure about something."

Fanculo! I am going to marry this girl. I know in my heart I will and I know the guys feel the same way. I slowly pull out of her and I look down and see my cum dripping out of her. I become a possessed man because the next thing I know I am scooping up all our juices with two fingers and putting them back into her. I know she is on the pill and won't do anything but god I wish it could. Once I am satisfied with my work, I collapse next to her and pull her to my chest.

"You're not mad that I am talking to your mom behind your back, are you?" She asks nervously.

"Absolutely not! It only makes me love you more," I tell her, and she turns her head so she can look at me to confirm that I am not mad. I have the biggest smile, so she relaxes into me. I bare my head into her mess of red curls. I start to feel her trace my tattoo on my chest. My whole body straightens and tightens from her touch. I want her to know everything about me, even the sad moments. I pull away slightly to look at her in her beautiful green eyes. They are a stunning mossy green and they are peering up at me through her long lashes but still keeping her hand on my tattoo.

"Would you like to know why I got it?" I ask her with a hard swallow. I never really talked about my dad with anyone outside my family. Not even Ivan. He knows what happens, but he knows I don't like to talk about it.

"I would love to but if it is too hard, I understand," she whispers. This only wants to tell her more. I take a deep breath to calm my nerves. Back into the hard shit.

"I got this when my father passed away," I tell her with a heavy sigh.

"How did he pass?" She asks with an understanding look.

"He had a heart attack. I came home from school and I was the one who found him. Luckily my brothers were little shits and had detention that day so they were coming home late, but my mother left to run an errand before picking them up," I tell her with sadness, and I can feel a tear fall from my eye. I turn away from Nikki embarrassed. She quickly moves her hands to cup my face so she can turn me back to look at her. She wipes my tears away with her thumb.

"I am so sorry, Mio Amore. That must have been so hard for you to find him," she says and kisses my tattoo.

"It was but it was harder on mamma. The doctor said if he was rushed to the hospital, they might have been able to save him. I wish he would not have told us that because she blamed herself because of it," I tell Nikki and she looks so shocked, but I see tears coming from her eyes now. Her shock turns to anger.

"Why the fuck would the doctor do that to her? She must have been so devastated," she yells, looking pissed that the doctor had the audacity to do that.

"It's okay Mia Amore, he was just making sure he was doing his job and giving us all the information about his passing. She struggled so I had to stand up and take care of my family. I tried to make it work. I still did school and hockey but when I had free time, I would take an odd job here and there to help put food on the table. Ivan helped us a lot with watching my brothers or helping them with homework. I wasn't the brightest kid so it helped them a lot," I tell her, admitting my insecurity. She hugs me and snuggles into my chest.

"You are so smart Dante! You should never sell yourself short," she practically yells it into my chest. I can't help but let out a soft laugh. Here I am telling her not to be insecure and I have them myself.

"I know that now, Mia Amore but it took a long time for me to come to terms with it," I tell her.

"If I can't have insecurities, you can't either," she says with a giggle looking up at me.

"I know, Mia Amore," I whisper with embarrassment.

"How did your mamma get better because she seems so happy now," she asks me and I just give her a shrug.

"She just threw herself into two part time jobs and was trying to be the best mom she can be when she saw me trying to help. When I tried to give her money the first time she actually tried to throw the money at me," I tell her with a chuckle. "I found ways around it. Since all her money went to the bill I would come home with groceries. I would use the money I got from my jobs and buy food and sneak it into the fridge and cupboards. I knew she was too frugal to throw away perfectly decent food away."

"See smart boy," she says with a smirk. She lets out a cute yawn. She must be exhausted from all that happened tonight. I kiss the top of her head.

"That's enough for tonight. Time for bed, Mia Amore," I whisper into her forehead.

"Ti amo, Mio Amore," she whispers and my chest swells at her declaration. Her breath starts to even as she falls asleep.

"Anch'io ti amo," I whisper as we fall asleep with Mia Cara in my arms.

Chapter 20

CARTER

I feel so much lighter. I know I have a lot of shit to do today but my sweet little princess shocked me. I told her of my past but now it really is coming back to bite me in the ass. It doesn't matter though because Nikki is here and she is choosing to support me. I snuck into Dante's room once they were finally asleep. I let him have his little moment for winning but now that she is living with us there is not a single night, I am not going to be with her as long as I don't have an away game, even then though I want her to come, but I can't be selfish. Her life is here, the club, Ian, Dante, and Ivan so I can't ask her to come to every away game. Dante didn't even realize I was sleeping in here and Nikki somehow ended up sandwiched between us. She is facing Dante, and I am spooning her back.

I let out a hard sigh because we need to get the day started. We have a ton to do. Well might as well use this morning wood to wake her up. I nestle my dick right between her ass cheeks. I place my hand on her hips and kiss her neck. I can feel her start to wake up and Dante peeks one eye open and groans. I let out a soft laugh against Nikki's neck. She burrows further into the pillow.

"Mio Amore?" She asks Dante.

"Hmmm," He moans like it is a question.

"There is an annoying intruder," she groans and I pinch her hip. She lets out a squeak. Actually squeaks. Oh my god, this girl is so fucking cute!

"A sexy intruder," I tell them with confidence.

"Why the hell are you in my bed?" He asks annoyed and pulls Nikki from me. Oh, hell no! I pull her right back and then it becomes an all-out war. Both of us keep pulling her back and forth between us.

"Because you need to share! I let you have your moment, but you can't blame me for wanting to be with my Princess!" I yell at him pulling her to me. He just tugs her right back.

"I share just fine!" He yells. Nikki laughs but has enough with our foolish asses. She sits up away from both of us.

"Stop tugging me like I am your dicks!" She yells and that has us both falling over laughing. She plops right back in between us groaning. She buries her face in the pillow, and we sandwich her again. "What fucking time is it?"

"It is nine, Princess. Time to get up!" I tell her cheerfully. I am not normally a morning person but waking up to Nikki in the morning has made me the happiest man on earth. I feel like I drank an energy drink after waking up with her.

"Fuck you! I thought you were just as grumpy as me in the morning! Now I gotta deal with three morning people," she yells into the pillow and it has me laughing even harder.

"Well waking up with you makes my morning much better," I tell her, pulling her out of bed. "Plus, you said you wanted to come when I file the report so I wanted to make sure that was still the plan."

"Of course, I want to come but that does not make me a morning person, Charming," She tells me with a roll of her eyes. "I need clothes and coffee."

"Ivan put your clothes in the wash last night so you will just have to go out naked," I tell her with a smirk. She just laughs like that is never going to happen.

"Like hell I do," she says and then makes her way to Dante's closet and grabs one of his button up shirts. It is a soft white, so it is not really doing anything to cover her but as long as she is happy. I shrug. Dante gets up and is naked. I turn away quickly.

"Dude! Cover the fuck up!" I yell at him. I turn to look, and he slides on some gray sweats. He just shrugs.

"Nothing you haven't seen before," he says bluntly.

"Just because I have seen it does not mean I want to see it besides when we are with the Princess!" I yell and grab Nikki's hand and practically drag her to the kitchen. Ivan decided to make her breakfast and we opted for protein shakes. Tot is waiting next to Ivan hoping he will drop some food but once he sees Nikki he rushes to her for pets. Once she sees Ivan though she bum rushes him letting go of my hand. She jumps on his back wrapping her legs around his waist. He just laughs and turns his head to give her a kiss.

"There is my big guy. I missed you," she says with a sigh.

"I missed you too. Don't worry, little one, we will have a lot of time together grabbing your things," he tells her and she slides down and looks around at what he is making and laughs.

"You know you don't have to make breakfast for me every morning," she says blushing.

"I know but I want to, plus it sounded like you need the calories dealing with these two idiots," he says pointing at me and Dante as he walks in. Finally dressed. Thank god the only time I want to see my friends' dicks is when we are with Nikki.

"Hey dick wadd! I resent that!" Dante yells at him. Ivan ignores his comment and just hands him a protein shake then follows up by handing me one. I sit at the island's breakfast bar and Nikki comes around, Tot follows by her side and goes to sit next to me, but I grab her hand to stop her.

"You know that is not your seat, Princess," I tell her sternly. She blushes and slides into my lap and Tot sits right below us. "That is much better. A princess on her throne."

"So, what's for breakfast, big guy?" She asks Ivan and he places her plate in front of her and to be honest I am jealous. He made her BBQ shrimp and grits. She looks at him in shock.

"This looks absolutely delicious. This is one of my favorite dishes from New Orleans," she tells him, digging in excitedly.

"I know, little one," he says looking amused. Wait, am I missing something? She never told me this! Well now I am going to have to look up restaurants when we go to New Orleans this weekend. I look at her and she has a shrimp hanging from her mouth, jaw gaping. It makes us all laugh.

"How do you know that?" She asks once she regains her composure. Ivan stops laughing and just shrugs.

"I text your dad all the time. He had some questions about my charity, so we swapped numbers the other night and I don't really know how to say this, but we are becoming best friends. Plus, I gave him the rundown about last night in case for some reason it gets leaked to the press. He knows the situation and knows you are safe with us," Ivan says, downing his shake. Damn he is going to give me such a tough time for being my fault. I look to see her reaction and she just smiles.

"I love that! It's no problem but do you really think this will be in the press?" She asks him, biting her lip nervously. She must have replaced that with twirling her hair. I hate that she is so scared of this. She is not scared of what they will say about her but of us. She is the most selfless person I know.

"Little one, I am not going to sugar coat this. Yes, that is a possibility and I know you said you are okay with going public but we can hold off if you have any hesitation about this," Ivan tells her and grabs her hand across the island. I wrap my arms around her waist as she thinks for a second on his word. I feel like this is a huge setback in her accepting herself. She finally started to feel confident about herself admitting going public but with all the events in the last twenty- four hours I can understand if she does. She finally takes a deep breath and relaxes into me.

"I am not worried about me. I am worried about you all. I should not have punched that bitch last night because if it gets to the press, it will affect you guys in a negative way but I don't think I would change what I did," she says and then let's go of Ivan's hand and turns to me. She turned awkwardly trying to straddle me to look me in the eyes. Once she is finally comfortable, she cradles my face between her hands. "She was just saying such awful things about you and I could not stand there and let her do that. I protect what is mine and you guys are mine."

"I just want you to be comfortable with this princess. Did I think it was hot as hell that you stood up for me? Yes, but you don't need to do that. I know that I have a past that does not paint me in the best light and I need to deal with that, not you," I tell her, barring my face in her red curls that are cascading down her neck. Her scent is always comforting when dealing with things. Like a sweet strawberry shortcake. She pulls my face up and I just get lost in her eyes. I try to count how many different greens I see. After a moment she let out a deep breath, pulling me out of the trance I was in.

"I still don't care about being public. I just don't want it just on you all. If you guys are ready then I am ready," she says with confidence. There is my confident sexy girl. She lets go of my face and Dante and Ivan come beside her and grab both her hands.

"We don't care about the press, Mia Cara," Dante says with an empathetic look. Ivan adds, "We only have ever cared what you think."

"Okay so how do we go public?" She asks with a smile. I can't help but give her a beaming smile. She has made me the happiest man on the planet.

"We will contact our PR people and managers so they can figure out the best way. You won't have to do a thing," I tell her and all three of us pull out our phones and text our managers and PR people.

Carter: I have something important for you to do. Me, Ivan, and Dante have moved forward in an unconventional relationship. We all love one girl, and she loves us. We don't want to hide it anymore so I need you to figure out how to release this, so it paints us in a better light.

Cindy (Manager): The press is going to have a field day with this.

Carter: Don't care. See that it's done.

Cindy (Manager): *Sigh* Okay stop by my office and we will figure this out.

I know this is a lot to ask her, but this is her job. I will make sure to make her Christmas bonus is nice and fat for dealing with it. Once we are done, we turn our attention back to her.

"It's done, little one," Ivan tells her and her eyes go wide.

"What? Already?" She asks, confused.

"Well, we just texted our people and they will work on the story for this. We will have to meet with them, but I am sure once we meet and explain the situation they will figure out the game plan and have it out by tomorrow. No more hiding, princess," I tell her. She turns around and goes right back to her breakfast but before she could get in her mouth, I steal her spoon and take a bite of shrimp and grits and moan as I eat it. I turn to Ivan, "This is good as fuck."

"Hey! That's my food!" Nikki yells at me and swats at my chest.

"Sharing is caring," I tell her with a shit-eating grin. She just scoffs and turns back to her food. "Also, instead of us going to the police I have someone coming here so we can keep last night on the down low, but make no mistake princess we are going public, but I don't think it would be good if they get a shot of us at the police station."

"When will they be here?" She asked, still eating.

"They should be here in fifteen minutes and then I have a private investigator and security coming so I can get more information on what Rachel has been up to and get security for you when we are not around, but I think I will still have them around when we are just to be safe," I tell her. She drops her spoon into her bowl and pops off my lap when she realizes the time.

"Fuck! Give a girl a warning! I only have a few minutes to get dressed!" She says running to the laundry room to look for her clothes and Tot follows her. She is starting to become his favorite person. The intercom by the door goes off. I go to it and hear our front door man Zach come over it. The guys go to get ready to leave to talk to their managers.

"Sir we have a police officer named Bill Olson that says he was expected. Should I let him through?" Zach asks.

"Yes, and I also have a private investigator and a security team coming today so you can let them through as well," I tell him and he hesitates before asking, "Is everything okay sir?"

Zach has been our door man for years and normally does not ask a lot of questions, but I am sure having all these people come in is concerning.

"It will be, but I will stop by with a picture of someone. If she ever comes you are to notify me and then call the police," I tell him. I make a mental note to ask the investigator to get an old and new photo of her just in case she changes her look again.

"Of course, sir. I will be sure to be on the lookout," he says and then there is a knock on the door. I opened it and let Officer Bill in.

"Good morning, Sir," he says with a raspy southern accent. He's an older gentleman. He has white hair that is in a military haircut. He is not fit at all with the beer belly to go with it.

"Good morning. I am sorry to have you come, but with the press I would rather be safe," I tell him and lead him to the living room. His expression softens.

"I completely understand. I am not going to lie I am a fan, so I volunteered to come so there won't be any issues for you," he tells me. I motion him to sit on the couch and we sit there for a moment. I don't want to start without Nik. Nikki and the guys walk in, and they both give her a sweet peck on her lips since Officer Bill is here and hug her goodbye. They leave and Nikki makes her way to us.

"Hello ma'am," Officer Bill goes to shake her hand and she obliges but grimaces at the fact that he called her ma'am. It had me letting out a soft laugh.

"Hello and please call me Nikki. Would you like tea, coffee, or water before we start?" She asks him.

"Tea would be lovely and sorry about the ma'am. Stuck in my southern ways I guess," he says apologetic. She just nods and heads to the kitchen to make some tea.

"So did the station tell you, our situation?" I ask, turning to him to give him my undivided attention.

"They gave me a little but not much. It sounds like you are getting followed by someone but that is really it," he tells me. Shit, I got to go through this whole thing again. Nikki walks in and hands him his tea and sits on the couch next to me and Tot could care less and hops right up next to her and puts his head in her lap.

"Well from what I have it looks to be more serious than that," I tell him, and he nods telling me to continue. Nikki stops petting Tot and grabs my hand for reassurance. "There was a trainer that worked for the team. She would try to flirt but I would always tell her to stop and it was a never-ending cycle of it. Then I met Nikki, so I told her not to flirt or to get handsy. I just told her I want to be respected and that I am with someone, so she needs to keep it professional. I know being a trainer she has to touch me, but her hands would get too close to areas that were not the issue. I got out right away and reported her to my coach and since they did not want one of their players to get sexually harassed, they fired her immediately."

I take a deep breath and Officer Billy looks at me in shock but then shakes his head and returns his facial expression to seriousness.

"So, I am assuming that is not all since I am here," he says.

"No, it's not. We went to Nikki's jazz club after my friend's hockey game. We were spending time together and then Rachel showed up. She changed her whole look to look like Nikki thinking I would leave Nikki to be with her. It was odd so we are thinking she is stalking me. She has never seen Nikki and we were careful because we were enjoying not being followed by the press. It was just very concerning that she showed up at her club and looked like her," I tell him, and he nods.

"Well, we can definitely file a report and get a restraining order started for you but I have to warn, if she is stalking you she is probably smart and is hidden till she makes her next move. Is there anything else from last night?" He asks, waiting for me to continue but Nikki chimes in.

"We may have one problem," she says and leans forward on the couch not letting go of my hand.

"Okay what is the issue?" He asks her curiously.

"She kept grabbing him and he was trying not to hurt her, so he just kept telling her to get away. I snapped and I am not happy to tell you I hit her," she says defeated. Officer Bill just looks at her for a second but then smiles.

"Don't worry about that. We can mark that as self-defense, if necessary, even if she tries to get you for assault it will not stick. I would still get a lawyer to be sure you are ready if she goes that route but I promise nothing will come of it and it is nice to see a strong female defend her man so he does not have to deal with hurting her," he says with a small smirk. Let's just add a lawyer to my never-ending list of things I need to do for this. This is seriously becoming a pain in the ass but if Nikki needs it, I will make it happen. I glance over at her, and she looks at him in shock.

"Really? That is not a problem? I thought it would cause issues with the report and restraining order," she tells him, biting her bottom lip.

"No, we can make sure you are involved as little as possible. You were just using self-defense, so Carter did not have to with a woman. Even if he did, we could still file the report and not take him in but I am glad it was you," he says and grabs the backpack he brought in. He pulls some papers out and hands them to me. "I need you to fill these out and I will take them down to the station. If I file today, which I will, I should have a restraining order for you by the end of the day."

I grab the paperwork and fill out the report for him. The sooner I get this done the sooner I can keep this woman at bay. When I am finally done, I hear another knock at the door. I nod to Nikki while Officer Bill looks over the paperwork. Nikki opens the door, and my private investigator walks in followed by three guys who I assume are a part of the private security team. Officer Bill gives me a nod.

"Well, that is all I needed from you. Looks like you got a lot on your plate so I will get out of your hair and get this ball rolling," he says and gets up. He shakes Nikki's hand goodbye and goes out the door. The

Lexi Haynes

investigator comes to me on the couch. Tot has been a good boy just staying by Nikki. People would just say he is a dumb dog just following his favorite person, but I know better. He is the smartest dog I know. He knows he needs to stay by her to protect her. I am half tempted to tell Dante to let Nikki take him to work.

"You must be Mr. Quinn. I am inspector Paul. I am starting to look into what we discussed on the phone but would like more information before moving forward so I know what to look for," he tells me sitting down on the couch. He is a small older gentleman, he has messy short brown hair with a scruffy beard. I fill him in on what happened and Nikki leaves the security in the kitchen with some leftover breakfast and coffee. They seem content enough. I keep going and Nikki is there with me.

"So, with this information, what would you like me to do?" He asks, wanting to know exactly why I hired him.

"I just need to know what she has been up to, so I know what we are dealing with. It is obvious that she is tailing me at least. I need to know what she knows basically," I tell him with a shrug. "Also, since she changed her look, if you could possibly get an old picture and new picture to give to my doorman and security that will be greatly appreciated."

"Yeah, it should not be hard to do that. Okay let me get to work. I can work from here if you like so the second, I find stuff I can update you immediately, but that is up to you," he tells me. We normally don't like people in the penthouse but if it gets the information faster, I am sure the guys will be all for it.

"I have an office upstairs, second door on the right. Nikki, if you don't mind showing the investigator where he can work and then come right back down so we can get your security squared away," I tell her and she nods. She rushes him upstairs while I go to the security in the kitchen. I shoot the guys a text to let them know how everything is going.

Carter: Hey, I just want to keep you guys in the loop. So I finished talking to the Police and they are filing the report also they are filing a restraining order so hopefully that helps. Also the private investigator is here and he is going to work in our office so he can get the info to us as fast as he can. I am now getting with the security team so we can coordinate with Nikki so she is safe.

Ivan: Good deal! Anything they need I should be home soon. Our managers coordinated and the article will be released tonight so Nikki needs top notch security. If you think these guys suck call another one. I don't care about the price because she is about to get a lot of attention.

I just roll my eyes because this is the most top-rated security I could get, so if they can't protect her no one can. A lot of them are ex-military or secret service. These guys can protect our princess. I laugh in my head because I think I should call them her knights since I am her prince charming.

Carter: This security team is the best in the country. It will be handled.

Dante: THEY BETTER BE! Make sure they know they are dealing with precious cargo!

God he is more protective than I am I swear. He's a fucking idiot.

Carter: So shouty! Calm down I will make sure they know and will let you all know how it goes when I am done.

Nikki finally makes her way down with Tot too far behind her. He eyes up security, but I guess since Nik is not freaking out about them he deems them not a threat. Yep, she is taking him wherever she goes. She comes into the kitchen by my side and holds my hand.

"Sorry to keep you waiting. Did I miss anything?" She asks me and the three buff dudes in the kitchen.

"No, princess. I was waiting till you got here since this is for you," I tell her, placing a sweet kiss on her forehead. The guys finally turn to us.

"Hello Mr. Quinn. We heard that you are in need of security," He says with a British accent. Now that I think about it, they all sounded British. How odd. All three men are tall and buff. One has long black hair in a man bun, the other has short brown hair on the sides with some length at the top and the other is a grumpy looking guy, short brown hair, and full beard. All three of them are covered in tattoos. I nod but then pull Nikki towards them.

"It's actually for her. I have plenty but it looks like I have a stalker problem and they are fixating on her, so I want the best protection for her," I tell them as a warning for Dante. Nikki just slaps my chest.

"Ignore him. The guys can be very protective of me like annoying little shits," she tells them with a giggle. "My name is Nikki and it's a pleasure to meet you."

She sticks out her hand and shakes the one with the man bun. He shakes it and she blushes. Yeah, this was a bad idea. Why couldn't the company send us ugly guys? I grab her and bring her close to me and they all nod knowing what I am doing.

"I am Cyrus, and these are my partners, Alexander and Clyde," the one with the man bun tells us, pointing at the men when saying their names.

"Nice to meet you. I heard amazing things about your agency," I tell them with a smile.

"That is kind of you sir, but we put in a lot of work for important people. So, you can rest assured that Nikki is safe with us," Alexander says.

"Well, we will need more information on what you want us to do. If it is a stalker, we do suggest twenty-four-hour security. We can take turns and then when you have to go out to work we will go in pairs just to be on the safe side," Clyde says to Nikki.

"Round the clock protection? Are you serious?" She exclaims in shock. I am shocked too but if this is what they are suggesting so be it.

"I'm sorry ma'am but it is that serious. Sadly, since the stalker has fixated on you it is most likely she will come after you and not Mr. Quinn. Once they are fixated on their target they develop anger towards that person. Once the investigator gets more information for us, we will be able to confirm that," he tells her with a frown.

"I have a private investigator upstairs that is finding more information on the person in question we can go from there," I tell them, wrapping an arm around Nikki. She is probably so scared and this is all my fault. I should have dealt with Rachel sooner and maybe then this would have been dealt with before meeting Nikki and she would have fixated on me.

"Okay so for today I think our plan should be I will stay here and then Alexander will check the security at the club and Clyde will work on your apartment. Most likely we will set up security cameras and alarms, you know the works," Cyrus says and then I clear my throat getting his attention.

"Nikki does intend to go out today. She is actually moving in with us and is going to the apartment with one of my friends that lives here who is also her boyfriend," I tell them and they all smile. I expect them to be shocked by saying she has more than one boyfriend, but they all give me and Nik an understanding look.

"Sounds good! We actually all share the same wife, so you won't get any judgment from us. When you go, we will all go with you so that way I can protect you and they can check out the club and your apartment," Alexander says with a smile. Me and Nikki's jaws drop in shock. Then she shakes her head, regaining her composure.

"Wait, you all share the same wife? Sorry if that is too personal but this is new to us, so I am just curious," she says to them. I can see her eyes wide with curiosity. They don't look upset or angry at her question but instead look amused.

"Aye we do. It is unorthodox but we all love her and instead of acting like children fighting over her we all decided to come together as a family.

Trust me some days I want to kill these blokes but then there are the moments when we are all together that it feels like a family. Those are the best moments," Clyde sighs dreamily like those are the moments he wants to relive every second of the day.

"Please tell me if any of my questions are out of line but can you be legally married to more than one person?" I ask them. I am not going to get down on one knee right now but I sure as fuck want to. The only thing stopping me is that I know Nikki will want all of us, so it is a conversation to have with the guys.

"I am not sure about the US but in the UK technically no, but we still had a wedding with our girl and exchanged vows. We see it as we are married in our eyes. We all have rings and call each other husband and wife. We even have kids, a boy, and a girl with another on the way. We decided that we all wanted one kid and our wife agreed saying she would not let a single one of us feel left out but they all call us dad and know that they have one mom. Kids are smart like that," Cyrus says. Nikki nods with excitement. I never thought that far with our situation, but I like that these guys are putting Nikki at ease with the situation we have. That we could be a family, get married in our own way and that one day we could even have kids.

The guys finally are back. They walk in to see a happy, excited Nikki and look with worry. I get it this is not a situation she should be happy about. I just nod at them with a smile to let them know everything is okay. They rush her and both hug her at the same time.

"Did you miss us, Mia Cara?" Dante says to her, kissing her forehead.

"Of course, Mio Amor! I miss you all any second we are apart," she tells him and Ivan with a big smile like she can't wait to tell them about her security.

"Are you ready to go, little one?" Ivan asks her.

"Yes, the security guys are going to come with us. One is going to stay with us and the other two are going to check the security at the club and my apartment while we are there," she tells him with a nod. "Oh, let me grab some shoes."

She walks off with Tot following after her. Ivan and Dante make it to the kitchen and introduce themselves. The security guys excuse themselves so they can talk to the investigator before they go. When they finally leave Dante and Ivan look at me with curiosity.

"Not that I am mad or upset about it but why did Nikki look so happy when we walked in? I would not expect that with a stalker on the loose and after her," Ivan says, and I shrug.

"We were getting to know the security guys and it looks like I hired the right guys for the job," I tell them with a smirk.

"Care to elaborate on that?" Dante asks and I shrug again.

"The three guys you just met have the same relationship that we have. They all share a wife," I tell them and they look at me in shock, jaws slacked.

"They share a wife?" Dante asks, confused.

"Yeah, all three of them have the same wife. They have a family and kids. I think it eased Nikki about going public knowing other people have a similar relationship and are making it work," I tell them and their shocked faces relax at the idea of being able to have everything.

"I was just enjoying being with her. I never really thought about our future, but it is great that Nikki now has people she can ask questions to see what can be offered in the future," Dante says happily. Now we are all thinking about it. We can marry her together, have kids one day. We have a future with this gorgeous woman, and it looks like a beautiful future. Nikki walks in with her shoes in hand.

"Ready to go, big guy?" She asks sweetly and we all just look at her with big smiles on our faces. We are looking at our future.

Chapter 21

IVAN

I thought Carter was going to blow it with the security agency but this is great. Not that it would have been his fault, but I just have trust issues when it comes to the people I care about. My own parents left me when I was young so letting strangers come in and protect Nikki did not sound like a great idea to me, but now that I know that she trusts them, I think I can trust them with her. Luckily though it is my off season so I don't have a tight schedule and can be with her all the time just to be sure. I still have odd practices and training here or there, but I will reschedule them till we get this stalker situation under control. I have already told my managers and PR that I will not be reachable the next couple weeks and explained the situation. They were understanding and told me to take all the time I need, but when training camp starts, they need my full and undivided attention. I told them that should not be an issue. That is months away and we want to deal with this quickly. Nikki walks up to me with a big smile. Oh, shit I lost my train of thought. She asked me a question and I was so lost in thought I do not even remember the question.

"What was that, little one?" I ask her. She looks amused.

"I asked if you were ready to go big guy?" She asks again with a big smile. She makes her way in front of me and slips on her combat boots.

"I am just waiting on security to come back down and then we can go," I tell her, giving her a big hug when she pops back up from putting on her boots. We finally saw a future to what we are doing and that makes me so happy and by the look on her face she is happy too. I release her from my big bear hug and then Dante grabs her to kiss her forehead again.

"What is all this for?" She asks with a giggle.

"We just like loving on you, Mia Amore," Dante tells her, but we are all beaming so she can tell something is up. She looks at us with an arched brow. I sigh because this woman knows us so well, she can tell something is up.

"We are just happy with your new security is all," Carter says with a shrug.

"So, it wouldn't have to be about how they are in the same type of situation as us and you're happy that there can be a true future for us?" She asks with a smirk. Yep, this little one is too smart for her own good.

"Maybe, it does help," I tell her honestly. No use in hiding it since she can see right through us. "We were just so focused on making you happy that we did not really think about our future and what it could entail for us but now we can, and we are all in. We know this relationship has been moving fast under this situation, but it would have led to that eventually and I am ecstatic that now you have someone to talk to about it to see what we can be in the future."

"What if I told you I am okay with the pace we are at?" She asks with a smirk and before we can ask her any questions, the security guys walk in.

"Okay we are ready to go when you are. I will ride with you guys while Alexander and Clyde will follow," Cyrus tells us. It is going to be awkward having these guys with us but I want our girl safe so I can deal with it.

"I do have one stop we need to make before we go to her place. Is that a problem?' I ask them because they probably want to keep a tight shift with everything going on.

"It shouldn't be but when it comes to Nikki's safety, in the future clear it with us beforehand so we can check it out and make sure she will be safe," Clyde says with a small smile.

"Sorry, that was my fault. It's a surprise for her but in the future, I will make sure to let you guys know to make your guys job easier," I tell them. At least they are taking their job seriously.

"It's no problem! Let's get going," Clyde tells us and leads the way to the door so he can go first and then the other two are behind us. Nikki looks at me with a smile and steps on her tiptoes so she can whisper in my ear.

"Come on, daddy. I cannot wait to see what you have in store," she whispers to me, so the security doesn't hear but not quite enough. The security guys don't look at us but smile when they hear her calling me daddy. I lean back down to her ear.

"Behave, little one," I warn her and plant a kiss on her temple. We make it to the garage and I grab the keys to my Jeep Wrangler. I hold open the door for Nikki and she slides in. I round the hood and put my seat up so Cyrus can sit in the back. He gets in and I push my seat back up right so I can slide into the driver's seat. I turn on the engine and check to make sure the other guys are ready.

"Okay so you can go but make sure you don't go too fast, so we stay in their line of sight when driving," Cyrus says to make sure they are there if anything happens. I take off for the city. I grab Nikki's hand while we are driving. I zoom through the city making my way to the church. The drive is pretty quiet with awkwardness but then Nikki finally had enough of it.

"Hey Cyrus, do you mind if I ask some questions about your relationship?" She asks, twirling a loose curl from her bun.

"Yeah, that is no problem. I can understand now that you are in a similar relationship," he tells her, letting out a chuckle. I don't think he is laughing at her though. His chuckle is because of her curiosity.

"Please tell me if any of my questions are inappropriate or you don't want to answer. So, what made you guys decide to have that kind of relationship?" She asks, still nervous. I squeeze her hand that I am holding to let her know that I am here for her. Her body relaxes a little but still a little tense.

"Well, that is a loaded question but me and my guys were in the military. We were a small special ops team. There were never really any girls, especially in the military at that time. We were extremely lonely. We came to an agreement that if one of us had the chance to bring a girl back to the tent we could and the other two would just maintain our distance but would still stay in the tent. Well that got our minds thinking about sharing a girl. We finally talked about it and offered it to Alexander's girl at the time. She said she was down and then we just kept doing it," he says with another chuckle.

"So how did you meet your wife? When you were in the military?" I asked because now I can't hold back my curiosity. Nikki looks at me with a small smile, happy that I am just as interested.

"Actually, no. We met her on a protection job. She is an actress in LA and we got assigned to come to America and protect her from some crazy fans that were giving her a hard time. All three of us fell in love with her. She played a spoiled bitch in the public eye but protecting her we figured out she was not like that at all. She is actually really sweet and nice when you get to know her. We all slept with her and then decided when the job was done, we did not want to leave her so we upped and moved to America for her so we could continue seeing her," he tells us with a sigh with a soft smile. He must miss his wife when he gets a job and has to leave her because I look in the rearview mirror and he looks so content with the memory of meeting his wife. I probably make the same look when I think about how we met Nik.

"So, your wife is in the public eye and deals with the press?" She asks, shocked because the similarities of our relationship are uncanny.

"Yes, the pops are awful to her saying it is wrong that we have kids that have three fathers, but I think it is great. She has a whole support system for our kids and they even brag at school about how they have three dads. It is pretty funny when kids try to pick on them for it because our children are like little adults and don't pick a fight, they just explain how much love they get having more than just a mom and dad. If you want, when we are not too busy, I can call her and ask if she is okay with me giving you her number. You can video chat or text so you can ask her questions. Actually, she has been wanting a friend that is in a similar relationship so she can have a girlfriend that understands. She has friends but they are in normal monogamous relationships so don't understand the struggles of being in this type of relationship," he tells Nikki and her eyes light up. She rushes to give him her number and I can't be any happier than I am right now. Now she has someone that understands our relationship and can even help her deal with pops and what she needs to do to deal with it. I pull up to the church and Nikki looks at me with an arched brow. I just let out a soft laugh.

"I wanted for you to see where I grew up, little one," I tell her, pulling into the church parking lot. I shut off the engine and climb out and let Cyrus out. Before I could open Nikki's door, she pops out excitedly. She runs over to me and grabs my hand ready to see my past. I lead her into the church with security right behind us. We walk into the church, and they must be using the money I donate because I see they have done some remodeling. It is a big church with a big stained-glass window with scenes from the bible. It lets in rays of rainbow of colors. There are rows of pews with red velvet upholstery. There is a big altar in the front. As we walk down the aisle there are three Nuns in the front. They finally look up and smile once they see me. Me and Nikki finally make it to them, and they look at her inquisitive but then turn back to me with a smile.

"Hello. It's nice to see you Ivan," Sister Christina says with a big smile.

"I just came to give my donation and show Nikki where I grew up," I tell them and they all look at her.

"It is nice to meet you. Ivan has never brought a girl here. Are you his girlfriend?" Sister Mary asks. She was always the rambunctious one out of the nuns. Nikki just gives her a small smile.

"I am. It is nice to meet you sisters," she says, offering her hand but Sister Mary just grabs her hand and pulls her into a hug.

"Sorry I am a hugger," Sister Mary says with an apologetic look. Nikki just nods her head and sister Mary releases her.

"Me too. Don't apologize!" Nikki says with worry.

"Well let's show you around," Sister Christina says to Nikki. They take us to the orphanage part of the church. The nuns show me and Nikki around with our security detail right behind us the whole way. The nuns introduce us to the kids. I signed some of their notebooks and took a few pictures. We make our way to the playground they have in the back for the kids, but they are doing their studies right now so not a kid in sight. Me and Nikki sit on a bench.

"So, this is where I grew up, little one," I tell her with worry. I have never brought anyone here. Sure, I met Dante here during Sunday Mass but I never brought anyone here that I truly care about.

"It's beautiful, Ivan. I can feel the love that the nuns give to the children," she says softly, holding my hand.

"I know I had a rough childhood, but the nuns really helped to show me all the love I didn't deserve," I tell her honestly.

"Ivan, what makes you think you did not deserve it?" She asks, almost annoyed.

"Come on, Nikki. Not even my parents loved me enough to keep me," I tell her with a sigh.

"Ivan, just because they let you go does not mean they do not love you. They loved you so much they did not want you to grow up in the situation they were in. They might have been broke and not in a good situation to raise a child, so they sent you here so you can grow up with other children and the nuns. They knew you would be well cared for here," she says and hugs me.

I am trying to wrap my head around her words. I never thought of it that way. I thought my parents were just dead beats that did not want a kid, but she is right. If they did not care about me, they would just call social services and I would be in the system. They cared enough to take me here where you can feel the love of the nuns as soon as you walk in. Nikki leans back so she can look at me.

"I know you think you are a lost soul, but I am glad that your parents left you here. You are not lost anymore. If you were not here we might not have met. You might have been lost when I found you, but you are not lost anymore," she says and I get lost in her beautiful green eyes. I understand what she is saying. I found myself through her. I might have been a lost boy when I met her, but I found my home in her and the guys.

"You are my home, little one," I tell her softly and then kiss her. I put all my passion into the kiss. All the love I have for her. It is not a kiss that you should have in or by a church, but I could care less. This is the woman I love and I will kiss her when I want and how I want. She pulls back and cups my face.

"We have an audience," she whispers looking past me. I turn to look and we have our three security guards and then three nuns blushing like crazy at what they witness. I just let out a soft laugh. I turn back to her and give a peck on her cheek.

"We will finish this later," I promised her.

"Promises, promises, daddy," she whispers back with a giggle. I love that sound and I am instantly hard.

"We need to go before I ravish you right here, little one," I tell her getting off the bench and pulling her with me. I lead her toward her bodyguards and nuns. I pull out my check and hand it to Sister Mary. She shakes her head.

"Now don't be stubborn. You know if you don't take it, I will just go give it to Father Macky," I tell her sternly. She just sighs in defeat and takes it.

"One of these days I am going to tear up your checks. We raised you because it was God's work. We didn't do it for your money," she says defeated.

"I know that is why I do it," I tell her with a smile. "We are on our way out. You sisters have a wonderful day."

Nikki lets go of my hand and pulls Sister Mary into a hug. She whispers a thank you to her and lets her go. We make our way out of the church to my Jeep. I open her door and buckle her seat belt. She laughs when I do but I look at her and her laughter dies.

"Why did you say thank you to Sister Mary?" I ask her with a stern look. Nikki just smiles.

"I was telling her thank you for taking care of you," she says in a soft tone. This woman is something else. I go to let Cyrus in the back and slide in to make it to Nikki's club. The ride is silent again because I am lost in my thoughts. How did I get so lucky? I found this goddess and she is so perfect for us three. I don't know what I would do if I lost her. She is my home.

We made it to her place. The security guys say they are going to check out the club's security first so me and Nikki can pack. Nikki takes the guys to the club and Donnie is already there. Nikki tells them that Donnie will show them around and we make our way to her apartment.

"So, what would you like to pack, love?" I ask her. She makes her way to her closet to grab some bags.

"I think at first I just want to pack the necessities and throughout the week I will grab some boxes and slowly bring stuff to our home," she says and then looks down at her feet, blushing.

"Our home? I think I like the sound of that, little one," I tell her with a smirk. I cross the room and gather her in my arms. I grow instantly hard with the sight of her. Her pulse quickens. I can see it at the base of her neck. Her flushed cheeks and chest. I go to kiss but then there is a knock on the door. I bury my face into the crook of her neck and groan. She just giggles.

"You think this is funny, little one?" I ask her with an arched brow. Her giggle turns into a full laugh.

"A little," she admits. I just bury my face further into her neck and kiss it softly. She gasps in response. Then there is a knock again. I groan again and go to her door. This better be important! I open the door to find Alexander there.

"Sorry to interrupt but I need to check out the apartment so we can get a good security system for Nikki," he says with a soft laugh, like he knew what he was walking into. I pull the door open to let him in and he walks through the apartment to check it out. I sigh and turn back to Nikki, and she has a goofy grin on her face. She walks up to me and wraps her arms around my neck and my hands instinctively go to her hips.

"Don't worry big guy. Now that we are living together, we have plenty of opportunities to ravish each other later," she tells me and gives me a quick peck on the lips. I just sigh.

"Okay let's get you packed so we can get you to our home and I can have my way with you," I tell her, picking up the bags she had. I make my way to her bedroom, and we get to it. We get her all set with clothes and then go to the living room.

"Want to bring any books with you?" I ask her and she shrugs. "Do you not want to?"

"It's not that. I am just not sure where I am putting all my stuff as is. I don't know where I would put them," she says with an insecure tone. She puts her bags down and looks at her feet. I go to her and wrap her up in my arms but put one hand on her chin so I can make her look at me.

"You can scatter your clothes between our three bedrooms, so you have clothes wherever you sleep and as for your books, what if I told you I have a secret door in my room that leads to a private library?" I ask her and her eyes go wide. I don't tell a lot of people about it because it is my safe space. The guys know I have a secret room, but they don't know what I use it for. They just know it is there and I had construction done on it. I like my solitude and they know that so they know not to ask too many questions, but I wouldn't mind Nikki using it.

"Are you serious? You have a secret dungeon?" She asks with complete shock. It just makes me let out a soft laugh.

"Not a dungeon, love. It is a secret library where I can read and listen to my music. It is one of my favorite places in the house to just relax," I tell her. Then I see something flash in her eyes. I am not sure what it is, but I can bet it is her insecurities again.

"I don't want to intrude in your space," she says as a whisper.

"I am only going to say this once, so you better listen good, little one," I tell her and her eyes widen, which confirms I have her attention. "I would not invite you into my space if I did not want you there. One of the things I love about you is that we could just sit in silence and enjoy an informative book. So I would love it if you would use my library. I could just see you locking yourself in it and I come in from a game and find you all cozy on the couch that is in it with a comfy sweater. So please use it."

I tell her and the last part does not come out as a question. It is an order. I know my little one loves to be bossed around by me. Her face softens a little.

"Okay, yeah, let's grab some books for me to take," she says, and I just give her a beaming smile. I pick her up and her legs go around my waist and carry her to her bookshelf. I put her down and turned her, so she was facing her bookcase.

"Pick as many as you like and I will put them in the car. Also grab the one about the baseball player, I quite enjoyed it and want to finish it," I tell her, placing a kiss on her temple. She just giggles and starts grabbing books. I take them to the car. I know she thinks this is temporary, but this is going to be permanent if I have any say, which I do. We get everything into our car and the security's SUV. Maybe bringing the Jeep was a bad idea but it is just instinct to always take my car when I can. Nikki comes out with the rest of her small bags, and I toss them in the back next to the security guard. She has one of her mischievous grins which makes me laugh.

"What is it, little one?" I ask her.

"Can we put the top down?" She asks with a big smile and before I can answer Cyrus chimes in.

"Please don't. It is an unnecessary risk because it is harder to see in with the top up," he says and Nikki looks disappointed, but I can't get mad he is just trying to do his job. I opened her door.

"Once this is all over, we can put the top down and drive on a beach. How does that sound?" I tell her and her disappointment disappears. She slides in and buckles her seat belt so fast with excitement.

"That sounds even better! I cannot wait till this is all over now!" She says, bouncing in her seat with excitement. I round the hood, slide in, and start the engine. I grab Nikki's hand again as we zoom through the city.

"Me too, little one, me too," I whisper. I just want the person I love most in my life to be safe and secure.

We finally made it home. The security team is nice and helps bring in the stuff but once we get settled and start to get her clothes unpacked in my closet one of them comes up to us.

"Ms. Nikki, is it okay if I get a key to the club and your apartment?" Alexander asks her. She looks a little taken back.

"Why?" She asks with curiosity.

"Well, we saw that you could use an update in your security, like cameras and alarms. We contacted Mr. Quinn and he said to update to the best system money can buy," he says rubbing the back of his head nervously. "The only thing is we need a key to get in."

She looks at him with shock and says, "You do not have to do that. I don't want you all to go out of your way. I am hoping this will be all over soon."

"Mr. Quinn thought you would say that and he told me to encourage you to still let us do it. Yes, we are hoping this issue is resolved quickly but still suggest for the future just to be sure," he tells her with a soft laugh. She just looks down to think about it but is taking too long because he looks at me for help. I need to step in and save this guy.

"Little one, please let them do it. If not for you then for us. We just want to make sure you are okay when we have to travel and it will make all three of us feel a lot better if you have it," I tell her, and she whips up to look at me. She finally turns to Alexander and smiles.

"Fine," she says annoyed. She stomps over to him like she is a child and hands over her keys reluctantly. Then she turns to me, "You have to be the most expensive boyfriends."

I just let out a soft laugh, "Little one, do you think we would make you pay for all this?"

"Yes! It is a security system for my club and my apartment!" She yells and Alexander just lets out a chuckle and leaves with a small wave leaving me to deal with a truly angry goddess.

"Yeah, that will be a no, love. We are the ones that put you into this situation so we will be paying for everything and please do not be stubborn on this," I tell her with a sigh and her jaw drops in shock. I laugh again and she shakes her head regaining her composure. When she looks at me, she looks angry. Her brows are furrowed, lips pursed and hands on her hips. I know I should be scared with this lioness, but she is just so fucking adorable when she is angry. I just give a smile.

"No, you guys will not! Who said they will pay for everything? You?" She asks, cocking her hip out. I have to think about this for a second. What is the best way to convince her that she does not have to deal with this by herself? Okay time to turn to daddy for this situation. I go to her and grab her hands. I move them to wrap around my neck and grab her hips.

"I did not, but if you think you are paying then you will bring out daddy," I tell her sternly. "If Carter wants to pay for it, you will let him."

She then shocks me. She looks up and has a mischievous smile. Not the reaction I was expecting but I will work with it. She places a peck on my lips and then lets me go.

"Thank you, daddy," she says and then runs out the room. I chase after her not understanding her thank you.

"Thank you for what?" I yell after her. She turns to me and walks backward to wherever she is going.

"You told me who was paying for it. Big mistake, daddy," she says and turns to go back to look for Carter. Shit! I fucked up! I chase after her.

"Flirt! Where are you fucker? You can't hide from me, puppy!" She yells as she opens his bedroom door. I come up from behind her. I grab her and we find Carter laying on his bed scrolling on his phone.

"You bellowed, princess?" He says, looking up from his phone with a smirk. He knew she would react like this. It just makes me smile. Now we can play with our goddess.

"I agreed for you to pay for the security but did not agree to the system they installed!" She yells at him. He gets up from his bed with a sigh and crosses the room, so he is standing right in front of her. He cradles her head and I tighten my hold on her hips.

"I said I would pay for security and that includes whatever they do, so I will pay for the security system, love. It was cute that you came in all angry in here thinking we weren't going to pay for it," he says with a soft laugh. She blushes in response because she knows he got her. I kiss her neck with a smile.

"I think it is time for punishment for that attitude you have, little one," I whisper into her neck. She trembles with excitement.

"You guys are not playing fair," she gasps out as I bite her neck. I laugh into her neck.

"Who said we would play fair?" Carter asks and then kisses her. She moans into his mouth which has my cock pressing into her ass. I pull her out of his arms and throw her over my shoulder holding her by her thighs. She squeals when I start to carry her to my room. Carter follows us.

"Put me down!" She squeals out, smacking me in the ass and kicking her feet.

"I don't think I will, little one," I tell her with a spank on her ass. I carry her into my room and toss her to the bed. She gasps when she bounces on the bed. Carter goes to sit on the bed, and he gives me a nod telling me I am captain. I go to the chest that is at the bottom of the bed. As I open it, I look at our goddess and she just smirks.

"Is that your play box, daddy?" She asks and I smirk at her.

"It is baby girl. I think I want to try something new," I tell her and her eyes go wide with excitement. I pull out a bullet vibe that I ordered just for my little one after the opera. It is a small one because I bought it for a particular hole of hers. I throw it on the bed and she looks at me with curiosity.

"And what's that?" She asks and looks at Carter who has a mischievous smile. He knows exactly what I want to do. I walk over to her and kiss her, hot and hard. While our tongues tangle in her mouth with intensity I snake my hand around to grab her ass. She moans but then I slip my hand in her jeans, and she tenses when I move my finger in her crack putting right near her hole.

"Have you ever had someone back there, little one?" I ask against her lips. She just shakes her head.

"No one has ever wanted to," she says softly. Carter groans and comes up next to her.

"How would you feel about riding me while my guy plays back there?" Carter asks her with a low gravelly tone. She quivers with anticipation while she thinks for a moment. We wait nervously.

"We can try and if you don't like anything we will stop. I promise, baby girl," I tell her and she looks at me, her eyes dilated with lust.

"No, I want to try because one day I want to be filled with all three of you," she says which has me and Carter groaning. God the image she just put in our heads is like a hot wet dream. I can't wait to make it a reality.

"Well then princess since you haven't, we need to work you up to it, but like Ivan said you say stop we stop," he says and pushes her chin up to look at him.

"I won't, but okay," she says to him and kisses him deeply. Almost to reassure him that she wants this more than anything. This woman really is a goddess in every meaning. I watch as they pull apart for air. Me and Carter both have the same look, like this girl is our entire world.

Chapter 22

Nikki

Fuck me! This is really happening. We all get off the bed to undress. The boys get to work getting their clothes off. You would think that it is a race. Then I understand why. Carter gets done first and then moves to me. He slowly starts to take off my clothes. He takes off Dante's jersey, that I feel like I have been living in for the last twenty-four hours. Luckily while me and Ivan were packing, I did change my bra and panties, hoping we would play when we got here. I put on my black crushed velvet bralette with black lace straps and matching black lace thong. I know I made the correct choice when I see their faces light up.

"Well don't you look like a snack, princess," Carter groans out. Ivan comes up from behind me and hooks his fingers on my thong on my hips. God, I am aching with need. I can literally feel my pussy pulsing as my men surround me but then I realize that Dante is missing. I stop both my men by putting a hand on each of their chest.

"Where is Dante? Shouldn't we invite him to the party," I ask them with a wicked smirk. They both let out a chuckle.

"He is at practice right now, so he is unable to attend this little party, princess," Carter says, grabbing my hips. I wrap my arms around Carter's neck and move to kiss him. I still feel sparks when I kiss him like it is the first time I am kissing him. Before anyone deepens the kiss, he pulls back. His hands go up to my face to cradle my head and he looks at me so deeply I get lost in his ocean blue eyes. They are not a perfect blue, there are glimpses of gray just like the ocean after a storm.

"Is this okay, Nikki?" Carter asks and I know he is being serious if he is not calling me princess.

"Why do you ask that?" I ask him. He looks like he is nervous.

"I know we have been waiting till you can trust me and then all this Rachel shit happened so I will understand if you don't want to s-sleep with m-me," he says and the last part he almost sputters out. He is scared that I don't want this. I need to do something dramatic to make him believe there is nothing more I want right now at this moment. I grab his hands from my face and bring them down. I wait till Ivan finally pulls down my panties and when I step out of them, I put my hands on Carter's chest. He looks at me with anticipation for my answer. I push his chest hard, so he falls on the bed and I hop up to straddle. His cock rubbing against my wet sex. He groans the second he feels how ready I am.

"Fuck me, princess. You are dripping!" He growls out. I rub myself on his shaft without it going in and he groans almost in pain. I hear Ivan let out a soft laugh behind me. I whip my head and he is right behind me. He places a kiss where I can feel my pulse racing at the base of my neck.

"Don't torture him, little one," he whispers into my skin. I turn back to Carter.

"Feel that puppy. I am more than ready for you," I tell him as I grind on his cock. Carter puts his hands on my hips to stop me.

"Sorry love I need to grab a condom before we do something we might regret," he groans but as he goes to sit up, I push him down on his back again.

"Princess?" He asks, concerned. I shake my head and push harder holding him in place.

"I don't want to use one. This is me showing how much I trust you. I am sure you get tested, and I am on the pill so as long as you are clean I want to show you because you don't seem to believe me when I tell you," I snap at him and his eyes go wide. He needs to get this in his head that I am in love with him so he will not have this insecurity. Fuck! They never let me believe my insecurities! His expression softens and his hands come up to my face again.

"I love you so fucking much," he says with such sincerity.

"I love you too and also never fucking doubt me again," I tell him. He and Ivan start to laugh.

"I won't be doing that anytime soon, love. I heard you loud and clear," Carter says with a salute.

"Can we get on with this? I am dying to play back here, little one," Ivan growls in my ear and then nips it with his teeth. I look at Carter and he has a mischievous look again.

"Put me in princess, I want to watch you sink down on me," he says and turns his attention to where we are almost connected. I reach between us and grab his cock lining it up at my entrance. I slowly start to sink down on him inch by inch. I turn my gaze to his and he is staring at me, stretching around him. His intense gaze is too much to handle. I close my eyes and sink down completely. As I was distracted, I felt Ivan grab my ass on both cheeks and move me up and down on Carter's cock. Is he really bouncing me on his friend's dick? I turn my head so I can see Ivan and he just gives me an evil grin.

"Don't worry about me, love. Focus on riding him. I need you nice and distracted for what I am going to do," he says, and I turn my gaze to Carter, he just snickers. Carter decides to start thrusting up into me hard. God he is hitting just the right angle. I scream out but then Ivan pushes me down between my shoulder blades so that way my face is on Carter's chest. Carter snuggles into the top of my head. I hum in contentment. How can this man be so adorable even during sex?

"Is my puppy coming out?" I ask with a soft laugh. He just growls at my question and thrusts up into me hard. My laughter gets caught in my throat as he thrusts up harder. I moan out his name and he moves his mouth to my ear. I shiver when his hot breath ghosts my ear.

"Am I a puppy when I do this?" He asks in a soft tone and then he thrusts up even harder.

"No," I cry out, out of breath. Then while he is distracting me, I hear a bottle cap pop and then feel warming and tingling liquid drip down my crack. I gasp at the sensation. I have never tried the tingling lube, but it is sure doing wonders for me now. While Carter is still thrusting into me, I start to feel Ivan massage around my hole with his finger. I gasp again when he starts to insert his finger. It is a weird feeling. I am not in pain, but it does not feel great either at the moment. I feel full. Then I have a hand on my face, pulling me out of my train of thought. Carter turns my face to look at him. He looks concerned.

"You okay, princess? We can stop if you don't like it," he says softly. I just shake my head. "Words, princess."

"Yeah, I am okay. I feel so full and he hasn't even put his dick in," I tell him with a small smile. He just laughs and places a kiss on my forehead. I shoot up though when I finally hear vibration behind me. Ivan just slowly pushes me back down with the hand that is not in my hole.

"Easy, little one. Just relax or this may feel uncomfortable. This is about trust," Ivan says, slipping in another finger stretching me out but I can't focus on that. His words ring in my ears. This is about trust. He is trying to be daddy and teach me a lesson. He is trying to teach me how it can be if I don't have control and have full trust in them. Like how they want me to with my security. I gasp as he runs the vibrator down my spine. He starts at my neck and runs it softly down my back to my crack. Once he has it there, he moves his hand that is in me out and runs the vibrator through my lubricated crack, getting it ready for me.

"Is this a lesson, daddy?" I ask him with my cheek to Carter's chest looking back at him. Our eyes connect and his green eyes are dark with lust. They normally look like a bright mossy green but with the heat in them, they look like a dark forest green.

"It is baby girl. Did you figure out what that lesson is?" He asks, his voice low and raspy. I nod but he gives me a look letting me know he wants me to say it aloud.

"It is about me not trusting you all to know what is best for my security. You are doing this to show me how good it can feel if I put all my trust in you in every situation," I tell him breathlessly. His chest puffs out triumphantly and a devilish smile grows on his face by my words.

"My baby girl really is so smart. Hey, Carter give her a good orgasm for being such a smart girl," he says with a smirk. I blush at his praises. I can feel myself get even wetter from his praises of being his smart good girl. Then I turn to Carter who has the same mischievous smirk as him.

"Got it, boss," He says and then lets me have it. He pounds into me hard and fast ruthlessly. Not giving me a moment to breathe. Carter cradles my head to his chest as he keeps going. I am so close. Just when I am about to yell, I am cumming I feel the vibrator again. Ivan is pressing it to my hole. Just as it slips in, I feel my release, I am cumming so hard I am shaking and I cry out.

"Fuck, Carter!" I scream and Ivan holds his movements for a moment till I come down. I am a sweaty shaking mess.

"How was that princess?" Carter asks, pulling my chin up so he can look at me. I am speechless so I nod letting him know it was good. "We are not done yet, love."

He's right. Now it is their turn. I start my movements slowly. I lean up but not enough that it would mess with Ivan and what he is doing. I arch my back and then start to bounce a little more on Carter. He flops his head back and moans. With my back still ached, I grab the headboard of the bed to keep my balance. Ivan goes back and starts to move the vibrator in and out of my ass. I moan. Now that it was completely in, it feels so good. As I pull up from Carter I push my ass back into the vibrator. Ivan lets out a soft laugh and spanks my ass, hard. I gasp.

"Remember this is a lesson. So don't worry about what is going on back here," Ivan says with another smack on the other cheek. I gasp when he does it a third time. He gives me a second while he massages the sore part of my ass. I start to understand he is wanting me to ride Carter and have him take care of me. I start moving again, this time faster. I hear Carter groan.

"Keep smacking her ass. Every time you do, she clenches my dick," Ivan growls at Carter. Ivan comes down on my ass hard and I feel myself clench like Carter says. Carter groans and snaps, "I am not going to last long if she keeps doing that so whatever you are going to do back there do it!"

I let out a soft laugh which earns me a glare from Carter. I go faster and harder for him. He starts to tense up and I know he is close. I keep going even as Ivan starts to put out the toy in my ass and replace it with his fat tip. He pushes slightly but I can feel him. He is not going to fully fuck my ass, he is just spilling his seed in it. Then I feel Carter. He pushes up hard and yells as he releases into me and Ivan does the same as his tip is in my ass while he pumps his hand on his base. I cum with them. How can I not? This feeling of both of them inside me is so intense and fulfilling. Once we come down from our high, we collapse to the bed breathless. Carter goes to get up, but I stop him by pulling on his arm.

"Where do you think you're going?" I ask him. He just puts a kiss on my forehead.

"I am going to get a washcloth to clean you up, princess," he says against my head. I pull him back to bed and cuddle up on his chest while Ivan cuddles behind me.

"Nope it can wait till after we take a nap. I just want to cuddle with my big guy and puppy. If you cuddle me properly, we can take a shower after our nap together," I hum into his chest. He relaxes and cuddles me back. I think about how life gets any sweeter than this as I drift off to sleep.

I feel like it was all a crazy wet dream. Ivan and Carter shared me. It was the most amazing experience I have ever had with all of them. I can't wait to add Dante to the mix. I start to stretch my arm over where Carter was, but I don't feel him. My hand just feels the soft and silky sheets. I shoot up and then realize I am not alone. Behind me, Ivan grabs me before I shoot off the bed and brings me closer to him.

"Where do you think you're going?" He asks while snuggling closer into me. I just sigh.

"I thought you guys left for a second and was worried," I tell him nervously. He just laughs into my hair.

"Well, that's the perk of having three boyfriends then. You will never wake up alone, little one," he says and then pulls me up standing. He leads me to his private bathroom, placing me on his sink counter to sit and turns on his shower. His bathroom is just like his bedroom, very minimalistic. He did so with a color scheme of black and white. The walls are painted a bright white but everything else is a tone of black. The shower is a black stone behind a wall but there is a window in it so I can see he turned it on, and the sink is black marble with ribbons of gold in it. Even his products on the shelves on the wall are in reusable black bottles. He has a white stand-alone tub on the opposite side of the sink. When he feels the shower is warm enough, he plucks me off the counter and pulls me into the shower.

The little sneak has my loofah and shower products on the shelves that are in the shower. He must have grabbed them while I was unpacking. The warm water hits me, and it feels so good. I am a little sore after waking up, but it is a good sore. I can live with being sore everyday as long as the sex keeps being that amazing. I feel like I am on cloud nine right now.

"How are you feeling, love?" Ivan asks, grabbing my shampoo. He lathers it in his hands facing me. He then starts to message it into my scalp. I hum at him. It feels so good I forgot that he asked a question. "Love?"

"Hmm, oh right. I am okay, just a little sore big guy," I tell him, still humming as he rinses my hair. He laughs which has me opening my eyes a little too soon because soap gets in them.

"Shit!" I yell and he wipes the tears from my closed eyes.

"I am sorry, little one. I was just laughing because when you are relaxed you are like a cute little purring kitten," he says, grabbing a washcloth that was hanging in the shower. He goes and wipes my eyes. I opened them up and he did an excellent job at getting it out because the sting in my eyes is minimal.

"You're okay, big guy. It was only a little, but it is pretty funny of you thinking I am a small kitten," I tell him as he keeps rinsing my hair. Then he grabs the conditioner. He rubs it through my ends, playing with my hair as he does so. I am humming again. That is my true weakness, when someone plays with my hair. I could fall asleep standing here as he does it. Maybe it is because he is so comfortable to be around. "If you keep playing with my hair like that, I might fall asleep."

"You can if you like. I will make sure you don't fall over," he says with a soft laugh.

We continue to wash up and hands start to roam. He is overly concerned about getting my breasts clean. When he grazes my nipple with my rough loofah, I let out a soft moan.

"Little one, I know you are sore, so I need you to stop making those little noises or I won't be able to help myself," he says with a growl. I know he growls a warning, but it is making me hotter. I have to clench my thighs to relieve some of the ache. His eyes drop as I hold my thighs together.

"I can't help it. You started this, daddy," I tell him with a giggle. I reach for his cock, and he is already hard and jetting out. I pump it once, twice and he is already groaning. I drop to my knees and water drips down my head and face. I look up at him and he smirks.

"Baby girl, you should see yourself right now. My perfect wet fantasy," he says with another groan as I pump him one more time. I kiss the tip of his cock.

"You said you were worried about being sore but what my daddy did not deduce is my mouth is not sore," I tell him and then gobble him whole while keeping my hand wrapped around his base.

"Fuck, baby!" He yells as his hand grips my hair firmly. I start to bob my head up and down on his incredible length. I move my hand with my mouth. As I do this, I think about how I want to unravel him under what technique I want to use. I decided I don't want this to be soft and gentle. I want to show him how much I appreciated last night. I pop him out of my mouth and that gets his attention. He looks down curiously with his emerald eyes.

"I want you to fuck my mouth, daddy. I don't want you to be gentle. I want you to show me why I call you daddy," I tell him, and his eyes go wide. Then his eyes soften but go dark with hunger. His pointer finger goes to my chin to force it up even more.

"You asked for it, little one," he says with a moan. He bends down to give me one last sweet kiss before popping back up straight. He reaches out the shower for something. I wait and then I see he has the black cushiony rope from his robe that was hanging next to the shower. I peer up at him with an arched brow wondering what he is planning.

"Put out your hands," he orders. Then it comes to me what he is going to do. "Now, little one. You know I don't like to repeat myself."

I put my hands out like I am on my knees praying. In a way, I am. I am praying he shows me no mercy. I am glad this material is soft because he ties it so tight it is almost uncomfortable. I hiss at the sting, and he looks at me carefully.

"Too tight, baby girl?" He asks with concern. I shake my head and lick my lips. His eyes dart to my lips as he licks his own. He then crashes his lips to mine like a starving animal devouring his prey. Our tongues battle as we both fight for dominance but we both know who is in charge right now. He pulls away slightly, his lips still grazing mine. "Since your mouth will be full of my cock we can't use a safe word so if it gets too much I want you to tap my thighs with your hands."

I shiver at his words with excitement and nod my head. I could tell that won't be enough. He just looks at me with a stern expression. My daddy is all about verbal consent. I whisper, "I understand."

"Good girl. My baby girl is learning," he says raspy. He stands now and moves his hand to my lips to part them for him. "Open up."

I do and he angles his hips, so his cock is right at my mouth. I place a quick sweet kiss before this gets rough. I am able to get his precum that was on the tip onto my lips and lick it off. His hands go to my hair and pulls on it so I am moved back a little back.

"Open wide, baby girl," he says in a low tone and I do as he says. I open my mouth with my jaw going slack. He slips his tip in and my lips automatically wrap around his cock. I hollow my cheeks sucking at his tip. He lets out a groan. Then he thrust into my mouth fully as I continue sucking. His rhythm is rough and hard. It is amazing. I can't stop myself, my fingers move to my pussy, rubbing my clit. It's a little difficult with my hands tied but I make it work. I look up and get lost in his hot green gaze.

"God baby you are so pretty on your knees for me," he says with a groan and thrusts even deeper. These are the moments I am glad I don't have a gag reflex because I am sure I would have been throwing up and gagging at his length. I can literally feel him hitting the back of my throat with each powerful thrust. There is no point holding back my tears as my eyes water. I probably look like a hot mess with tears and spit slipping from my mouth as he mouth fucks me. He must have read my thoughts. He pulls himself out and I make a popping sound as he pulls free.

"You are beautiful, baby. I want to hear you say it," he says. I am stunned and silent. I don't know what to say to that because at this moment, I am a hot mess. He just waits. "You don't get my cock till you say it."

"I am beautiful," I whisper, staring at his intense gaze.

"What was that? I didn't hear you baby," he says with a soft laugh. I just roll my eyes but then he pulls my hair tightly.

"Say it loud and proud baby and don't roll your eyes at your daddy," he says, not breaking his firm expression.

"I am beautiful," I yell out. He finally has a satisfied smirk on his face. He pulls me forward with my hair and thrust even harder in my mouth.

"Fuck. Your mouth is heaven," he groans out, thrusting into my mouth. I finally put two fingers in my dripping pussy, and I moaned around him. His words alone could make me cum.

"Yes, baby. Make yourself feel good while you are being daddy's good little slut," he grows out and I whimper. This sends me over the edge. I cum almost yelling into Ivan's dick. The vibrations must be to his liking because he cums down my throat. His cum coats the back of my throat and fills my mouth where it spills out a little. I remove my fingers from my pussy. He pulls back and kneels in front of me. One hand gathers what was on my chin onto his finger and slips it back into my mouth.

"Swallow," he growls with his finger still in my mouth. It is too much, and he can tell. His other hand goes to my neck, massaging it to help get it all down. He repeats himself but comes out with a firmer tone, "Swallow."

I swallow every last drop. I have to gulp it down with it being such a big load.

"Good girl," he says and kisses me. I whimper from his praises and he chases the taste of himself on my lips. I love it when they praise me. It's like I am a flower, and their praises are the sunshine I desperately need to survive. I giggle against his lips. He pulls away and picks me up, so I am standing and he is holding me up.

"What's so funny, little one?" He says looking at me amused. I just giggle harder.

"I think we are going to have to shower again," I say, smiling up at him. How did I get so lucky?

Chapter 23

Nikki

This week with the guys is flying by. Carter and I leave for New Orleans tomorrow. They have been relentless about protecting me. They even convinced me to take last night off from the club. Well, they convinced me with orgasms, so it wasn't that hard. Dante and Ivan were in the middle of sharing me in the middle of the kitchen and said I could not cum till I agreed to take the night off. Now I am here at Carter's practice watching him with one of my bodyguards. He said until we find Rachel he wants to keep an eye on me. This is so frustrating! I feel like I am losing some of my independence that I am so used to having. I couldn't say no when he gave me his puppy eyes snuggling me in bed. I know with this, I am going to be late for the club again so I have to call Chloe so she can open.

"Don't worry about anything. With everything going on you should take as much time as you need," she tells me. She is not wrong. The article about me and the guys got released and everything has been crazy. My social media went up in followers and the club is even bat shit busy. I really need to go to the club tonight because I feel like I am going to have to double my orders and work on hiring even more help. I look to the field and Carter flashes me a big smile and waves his arms in the air. Like he doesn't have my attention already. I just roll my eyes at him and give him a wave back. That has him beaming as he slides his helmet back on looking like a god in his football uniform. I can't help but stare at his ass in those football pants as he runs back on the field. Chloe noticed my silence.

"Hey are you busy?" She asks with a giggle.

"No, I am good. So how bad was last night?" I ask her worried that if I am not there for a second the place would burn to the ground.

"Will you chill? Everything is fine. We are a little busier than normal but nothing we can't manage. You trust me, right?" She says it with hesitation on the last part. I don't want her to think I don't trust her but some days the club felt like my safety net. Like it was the only thing that brought me joy before these guys came barreling into my life.

"I do trust you! Fuck your one of the few people I trust with the club!" I yell into the phone. It's true. There are very few people I would trust to keep the club going and she is one of them. "Actually, there is something I want to ask you since we are on the topic."

"Really? What is it?" She asked with a perk in her voice.

"Well…. Fuck! I want to give you something and I hope you like it," I tell her with hesitation. This is a big step for me. I take a deep breath preparing myself to let some of my control issues go.

"You have me on pins and needles here," she says with a small laugh.

"How would you like to be a partner of the club?" I ask her, closing my eyes. I wait for her answer but she is stunned silent. I feel like a few moments go by and I lost her. "Chloe?"

"I'm here. Sorry, I am just in shock. The club is your baby and never thought you would ask anyone to help with the club. I am sorry but I don't have the money to be a partner right now," she says with disappointment in her voice, and I just laugh. "What's so funny?"

"I am gifting the partnership to you. You're not buying in. I want you as a partner and with everything going on I can't be at the club twenty-four seven like I used to. I am starting to get really busy with the guys and know I can't keep babying the club. They need my attention," I tell her.

"Yes, we know you have three boyfriends! Stop bragging bitch!" She complains and makes me laugh again.

"I am not bragging. I just want to slow down for them. The club is not the only thing I have anymore. I have made my own family, plus with everything going on with the bitch, going to the club every day is an unnecessary risk. At least that's what the guys say," I say with a scoff. Then I continue, "I just want someone I can trust so I know my club will be safe and sound. I don't want you to feel like you need to buy in because that club is just as much yours as it is mine. Fuck! You left Broadway when I did because you are so loyal to me and helped me create an amazing club."

"Shit! I don't know what to say!" She yells with excitement.

"Say yes!" I yell back at her with a laugh.

"Yes! Yes! A thousand times yes!" She screams.

"Okay so what I am going to do is hire us both lawyers and have them draw up the contract for us and if you don't like the lawyer I pick, you can pick someone else but I will cover the lawyer fees for you, that is not up for discussion. I just don't want you to have to pay for a thing and I don't want you to think I am taking advantage of you," I tell her, trying to be stern like Ivan always is.

"I would never think that. Did you pick them already?" She asks with excitement.

"Yes, and they drafted up the contracts already. I will have fifty-five percent and you will have forty-five. I hope that is fair. I wasn't sure but the lawyers said that was fair and still gives me comfort with decision making but I told them I trust you and I know if there are any changes you want to make to the club you will run it by me first. So, if you want more, please feel free to tell me and I will have them draw up new documents," I tell her.

"Holy shit balls! That is more than enough! That is too much actually!" She yells with anger in her tone. "I don't want you to give almost half your club to me. It is your baby! I would have been happy if you just made me a manager, but this is so generous."

"It is what I feel like you deserve. You helped me build the club up to be honest, so you deserve fifty, but I just get so nervous about giving people control that the lawyers suggested this and, in the contract, you will see in the next couple of years we will assess the club and give you more. With how fast me and the guys have been moving in our relationship I would not be shocked if I want to give you more than fifty," I tell her shaking my head because I am sure in the next couple years me and the guys will want to start a family with how everything is moving. If we do, then I want that to have my full attention. Not a lot of people know this. When my dad found out about my mom splitting, he took a break from fighting. He wanted to give me all the love and attention I deserve and if I have kids, I want to do the same. Chloe sighs with contentment.

"You really must love these guys. Not that I would ever doubt you, but you are willing to give up a portion of your club just so you can spend time with them. That is a huge deal for you, and I am just so happy for you," she says softly and longing. Chloe has told me that she used to be in love with someone. He was a professor at a university. She always did have a thing for older men. They were mature and smart until one day the guy left her for a younger grade student. He told Chloe that the girl he was leaving her for was so smart and intelligent and they could have meaningful conversations that he couldn't get with her. The guy was a dip shit. Chloe is so smart and bright. I mean for fuck's sake the woman can speak in four different languages. Yeah, she is not a rocket scientist, but you don't need to be a brainiac to have a meaningful conversation. Since then, she only ever had physical relationships with men. She said she could not go through such a hard heart break again.

"You know you will find happiness too one day," I tell her in a soft low tone.

"Girl, I do not need a man to make me happy. I just need my friends," she says with a sass.

"Okay, okay, I won't get into this again, but I cannot wait for the day some guy wants to be your white knight and sweeps you off your feet," I tell her with a giggle. She just scoffs.

"Yeah, that will be the day," she says with reluctance but I already know for a fact someone wants to be that. Apparently Quick will not leave Dante alone about her. He keeps texting him asking questions about her and wants to make the club the place they go to after home games so he can have a chance to see her. It would take an idiot to not see what he is doing but I don't want to tell Chloe. If it does happen it should happen naturally and on her terms. I told Dante to agree about the club but that is the only thing he is getting out of me. He is going to have to put in the work himself to show he is worthy of the goddess, that is Chloe.

"Okay so when I come to the club tonight, I will bring the papers so you can sign and then you will be co-owner of the club. It is perfect timing too with me going away this weekend," I tell her. Yes, I won't miss much but it is reassuring that when I am out of town she will always be there for the club.

"You will not regret this! I promise!" She yells and I can hear her jumping up and down.

"No, I don't think I will," I whisper. "Also, me and Ian are not having breakfast this Sunday since I will be out of town, but I already talked to him and we wanted to invite you to the next one though."

"Are you serious? You never let anyone go to the Diner with you and Ian!" She yells.

"Yes well, it has been a long time coming. Me and Ian learned at a young age we like our privacy but we would love for you to come. We trust you and you are our friend," I tell her truthfully.

"I will be there! I have to go! I really want to dress up for tonight at work so mama needs to go pamper herself. Love ya, Nik," she says with a laugh.

"Love ya too. See you at the club later!" I tell her and we hang up. The team is finally done with practice so me and my bodyguard make our way towards the waiting area. It is still so weird having someone follow me everywhere I go. In fact, New Orleans is going to be really weird because all three are coming. The private investigator still has yet to find anything on Rachel. The cunt is smart and is in hiding till she makes her next move. The investigator found out a lot from her past though. She was an orphan like Ivan, but her story took a darker turn than his. She was in foster home after foster home never to be adopted. Her homes were never that great either. There were reports of mental and physical abuse while she was in them. I could never imagine going through something like that. To never feel loved by a single human being or having one not give a rat's ass about you. It makes me so thankful that Dante found Ivan and then they found Carter. Who knows where Ivan would be if the guys never found him, or his parents did not drop him off at the church?

I am so deep in thought that I did not realize the team was leaving the locker room. Carter sneaks up behind me and wraps his arms around my waist and puts his chin on my shoulder.

"What's got you so deep in thought, princess?" He asks, placing a kiss on my neck.

"Nothing really. Just thinking about everything going on. I made a business decision that's going to give me some more free time on my hands," I tell him with a giggle. He turns to me, so I am facing him and he looks at me with worry all over his face as he waits for me to tell him. "I am making Chloe part owner of the club." His face lights up.

"That's wonderful love!" He exclaims and picks me up to spin me around. Then we hear someone's throat clear, and we look to the side. There are two huge football players standing there with smug smiles on their faces.

"You gonna introduce us to your girl," one says. He is African American and is even taller than my guys. The guy is huge with dreads in his hair.

"Yeah, we want to meet the girl that made the famous fuckboy change his ways," the other chimes in with a laugh. This one is a pretty boy like Carter. Short brown hair, tan skin, and a dazzling smile.

"Fuck off," Carter growls out, but it makes me giggle. I tear myself out of his arms and walk right over to them.

"Hi, I am Nikki," I tell them, putting out my hand. The guys look at my hand and laugh. The big guy grabs my hand but instead of shaking it he pulls me into a big bear hug. I swear he squeezes so hard I think I hear my back pop.

"Don't crush my princess!" Carter yells at them. They both laugh and the big bear plops me down on my feet.

"Sorry, princess. I am a hugger," he says with no apologetic tone in his voice.

"You don't get to call her princess!" Carter yells and punches him in the arm. He doesn't seem affected by the punch though.

"What else are we supposed to call her! That's literally the only name you call her, so I was just rolling with it," he says with a shrug. They are fucking with him and I am loving every second of this. It feels almost like we are getting back to normal with all this crazy shit going on around us.

"She just said her name is Nikki so that is what you call her!" Carter says with shaking anger. I laugh and grab his hand. He turns to me, his expression softening.

"How are they supposed to know when that's all you ever call me, puppy?" I say and then he glares at me. The guys fall to the floor laughing. Yep, I'm fucked!

"She really calls you puppy! That is so fucking hilarious!" The one with brown hair says.

"Nik these two dip shits are Xavier and Jaden, and you will deal with that puppy comment later," he says with a wicked grin. I feel my body shiver with the dirty promise he made me. The boys get off the ground and straighten up.

"Xavier, the best middle linebacker in the NFL," the big guy with the dreads said, sticking out his hand but I giggled at him.

"I think I learned my lesson last time, big guy," I say and that has him giving me a smirk. He puts up his hands in defense. The other guy scoffs.

"I am Jaden, and I can openly admit I do not think I am the best quarterback and won't break your back over a hug," Jaden says, holding out his hand. I grabbed it and instantly pulled into a hug but not as tight as Xaviers. I giggle and hug him back.

"Okay that's enough," Carter says and pulls me into him.

"What's up Quinn? Think I will take your girl?" Jaden asks with a flirty smile and just to really fuck with Carter he throws a wink my way.

"Didn't you hear, I have three dicks. I don't really want to add a fourth in the mix," I say laughing so hard, but it gets caught in my throat when I look at Carter who has the biggest grin of pride.

"Damn right you don't. I have a hard enough time sharing you three ways as it is," Carter says, putting his arm around my shoulder. "I am so excited you are coming to New Orleans with me."

"Oh shit! Little Miss is coming to New Orleans with us? This just turned into a hell of an away game," Jaden says to wind up Carter again, but I think it is time to put a stop to this before Carter kills one of his teammates.

"Okay boys if you are done messing with my Charming, I would really like to go home and pack for the trip and finish up some orders for the club," I tell them patting both their cheeks.

"I like her. Bring her around more often," Xavier says as they go to leave.

"Bye little miss! Can't wait to see you at the game," Jaden calls when they are a little further away. I turn to Carter, and he looks sad.

"What's wrong puppy?" I ask him, wrapping my arms around his neck. He just pouts even more and it is so adorable.

"Why are you going to the club?" He asks, looking down at me with his big blue eyes. His hands are gripping my hip like if I go to the club, he won't ever see me again. "At least let one of us go with you."

"Carter, you hired a whole security team. It just feels like I am losing what little independence I have with having to be watched twenty-four seven. Let me have this one thing. I have to square away Chloe's ownership and show her a couple of things so that way I can stay by your side all weekend. It will only take a couple of hours. It's a small risk but after this I am all yours. Plus, I am sure you guys will get tired of me eventually," I tell him scratching the back of his head to sooth him. He just doesn't understand. My whole life I have always been on my own. Yeah, I had my dad and Ian but they are not around twenty four seven. So, the past couple days have been awkward with the guys and my bodyguards following me around. I just need a breather.

"Fine, but you are taking all three of them," he says and points to my bodyguard that is ten feet away. I roll my eyes and he takes his hand and reaches around to swat my butt. I squeal at the sting. "Please princess."

"Fine, but just to make you feel better," I tell him with a sigh and then give him a sweet kiss on the cheek. When I look back, he has a mischievous smirk on his lips.

"I might need some more convincing," he says and grabs the duffle bag he put on the ground.

"Oh, really and what is going to convince you?" I asked, wanting to know what he was thinking. He goes and pulls out his official jersey. I smirk at him knowing this has been his fantasy since we met.

"Pictures with you in this and nothing else," he says with a growl. I smirk at him and grab the jersey. I break out of his hold with the jersey and run to the car with him right behind me.

"Come on, Charming. Time to fulfill your wildest fantasy," I yell back at him, and he catches me spinning me and throws me in his fancy car. Well, I am going to be really late for the club.

We finally make it home and Tot bum rushes to the door so excited to see me as well as the others. Dante and Ivan are not far behind him. Ivan turns the corner and looks so happy to see me. He pushes Dante and Tot out of the way to buddle me up in his arms. I swear it is like they are all cute little puppies so excited to see me.

"Well, hey there big guy," I say in his ear, hugging him back.

"Ivan, share," Dante says behind him in a stern voice. Ivan reluctantly lets me go and moves out of Dante's way. Dante moves to hug me, and he dips his head down to my ear. "Missed you, Mia Amora."

"Miss you too, Mio Amore," I tell him, hugging him back. Then quickly Carter grabs my hand to lead me to his room.

"Well, you are going to miss her for a little longer! Bye guys!" Carter yells at them and I hear them both complain as he pulls me into his room. He slams the door shut and makes his way to me. His hand moves to the center of my shirt and then I feel him bundle it up in his fist.

"Off," he growls out like it is ridiculous I have left it on this long.

"Well, that was not nice, puppy," I tell him with a giggle. He looks at me confused.

"What was not nice?" He asked with an arch brow while taking my shirt off. I roll my eyes when he slides his jersey on me.

"Didn't you learn to share your toys when you were little?" I ask him with a condescending tone. He kneels down and slides off my shoes but then pauses when he is done and looks up at me with those amazing blue eyes.

"You are not a toy, princess. Tell you what, once I get a few pictures of you in my jersey then you can call them up here," he says with a soft laugh. He undoes my jeans and slides them off but leaves the blue lace thong I have on that goes with his team's colors. I might have planned that this morning when getting ready. He stands up and is standing chest to chest with me. His arms wrap around my waist and his hand makes it to my ass. I wrap my arms around his neck as he picks me up by my ass. I giggle as he tosses me to the bed. I bounce so high when I hit the bed I can't help but turn my giggle into a full blown laugh.

"Get up on your knees for me, love. I want to take some beautiful pictures of you in your new favorite jersey," he says with a beaming smile. He takes off his shirt and I can't help but stare. These men all look like Greek gods to me. His muscles ripple and shine with sweat from his practice. He catches me staring at him as he pulls out his phone. I blush in embarrassment and look down towards the bed. I hear the camera snap a picture which has me snapping my head up to look at him. He is not even looking at his phone. He is looking at me with hunger and I blush even harder.

"You are so beautiful when you go all red," he says with a growl. He snaps one last photo and then tosses his phone on the floor.

"What about all the pictures you wanted?" I ask because this is his fantasy. He looks at me and I get lost in his eyes, They go dark with lust, his pupils dilated. The blue almost looks navy in this light.

"I just realized, why get so caught up in pictures when I have the real thing in front of me. You make me want to live in the moment and not worry about anything else. I love you, princess and I don't think this is a time to be selfish when I get you all weekend to myself," he says and moves to the door calling for Dante and Ivan. I swoon at his words. All I can think is how could I get so lucky? This man has proved himself repeatedly. Both Dante and Ivan walk in shirtless and ready to play. The guy's whisper between each other for a moment as Carter closes the door. This has me curious.

"Why are you all whispering? You know it is rude to keep secrets from a lady," I tell them with a playful tone. They turned to face me looking a little embarrassed which makes me even more curious.

"Well, little one, when we share you, we like to talk so we are not clumsy through all of this. So, the first time we did it we decided that we would agree someone would be the one to take charge and we were thinking you could this time," he says, rubbing the back of his neck nervously. Well, that won't do. I hop up from the bed and stand right in front of him. Dante is on his right side and Carter on the left. I wrap my arms around his neck and kiss him deeply showing him how much I appreciate all that they do. We get lost in our kiss till I feel the other guys on each side of me. I pull away to look at all three of them. They all look so devoted to me, like if I asked them to get on their knees they would. Ivan cradles my face in his hands and looks so deeply into me it is like he is looking into my very soul.

"You're in control, baby girl. What do you want?" Ivan asks and my head whips to look at Carter and Dante and they are both nodding at me. I take a deep breath because what I am about to ask is going to be a lot for all of us and it is hard for me to have the courage to ask them. A wave of emotions hit me. Every guy telling me I am not worth it, every man leaving me telling me I am not enough. I don't even realize that it has been a few moments, and the guys are staring at me. Dante goes and grabs me out of Ivan's grasp. He pulls me into the biggest hug and kisses my forehead.

"You remember that phrase we have been practicing, Mia Amore?" He whispers. I can still feel his lips ghosting my forehead. I nod to him and he pulls away with a beaming smile. This mother fucker is going to make me say it in front of all three of them. Well, I guess this is one way to get over this trauma. "Say it, Mia Amore. I want to hear you say it and for them to hear it."

"Io sono abbastanza, Mio Amore," I whisper so quietly I am sure Ivan and Carter can't even hear me.

"Louder, princess. We did not hear you," Carter chimes in and I whip my head to glare at him. He just gives me his cocky smirk.

"Fine," I snap and then take another deep breath. This is really hard for me. They can all tell too as they do some sort of group hug to calm my nerves. They all pull away slightly, but their hands are still on me to support me. I try to puff up my chest and put some base into my voice as I say it again. "Io sono abbastanza."

It's Carter's turn to pull me. He turns into his puppy self. He bends down to nuzzle into my neck. He nibbles at the base of my neck, and I can feel my pulse quicken.

"What do you want, princess? We will do anything you want," he says, kissing along my jaw up to my ear. My whole body is shaking with nerves. I know what I want and I know I can trust them enough to tell them and not run away.

"I w-want all of y-you at once," I stutter out but they all pop into my view looking excited. Carter is practically jumping like an excited puppy. Ivan grabs my hands and pulls them to his chest.

"Who do you want where?" He asks softly. They really want me to take charge and have every say that goes on. I look at them and try to decide how I want to do this. I look at Ivan.

"I want to ride Cater, you in my ass and Dante in my mouth," I tell him with more confidence. I need to get over these insecurities and I need to do it now. This is all I have ever fantasized about, and these men love me enough to give it to so there is no reason to be scared. Carter goes to pull me to his bed. He plops down with his head on the pillow and me straddling him. I go to kiss him deeply. He responds with a groan and pulls away but lips still grazing mine.

"Get these pants off me, princess," Carter says with a growl. I go and unbutton his jeans and pull them down with his boxers. I lick my lips when I pull them off and his dick stands to attention hard as a rock. He looks at me with his beautiful blue eyes, dark with lust. "Come here, princess."

I move crawling up him slowly. I straddle him as the other guys get undressed behind me. I feel like a little minx when I grind on his hard cock so my juices could spread all over him. He moans when he feels how wet he makes me. He moves so quickly pulling the jersey off of me and removing my bra. Once I am fully naked, he looks pleased with himself with that cocky smirk I love. I reach between us and guide his cock in and apparently, I am taking too long because once I finally put the tip in he thrust up into me completely.

"Fuck, charming," I moan out and he lets out a moan as he keeps his thrust slow and hard. He pulls me down to him, so my boobs are in his face. He licks at one nipple while he pinches the other hard. I moan at the pain as he bites down on the one, he has in his mouth. He spread his legs just a little so Ivan then can come up behind me. I feel Ivan kiss up my back and he works all the way up my neck. Once he is there, he joins Carter in leaving marks on me. He nibbles and then sucks hard, claiming me as theirs.

"You know if you keep doing that, I am going to have to wear scarves every day, daddy," I tell him, and he lets out a growl. He turns my head so he can look me in the eyes.

"You will do no such thing, angel. You are ours and I am just letting other men know by marking you," he says with a soft laugh and releasing my face, so I turn back to Carter. Carter keeps his thrust slow and hard as I feel a warm lube running down my crack.

"Please, daddy I feel so empty," I beg him. It is the truth ever since they both filled me, just sex is underwhelming. I can still get there but nothing beats when I have them together.

"Just relax, little one. Focus on Carter while I play, like last time," he tells me and pushes between my shoulder blades, so I am chest to chest with Carter. Then I hear soft music in the background. Ah, there is my Dante. He must have been grabbing a speaker, so he has tunes going while we play. He loves music more than me, it makes me giggle. He is nude now and comes right up to me and Carter by the bed. He stands there while grabbing at the base of his cock.

"Something funny, Mia Amore?" He asks with a smirk. I shake my head and he drops his head to give me a kiss. I get lost in the kiss because it is hot and heavy. Our tongues battle as I feel Carter thrusting into me and Ivan working two fingers in my back hole. I want more so I pull away from Dante and grab his shaft. I pump twice before pulling slightly harder to bring him right to my mouth. He hisses when I pull. I kiss up and down his shaft and that has his hiss turning into a moan. Carter laughs.

"What have I told you? Our cocks are not leashes that you can pull," Carter says with a laugh. I lick Dante, base to tip, and then turn to Carter.

"He doesn't seem to mind, puppy," I tell him and then suck on Dante's tip. He groans and thrusts his hips, so he goes a little deeper in my mouth.

"Hurry the fuck up back there. I am not going to last long with Nik literally dripping on me," Carter snaps at Ivan. Ivan just lets out a soft laugh and moves towards me. I gasp around Dante as I feel Ivan enter me slowly. Fucking Christ, I feel so full and he is not in me completely. Carter finally picks up the pace when he knows Ivan enters me. I am so distracted that I am giving Dante the worst blow job ever. I give up. I pop him out of my mouth, and he groans in protest. I look up at him through my lashes.

"Fuck my mouth, Mio Amore," I tell him breathless. He narrows his eyes a little contemplating it. I roll my eyes at him because he is scared, he is going to hurt me. "I will be fine, Amore. I just have so much going on I am overwhelmed and need you to do the work."

He apparently does not need to be told twice. He grips my hair to move me closer and pushes his tip at my lips. I open up for him and he makes quick work. This is not the most comfortable position with these three men, but I could give a rats ass. This is the most amazing feeling. I feel all three inside me at the same time. I moan as all three find a rhythm and thrust into me all at once. I am so close. Carter then reaches between us to circle my clit with his thumb. I scream around Dante while the boy's keep thrusting as I am cuming. I am cumming so hard. I don't think I have ever cummed harder in my life. Carter swears and then I feel it.

"Fuck, I'm cumming, princess," he says as he fills me with his seed. Ivan is not far behind from what I can tell.

"God, you are so tight back here. I can feel your tight ass squeezing my cock," Ivan says and since I am one man down, I grab Dante's hips and bring him as close as I can. Carter leans up and starts to suck on my tits as I take Dante as deep as I can.

"Shit," Dante swears and then shoots in the back of my throat as Ivan releases his seed in me. I eat up all of Dante and swallow. He pulls back when he knows he is done. Simultaneously they all lean in and kiss me in different areas. Carter leans up to kiss me on my mouth, Dante kisses me on my neck and Ivan leans down and kisses the shoulder opposite Dante. I sigh in contentment. Ivan lifts me off of Carter and places me next to him, so I am sandwiched between Carter and Ivan cuddling. Dante leaves the room for a moment and comes back with a warm damp washcloth. He cleans me up and I moan when he is wiping between my thighs.

"How was that, Mia Amore? We weren't too rough with you?" Dante asks as he throws the cloth in Carter's hamper. Carter moves to his favorite sleeping spot, his head on my tummy and his body between my legs. Dante goes to the side Carter was on. "Amore?"

"Sorry, I am just so happy and content I forgot to answer," I tell him with a giggle. I yawn, exhausted from our activities. "I need a nap before I head to the club though."

All three laugh but Ivan reaches for his phone and says, "I will set an alarm, love. Don't worry we will make sure you are up with enough time to get ready."

Carter grumbles into my stomach with protest.

"I still don't like the risk of you leaving," Carter grumbles out. I giggle and start to play with his hair, running my hands through his short golden locks.

"I promise after tonight I won't leave without you guys. I just need to make sure Chole signs the papers and show her a couple things. Like I told you I need a moment for myself to breathe and then I am all yours," I tell him and he sighs in defeat. He cuddles as close as possible.

"You already are, princess," he says softly into my belly. I can't argue that I am all theirs, so I stay silent as I fall asleep.

Chapter 24

NIKKI

The club is really busy when I walk in with all three of my security guards. Carter was pestering me to take all three of them, so they know I am safe. I am so excited the club is doing well but feel bad because all this new business is all about the guys. They made my club the new IT club, but I don't ever want them to think going public was about the club. I make my way to my office to get the papers for Chloe. I hope I am doing the right thing. This club is my baby, so it is really hard to give up a portion of it, but if anyone deserves this, it is Chloe. She has been there for me through thick and thin. I hear a knock on the door.

"Come in," I yell at the door as I flip through the pages on my desk. Chloe walks in with a big smile.

"Hey, bitch," she says happily.

"Hey! So, I have the papers here if you want to look over them and then I will send them to the lawyer and you will be part owner," I tell her. She sits down opposite my desk.

"Love, I just need to know where to sign. I trust you and don't think you would do anything bad," she says, grabbing my hand. "I know this is hard for you, but I promise to never over step. If there is anything that comes up, you have final say in the matter."

This woman is so sweet. She knows this is going to be hard for me, but I need to do this. I am doing this because this club is not the only thing I have. I have my men and they deserve my undivided attention like they give me.

"I know you won't, but there are a couple of things I want to work out. So, this will be mainly your office. I will try not to mess anything in here when I do stop by, but you can do what you like here. Feel free to redecorate how you see fit. Also, with me moving in with the guys, I figured I would also include my apartment for you. It helps when you are super busy and need to get away. The apartment is included in the club's lease so it is yours if you would like," I tell her and her jaw drops in shock. I just give her a humble smile.

"I can't take your apartment! Now you are really being too generous!" She exclaims and then bites her lips with nervousness.

"Listen, I just moved in with the guys. I still have some stuff there but I'm moving that stuff once this bitch is caught. Really it comes with the club, and I am not using it, so I want you to use it. You would be doing me a favor, so it is not just sitting there," I tell her with a shrug trying to play it off like no big deal.

"Fine, I will use it, but I will wait till you are completely out. Also, if you ever feel like you need to come back you will always be welcome. Plus, it is a two bedroom so if anything happens with the guys, know you will always have a place there," she says with a soft smile.

"That's fine if you want to think that way, but once you are finally in, please feel free to redecorate. I know you are more of a pink girl," I say with a giggle. She has an obsession with pink like mine with purple. She giggles with me.

"Sounds good, where do I sign?" She says grabbing the papers. I point out where she needs to sign. She signs the papers and I scan the documents to send to the lawyer.

"You are now part owner. Now that all the hard stuff is out of the way, what is going on with you and Quick?" I ask her with an arched brow. She blushes so brightly and looks down at the ground.

"There is nothing to tell," she says embarrassed. Okay no, there is no way there isn't something there.

"Cut the shit. I saw him with you the night the guys came in. He followed you around like a lost puppy," I say sternly. She rolls her eyes.

"Yes, he followed me around like a lost puppy but Nik he is twenty-one. He is a baby compared to my thirty-five," she says annoyed. Huh? Interesting.

"So, the only reason you are not giving him a chance is because of his age? Nothing else?" I ask her. She can't look me in the eye for some reason. She is hiding something about him, but I am not sure what.

"No, that is not the only reason, and you know that. He told me he is a serious relationship kind of guy, and you know I can't do that. The last time I had a relationship like that it broke my heart beyond repair," she says with a sigh of defeat. This poor woman is going to miss out on a great guy that wants to give her his heart over some asshole from her past. She is just like me before the guys barreled through me.

"Listen, I know you are scared but Quick is a great guy. I met him a couple times and Dante talks about him all the time. He won't hurt you on purpose," I tell her, moving to comfort her. I kneel in front of her and grab both her hands. "Just know whatever you decide, it is your choice. I just don't want you to miss out on a great guy that will show you how much love you deserve."

"Okay let me think about it. We know you have enough on your plate. How is the Rachel thing?" She asks, changing the subject. Fine, I'll let it slide this time, but this bitch has another thing coming if she thinks I won't ask her every Sunday at brunch.

"It's going. The bitch is hiding it out for right now from what the investigator told me. Coming here was a risk but I have three big buff security guards for a reason," I say with a giggle.

"No kidding. Those men are sex on a stick!" She exclaims laughing.

"Hey back off. They are married to their wife," I tell her, grabbing a drink of whisky from my decanter on the shelves in my office.

"Hey, I am not that much of a hoe. I know only to look and not touch. Anyway, let me go check out the front to make sure everything is going smoothly and then check back in so we can work out the orders," she says standing.

"Okay, sounds good! I will get started then show you how it works," I tell her. She leaves while I get to work. I take sips of my whiskey while working at my desk. I am going to miss coming here so often but I will have the guys while we build our lives together. I know it is soon but I know I want to be with them forever. I know it is not legal, but I want to marry them. We can still have a ceremony and exchange vows in front of our closest friends and family. We can even do it at the church Ivan grew up at if they let us. God, I need to slow the fuck down. My phone starts to ring. It is my dad. Huh? He was supposed to be on his flight back to New Orleans. I accepted the call worried that he did not make his flight.

"Daddy? Hey, I thought you were flying to New Orleans tonight," I say with a worried tone. Then I hear a voice that sounds familiar.

"Well hello to you too," A female voice says on the other end with a cackle of laughter. Something is not right.

"Who the fuck is this? Where is my dad?" I ask, practically yelling on the phone.

"Well, I thought you would remember my voice. Am I really that forgettable?" She yells her question and that makes all the pieces come together.

"Rachel?" I ask and she just laughs.

"Who the fuck else could it be? I bet you have a lot of women after you, but it is just little old me," She asks, annoyed. Fuck I hate this bitch with my whole soul.

"How do you have my father's phone?" I ask her, worried. She just laughs.

"Well, I went to your father's fight and we hit it off. Sadly, I went to find you, but I found the next best thing. Pretty sad how his own daughter did not come and support him to maintain his title," she says with a snarky tone.

"Well, I wasn't there because a certain crazy cunt is after me!" I yell, but she is right. If I were there then she would have come after me and not my father. I should have had Carter set my dad's own security. Now he is dragged into this bullshit because of me. "What the fuck have you done to my father?"

She lets out a cackle of a laugh. I am going to kill this woman if she has done anything to him. He was the first man to ever love me, and I will protect him. My father does not call me his little lioness for nothing.

"Well poor guy just can't hold his liquor. We went out for drinks last night and now he is passed out. It might help that I slipped something in his drink and that I look like his little lioness. He would not shut the fuck up about how much I look like you," she says, annoyed and I see red.

"You're the one that changed your looks to look like me! What the fuck do you want you, psycho?" I ask her.

"I want my life back you bitch! I had everything! I had a fantastic job and was warming Carter up to date me. Now I have no job and no one to vent about losing my life!" She screams into the phone.

"You can get a job! It is not my fault no one will hire a sexual harassment cunt!" I yell at her. God, I need to figure out what to do. I probably should not be egging her on, but I don't know what to do. It is one of the few lines of defense I have.

"Carter would not have done that if you weren't in the picture!" She yells and then I hear a man groan in the background. Shit, shit, shit! It sounds like my dad. Her tone turns flirty. "Well look who is up?"

"Where the hell am I?" My father says groggily. He groans again. She better not fucking hurt him!

"You better not touch one hair on his head!" I scream and my father can hear me. She must have me on speaker.

"Little lioness?" He asks, trying to figure out what is going on.

"I am so sorry daddy! This is all my fault!" I scream so he can hear me.

"Why am I restrained to a bed!?!" He asks Rachel. I hear him pulling and struggling, trying to get free of his restraints.

"Oh, shut up," Rachel says, annoyed.

"I am going to ask this one more time! What the fuck do you want?" I ask her, gritting it through my teeth. I am done playing games with this woman. Whatever she wants she can have as long as she does not hurt my daddy.

"Oh well now that you asked. I want you to fix my problem. I want money and lots of it," she says.

"Fine! How much do you want?" I ask her.

"Don't give her a penny, little lioness!" My father yells. Then I hear him groan as Rachel smacks him.

"Shut up, the adults are talking! Now where were we? Oh yes, I was going to tell you how much money I want," she says and continues, "I want at least one million."

"I don't have that much!" I yell at her. I am in no sense a millionaire.

"Well, you better figure it out and don't even think about asking your harem for the money! I will know!" She snaps at me.

"I can get you around seven hundred thousand and that is emptying my bank account and cleaning the safe at the club," I explain in a calm voice. I need to stay calm now that I know she is not above hurting the people I care about.

"Fine and I need you to lose the bodyguards," she tells me.

"How do you expect me to do that?" I ask her, annoyed. She lets out a snicker of a laugh again.

"Not my problem but if they figure it out say bye-bye to daddy," she says.

"Fine but I will need time to get the money and lose them," I tell her.

"Oh no. That will not do. I have a driver behind your bar and if you are not out in an hour then I hurt the only man who has ever loved you," she tells me. I roll my eyes because I know so many people that love me but now is not the time to point that out.

"Fine. I will be in that car in an hour, but I need them to drive me to the bank to get the rest of your money," I explain. I don't think all she wants is money, but it is the only thing I can give her at the moment.

"Oh, they will. They already know where to go, so all you have to do is get the money you promised," she says and then hangs up. I drop my phone on the floor. Okay breath Nikki, you can do this. I rush to my apartment to grab a duffle bag and rush back to the club. I open the safe and start dumping the money in the bag. Then I hear the door open. Chloe walks in and her jaw drops in shock. Fuck, I forgot I told her to come back to show her how to do the orders. She is frozen for a moment and then she rushes to close the door and turns to me.

"What the fuck is going on, Nik?" She asks worriedly. I can't blame her, this is out of character for me. I take a deep breath before explaining.

"That cunt just called me from my father's phone. She said if I don't get her money then she is going to hurt him," I say and I burst into tears. I fall to the floor in defeat with my head in my hands. She moves to kneel in front of me.

"What do you need me to do?" She asks with a serious tone. My head whips up to look at her. She does not show pity in her eyes, just determination to help me.

"I have to get out of here without my bodyguards. I don't know how I am going to do that," I tell her, wiping the tears from my face. When I get to Rachel I don't want to show her any weakness.

"Okay, I can distract them while you get out. Is there a certain way you need to leave?" She asks. She reaches for my hands to get me off the floor. Once I am up, she goes to the safe and puts the rest of the money in the bag.

"I need to l-leave out the b-back. She has someone with a car to drive me to the bank and then to her," I explain, stuttering out the first part. She hands me the bag.

"Okay. I will distract the guys, so they come out front. How would you feel if I start a bar fight? That should give you plenty of time to sneak out the back. Any furniture damage can come out of my portion of my check next pay period. I am just trying to make sure we follow her rules, so your father is safe," she explains. I could really care less.

"No, it will not come out of your check. We will figure this out later. To be honest if it keeps my dad and the guys safe you could burn the place to the ground for all I care," I tell her with a serious tone. That has her stunned.

"But this club is your baby," she says softly. I turn to her with the duffle in hand.

"This club is not the only thing I have anymore. I have friends and family that love me. That is all I need, not this fucking club," I explain, grabbing her hand and squeezing in reassurance. She gives me a soft smile knowing I include her in that group.

"Okay, let me get the bodyguards distracted. When you hear a commotion, run for it. Then I will call the harem, so they know what is going on," she says and I stop in my tracks.

"No! She says if I tell them she will hurt my dad. You cannot tell them," I tell her worriedly. She just smirks.

"She said you not me," she says and leaves, closing the office door.

I pick up my phone, make sure it's on silent, and shove it in my bra, praying to god they don't try to search me in all this mess. I just wait at the door of my office. The seconds feel like years right now with how my anxiety is. I wish the guys were here. They always know how to calm me when my anxiety is eating at me. Then I hear it. Yelling and people chanting for the fight Chloe started. I move quickly, I peer out of the office and don't see anyone, so I make a run for it. I run past the cooks praying they don't stop me. I make it out the back and see a black SUV there with dark tinted windows. A big guy comes out of the driver's side and opens the back door for me. Then I see that the guy that kind of looks like the guy my dad was supposed to fight. He has short black hair, tan skin, and crazy muscles like he lifts on the daily. I look and he has a black eye and a cut on his lip. Oh my god it is him. It's Rodrigez.

"What the fuck? How do you benefit from helping that cunt," I exclaim moving towards him. Then I feel it before I see it happening. He slaps me and my hand goes up to my cheek where he hits me. He moves close and bends down so his mouth is ghosting my ear.

"Are you kidding me? Your father embarrassed me in front of the world, beating me in that fight. It was obviously rigged so this will put him in his place," he whispers and grabs my arm to toss me in the back of the car. He slams the door and moves to get in the driver's seat. He confirms my bank and all I can do is nod. He puts the car in drive and takes off. I am in the back seat thanking god that he did not ask about my phone.

We rolled up to the bank. We get out and Rodrigez grabs my arm to haul me into the bank, but I pull away.

"Listen if you walk in there with me, they are going to have questions. Just stay out here and I will get the money and we can take it to that cunt," I spit out angrily. He moves and smacks me again. Luckily he parked in the back of the lot so no one is around to see him do this. Even if they did, this is New York. They will pretend they did not see it and go about their day. He moves closer and grabs my arm again. He is grabbing so hard I am sure I am going to have bruises.

"If you think you are going to go in there alone so you can escape, think again," he says with a growl of anger. I roll my eyes at him.

"The bitch has my father! You think I am just going to run away like a piece of shit like you," I snap at him. He goes to smack me again, but I catch his hand this time. I am just trying to be a good hostage by letting him smack me but there is only so much I can take. He yanks his hand back.

"I am going in with you. If they ask to speak to you about your crazy withdrawal, I will hang back, but I will be watching you and staying close," he grits out. He grabs my hand this time and leads the way. God, I thought him grabbing my arm was bad but him holding my hand makes me want to throw up at the intimacy it displays. We walk hand in hand, and I figured he is trying to show intimacy, so the bank thinks we are a couple and did not see me as a hostage. One of the tellers smiles at us and waves to call us over. I do my best to plaster on a smile as we walk up.

"Hello, how can I help you today?" She asks sweetly.

"I have a very odd request, but I would like to withdraw all my money from checking and savings," I tell her in a soft, even tone. She looks at me in shock.

"Is there something wrong?" She asks worriedly, eyeing Rodrigez. Fuck me I am going to have to sell this. I lean into Rodrigez and he leans right back knowing what I am planning.

"No, nothing is wrong. This is my fiancé and I am going to join his bank so we can consolidate our assets. We were going to look into buying our new home and our real estate agent suggested it," I say with a big smile trying to sell this.

"Okay, we may have some problems doing this. We have to follow our policy so if you could follow me, we will talk to a manager," she says. We followed her to a back office. I walk in and Rodrigez stays just outside. She closes the door behind us. I sit in the chair that is at the desk waiting for the manager. I am so happy that I don't use a modern bank. There are no windows so Rodrigez can't see in. Now that I have a moment, I pull out my phone and of course I have a million texts and miss calls from the guys. I look over the text.

Dante: Hey Mia Amore! How's the club going? Miss you.

Dante: Mia Amore! Please answer! We heard from Chloe!

Ivan: Please tell us what is going on! We just need to know if you are safe.

Ivan: FUCKING answer the god damn phone!

Carter: Princess! Come on, please answer! We can figure this out together. Chloe told us she has your dad and that she will hurt him if you tell us but Chloe told us, so it is a mute at this point. I love you and don't want you to get hurt because of my past. It will kill me!!

Then I see Carter calling me. This is risky but I need to let them know I am still alive so they will stop calling me. I answer the call.

"Princess?" Carter yells, shocked that I even answered. I take a deep breath.

"I am alive. Do not call again. I have been able to keep it from Rodrigez that I have my phone so you can track it," I whisper and hang up before he responds and shove the phone back into my bra. I am praying that he heard all that and gets moving because I highly doubt that Rachel is just going to let me go once, she has the money. There is a knock on the door, and I am guessing it is the manager that walks in. He goes to his desk with a serious look on his face.

"Miss. Bell, am I to understand you want to withdraw all the money out of your account?" He asks with a worried tone. I swallow hard and nod. "Well, that is not how we do things sadly. You will need to slowly take money out and then once it is cleared then we can discuss closing your account with us. It is state law if you withdraw or deposit an excessive amount, we are to notify authorities to prevent any fraud or illegal activity."

That has me sitting straight up. This is perfect! If I withdraw all this money, they will notify them and then hopefully the police will find me when I am with Rachel. Even if they don't, I know my men are looking for me, even if Carter did not hear me, they know I have my phone so they know to track it.

"I don't care if you notify them. Please I am begging you just get me the money and I will deal with the repercussions," I beg the manager. He thinks for a moment, and I can see him putting the pieces together. He gives me a stern nod. I hand him my bag that has the other money in it, and he goes and leaves the room. I hope he gets the money before contacting the police so I can get to my father before they intercept me. I sit there and wait filled with adrenaline. I pull out my phone again and it makes me feel a little calmer.

Carter: We are not far behind you. We will be there to save our princess and her father.

Don't get me wrong, my nerves are still crazy, but that text does make me feel a little at ease. It means the guys are coming and not only for me. They know my dad and I are a package deal. I can also tell Carter is being serious because all of his texts are missing emojis. I let out a breath of laughter because of it. I hear the door open, and I am quick to hide my phone and recompose myself in case it is Rodrigez. The manager walks in with my bag.

"Okay so here is all the money and I will notify the police once you are off the premises to give you time to get where you need to go with the money," he says with a knowing smile. I grab the bag and before I leave, I give him a hug.

"Thank you so much," I whisper in his ear and rush out, but Rodrigez grabs my arm to stop me.

"And where do you think you're going?" He says with a condescending tone. I rip my arm out of his grip.

"I was rushing to the car so we can go see my father now that I have Rachel's money. So, if we could get a move on," I tell him in a sassy tone in my voice. I will not show fear to this piece of shit. The second I do he is going to take advantage of that fear to manipulate me.

"Fine let's go," he says, gritting through his teeth. We go out and get in the car. Rodrigez is speeding and all I can think is, I am coming dad. Just hold on a little longer.

Chapter 25

CARTER

"God I am so fucking bored without Nik," I yell in the penthouse. I loved having her at practice and she is always here, but I know she needed to go. This is a big step for her and she needs to do this on her own. She is releasing some control giving Chloe part of the club and I know that is difficult. Her whole life she has been in control of everything. Her dad even told us at one point in time she controlled who he fought, making sure she had some say in the outcome. She was always scared he would get hurt in a fight and to help her he would include her in the decisions if he fought someone or not. I know she is doing it for us even if she did not say it. She is wanting to be with us more and in her mind, to do that she has to do this so she has someone she trusts at the club.

Me and the guys want to celebrate this milestone in her life, so we cooked her dinner and decorated the penthouse. Ivan cooked her steak, lobster and salad as a side and mac and cheese. Dante is decorating. He has a thousand candles lit in the dining room and then he scattered purple and black rose petals throughout the place. He even went as far to get purple balloons and a banner that says congratulations. We all dress to impress because Nik has commented how good we look in suits. We match too, in black slacks and dark purple button ups. Dante got Tot a purple bow tie collar that even I think is cute. Ivan is facing the stove so I cannot see his face, but he rolls his eyes so hard I actually see his head move with his eyes.

"You know if you are bored you could fucking help, asshole!" He yells from the kitchen.

"Hey, I did my job dick! I was in charge of the wardrobe and getting Tot ready!" I yell back. It was a pain in the ass to bathe him and blow dry him. Next time he can do it! I am starting to get nervous. Nik said she would only be at the club for an hour or two and we are well past that. I keep checking in with her security and they say all is quiet, but something doesn't feel right. Even Dante has asked me about her and her security. I am brushing Tot to make sure he is nice and pretty for our princess. My phone rings and it is one of Nik's security guards. I answer and put it on speaker.

"Hey Alexander, what's up?" I ask nonchalantly. They call a few times to check in when they are out with her, so I think nothing of the call.

"Sir, we lost her," he says and I am sure I heard him wrong.

"What did you say?" I asked in shock and that has Dante and Ivan coming towards me to listen.

"I said we lost her, sir," he says in a nervous tone.

"What the fuck do you mean you lost her?" Dante yells into the phone. Fuck! I knew something was wrong.

"There was a bar fight and we moved quickly. Miss. Bell was in her office, and it was locked so we yelled at her to stay put so we could check to make sure it was not Rachel. When we went back to the office she was gone," he tells us, and I can hear the other guys in the background trying to search for Nik. My heart drops. She is gone and has no protection. I am frozen so Ivan grabs the phone and gives me a reassuring nod.

"Okay how long was she alone and is there anything in the office to lead us to her?" Ivan asks him in a serious tone. These are the moments I am grateful we have Ivan. He is better in these types of situations because he had so much hardship growing up. He is always calm, cool, and collected. I am useless. I can't even function. I am so shocked and scared. Even Dante is texting Nik to try to get a hold of her. What if Rachel hurt her? What if she got a hold of her and threatened her? What if this is not even Rachel and she just left us? What a fucking dumb thought! Of course this is Rachel. We have been waiting for her to make her move and I guess she did. I shake my head and see red now. I will fucking kill Rachel if she hurts one little hair on her head!

"She was alone for twenty minutes, but we did see she cleaned out the safe in the office. We can only assume someone is holding her for ransom if she cleaned that out," he says. Then the investigator rushes in with a worried look. We all turn to him.

"What is going on?" Dante asks, dropping his phone, forgotten.

"Nikki's dad missed his flight. At first, I just thought he was running late but he is not at the airport and I can't locate him. I just have a bad feeling about him," he tells us with a worried tone. Everything is clicking. Her father is missing, her missing and now the safe is cleaned out. Then I hear Chloe trying to get the security guy's phone.

"Give me your phone!" She yells at him.

"Miss, please calm down, we have a situation," he explains to her. If anyone knows what's going on it is that sassy pink hair girl.

"Give her the phone," I ordered him. He sighs and sounds like he hands her the phone. "What's up Chloe?"

"You guys have to hurry. This is the gist of it. Rachel got a hold of Nikki's dad and is holding him for ransom. She cleaned out the safe and is on the way to her bank for the rest of it. I am sorry I distracted the security guys, but she did not know what to do. She threatened her dad if she told you all and if she did not do this alone," she explains. My heart drops in my stomach. Rachel thought of everything. My beautiful princess is alone and scared. We need to think of everything too. I turned to the investigator.

"We need to switch up our strategy. I need you to look into Nik and her father. See if there is anything on where Rachel has her father and find out the bank Nikki uses," I tell him and he nods. He leaves to go to the office we have set up for him.

"Chloe, thank you for being there for her. I understand you had no choice and I appreciate that you did what was best for Nik and her father," I said into the phone.

"It's no problem but I got to go. I need to close the club and call Ian to tell him what is going on," she says and hands the security back the phone.

"We are coming to you so when we find her, we can go instead of you guys," he tells us and before he hangs up Dante grabs the phone.

"Like fucking hell we are not going! You lost her not us, so we are getting our girl back. You can come with us to watch our backs," Dante yells and hangs up. He's not wrong. There is no way in hell we are not going when we figure out where our girl is. We spend the next twenty minutes trying to get a hold of Nikki. I am sure it is probably a long shot, but it is the only thing we can do while we wait for more information. I keep calling and texting and so do the guys. We take turns calling her. It's my turn. I hit the call button and after the second ring she picks up. She is quiet for a moment and I realize it could be someone else. I put the phone on speaker and ask, "Princess?"

"I am alive. Do not call again. I have been able to keep it from Rodrigez that I have my phone so you can track it," she says and then hangs up before I could say anything else. I look at the guys.

"Who the fuck is Rodrigez?" I ask them and they both look down and think. Ivan's head whips up.

"Isn't that the guy that her dad fought?" He asks. Me and Dante look at him with arched brows.

"Why the fuck would he get involved?" Dante asks.

"You guys did not read the news about the fight. Rodrigez talked shit all the way up to the fight and Nikki's dad knocked his ass out in the third round. Nikki's dad embarrassed him, and the news is really tearing him a new one. If Rachel took her dad like Chloe said then he could get something out of it," Ivan explains. Okay this is good we have even more. We rushed to the office with the private investigator.

"We have more information that we need you to get on," Ivan tells him. "We learned that the fighter that Nikki's dad fought is helping Rachel and that Nikki has her phone. We need to check into the fighter Rodrigez and track Nikki's phone."

"I am on it. I will get the phone tracking done first so we can keep an eye on her. I need her phone number," he demands and I give it to him. He gets to work and he gets her location really fast but we decide to wait till security is there before we get moving. Plus, we do not know where they are going to take her after she gets the money. Now that he is tracking her, he moves onto finding information about Rodrigez. He takes a few minutes then looks at us.

"Well, this makes sense," he says to us and we all focus on him.

"What is that?" Ivan asks, ready to get moving.

"So, it looks like he has a hotel room and I found photos of Rachel and Rodrigez together at a bar the day after the fight. This is why I could not find anything on her. She is using him so we can't find her, but I bet she is at the hotel room he is staying at and has Nikki's father there too," he says and gives us the location and room number in which they are staying. We go and get changed into jeans and t-shirts because if we have to fight I really rather not do it in a suit. When Ivan and I make our way downstairs,

Dante is already waiting with security but what has me and Ivan shocked is he has Tot on his leash like he is coming with us.

"What the hell? Why are you bringing Tot with us?" Ivan asked. Dante rolls his eyes.

"Because he is with Nikki twenty-four seven. He will protect her once we get to her and you know it," he explains with a hiss. He is not wrong. I have even thought about Nik taking Tot everywhere because of it but she shot it down real quick. Ivan looks at me to argue the idea but I just shrug.

"Fine, we get in and Nikki gets Tot, and we deal with the situation," Ivan says in a deadpan tone.

We make our way to the garage and security lays it out the pan for us, probably because they think we will fuck it up. I know we won't though, there is too much on the line for us to fuck up.

"Okay we will split up Dante, Tot, Clyde, and Alexander in the SUV and then I, Carter and Ivan in Carter's car. It is fast so if we need to make a quick getaway it will be good to have," Cyrus tells us. They are locked and loaded. They all have guns and whatever they need if things go sideways. We get into our cars. The security guys already called the police while we were getting ready and hopefully will be there when we get there. I decide to shoot Nik a text even though she might not get it.

Carter: We are not far behind you. We will be there to save our princess and her father.

I hope she gets it. It might put her mind at ease a little that we are on the way. I get a call from the investigator, so I answer.

"What do you have?" I ask him.

"Looks like Miss. Nikki has made it to the hotel so she will most likely be with her dad and Rachel when you are there," he tells me. Good, I don't want to run into them in the lobby and then not be able to get to her dad.

"Good. Keep me posted if they move at all," I tell him and hang up. We finally made it to the hotel, but the police are not here yet. When the valet greets us, I hand them a hundred-dollar bill and tell them to keep the cars out front. We make our way into the hotel lobby. This hotel is pretty fancy. There are white marble floors but in the waiting areas they have big Persian rugs with vintage furniture. There are several people waiting there that look like businessmen. I turn to look at the front desk and it is massive with a polite young lady behind it. She looks at us with a curious look, probably because of Tot but she has a few people waiting on her, so she goes right back to work. Me and the guys turn to the security guys to figure out our next move.

"Okay since the police are not here, we need to wait before barging in," Cyrus says.

"Yeah, that will be a fuck no!" Ivan yells. "We are not just going to sit here and wait when Rachel could be hurting Nikki."

"Yeah, I am with him," I agree and Dante nods. The security guys sigh in frustration but they know we will go even if they don't agree. This is my princess, and I really am going to be her white knight.

"Okay we will go up but stay outside the door and do not go inside till we can assess the situation," Alexander says. Yeah, we all nod but we know if Nikki is in serious trouble we are jumping in that room. We make our way up the elevator and wait patiently with Tot. I dare someone to give us trouble that our dog is here. I start to tap my foot. This is the longest elevator ride I have to sit through with awful elevator music playing in the background. I knew we should have taken the stairs so I could run. The doors open and one of the security guys puts a hand on my chest. Probably because he knows I am about to jump out of my skin if we don't get to Nikki soon. Two of the security guys are in front of us and one behind to watch our backs while we make our way to the room. We move down the hallway and I pray no one comes out of their rooms and asks questions. The hallways are pretty simple with white walls and doors. There are simple brass light fixtures on the walls in between rooms and they let off a yellow hue. The floor is at least a red carpet and that keeps our footing pretty quiet as we make it to the room Rodrigez has rented.

We get there and the door is cracked for some reason. Then we hear it. My beautiful princess screams. I go to move but Tot pulls Dante, and he must not have a good hold because Tot is gone and into the room where Nik screamed.

"What the fuck?" I hear a male voice yell. Well, there goes my plan to rush in.

Nikki

When we make it to the hotel, I observe everyone in the lobby. Checking for all exits and how busy it is. There is pretty tight security here, I see two by the front door and I see one at the front desk. This may cause issues if we have to make a quick run for it and they may try to stop us with questions. The lobby is pretty busy filled with businessmen and socialites. Damn, for someone who just lost, Rodrigez must really like to blow his money on this fancy hotel. We get to the elevator and me and Rodrigez ride up in silence. The only sound is of the terrible elevator music that is playing on the speakers. I much rather this than him smacking me. The doors open and he puts his arm out for me to exit first.

"Lady's first," he says with a snicker. I can't help the eye roll I give him. He can play the gentleman all he wants but I know all he will ever be is a piece of shit. The halls are white but very dimly lit from the yellow lights that are in between rooms. We both walk down the hall to a room at the far end of the hallway. He pulls out the room card and waves it at the lock and opens the door. He goes in first so when I go to close the door, I leave it barely cracked. The guys said they were coming so I don't need something like a locked door getting in their way.

I walk further in from the entryway of the room and then my jaw drops when I turn the corner. My poor dad looks worse for wear. His hair is messy which never happens. He is shirtless for some reason, but I am not going to address it. It also looks like Rachel has been smacking him hard with how red his cheeks are. I am going to kill this bitch. She is sitting on the edge of the bed with her legs crossed and a gun in hand on her lap. Shit! This complicates things. I don't think she would be dumb enough to shoot me in a hotel but with this crazy bitch you never know. She is sitting there with a smug look on her face. She is in a basic black t-shirt and jeans and has a black ball cap on. She still has my hair color, but she lost the green contacts. Her eyes are brown, but I can still see the crazy in her eyes.

"Finally. Took you long enough," she says with an annoyed tone. I could care less. I turn to my dad. He pulls on the ropes that have him tied to the bed and leans forward trying to fight his way to me.

"Are you okay?" I ask him. He nods.

"I told you not to come, little lioness," he says with such sorrow. I roll my eyes at him because he knows I would come no matter what he said. He has always been my protector, so it is probably eating him up inside that I have to protect him.

"You would have done the same for me. I am just sorry you got dragged into this," I tell him softly. I mean it. I hope he can forgive me for this mess that I caused. Carter can say it is his fault all he wants but if he did not meet me, he would have not reported Rachel. This is all on me.

"Fucking Christ! Can we stop with the sappy shit!" Rachel yells. I whip my head to her and toss her the duffle bag at her feet.

"Here! All the money is there. Feel free to fucking count it," I snap at her. She drops the gun to the bed and picks up the bag to open it. She snickers when she sees the money. "Now that you have the money, let my father go."

"Oh, this was never about the money, it was just a bonus," she says with an evil laugh. Shit, I knew it.

"Then what the fuck do you want! I gave you everything I have," I snapped at her again. I notice out of the corner of my eyes that my dad is still trying to wiggle out of the rope in a softer approach instead of trying to rip the rope with his brute strength, but it is tied pretty tight, so I don't think he is going to be able to help.

"Money is nice but really I just wanted you away from your security and Carter," she says, and I don't like this one bit. She is not after my dad. She is not after my money. She is fully fixated on me. This is not going to end well for me. I know that much.

"Well, you have what you want now what?" I ask her, annoyed. I am not trying to show fear, but I am terrified. I can feel my body shaking like a leaf and with the smile she has, I bet she can tell.

"I just want to know how a nobody like you grabbed Carter's attention," she says with an evil grin.

"Are you fucking serious? Of all the things you could possibly want, you want to know how I flirted with a man. How should I know?" I ask her with anger in my tone. She must not like my answer because she pulls out a knife and stalks toward me. I hold my hands by my side but ball them into fist, ready to defend myself if need be. The knife is a small pocketknife with a black hilt so I highly doubt it can do anything fatal but I bet it will hurt like a son of bitch if she cuts me with it.

"I don't think you are telling the truth. I am sure that he has given you some inkling of what he likes about you," she says, and lays the knife flat on my cheek. All she has to do is turn the knife a little and she can slice my cheek. I take a deep breath trying to think of something to give her. I need to give her something she wants to hear but my dad cuts in.

"Her voice!" My father yells. This has Rachel snap her head to him removing the blade from my cheek. I let out a sigh of relief. I am no way out of the clear, but I will call this a small win in this situation. I feel a ping in my stomach when I see her stalk towards him. She gets on the bed and straddles him. I feel like I am going to throw up. I need to get her away from him.

"What do you mean, her voice?" She asks him with a purr. My father looks at me with an apologetic look and then focuses right back to her.

"The night they met she was singing at her club. That is when she got his attention. Have you heard my little lioness sing? She has the voice of an angel. I also text with the guys and they all rave about her singing talent," he tells her. I am a little shocked myself. I knew he texted Ivan, but I didn't know about the others. I didn't even think my dad liked Carter. He gives me a knowing look, giving me an indication he is lying but I try to hide my emotions. He turns back to Rachel. "Now you got your answer so let her go."

"Oh, that is not all I want. I want to make your daughter pay for taking what was dear to me," she says and goes to straddle my father on the bed. I keep reminding myself to stay calm till I see my opening, but it is so hard to hold back. My father's anger is released, I can tell. Since he is tied up all he does is spit in her face. She does not flinch, she just laughs in his face as she wipes off the spit with her hand. She turns her head slightly but does not get off my father. "Because you took what was dear to me, I am going to hurt what is dear to you."

My eyes go wide as I see her lift the knife to my father. No! No! This is not happening. I did what she had asked. When she digs the knife into my father's shoulder, I can't hold the scream that I let out. He groans in pain but looks at me with reassurance that he is okay. Then all of a sudden something rushes into the room. It is the last thing I expect. Tot rushes to me and stands in front of me and growls at everyone else in the room.

"What the fuck?" Rodrigez yells and heads right for Tot to grab him. Big mistake on his part. Tot thinks that Rodrigez is coming for me so Tot jumps up and bites down his arm. He is such a good boy protecting me I will have to sneak him some human food later as a treat.

Everything is moving so fast my head can't keep up. First, Rodrigez yells out in pain and tries to get Tot off but fails. Then I see dad, he must have been trying to figure out how to get out of his ropes the entire time he was pulling at them and squirming. He gets out of his bonds and grabs the knife from Rachel. He flips her so her back is to his chest and pulls her to him and holds the knife to her throat. Then the guys, with the security team, rush into the room. Ivan, Dante, and Carter rush to me as I fall to my knees out of breath. With everything that is going on panic is finally hitting me. The security goes to deal with Rodrigez since my dad has Rachel. The whole thing is a blur until Cater kneels down to me and puts his hands on my cheeks. He looks me over to make sure I am not injured.

"Are you okay?" He asks softly. I don't answer him with words. I yank him down to me and place a hard kiss on his lips. I can feel him tense at first but then he softens into the kiss. He leans into me and then I feel my other men kneel on both my sides and hug me. I pull back and look at my men.

"Little one, please tell me she did not hurt you," Ivan says with concern written all over his face. My poor big guy was probably so worried about me.

"She didn't," I tell them with a shake of my head and a frown.

"But we heard you scream," Dante says with hesitation like he does not believe me. Then I think about everything, and worry hits me, my dad.

I rush to get up to get to him, but he is still holding Rachel. I keep my distance but look him over. He has blood on his shoulder and I feel all the color fall from my face. I think I am going to be sick. The guys follow my stare, and they look mortified but don't want to move Rachel away in case she gets away. Finally, my security gets Rodrigez in their handcuffs and one holds him on the ground. The other two go and move towards my dad and Rachel. They grab her and put cuffs on her as well. As soon as she is out of the way I tackle my dad in a big hug and then he lets out a muffled groan in pain.

"I'm sorry!" I squeak out and pull away from him as fast as I can.

"It's okay little lion, just a little sore. This is just a flesh wound, probably won't even need stitches," he says with a soft laugh and then groans. It is not just me concerned about the groan, it also has the guys rushing to him to help him. Dante pulls off his shirt and puts pressure on his shoulder. Carter pulls out his phone to call the police and luckily, they already got an ambulance on the way since it was a hostage situation. Cater goes to my dad and checks him out.

"Stay awake and make sure not to move too much. The paramedics are on the way up," Carter tells him. My father rolls his eyes.

"Listen punk, you're lucky you saved my daughter, or I would tell you to fuck off with ordering me around like that," he says with a soft laugh. We all burst out laughing knowing it was a joke. I am crying with laughter. He is okay, my men are okay, and I am okay. I don't know if my crying is because of all the trauma or from being so happy now that this is behind us. Rachel has to ruin this happy little bubble by opening her goddamn fucking mouth.

"You bitch! I will ruin you!" She yells at me squirming under the security guy that has her. I am about to scream at her that she almost ruined my whole world hurting my father but then Carter steps in. He grabs both my arms from behind me, but I can feel him shaking with anger. I take a deep breath and back off a little calming down my inner lioness. He needs this more than I do. He needs to confront this demon straight on and does not need me to fight it for him. He releases my arms and moves to the side of me.

"You will do no such thing. Your happy ass is going to jail," he tells her with all the anger.

"We could have been happy! The only reason we aren't is because of that conniving cunt!" She yells squirming. I can't hold my anger back anymore. Ivan goes to grab me because he knows what I am about to do but I move out of his reach. I go and punch her in her eye.

"Listen here! You will not talk to Carter. You will not even think about him when the police officers come and get you and do you want to know why? Because if you do there will be no jail that will keep me out to finish this. Also, I want you to know I was not fighting you because you had my dad. If it was just me and you, I would have killed you with no regrets," I tell her and the boys move to me. Carter gets between me and her.

"Stop, princess. She is not worth it. You will never have to deal with her ever again. I will make sure of it," he promises me. I sigh because I know there is nothing, I can say to him to make him realize it is not his fault. I wrap my arms around his neck.

"I will as long as you promise not to blame yourself on this. None of this is your fault or mine. It is her's," I say pointing to Rachel. He shakes his head.

"No, love, this was all on me. If I did not act out in my past then she would not have been so obsessed with me," he says with a hard swallow.

"But do you know that for sure?" I ask him with curiosity. He thinks and he knows I have him. "See you don't. If you were sweet and nice it could have made her even more obsessed but there is no way to know. So, I will stop if you will."

"Okay, you win princess," he says with a sigh, but this has me smiling like crazy. When he sees mine, he gives me his big flirty smile. The paramedics and cops come in. The police officers are pretty quick in taking Rachel and Rodrigez away and the paramedics look over my dad.

"Good news. She did not cut deep. All you will need is a couple of stitches and then you will be good to go home. Let's get you to the hospital," one of the paramedics says to him. Thank god! Me and the guys follow the paramedics on the way to the hospital. Dad was adamant that I did not have to go, but I told him to shut the fuck up and let us come. He blushed in front of the pretty female paramedic when I said that. It made the boys snicker. Of course, the boys took care of everything. They reached out to my dad's promoter and publicist to let them know what was going on. They had security go before us so they could get rid of any reporters that were at the hospital. Carter even called the hospital ahead of time to reserve a private VIP room, so we don't have to deal with anything. It is the most caring and romantic thing. They care and love me so much they are making sure the only family I have ever had is comfortable and loved as well. My dad actually got cleared to fly back home tomorrow shockingly.

"Thank god! I have been itching to go home!" He tells the doctor and then turns to me. "No offense, little lion but New York just isn't my cup of tea."

I laugh because I know. He misses home and to be honest I can't wait to go back home too. It will be nice to be in New Orleans without having to worry about what is going on here with Rachel. I tell him, "None taken dad, but Carter agrees, you are not flying back without us just so I can keep an eye on you while you heal. He got us a private plane and cleared it with his coach so he can fly with us and I made arrangements so that Ivan and I can stay in New Orleans with you for a week."

He rolls his eyes, but I can tell he is excited for multiple reasons. One, I will spend the week with him. Since I moved to New York we don't get to hang out a lot so I know he will love having me in New Orleans for a little while. Two, out of all my boyfriends, Ivan has a clear schedule, and he just so happens to be my dad's favorite so they can have their little bromance. Last but certainly not least, he and I have never flown on a private plane before.

Luckily Chloe has not moved into the apartment yet, so he is going to stay there till we leave tomorrow. I offered him to stay at the guy's house, but he said he has had enough of our lovey dovey shit. It makes me giggle but me and the guys make sure he is comfortable at the apartment before we go to our home. Huh, our home.

Chapter 26

DANTE

She is safe. Mia Cara is safe. It is still hard to believe. We are making our way back home. We opted to take the SUV to fit and the bodyguards are going to drive Carter's car home. Me and Ivan were shocked. He never lets anyone drive his car, but we also understand. None of us want to be separated from Nikki right now. Ivan is driving and Carter is in the passenger seat. Me, Nikki, and Tot are in the back. She is loving on Tot right now. I can't blame her, the little guy did good protecting her. He is soaking up all her affection.

"Who's my good boy?" She asks him, petting and kissing his head. He barks in approval. "I am going to give you a human treat when we get back."

"You will not. I will have to clean up whatever comes out. Either from the front or back," I tell her with a frown. He does not do great with human food unless it is just straight meat without any seasoning on it or tater tots for some fucking reason. I really don't want to clean up throw up or shit later when I am trying to love on Nikki.

"Pretty please? He was such a good boy protecting me," she asks with a pout and eyes wide filled with sadness. Damn it! I really have a challenging time saying no to her plus, he did a really good job at protecting her.

"Fine we may have some leftover tots in the fridge for him," I say with a sigh, and she smiles from ear to ear. She turns back to him to scratch his head.

"My good boy is getting a treat later," she says excitedly and even Tots ears perk up at the word treat.

"I thought I was your good boy?" Carter says with a big smile looking at her in the rearview mirror. She rolls her eyes at him and turns back to Tot. "Is Carter crazy? Yes, he is. He didn't bite the big bad man for mommy."

I can't hold back my shit eating grin. Her words make me so happy. Mommy? Hell fucking yes! If I have any say, she will be more than just a puppy mommy in the near future. She sees my grin and falters a little with a frown.

"What's wrong, Mia Amore?" I ask her, worried. Maybe they did hurt her, and she is in pain. I grab her hand and she looks at me with a soft smile.

"I probably shouldn't call myself his mommy. He's your dog," she says, and I put my other hand up to stop her.

"No, you are. I already knew that but today was just proving it to you," I tell her and I bend over Tot who is lying in between us. I place my lips on her to give her a sweet kiss and I can feel her lips turn up in a smile. She goes to deepen it, but I pull away with a soft laugh. "Mia Cara, as much as I want to get my hands on you. I don't want us to make out over our dog."

"Okay, I think I can wait till we get to our home," she says with a giggle. Our home?

"Little one, did you just say our home?" Ivan asks her with an arched brow. She blushes for him calling her out.

"Oh, I'm sorry. Am I not staying? That's fine. I know I was only there because of Rachel," she says shyly.

"No!" Me, Carter, and Ivan yell in unison. Carter goes and unbuckles his seat belt even though it is against the law and turns himself in his seat to look at her.

"No, you are not leaving, princess. We told you even if Rachel wasn't a factor we would want you to stay. So please stay?" He begs her. She puts her finger to her chin to think for a moment and the suspense is killing me. We just got her to move in which is a huge step. If she moves out, then it would feel like we are taking ten steps back. She gives him a soft smile.

"Okay," she says softly.

"Okay?" I ask her. Nikki loves her independence so much. I figured she would argue with us on this more.

"Yes, Mio Amore, I will stay," she says, squeezing my hand in reassurance. "I love you guys and want to be with you always. Why do you think I gave Chloe a substantial portion of my club? It was so I can stop focusing solely on work and put more effort with you guys."

"We would never ask you to do that, little one. We know how much the club means to you," Ivan tells her with a serious tone. She shrugs.

"I know you won't. That is why I just did it. To show you how much I love you. I want to be able to go to your games whenever I want or if we want to travel or have date night. Owning the club by myself, I could never do that. I would always have something to do. Now I have a partner I can trust, so I can really start to live my life with you guys," she explains. Tot hates that he is not the center of attention, so he leans up to lick her face. She smiles down at him. "I have a family now that is more important than some club."

Ivan pulls in and parks in the garage. We all get out and before me and Carter even try, Ivan is there throwing her over his shoulder to carry her up to the penthouse.

"You know I can walk right? This seems to be an ongoing issue that you think I can't," she says with a giggle. We made it to the elevator. Ivan swats her ass as we all pile in.

"Little one, are you sassing your daddy?" He asks her with a mischievous grin. She can't see it, but she snorts knowing it's there.

"What if I am? What are you going to do about it?" She asks him back with an attitude. Jesus Christ, I am hard as a rock and seeing Carter adjust himself, I am guessing I am not the only one. The door opens and Ivan books it to the stairs.

"Oh, there is plenty I can do," he says and swats her ass again. She puts her hands on his ass to look up at me and Carter but then looks shocked looking around the apartment. Shit, I forgot we decorated everything to celebrate.

"Ummm, guys? What is all this?" She asks us, whipping her head around to look at everything. It looks a little weird now and not the grand gesture it was supposed to be. The helium in the balloons are starting to go out of them so they are sitting low on the ceiling and I blew all the candles out before we left so we didn't have a house fire. Ivan put the dinner up but left the dishes in a hurry so there is a mound of dishes in the sink.

"Oh shit! With everything going I forgot we did all this," Carter says with a laugh. "Surprise, princess!"

"Okay and what are we celebrating? Because that banner says congrats," she asks and looks at me.

"Well Carter told us about how you were making Chloe a partner. We did not understand why but Carter told us you were so happy about it we, so we felt like celebrating. So, when you were at the bar Ivan cooked and I decorated while this guy did nothing," I say and point to Carter.

"Fuck you man! I got our matching outfits and got Tot ready. Do you know how much of a pain in the ass Tot was in the bath!" He yells and shoves me. I roll my eyes.

"Yeah, I wanted to give you a job I know you could not mess up," I tell him and that has Nikki laughing hard. Ivan finally makes it up the stairs and goes right to his room. I could care less who's room we are in. I just need Mia Cara on some kind of flat surface. Ivan tosses her to the bed. She bounces so high it makes her laugh again. I love the sound of her laugh. It's intoxicating to me. She goes to remove her shirt. She dressed down since she thought she wasn't going to be at the club long. She is wearing a band t-shirt that she made into a crop top that she wore the first time we met her and high waisted tight black shorts. She goes to remove her shirt but before she does Ivan is there in an instant, ripping it down the middle. Damn, that was hot.

"Hey! That was one of my favorite shirts, dickwad! It was a real vintage ACDC tee," She yells pissed. I will buy as many of those t-shirts I can get my hands on so I can try that move. He scoffs.

"I will buy you ten new ones exactly like it. Sorry little one you were wearing too much clothing," he explains and rips off his as well. Me and Carter decide to be normal fucking people and take ours off without ruining them. Ivan gets to work on taking off Nikki's shorts. Pulling them down slowly. She is wiggling in need. She reaches for her panties. Ivan smacks her hand away. She looks up in shock at him but then her bright green eyes go hungry with need.

"The only one to undress you right now is me," Ivan growls at her. He waits for her to verbally agree and when she doesn't, he demands it. "Say you understand."

"I understand, daddy," she says with a whimper. Ivan moves away from her and goes to the trunk that is at the bottom of the bed. When he opens it, my jaw goes slack from shock. This kinky bastard has a chest filled with toys and playthings. One day I am going to have to look in there when he is not looking. He grabs the ropes and a blind fold. Well shit, this just got more interesting. He tosses the blind fold to her but keeps the rope in hand.

"Lay on your back and put that on, baby girl," Ivan demands. While she gets in position and puts the blind fold on, we all finish getting undressed. Ivan tosses one rope to me and two to Carter. Me and Carter nod and understand what he is telling us to do. Me and Ivan go to the headboard and tie each of her hands to the post. We try to make sure we give her some slack but not enough to where she can move freely. Carter ties each ankle to a bottom post, so she is spread out for us like a feast. We all move to the bottom of the bed so Ivan can whisper what he has planned.

"We are going to take turns eating her out and teasing her but do not let her cum," he whispers so Nikki cannot hear. Me and Carter nod understanding. Well, that's no fun, I wanted her cumming on my tongue all night, but Ivan is Captain. We watch Nikki pull at the ropes for a little, she is testing to see how much movement she has. Ivan looks at me and motions with his head to tell me I can go first. I am so excited that I dive face first into her wet pussy. She screams out in pleasure. Ivan and Carter move up, so they are lying on either side of her. I don't bother with them and get to work eating her out like a king enjoying a feast. The delectable taste soaking my tongue with each lash of it. She always tastes sweet and tart like a fresh strawberry. Ivan and Carter are sucking each a tit. I move my hand so my thumb can circle her clit. This has her panting.

"More, please," she gasps out. She is so close, I want to taste her cum so bad, but Ivan has different plans. He moves next to me and taps my shoulder.

"Move," is all he says. I reluctantly get up and move to Nikki's side as Ivan gives her a minute to bring her down. Then he devours her. When she is close, he pulls away and motions for Carter to take his place. We keep her on edge for well over thirty minutes. She is crying out begging for more.

"Please, I need to cum!" She cries out pulling at the ropes. I am in the middle of my turn. I pull away slightly and look at Ivan. He nods but holds up a finger to tell me to wait. Oh, I can tell this is about to get good. Ivan bends down so his lips ghost her ear.

"If you want to cum, I want you to promise me something, baby girl," he whispers in her ear. She is shaking with need. Ivan could ask her anything and she would give in just so she can cum. I make a mental note that if I ever need her to agree with something to hold off her orgasms.

"Anything, daddy. As long as you make me cum," she says, nodding her head rapidly.

"I need you to promise if you are ever in a situation like that again, you call one of us so we can help you," he tells her sternly. Oh, this is one of his daddy lessons Nikki has told me about but I am not mad about it. She should have called us the second Rachel called her. Then we could have been there for her through the whole thing, protecting her.

"But there was no time plus she threatened my dad if I told you guys," she gasps as my thumb circles her clit again. I am trying to edge her on. If she makes that promise I will be more than happy to let her cum.

"Promise, Mia Amore," I ordered her. She nods her head at me but then Carter cuts in.

"Words, Princess," Carter barks at her and then bends down to kiss her neck. I bend down to force it out of her. I lap her up once from the bottom to top.

"I promise! For fuck's sake please I need to cum," she yells out in frustration. That was all the confirmation we needed. I place my face as close as I can and devour her and slip two fingers in her wet folds till, she is screaming in release. She is shaking and I lick her through it till her body calms down slightly. Then I sit up a little and remove my fingers from her wet warm entrance.

"I think you guys broke me!" She yells and swats at Carter's chest. We all laugh. Carter goes and yanks the blindfold off of her. She lets out a giggle, "Done with the kinky stuff."

Carter lets out a growl and tells her, "I want to look into your eyes when I make you cum."

We move fast as we untie her. Her body was shaking from the most intense orgasm. She curls into a ball shaking. Ivan puts his finger under her chin, so she has to look up at him.

"Who do you want where, love?" He asks her softly. She looks at all of us thinking.

"Carter in my pussy, Dante in my ass and you in my mouth," she says with a big gulp. I peered up at her with excited eyes. Ever since Ivan told me he had her ass I have been wanting to do it myself. We arrange ourselves accordingly. Carter lays on his back for her. She rushes to straddle him. Ivan tosses me a bottle of lube from his little trunk. I am going to have to look in that trunk another day, right now Mia Cara needs me. Ivan goes to the top half of her, kneeling on the bed for her so she is not straining her neck. Carter slams into her once before slowing his pace so I can start. I squirt lube all over her and myself. I want to make sure I don't hurt her. She just started this, so she is probably still tight as hell. I position myself and rub myself through her slick crack getting her ready. She moans and pushes back into me trying to edge me on. I finally sink into her. I used enough lube that I slid right in. She lets out a moan the same time I let out a growl. Fucking Christ, she is tight back here. I move though, slowly feeling Carter start to move as well.

"Fanculo! You are so tight back here!" I growl out loudly. She moans but it is muffled. I look up and Ivan is already in her mouth. He moans at the vibrations he is feeling as she gargles him down. She is giving him the sloppiest blow job I have seen. To be honest it is the hottest thing I have ever seen. There is saliva dripping from her mouth and her make up is all smeared from her tears running down her face. She is the most beautiful woman I have ever seen. I start to feel my balls tightening knowing I am close.

"I am going to need you guys to hurry the fuck up because I am so close with this tight ass," I groan out. Carter reaches down in between him and Nikki. He slips his hand between her slick folds.

"Fucking hell! She is dripping on me," he yells out and then is cumming a few seconds later. He screams her name as he empties himself into her. Me and Ivan are not far behind him. I cum so hard I think Mia Cara can feel it shoot into her. She groans around Ivan as she cums with me and that has him shooting down her throat. She gobbles up every last drop of him. We all slowly pull out of her, and she collapses to the bed exhausted. I go to Ivan's bathroom and find a few washcloths and I damp them with warm water. I go back in and toss Carter and Ivan a washcloth. We all clean her up. I clean up her ass while Carter cleans his area. Ivan washes her face with the damp cloth. When we are done, I throw the washcloths in Ivans hamper. She hums in content as we get into her favorite cuddle position. Carter between her legs, hugging her stomach, me at her front and Ivan spooning her.

"How are you feeling, Mia Amore?" I ask her as she continues to hum as Ivan plays with her hair.

"Perfect. You know a girl could get used to this," she says softly. That has Carter bark a laugh.

"You better, princess, because we are not letting you go," he says nuzzling in her tummy. She has no idea how right he is. We are going to marry this girl. Yeah, it won't be official but I don't care. I want us to be tied to her in every sense of the word. As we fall asleep, I think of ways to make this happen as soon as possible.

Nikki

Well, we are finally here. Me and my dad made it to New Orleans. We are walking into the New Orleans stadium where Carter is playing. Ivan and Dante were able to come too. Carter made sure we traveled in style. He had to travel with the team, which I completely understand but he got us a private jet. The original plan was for him to travel with us, but his coach gave him a hard time about it saying he needs to be with the team. I told him I was okay with it and that if he travels with his team, I would make it up to him later. Normally I hate it when they buy things for me or spoil me but not having to ride in a stuffy plane in coach was amazing. There was even a bedroom on the plan. Ivan tried to convince me to join the mile high club, but I shut him down. It would have been weird since my dad was on board. I did make him a promise to try on the way home though. He is excited to get this underway so we can fly home. Him and Dante have been acting weird since we got here though. Dante has been busy running errands but won't tell me what and Ivan has been really quiet. Like he is lost deep in thought. I have called both of them out on it but never got an answer. Maybe they are starting to resent me for the type of relationship we have. I tried to confide in my dad about it. He just laughed and said there is no way that would happen. This made me think he was also involved in whatever they were doing.

"Is everything okay?" I ask Dante and Ivan as we make it to our seats. Carter changed his mind about a private box. He got us fifty-yard line seats. We are so close it is crazy. Ivan sits on my left side and Dante on my right. They both grab one of my hands and squeeze with reassurance.

"Everything is perfect, love. Everything will be explained soon, I promise. Now no more questions and watch the game. I don't want to ruin the surprise," he says sternly. I roll my eyes.

"Fine daddy, you win this time," I tell him, and he gives a beaming smile. My dad chimes in which makes me blush.

"You guys know I am right here right," he says with a laugh. Dante and Ivan laugh but then focus on the field. Carter is warming up and I have to clench my thighs together when I see him. His ass looks so good in his football pants. He catches me staring and sends me a wink. He turns and points to his name on the back of his jersey and then points to me. I look at him confused and he rolls his eyes and runs up to us. He hops the barrier and I gasp in shock. He gives me a beaming smile.

"You look hot with my last name on you, princess," He says with another wink and hops down to rush over to Jaden and Xavier. It looks like they are giving shit about me again, so I just laugh and he does too and punches them in the arm. The game goes really well. I am not a football fan but when I ask the boys a question about something they take their time explaining it to me. I still know enough though to know Carter's team is killing it. The score is twenty-one to seven, Carter's team is winning. I still cheer for him when I know I should, and he gives me a beaming smile and waves when I do. We finally make it to half-time and I am excited. The boys just explained to me that they are doing a half-time show, and it is one of my favorite bands. They put a small stage in center field. I am jamming out to the rock music. Then the guys grab my hands and shock me by picking me up and lowering me to the field.

"What the fuck are you doing? We are going to get in trouble," I yell at them and they laugh.

"We won't, I promise," Ivan says laughing.

They hop down with me and the music stops. I turn to the small stage and Carter is there giving the singer a hug and grabbing the mic. I am so shocked that the guys have to pull me to the stage. I am frozen when all three guys stand before me. I swallow hard when they all get on one knee. Then they all pull out ring boxes which have tears forming in my eyes. This feels too soon but then I think about it and it doesn't in a way. We really only have been seeing each other for a week and know each other for two but it feels like with the week we have had that we have known each other forever.

"Baby you can't cry yet. We haven't gotten to the good part," Carter says with a snicker. I laugh but I am bawling my eyes out now.

"Can't help it after everything we have been through," I tell him. Carter goes first. He opens the ring box and brings the mic to his lips.

"Princess, I know we have not known each other that long but me and the guys agree. We know we are yours and you are ours. We know it is unconventional, but this is us. I don't think it would work if we were anything else, but you never once judge me for my past mistakes no matter how much it affected you. You stuck with me no matter how bad it was. I also know that we can't get officially married but we can still have the vows and promises that come with it so please marry me, princess?" He asks and then I look at the open box and gasp as the ring. It is a thin black titanium band with amethyst gems and diamonds lining the black band. I am taken back. It is so simple but so perfect and unique. He lifts his eyebrow waiting for my answer.

"Yes, of course charming!" I yell and crouch down to hug him. I pull back and he puts the band on my finger. I did notice the engraving on the inside of the band before he slipped it on. It says Princess. I don't know how he knew my ring size, but I don't care. Then I hear Dante clear his throat next to him. Carter hands him the mic and I move to stand in front of him and he opens his box, and it is another black titanium band but in the middle it has a huge purple diamond. Good fucking lord do these guys not understand about keeping things simple. Maybe I am just cheap. Dante laughs at my wide eyes.

"Mio Amore, you should know us better than that. We were not going to cheap out on your rings and you know it," Dante says still laughing. I giggle because he is right. He continues, "Mia Cara, I have been looking for what my parents had in someone. I started to get frustrated thinking I would never find it but then you waltzed into my life. I can openly admit that it was love at first sight. The first time I saw you and heard you sing I swear my whole world shook. Please make me the happiest man on earth and marry me?" He asks and my tears just won't stop. I drop down to him and give him a hard kiss till we have to separate for air.

"Si, ti amo tesoro mio," I tell him and he slides it on the same finger. His engraving on the inside says Mia Cara. They fit perfectly together. He looks at me like he said, like I made him the happiest man in the world. Time for the last one. Dante passes the mic to Ivan now and I move in front of him. My whole body is trembling with excitement. He grabs both my hands to calm my nerves.

"Baby girl, when I came to you, I thought I was broken. I had no family and was a lost soul. You made me see that I wasn't. Family is not blood, it is what you make it. We made our own little family with you, Carter, Dante, and me. This is where I belong with you three. I did not realize how lonely I was, and nothing would make me happier than if you will marry me?" He asked me and he let go of both of my hands to grab his box out of his pocket. When he opens his I gasp. His looks similar to Carter's, it is another black titanium band with amethyst stones and diamonds but his almost comes to a point so it will fit on top of Dante's band, and I can still see it.

"Yes, love! I will marry all three of you," I tell him and he plucks it out of the box to put it on my finger. The engraving on the inside of the ring says little one. I love all the rings so much. They all have their individualized touch, but it comes together on my finger just like we do. We are all great as individuals, but we are even better when we all come together to make our little family. I pull all three into a group hug. I don't know how I got so lucky, but I am not going to question it. When we first came together it was all about fulfilling my fantasy but not only did, I find three guys that fulfilled my fantasy but we fell in love and nothing can make me happier.

My dad rushed to the stage as fast as he could injured. He hugs me in a big bear hug and groans in pain. It is amazing that he was able to be here and when I pull back a little to look at him, he has a knowing smirk. He knew the fucker. He snickers at the glare I am giving him.

"You knew," I tell him more like a statement and not a question. He laughs as he lets me go and turns to the guys.

"Of course, princess. We had to ask him for his permission. I was actually scared he would say no to me," Carter says with a laugh. I laugh too because he is right. I would never guess that my dad would say yes to him. My dad turns to him with an apologetic look.

"I know I gave you a harder time than the other two guys but from what I experienced in the last week you have proved that you are putting your fuckboy ways in the past and focusing on my little lion. Don't get me wrong if you hurt her, I will still fuck you up," my dad tells him with a shit eating grin. Ivan and Dante bust out in laughter as Carter looks like he is going to shit himself. I move to Carter and wrap my arms around his neck.

"Don't worry, Charming. I won't let him kill you," I tell him with a snicker. He has a big smile and leans down to kiss me. The crowd goes crazy as he picks me up and I wrap my legs around his waist. He pulls away a little but puts his forehead against mine.

"I can't wait to spend the rest of my life with you, Nikki," he whispers. It is a promise that makes me so happy.

"Me too, Carter," I tell him.

Epilogue

Nikki

18 Months later

We had such an amazing year. I am walking into Ivan's stadium for his first game of the season with my security. Carter said he wanted to keep my security team just as a precaution. The guys moved to New York with their wife, Claire. She was thinking about retiring as an actress anyway so she can spend more time with the kids. I love their wife and she became one of my best friends instantly. She is even part of our breakfast club that goes to the diner on Sundays. We are able to vent about the frustrating points with being with more than one man but also talk about the benefits too.

Me and the guys got married four weeks after they proposed. They said they did not want to wait. Carter told me in his vows we did it so soon because he did not want to give me time to change my mind. Little does he know, I would never do that. It was a small wedding. Just me and my men with Chloe, Ian, and my dad. Dante's mom and brothers were there, and his mom was pissed it wasn't a big Italian wedding, but she dealt with it. I am not a big wedding kind of girl, and she knows that. I hate dealing with crowds and the press that comes with the guys, but I will deal with it every day if it means being with them. I did, however, let Dante's mom plan the rest of it to make up for it. She planned a small wedding and rented out the whole diner for the small reception. She almost had a cow though when I messed with my dress a little. I got a big white gown, but I knew someone who specializes in dip dying dresses. My girl was able to dip the bottom half of the skirt purple, so it was white but ombre to a bright purple. We actually got the sisters to convince the church to have it there. It was the most amazing wedding anyone could ask for.

With the busy year I have had with the guys I gave Chloe full control of the club, so I try to make it to all the guys' home games if I can. Chloe is officially the main club owner. I gave her a new contract the second we hit the one-year mark of her being an owner. To celebrate her first year as an owner, the new contract stated that she will own sixty percent and I would own forty. Of course, she tried to fight me on this, but I told her that me and the guys are trying to have a baby and I would not have time for the club when it finally happens, she was so excited to be Aunty Chloe she could not argue. We have been trying but had no such luck till recently. We discussed how we should pick someone and only they are allowed in my pussy. I thought the guys were going to argue forever on who gets to have the first kid but then Ivan said once he has a kid, he was going to retire so he can help me and focus on our family while the guys keep playing. That made me step in and tell the guys Ivan is first then. So, the other guys backed off and my pussy for the last few months was only for Ivan. That didn't mean the other guys couldn't play with me too though. They got blow jobs and fucked my ass. I know we could have just used condoms with them, but I would rather be safe. They did not complain at all though when they got to my ass.

I am walking toward the locker room. I have a surprise for the guys, and I needed all the help I could get. Ian, Chloe, and Stan are already there waiting for me. I run as fast as I can so we can get the ball rolling before Ivan comes out. I have Ivan's jersey on with some jeans and the high heels that Ivan bought me on our first date. I was going to have my hair down but it is unusually hot for spring in New York, so I tossed my hair in a ponytail and a ball cap with Ivan's team logo.

"Hey guys," I say and hug Ian. He laughs and hugs me back.

"Hey bitch!" He shouts, but me and Chloe shush him. He snickers at us.

"Keep your voice down asshole! Ivan is just behind this door!" Chole whisper-shouts at him and points to the locker room.

"Sorry," he says and looks at me apologetically. I sigh.

"It's okay, I understand. Future Uncle Ian is just excited," I whisper with a soft laugh. Then I get scared when the locker room door opens but I let out a sigh of relief when it is Ivan's teammates and not him. It is Rick and Cole. Rick is the shortstop for the team. He has long brown hair that is tossed in a man bun and a clean-shaven face. I always make fun of his man bun. Then Cole has medium length golden blond hair with a five o'clock shadow. He is the catcher of the team, so he and Ivan are pretty close. Once I told Cole my plan he has been threatening to tell the whole team besides Ivan so he could hold it over his head. They are the ones helping me with part of the surprise. They organized it so during the first pitch I would throw it and then tell him my secret. Dante and Carter are at our seats. I told them I wanted to wish Ivan luck and then would be at the seats. They were hesitant at first but then agreed.

"Hey trouble," I say and hug Cole. He laughs in my ear and lets me go.

"If I was trouble, I would have told the whole team like I said we should," he says with an evil smile.

"And I told you if you did, I would kick you so hard in the balls that I would ruin any chance for you to have kids," I warn and he laughs again so I pull back my leg just to make sure he knew I was serious. He grabs his junk to protect it.

"I swear to god I did not tell anyone. You can even ask Rick! Don't hurt my family jewels!" He yells backing away from me. I turn to Rick with a glare and he laughs at his pathetic friend. He comes up to me and gives me a quick hug.

"I promise I have been keeping him away from Ivan all day. I am not going to lie, he almost slipped this morning, but I covered it," Rick says with a scoff. I turn back to Cole.

"You better have not ruined the surprise or I am coming after your balls," I tell Cole with a growl. He backs away a few more feet but Chloe steps in to save the man.

"Okay, okay leave the guy's nuts alone. We have to deal with enough as is without you guys tormenting each other," she says and grabs my shoulder to pull me softly away from him. Fuck she is right. Eyes on the prize Nikki.

"Fine. Okay Cole your future babies are safe for now," I tell Cole laughing as he looks like he doesn't trust me. He shouldn't because if I find out that he ruined the surprise I am running across home plate and kicking him square in the nuts in front of all his fans. "So, you guys were able to get your people to agree to let me sing the national anthem?"

That was my original plan but the guys had a hard time convincing the owner to let me, so the first pitch was the backup. They look at me with dazzling smiles.

"What?" I asked them, worried. They are just acting too weird. Cole finally stopped cowering away. He walks right up to me and grabs my shoulders.

"I hope you are ready to sing your heart out kid," he says and my jaw drops in shock. I am stunned, silent with everyone just gaping at me waiting for an answer. I shake my head to bring me back to reality.

"Are you kidding? You really got them to agree?" I ask them skeptically. It wouldn't be the first time Cole tried to fuck with me. He's like an annoying big brother I never wanted.

"Nope, not kidding kid. You will sing the national anthem and then we got someone to fill in to do the first pitch," Cole tells me.

"Oh really? Who did you get to replace me? They better have a wicked fast ball like me," I tell him with a laugh. Then Ian chimes in.

"Well since I am the best best-friend you could ever have I convinced your dad to come up and do the first pitch. I told him his daughter and son in laws miss him so much that this would be an amazing surprise for you when really you get to tell him too," Ian says with a smug smile. I can't blame the man for being smug. The bitch killed this, so it is absolutely perfect. I grab him for another hug.

"Thank you! You made everything perfect," I whispered in his ear and let him go. "Do we have a way to get the other guys to the field when I am done with the anthem?"

"I got that covered. I am going to grab them and tell them you have a surprise for them and lead them to the field," Chloe says. I take both her hands.

"Thank you, all of you," I tell them with a soft smile. I could not have done this without them. Ivan was right when he proposed, we really made a little family for ourselves.

My whole body is shaking with nerves. I have a mic and watch Ivan warm up on the side. I am waiting for them to call me for the national anthem. I have never sung in front of a stadium of people. Sure, I sang on Broadway, but this is a whole new level of crazy. Luckily, I have been practicing, hoping that Cole and Rick could make it happen. I still sing at the club every so often and after that I would run up to Chloe's apartment and practice so the guys wouldn't know what I was up to. I think I am so nervous not because I am afraid to bomb the national anthem but to finally tell the guys my little secret. I never kept anything from the guys since the Rachel incident. I learned my lesson, but this is a good secret.

Lexi Haynes

Both teams line up outside the dugouts, and I know it is time when the announcer comes on.

"Ladies and gentlemen, if you could all please stand for our national anthem," he says over the system. Both teams take their caps off. I take one last deep breath before he continues, "Please join me and welcome our very own starting pitcher's wife who will be singing it tonight, Nikki Bell."

I walk out to the pitching mound and turn on my mic. Before the music starts, I grab one quick peak at Ivan. His jaw is slack, and his beautiful green eyes are wide in shock. I can see him thinking and processing what is going on. He probably thinks this is why I have been acting weird. He has no idea. The music starts and I look by the dugout and there stand Dante, Carter, Ian, Chloe and my father. The guys and my dad look as shocked as Ivan. I giggle before I start to sing. I am sure I am butchering the high notes through the song with how nervous I am but when I look at the people, I care for they all look so proud. When I hit the last note, the guys couldn't help themselves. They run straight to the pitch mount. Dante and Carter hop over the barrier and Ivan makes it to me first since he has nothing holding him back. When I am finally done the crowd cheers. I almost fall to the ground when Ivan tackles me for a hug. Dante and Carter join him, so we are in a group hug. These are my favorite types of hugs. They surround me with all the love and affection that they tell me I deserve. They pull away slightly but keep their hands on me and that makes me happy. I am so uneasy I might fall with what I am about to tell them. I switch off the mic so the crowd doesn't hear so we can have our moment.

"Mia Cara, that was Bellissima," Dante says loudly to talk over the crowd.

"Princess, you did amazing!" Carter yells with excitement but then I turn to Ivan.

"Is this why you have been acting weird, baby girl?" Ivan asks me with a big smile.

"It is not the only reason. I have one more surprise for you. Turn around for me," I tell them with a nervous laugh. They are facing the big screen which was not in my plan. I was hoping they came up behind me but I had a backup plan if they didn't. I told Cole the backup plan so the guys that run the big screen knew. The guys look skeptical for a moment but do what I say. They turn and face the dugout and I check the screen to make sure the message is big for the guys to see.

"Okay you can turn around," I tell them. They turn around and almost trip when they do. They look at the big screen in shock because in big bright lettering is "I am pregnant." I give them a minute to process what they are seeing and laugh. The next thing I know I am tackled to the ground by all three of them. Ivan kisses me as we fall in a hot hard kiss. Not the kind you want to do in front of thousands of people, but I could care less. This is our moment and if he wants a hot make out session who am I to deny him that. He pulls away and then Dante and Carter, both give me a sweet kiss on the lips. Ivan is still on top of me, and his eyes go feral with need. I swallow hard because I can feel myself get wet just with his gaze.

"You are so lucky you did this in front of thousands of people," Ivan warns. I am so glad I turned off the mic when I did because my daddy is looking at me like he will devour me.

"Oh, really and why is that daddy?" I ask him with a mischievous grin. He makes a feral growl sound in the back of his throat.

"Because if we were alone, I would show you how much I love you and this surprise," Ivan says with a growl.

"You calling him daddy has a whole new meaning now," Carter says with a loud laugh. I laugh as everyone from our little family rushes over to congratulate us. This has always been my dream and now it is a reality. I am surrounded by people I love, and I could not ask for anything else in my life.